Dear Reader,

Truth and consequences is this month's theme for Harlequin Duets. In volume #19 Julie Kistler tickles the funny bone with her arrogant Jones boys, heroes used to getting whatever they want in *Calling Mr. Right*. However, when they buy and transform a radio station, Griffin Jones finds himself assuming a false identity to help Nell McCabe keep herself from getting fired—by himself! Complications ensue and emotions run amuck. Then Connie Flynn weaves a tale of comic adventures and misadventures in *The Wedding Dress Mess* as the hero tries to protect his mother from the consequences of her folly.

In volume #20 Charlotte Maclay returns with *Not Exactly Pregnant*. Is she or isn't she? turns out to be the frequently asked question in a town that is overrun by pregnancies. But what happens when a very good girl and the ultimate bad boy are about to become parents? Then we welcome Liz Jarrett to Duets with her first novel, *Darn Near Perfect*. When workaholic Michael's boss decides he needs to learn how to be more altruistic, to learn that it truly is better to give than to receive, Michael gets a lot more than he expected when he hooks up with a group of matchmaking senior citizens.

I hope you enjoy this month's Duets.

Malle Vallik

Malle Vallik
Senior Editor

Calling Mr. Right

Nell McCabe

Thanks to the owners of my radio station—the arrogant Jones brothers—I'm a sex vixen!

Well, actually, a sex *victim,* as I've just become the host of *The Hot Zone!*

Now I have to find the perfect woman for Dr. Jones or lose my job....

Dr. John Jones
(aka Griffin Jones)

W109's ratings are down the toilet, but after meeting Nell McCabe I'm rooting for her to succeed—

So I made this stupid bet with my brother that Nell could turn around the station's numbers.

Except, when her show didn't have any callers, I picked up my cell and dialed in, and assumed a new identity… only now I'm really hot for Nell and in too deep!

For more, turn to page 9

The Wedding Dress Mess

"Haven't you ever seen a naked man before?"

"Of course I—" Vicky shook her head. "That's none of your business!"

Duncan's amusement faded. "Look, Ms. Deidrich, you're in my house in the middle of the night. Can you give me one good reason not to call the police?"

"How about that your jig is up?"

"My *jig?*"

"Yes."

He scowled as fiercely as a bronze warrior, and for the first time Vicky realized the precariousness of her situation. A man who'd commit fraud— what else might he do? Slit the throat of an inexperienced insurance investigator? Bury her body in the backyard?

Then the scowl burst into a true belly laugh. The antique blanket he'd used to cover himself slid low on his hips.

"This is nothing to laugh about. If you're going to kill me, do it now!"

His laughter escalated. "Kill you?" He moved in closer. "The only intention I have is to kiss you."

For more, turn to page 197

HARLEQUIN DUETS

ISBN 0-373-44085-5

CALLING MR. RIGHT
Copyright © 2000 by Julie Kistler

THE WEDDING DRESS MESS
Copyright © 2000 by Constance K. Flynn

This edition published by arrangement with Harlequin Books S.A.

® and TM are trademarks of the publisher. Trademarks indicated with ® are registered in the United States Patent and Trademark Office, the Canadian Trade Marks Office and in other countries.

Visit us at www.romance.net

Printed in U.S.A.

JULIE KISTLER

Calling Mr. Right

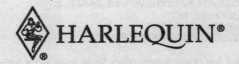

HARLEQUIN®

TORONTO • NEW YORK • LONDON
AMSTERDAM • PARIS • SYDNEY • HAMBURG
STOCKHOLM • ATHENS • TOKYO • MILAN • MADRID
PRAGUE • WARSAW • BUDAPEST • AUCKLAND

Dear Reader,

Romantic comedy is my first love. Well, actually, the boy who sat in front of me in kindergarten was my first love, but when it comes to movies, give me romantic comedy every time! That's why I'm so delighted to present my first Harlequin Duets novel, about a plucky radio host named Nell, and what happens when Valentine's Day 2000 approaches and her show gets turned into a matchmaking extravaganza called *The Hot Zone.* Her life is really up for grabs when adorable, arrogant Griffin Jones calls in, pretending to be Mr. Right. It doesn't occur to him—or Nell—that he really *was* Mr. Right all along!

I had a great time with Griffin and Nell, and I wish you all as crazy and romantic a V-Day 2000 as theirs. Happy Valentine's Day!

Julie Kistler

Books by Julie Kistler

HARLEQUIN LOVE & LAUGHTER
65—50 WAYS TO LURE YOUR LOVER

HARLEQUIN AMERICAN ROMANCE
690—TOUCH ME NOT
740—TUESDAY'S KNIGHT
782—LIZZIE'S LAST-CHANCE FIANCÉ

Don't miss any of our special offers. Write to us at the following address for information on our newest releases.

Harlequin Reader Service
U.S.: 3010 Walden Ave., P.O. Box 1325, Buffalo, NY 14269
Canadian: P.O. Box 609, Fort Erie, Ont. L2A 5X3

1

July 1999

"DAMN THOSE JONES brothers!" Nell McCabe, known throughout Chicagoland as the calm, unflappable host of the morning advice program called *Tell Nell*, crumpled the memo from marketing, threw it on the floor and stomped on it. Twice.

Amy, her producer, stopped halfway in the doorway. "Is this a bad time?"

"Every time is a bad time since *they* bought the station. And it's getting worse."

With a little shriek of dismay, Amy bent to snatch the paper out from under Nell's foot. "Oh, no! Don't tell me now they're firing *us,* too?" As she attempted to smooth it enough to read the lines, Nell began to pace.

"It would almost be better just to get the ax and get it over with," she muttered. "Hmph. Trying to goose my ratings. I liked my ratings just where they were. But hey, I went along with their stupid ideas, didn't I?" Her voice rose. "They said my image was too stodgy, so I had to get new photos. I'm thinking, *photos?* What do they care what I look like? I'm on the radio! But it's good PR, they said, and I thought, play nice, Nell. Go along, Nell. Give them a chance, Nell. That was before I knew they were going to ambush me with makeup and hair and that horrible dress.

God only knows what I'm going to look like in those pictures. Ridiculous, that's for sure.''

Amy raised an eyebrow. "Nell, the idea for the sexy photos and this memo both came from that slimy Drake Witley, the new director of marketing. I don't see what this has to do with the Joneses at all. Besides, it just asks you to come to a meeting. What's so bad about that?''

"But the Jones brothers hired Drake the Snake, didn't they? And I got this memo at two twenty-five, when the meeting started at two." She pointed to the clock. "I'm a half hour late before I even get there! I know a trap when I see one. They're going to lie in wait for me and hit me with some new scheme, and I'll be late and flustered and unable to fight back. It's just the kind of underhanded maneuver the Jones Boys are famous for.''

"Nell, you're starting to sound paranoid.''

Nell shook her head. As the host of *Tell Nell*, she dispensed advice to all the lovelorn and relationship-challenged people who cared to call in. She made it her business to listen to everyone's troubles, to remain kind and sympathetic in the face of unpleasantness and hysteria. "Tell Nell all about it," her promos said soothingly. "Together we can pave over some of the potholes on the bumpy road to love.''

But in a few short weeks, she'd lost every shred of her calm, her cool and her sympathy. Now she was ready to pound someone. Preferably one of the two globe-trotting, company-plundering, womanizing *pirates* who'd gobbled up her radio station. The Jones Boys.

"For all we know," Amy put in sensibly, "the Jones Boys aren't even in town. I've never seen them, have you? Paris today, Rio tomorrow. Do they really have time to come to Chicago to fool with little old W-109-on-your-dial?''

''Somebody has certainly been fooling with it. *Marvin's Meteorology Minutes*—gone!'' Nell lamented. ''And for what? For a whole hour of *Glittertown Gossip. Yecchhh!* Paddy O'Herlihy and the *Gaelic Hour,* gone. And in his place, we get the *World's Most Gruesome Urban Legends.*'' She threw up her hands. ''Now they're dragging me to a marketing meeting to...'' She narrowed her eyes, recalling the exact words in that odious memo. ''To discuss ways to make my show hotter and more 'happening.' It's insane.''

''Come on, Nell. It's just a meeting. And you don't even know what they're going to say.''

''I know *Tell Nell* is neither hot nor 'happening,' and that's just the way I like it.''

She loved her job, really she did, at least until the Jones brothers got their grubby mitts on it. She'd always felt she was performing a useful function in society. Everyone needed someone to listen, didn't they? Maybe even hot, happening people needed someone...

No. She was not going there.

Except that Amy was already pushing her out the door and down the hall. ''Just go to the meeting and hear what they have to say,'' her producer advised. ''Maybe it's some fun new summer promo package and you'll really like it. Look on the bright side— unlike old Marvin and Paddy O'Herlihy, we're not getting canceled. I mean, if they're spending money to make you hot and happenin', they can't be pulling the plug, can they?''

''Oh, lord, I hope not,'' Nell said under her breath. What would she do without *Tell Nell?* She'd been

dispensing advice on the radio since she was a mere
child of twenty, when she'd sort of accidentally gotten
her own show on the college's educational station.
Forget college—she'd left after her junior year to go
to Chicago with the show.

At this point, she wasn't qualified to do anything
else.

She didn't even want to think about trying to find
another job at the advanced age of twenty-seven. But
what if marketing really was planning to come up
with some new stunt—something even worse than
tacky publicity pictures—and they told her to get with
the program or hit the pavement? What would she
choose? How far could she bend her principles?

She wished she'd had time to think it through. But
she could hear voices from inside the conference
room. Impatient voices. "Where is that damned
woman?" came hissing through the door in the whiny
tones of Drake Witley.

She had nowhere to go but in.

With a deep breath and a final small prayer to any
gods or goddesses who looked out for lowly radio
hosts, Nell twisted the door handle and slipped inside.

Two strangers stood in front of the windows. Her
jaw dropped. Her pulse pounded. She felt as if she'd
entered a dimension where time moved very slowly
and she couldn't move at all.

The Jones Boys.

She'd never met them before, but it wasn't hard to
guess these guys were the dynamic duo. They were
both beautifully dressed in smashing, cutting-edge
suits, and one of them even had sunglasses on, as if
to underline the fact that he was too hip for the room.
The other one had a trendy little beard, the kind that
Hollywood folk were so fond of. They were biding

their time throwing darts at a flimsy dartboard left over from a W-109 giveaway promotion. The conference room was spacious enough that they were nowhere near Nell, but it didn't matter.

Big. Noisy. Gorgeous. Overpowering.

She would never have believed it was possible for a couple of men—even broad-shouldered, handsome, arrogant ones—to suck all the air out of a room.

The darker one—he was the one with the goatee and *very* blue eyes—looked over and grinned when the door clicked shut behind her. His gaze and his smile held her for only a second, yet she felt as if she'd been knocked back and pinned to the wall by the sheer force of his personality.

Lordy, lordy. No wonder they always got what they wanted. Who could fight with that much blatant masculine energy simmering in one place?

But the big question was—what were they doing here? Even when she'd told Amy that these two were pulling marketing's strings, she hadn't really expected them to show up in the flesh. In the sensational, sinful, drop-dead gorgeous flesh.

Nell forced herself *not* to look anywhere near the windows. There still seemed to be a lack of oxygen around her, but she would just have to take shallow breaths as long as those guys, with their impossibly white teeth and devilish smiles, were still in the room.

Her gaze ricocheted over a few members of the marketing department who were milling around, coming to rest on evil little Drake Witley, their newly crowned king. He hovered behind the conference table, gripping the back of a chair, sort of glaring at her and smiling at the same time, which was kind of creepy.

"It's about time, Ms. McCabe," he said, pursing his lips. "We've been waiting."

She tried to explain, "I just got the memo—" but he cut her off, waving a hand in the air.

"Forget it. What do you think?"

"I think the..." She stopped herself before she said, *I think the Jones brothers are even more amazing than all the newspapers and magazines say. I think I want to become the love slave of a Jones Boy.* Confused, she asked, "What do I think about what?"

"About *that!*" Witley snapped, jerking a thumb over his shoulder.

Nell's eyes widened. With all the testosterone flying around over by the windows, she'd somehow missed the monstrosity on the opposite wall. The whole wall. It was a picture of a reclining woman, in a very brief red dress, tossing back her tousled blond mane as she nestled into a velvet settee and whispered seductively into a phone.

She moved closer. She backed up. "Oh. My. God."

It couldn't be, could it? *Her?*

No, it couldn't be. She squinted. The wild hair, the bedroom eyes, the luscious lips... Had they put someone else's head on her body?

But then she got a gander at the body. It wasn't worthy of *Playboy* or anything, but still... Creamy white skin spilled from a rather daring scrap of scarlet silk. Nell felt her face flame. There was cleavage there that she definitely did *not* own. Had they put someone else's body on her head?

"That's not *me,* is it?" She remembered the slip dress very well, and she recalled posing against a couch like that, and even holding a telephone receiver. So it had to be her. But holy smokes! Even her own mother wouldn't recognize that slitty-eyed vamp! She whispered, "Thank goodness for small favors."

"Well?" Drake prompted.

"It—it's huge," she said with a gulp.

"Of course. You have to go big when you go on buses."

"Buses? Not…" What was that rushing sound in her ears? "You don't mean that this…this *thing* is going to ride around on the side of a bus?"

"Not a bus. Buses. Lots of them. Also billboards. We want you to be the talk of the town." From the corner of her eye Nell could see that the lazy, amused voice—accompanied by the *thwap* of a dart slapping into cork—came from the blue-eyed Jones brother, the one with the goatee and the sexy smile. She didn't dare look directly at him—the monster picture was making her feel faint enough—without bringing Mr. Prime-Male-Flesh-on-the-Hoof, whose voice sent shivers up her spine, into things.

"Fabulous pic," Drake Witley mused. "I don't know how he did it. The photographer is a genius at touch-ups, I guess. Or would that be special effects?"

She wasn't exactly sure how to respond to that, but she didn't have to.

Off to the side, the brother in sunglasses fired a dart into the board and declared, "Bull's-eye!" which made everyone in the room jump. Then he crowed, "That's it—it's all over, sports fans. You lose, Griff!"

Blue Eyes—Griffin Jones, who even Nell knew to be the older of the two famous brothers—objected immediately. "Look at it, Spence. It's on the line. No way that's a bull's-eye."

"It's not my fault it's not a regulation board and the lines are open. Face it, bro—I win, you lose.

What'd we say? Winner gets a hundred bucks and the house in Palm Beach?''

Silly men and their silly game! Didn't they realize she had a crisis going on here? For all she knew, the damn bus poster was *their* idea.

As they fought over their darts game, Nell fervently wished for lightning to come zapping in the window and scorch them both where they stood. And to set that big, trampy picture ablaze as well.

No such luck.

"Okay," she said, trying to be as calm and collected as she could under the circumstances. All she knew at the moment was that she wanted to get out of this crazy conference room, where everything seemed bigger than life. Backing up a step, she said, "So, Mr. Witley, you called this meeting to show me the poster, right? And I, uh, saw it. So we're all done here?"

"Done? Not at all." Drake smiled, exposing tiny, sharp teeth. No wonder he reminded people of a snake. "I haven't told you the best part yet."

After adjusting his tiny wire rims, he pulled a chair up to the conference table, motioning for his secretary and several of the other marketing people to join him. As they handed over folders and pie charts, he commanded, "Sit. Sit, Nell. We have things to discuss."

She didn't really have a choice. Choosing to put the Jones Boys at her back meant she was staring straight into that awful picture, but she did it.

Witley launched into a rather windy explanation of who they thought was listening to *Tell Nell* as opposed to who should be listening, and how they thought they could best reach their target audience, who sounded like some mythical group of sixteen-year-old misfits with their own cars and too much spending money.

Nell tuned him out. She really didn't care about demographics and market shares, although she did blanch a little when she caught something about her ratings being pitiful and how they definitely thought there was room for improvement. But she held fast to the notion that if she gave herself a minute to breathe, she could come to grips with the dilemma of the monster bus poster and the incessant tinkering with her show. After all, Drake seemed sure that this new campaign would increase ratings, which was a good thing, right?

Plus there was the sticky little fact that her contract gave the station complete control over advertising and promotion, as well as use of her public image, which meant she already knew she didn't have a leg to stand on....

"And that brings us to *this*." Drake Witley patted the front cover of a glossy folder that one of his minions had hurriedly set in front of him. "You're going to love it," he assured Nell. "As you know, ratings have been dire across the board at W-109. We've tried to create some excitement with programming changes and we're making headway. But that's not enough. So, with the backing of our new, hands-on owners..."

He inclined his head toward Griffin and Spencer Jones, who seemed to have started up another round of darts to settle the dispute over the last one. Hands-on? The only thing they had their hands on at the moment were cheap darts and a ridiculous competition with each other.

But Drake continued, "We've come up with a new concept for you that we think listeners are going to love."

"A new concept?" Nell asked carefully. "What does that mean?"

"Everything." He flipped open the folder with a flash. "Ta-da! *The Hot Zone*."

She let the words hang there for a second. "The... *Hot Zone?* And what exactly is that?"

"No more *Tell Nell*." After drawing out the name of the show to make it sound nasal and snide, he shrugged. "That's old, that's yesterday, that's blah. But when we invite callers to enter *The Hot Zone*, wow! Heat, passion, drama! That's somewhere they want to go."

Sounded like normal marketing baloney to Nell. "So you're basically talking about a name change?"

Restless, Witley stood up to his full height, which brought him to about five-four. "It's the concept, babe. Think concept. *The Hot Zone*. Where callers are encouraged to share their steamiest secrets, to sizzle those airwaves. So we plaster your poster around the city, with a banner headline—blazing red script that reads, Call Me! And then we add one of our new tag lines. My favorite is *The Hot Zone*—you may need oven mitts to hold the phone. Great, huh? We've got a whole slew of 'em."

"Oven mitts? For *my* show?" she asked doubtfully.

"Not overnight, of course." Again, he frowned. "We'll work on how to ease the program content toward the hipper, more happening audience. But first, we'll get the new ad campaign rolling. And then..." He leaned in and dropped his voice, as if he were getting ready to announce the D-Day invasion or something. "We're really going to pull out all the stops. On-air giveaways, a little matchmaking among your callers, and to underline the romantic angle of

The Hot Zone, we're going to gear our efforts toward the big payoff—V-Day 2000.''

Nell blinked. ''V-Day? What's that?''

''Valentine's Day,'' he replied irritably. ''*The Hot Zone* will host a bash to end all bashes, thrown in honor of Valentine's Day 2000. It will be a once-in-a-lifetime lovefest.'' He hurried to add, ''Of course, we'll take care of all that. But you'll be right there, on the front lines, when V-Day 2000 comes down, when this promotion for *The Hot Zone* goes over the top. You and *The Hot Zone* will *be* V-Day 2000.''

''Wow.'' She took a deep breath. Her show had never had any promotion to speak of, let alone posters on buses and bashes to end all bashes. ''That sounds, well, interesting.''

Drake Witley stretched his thin lips into a smile. ''Exciting, dynamic, *hot.* That's what we're going for.''

''Oh, yes. Of course,'' she murmured.

''Well, well, plenty of time to worry about the details,'' Witley declared suddenly. He jerked his head to the side, which apparently signaled one of his associates to run over and whip open the door. Everyone seemed to be gazing expectantly at her, and Nell got the idea that she was being excused. ''Great to have you on board as the centerpiece of our *Hot Zone* campaign.''

''Great to, uh, be on board.'' As she rose and made her way toward the exit, she was still trying to wrap her mind around the idea that she, Nell McCabe, would be hosting something called *The Hot Zone.* Not to mention participating in a ''lovefest'' on Valentine's Day 2000.

Valentine's Day, of all things, when she usually sat home in her robe with a pint of cherry chocolate chip ice cream to drown her sorrows. It was mind-boggling.

As she entered the doorway, she turned back to offer a quick exit line, but she accidentally glanced back to where Blue Eyes and his brother stood. Oops. Her gaze caught that damn Griffin Jones for just a millisecond. And he winked at her. *Winked.*

He might as well have bitten her. She felt like she'd just caught jungle fever and her temp was already rising. She spun to look at Drake the Snake instead, and mumbled, "Thanks for bringing me in on the meeting."

"You bet, Nell," Witley said briskly. "You're on the team. We'll keep you up on what's happening every step of the way." He nodded to an aide, who carefully edged the door shut behind her.

Nell was plenty glad to be out of there, away from all that maddening manliness, and she had every intention of racing back to report to Amy on the fact that the Jones brothers really had been there and they were worse—and better looking—than anyone thought. But she paused a second, just outside, long enough to hear Drake gripe, "She's got a bad attitude. Maybe we need to replace her. Surely we can find another blonde who looks vaguely like the picture."

What? So much for team spirit. Nell stopped where she was, tilting her ear closer to the door. A different voice, one she knew must belong to Griffin or Spencer Jones, interrupted. "I like her. She looks great in the poster. I'd call in if I thought I was talking to *her.*"

Okay, so that was probably the one who'd winked at her. She blushed just thinking about it.

"Yeah, right," the other one said with a laugh. "You, calling in for romance on the radio? Like that would happen in a million years. I say we cancel her.

It's a show for losers, and some lame ad campaign with an even lamer party attached to it isn't going to fix anything. Can the show now. Put on pro wrestling instead.''

A derisive hoot greeted his words. "Wrestling, Spence? This time you really are out of your mind. Wrestling, on the radio. That's a new one.''

"It could work.''

"Care to put some money on it?''

"I'm always up for a little wager, Griff. You know that. We put on pro wrestling and it tanks, I'll give you back the house in Palm Beach I just won. But if *I* win—''

But Drake's whiny voice cut in before Spencer Jones could list his terms. "Gentlemen, gentlemen, please, let's stay on track, shall we? You agreed to let us try *The Hot Zone* through February fourteenth, until we see if this new promotion and the Fantasy Bash bring the numbers up. That's still our deal, right?''

"Absolutely,'' said brother number one. "But only if you keep the girl. No replacements.''

"Waste of time,'' grumbled brother number two. "But, yeah. Until February. Come on, Griffin, let's get out of here. I told Tanka I'd be back in Stockholm in time to have breakfast.''

"Breakfast?'' Griffin Jones echoed. "Is that what you're calling it these days?''

They were laughing. Laughing, damn them, about the possible demise of *Tell Nell,* aka *The Hot Zone.*

Nell hustled to get out of the hallway before the Jones Boys caught her eavesdropping and marched back to her office in a grim mood. Even reconstituted, reformatted and reduced to the lowest common denominator, her beloved show was still hanging on by a thread. *Until February.* That was all the time she had to get the ratings up, make *The Hot Zone* something she could live with and save her place on the airwaves.

It was terrible. And she couldn't help but think it was all the Jones Boys' fault.

2

"VALENTINE'S DAY 2000 is practically here," lamented a petulant female voice on the radio. "And my love life is colder than the ice chunks in Lake Michigan."

Griffin Jones clenched his jaw. He'd been back in Chicago for only a few hours, but that was long enough to have heard *The Hot Zone*'s promotional spots three or four times. It was also plenty long enough to have formed an opinion on just how lame they were.

The plastic voice on the radio continued mournfully, "Tom won't return my calls. Dick moved to Alaska. And Harry is too, well, hairy! I'll never get a date in time for V-Day. What am I going to do?"

"Are you *kidding?*" demanded another, even phonier voice. This one was trying to sound jiggy and jammin'. It was pitiful. "Girlfriend, we are going to turn up the temp. We are going to enter *The Hot Zone!*"

Griffin listened to every misconceived word, feeling more and more irate. For what they were paying Drake Witley to bring up the ratings at station W-109, these ads were practically criminal.

Back on the radio, the dialogue continued. "You have heard of *The Hot Zone*, haven't you?" the second woman asked. "It's hosted by Nell McCabe and there's always some amazing guy calling in, steaming up the line. And now *The Hot Zone* is—are you ready?—sponsoring a V-DAY 2000 Fantasy Bash in the ballroom at the gorgeous, all-new Arcadia Hotel. And we're going to be there!"

"We are?"

"We are!" The second voice picked up speed. "Look out for the smokin'est party of the millennium—majorly cool music, fab drinks and eats, all kinds of awesome prizes, such as flowers and chocolates and lingerie, even free nights at the spectacular Arcadia Hotel... How can we not go?"

"But I don't have a guy!" the chirpy one cried. "There won't be any Fantasy Bash for me without a date."

"That's the best part," the other one shot back. "Nell McCabe from *The Hot Zone* will be matching up dates, right on the air, starting next week. Even better—if you get a match, you get free tickets to the Fantasy Bash. One little phone call and you can win a free pass to romance—a super-sizzling V-Day 2000 date with Mr. Right!"

"Wow. That sounds great. A date for Valentine's Day *and* free tickets to the Fantasy Bash. I'm goin' for it!"

"Griff, could you please turn that thing off?" Spencer begged from the far corner of the loft. Slapping his cell phone shut after a lengthy business call, he dropped to the edge of the bed. "I can't stand it."

Spencer's attitude didn't bode well for whatever deal he'd been working on, but Griffin ignored his brother's request and the perky radio voice continued.

"Stay home, call from the car, listen at work—whatever you have to do!" it urged. "But don't miss your chance.'' There was a sort of rough, raspy sound, followed by a whoosh, as if a huge match had scraped across sandpaper before it burst into flame. That was followed by a sexy whisper that breathed, ''*The Hot Zone*—strike a match.''

''Well, the last part's not bad.'' Griff turned off the radio, and meandered over nearer his brother. ''Okay, let's hear it. Who was on the phone?'' Spencer's expression was grim. ''Don't tell me—Seaboard Development.''

''Yep,'' Spence said gloomily.

''Not going well, I take it?'' It should've been a slam dunk, an easy deal. Stopping in Chicago to fool with the radio station made it a little trickier, since the Seaboard project was outside L.A., but still... It was a no-brainer.

''Actually, it was going fine. I've got all the permits, the zoning, the contracts... Everything but one lousy parcel of land.'' Spence frowned. ''Miss Brody's Academy is hanging tough.''

Griffin glanced over at his brother. ''Hoity-toity boarding school for girls, great view of the ocean, right where our third golf course is supposed to go? That land is key, Spence. So buy it, level it and break ground for the eighteenth hole already.''

''They won't budge.''

''A *girls'* school?'' Griff repeated derisively. ''And that's holding up a six-billion-dollar resort? Get rid of 'em. If they won't sell, convince them.''

''I've tried—''

''You know what to do,'' Griff cut in. ''Convince harder. Sic the health department and the local authorities on them—there have to be violations all over the place if they look hard enough. Not enough chlorine in the pool, dangerous lacrosse fields, school uniforms that burst into flame... I don't care. Oh, and find out who the competition is. Maybe we can fund a couple of chairs there and hire away Miss Brody's best teachers.'' He shrugged. ''One little girls' school is not going to stand in the way of our biggest resort ever.''

''I'm on it.'' But Spence fell back onto the giant bed, knocking a flurry of small velvet pillows onto the floor.

Griffin leaned over to retrieve a small, vaguely oval purple pillow, and tossed it negligently at his brother. ''What the heck is this supposed to be?''

''I think it's an eggplant,'' Spencer noted absently.

''I meant this whole place.'' Looking around at the eccentric loft he was supposed to stay in while he was in Chicago, Griffin shook his head. ''Last time I let you be in charge of housing.''

The place was all high ceilings, gaping empty spaces and wacky furnishings, as if someone had ripped off a white elephant sale and then scattered their booty every which way. There was even a sled with the word ''Rosebud'' on it fastened to one brick wall, not to mention a grand piano, a full-sized cutout of actor John Wayne in cowboy regalia, a carousel horse, a huge clock that was also a window and a basketball hoop.

The big, round bed sat on a raised platform over in the corner, and it was littered with tiny pillows, all shaped like vegetables.

Spence shrugged. ''Since we got this place thrown in on the hotel and condo deal, and nobody seems to want to buy the damn things, I figured we might as well use a couple of the lofts.''

''And is yours as weird as this one?'' Griffin inquired.

"Nah, I gave you the good one. You know, if we're going to be here through February, it'll be good to have a little room to spread out." He grinned. "We can play tennis lengthwise if we move the rowboat and the hammock."

"Great. Just what I want to do—play tennis in my apartment."

"We don't have to stay, y'know. We could always unload that worthless radio station," Spence offered. "Without it, we have no reason to be here. We could catch the next boat to Fiji, Hong Kong, wherever."

Griff lifted an eyebrow. Sometimes his brother was so transparent. They'd put a small wager on whether W-109 would improve its ratings before February fourteenth, and now Spencer was trying to maneuver Griffin into a default. If they sold the station before the bet deadline, it wouldn't make any difference whether the ratings rose or fell. "No way. We promised Witley we'd give him until Valentine's Day. I'm not going back on my word."

"Weather's a lot better in Fiji."

"But W-109 is here, little bro. And so are the other ten buildings we bought, all of them in various states of renovation. Like the beautiful Arcadia Hotel, for one, where this Valentine's shindig is supposed to come off." He sat down a little gingerly in a grand wooden throne with paws for arms and a big lion's head curving over the top. Just to annoy his brother, he said, "You know, I'm starting to like this place."

"And here I thought I was doing you a favor," Spence muttered, sitting up, weighing a pillow that looked like a plump tomato in one hand. "Letting you off easy. Listen to those ads, Griff. No way they lead to anything but disaster."

Unfortunately, Griffin agreed. He pulled himself up

out of the lion throne and went in search of his brief-case, where he'd stuffed the last ratings report his assistant had faxed him.

"Man, I don't know what we're doing with that station, anyway," Spencer grumbled. "It was just a whim—"

"Your whim."

"Okay, my whim. But as soon as I listened to a couple of their shows, I knew it was a mistake."

Griffin grinned, setting aside a folder. "And as soon as I listened, I thought it was a good idea. I kind of like plucky little W-109. And I especially like Nell McCabe."

"Come on, Griff. Her show was terrible then and it's terrible now. Dullsville."

"I disagree. I think there's a hit there, waiting to happen."

"You always disagree, just on principle. You know, Griff, if you weren't related to me, and if you didn't have such a damn fine knack for making money, I would seriously wonder about you." Spence lobbed his tomato pillow at the basketball hoop, and it swished through. He raised his arms and crowed, "He hits the three!" before getting back to the subject at hand. "As far as Nell and her program go, we both know that nobody in their right mind is going to call in to get a date. They might as well have Loser stamped on their foreheads. And if nobody calls in, then the Fantasy Bash is sunk, too. Throwing a party nobody comes to is not exactly good PR."

"Hold on a sec," Griffin interjected. He rifled through his briefcase, pulled out a file and rose to his feet. "The ads may be losers, but I still think the matchmaking idea is a winner. Women love that kind of thing. Plenty of them will be dialing in looking for dream dates.''

''Maybe.'' Spencer narrowed his eyes as he pitched a small mushroom at the hoop, but missed by a mile. He reached for a carrot. Swish. ''But what kind of man would stoop that low? Dialing for dates? That's sad.''

Griffin shook his head, impatient, as always, with his thickheaded brother. ''Think about it. There are a lot of men out there savvy enough to call in and go down the list and say all the things women want to hear—''

''The list? What list?''

''It ain't hard,'' Griffin returned darkly. ''Let's see. Some guy calls in, claims to be good-looking, lonely and rich. He can be pumping gas for a living, you understand, as long as he says for five minutes on the radio that he's a brain surgeon. Rich, but caring. Good-looking, but modest. Plus he's lonely, vulnerable, a little gun-shy. Why? Maybe he's been hurt in the past, like his girlfriend dumped him.''

''Don't you think that makes him sound like a wuss?''

Griffin offered a cynical grin. ''Women eat it up. What else?'' He lifted his shoulder in a careless shrug. ''Caring, wounded, rich… I think that'll do it.''

''I think any woman with a brain would see through that in about five seconds.''

''Since when do you know anything about women with brains?'' Griffin asked dryly. ''I think any man who plays the game can have his pick of dates. And after one man does it, the rest will be lining up.''

''No way.''

''Yes way.''

''You're wacked.'' Starting to look a little frustrated, Spencer began to pelt velvet veggies at the backboard. "I still say nobody's going to call in for a fix-up, and the Bash will be a bust."

"Yeah, well, I guess it's lucky for me then, that the Bash wasn't in the bet." Griffin tossed the ratings report on the bed. "We said ratings and ratings alone. What was it? *The Hot Zone* was supposed to have a twenty percent increase between last July and February fourteenth. So, read it and weep. Because the numbers jumped twenty-seven percent once the name change and the posters kicked in."

"And fell back down," Spencer noted.

"Yeah, but they're still fourteen percent higher than they were."

"There's a lot of room between fourteen and twenty, and not a whole lot of time to do it," his brother argued. "Besides, they were so anemic to start out with that one more guy listening in his basement would've been a fifty percent jump."

"So? Up is up. A jump's a jump." Griffin's smile widened. "I think a twenty percent increase is a sure thing after the Fantasy Bash. Looks like the house in Palm Beach will be coming back to me after all."

"Aw, that thing has changed hands so many times, who cares?" Spencer met his brother's gaze intently. Griffin knew what was coming. "What do you say we make this more interesting?"

"How?"

"My new plane. The Learjet. One-of-a-kind, specially built for me. And a lot more fun than the Palm Beach property, don't you think?"

"You know I do. I've been trying to get you to let me fly the thing for a month. I'm listening."

"Okay, here's the deal." With a crooked smile that Griffin knew better than to trust, Spencer continued,

"I say we put everything back on the table, not just the ratings, but the matchmaking *and* the party."

"Keep talking."

"It's easy. If it goes your way—the ratings increase twenty percent, the show gets hot, lots of mopes call in to get matched up and the party's a hit—then I turn over the keys to my plane."

As intensely competitive as they were, Griffin was quite used to Spence and his sucker bets. "No way. None of that is verifiable except the ratings."

Spencer considered. "Okay, we'll name a referee, somebody to make an independent call. How about Hildy?"

As Griffin's longtime assistant, Hildy Johnson might've been presumed to have a bias. But they both knew she was as honest as the day was long. The perfect choice. "Okay. I can go for Hildy as referee. She's flying in tomorrow, anyway, to set up an office for me here, so if we do this I'm sure she could monitor the show and the Fantasy Bash without too much trouble. But your terms still need work."

"Listen, if it comes down the way I know it will— little Nell sitting there without call one, the party a flopola and the whole thing a laughingstock in the papers, then..." Spence put an arm around his older brother. "Let's say that if any one of the three fizzles, then you give me the *Truelove*."

"My yacht? No way!"

"You sounded like you thought this was in the bag. What's the matter, Griff? You don't trust your girl Nell to pull it off?"

"I think she'll do just fine." He frowned. "But come on—you have to go at least two of the three. Ratings, callers and the Valentine's Day party. Two out of three bomb, you win. Two out of three fly, I win. And if you want me to put up the *Truelove,* you're going to have to sweeten the pot.''

"Maybe." Spence took his time to ponder the question. "Okay, this is my final offer. If two of the three make it, then I hand over my plane and the house in Palm Beach." As Griffin began to interrupt, Spencer waved him off, adding, "*And* I'll throw in another bone—solo ownership of the station. All yours."

"Okay. Now you're talking."

"But if two of the three flop, then *I* win. I get the yacht and…" Spence paused, smiling shrewdly. "And Nell McCabe gets her fanny fired, while Tanka gets her time slot. Maybe she'd like to host a show about supermodels."

"A fashion show on the radio, hosted by a woman who barely speaks English? That's worse than the pro wrestling idea."

"Is it a deal?"

Griffin considered his odds. Pretty damn good, as he saw it. "Deal."

His brother's smile grew more cocky. "I can't wait to get my hands on the *Truelove.* And Tanka is going to love having her own show."

"Your chickens are a long way from hatching," Griff said flatly. He scooped up a bright green pea pod pillow and gave it a high arc toward the hoop. Nothing but net. He grinned. "When have I ever lost anything to you, little bro?"

Never, Griff answered himself. Oh, there might have been a few trifles here and there over the years, but when it came to things he actually cared about, Griffin Jones never, ever lost.

And he didn't plan to start now.

Monday, January 31
Two weeks till V-Day 2000

NELL PROPPED HER head in her hands and stared at her Rolodex. "Amy, are you positive there's no way to get out of this?"

"You're stuck," her producer said flatly.

"But, Amy, I'm supposed to be the centerpiece of the whole Fantasy Bash, and that means a boyfriend, an escort, something. Who am I supposed to take? What am I supposed to do?"

"Hey, you know what I just realized?" Amy sat up straighter. "You sound just like the promo we're running, the one with the girl who doesn't have a date. We were just talking about how cheesy that ad is, and here you are saying exactly the same thing."

Nell sent her producer a dark look. "Not funny." She gave the Rolodex directory a shove to the back of her desk, pushing it behind the pencil cup and the box of tissues, where she wouldn't have to see it.

"That won't help. You have to call somebody. You have to have a date," Amy put in sensibly. "Come on, Nell. I know your love life hasn't been exactly steamy lately, but you've had dates. There must be somebody you can call."

"But that's the whole point. I don't want *some-body*. I want…" It was something she'd been thinking about ever since this whole campaign began. V-Day 2000. It was ominous, somehow. "We're talking Valentine's Day 2000. Not just any old Valentine's Day. But *2000*. I can't help but feel that's pretty significant. It should be someone special, someone you feel is worthy to help kick off a whole new century."

"Oh, no. Not The One again." Amy shook her

head sadly. "Nell, you've only got two weeks. You'll never find 'the one' in two weeks."

"Well, you never know," Nell declared with a bit more spirit. "You never know when the right guy is going to cross your path."

"Uh-huh. Which is what you've been saying since July."

"Yeah, well, that doesn't change the fact that I don't have time to do anything about it now." Nell glanced up at the clock. Only half an hour till show-time.

"Look on the bright side," Amy suggested. "At least worrying about your feeble social life has kept you busy enough to *not* worry about the rest of it. As in, today. As in, first day of Operation Strike-a-Match."

Nell lowered her head despairingly, and clonked it on the hard surface of her desk. "Ouch. I wish you hadn't said that."

"Two more weeks and it will all be over, one way or the other."

"That's true." She brightened. "Plus I've already made it through being the poster child for smut on buses, and that's no small feat—"

"Through?" Amy interrupted delicately. "You're not through, hon. The posters are still out there. Well, the few that didn't get stolen, anyway. Drake said they're rushing to print more. Apparently they're collectors' items."

"For twelve-year-old boys." Nell groaned. "You knew that my mom is a principal at a middle school out in the suburbs, right? She says I'm a hot item with the students. They go downtown and steal the posters right off the buses. Just what I always wanted to be— a pinup for juvenile delinquents."

"Oh, come on. At least it doesn't look that much like you."

"You know, that's what I thought, too." Nell scrunched up her face as she studied her reflection in the side of her metallic tape dispenser. "But a lot of people are stopping me on the street lately and telling me that they recognize me. A couple have even asked for my autograph. It's very weird."

"Any of them cute guys who want to go to the Fantasy Bash?" Amy asked hopefully. "No, huh? Well, it still means things are on the upswing. The poster did its job, ratings are rising and you're going to get a million hot callers today, all ready to find a dream date."

Nell shook her head, feeling the familiar anxiety surface. "I don't know if I can do this. Making couples out of perfect strangers, sight unseen? I feel like a madam."

"A what?" Amy giggled. "Hey, listen, I just had an idea. Why don't you get a guy for yourself off the radio?"

"Oh, right. For one thing, I think the legal department put it in the rules that I can't. For another, that wouldn't be *too* humiliating, would it?" Nell sighed. "Can you imagine the reaction if the big love-and-romance adviser confessed on the air that she didn't have a date for Valentine's Day?"

"Nell, your audience will understand if you don't have a date. Buck up, will you?"

"I'm trying, Amy, really I am. It's just…" Nell paused. "The thing is, not being in a relationship, not having any particular credentials, I'm not sure that I, of all people, should be playing Ms. Matchmaker. I mean, I'm not a doctor or a psychologist or anything.

I never even finished college. Everything I know, I learned on the radio!''

Amy crossed her arms over her chest and fixed Nell with a quelling stare. "Snap out of it. I say you go out there and do the best damn matchmaking anybody ever saw." She handed over the typed intro and schedule for the day's show. "Get to it, Nellie. We've got a show to put on."

Nell took a deep breath and rose from the desk, squaring her shoulders and angling her chin high. Amy was right—it was time to show Drake Witley what she was made of. She knew very well he'd just as soon replace her with someone who was sexier, sleazier and more agreeable. Hadn't she overheard him refer to her "bad attitude" with her very own ears? Everybody knew that "bad attitude" was just a euphemism for too smart and too uppity.

Well, if he was going to yank her out of her job and stick in some bimbo, at least she wasn't going to make it easy for him.

Thank goodness the big bosses—the Jones Boys—hadn't paid a return visit since that meeting last summer. That really would've put the icing on the cake. Nell had finally decided that they were too busy globe-trotting, company-plundering and supermodel-seducing to bother with little old W-109, and that was just fine with her.

So she could happily blame Drake the Snake for all her woes.

As she stomped down the hall to the broadcast studio, she was so occupied with All the Ways I Hate Drake Witley that she almost forgot she was going on the air in a few minutes. Almost. The slot before hers was a prerecorded hour of Top 40 hits, so there was no DJ or host already there waiting for a switch-over, just an empty studio. Nell settled into her usual chair, hooked up her headphones and tested her equipment, laid out her script and waved to Amy in the control booth. And all the while, she felt the flicker of some serious nerves.

On the air. Three minutes. She knew what was coming. Her feeling of dread grew as the second hand ticked off numbers.

Very soon, she would listen to as many lonely hearts as she could beg, threaten or blackmail into calling, she would match one to another, she would interject fizzy pop announcements for the Fantasy Bash and she would try to project a bright, capable, aren't-we-having fun persona. And if didn't go well, she might just be listening to her whole professional future go down the tubes.

"Nell? You ready?" Amy's voice asked over the headphones. "Thirty seconds."

She was as ready as she was ever going to be. "Let's go."

Operation Strike-a-Match was about to begin.

3

ALONE IN HIS LOFT, Griffin leaned forward on the sectional sofa. Frowning, he drummed his fingers against his leg, wondering what in the heck he was so nervous about. It wasn't *his* show. Well, technically it was, since everything at the station belonged to G&S Enterprises, but he didn't think that really counted. He'd witnessed the demise or dismantling of bigger concerns than W-109 without shedding a tear.

So why was he so anxious for *The Hot Zone* to be a hit, to fix up lots of blind dates and sail into Valentine's Day like a champ?

"That stupid bet," he said out loud. Why had he ever let Spence talk him into wagering on something this iffy in the first place? Pride. Sibling rivalry. Just plain insanity that ran in the family.

He didn't want to lose his beloved yacht, that was a given, and he also didn't want Spence acting like a jerk and firing Nell McCabe to make room for some dim Swedish supermodel. It offended Griff's better nature. He grinned. "Not that I really have one."

Right now, he was operating under the influence of his less scrupulous impulses. Knowing the call-in matchmaking campaign premiered on Monday, he'd sent his brother off to L.A., ostensibly to muscle Miss Brody and her academy out of existence. And if that kept Spencer out of town long enough for this radio campaign to debut, so much the better.

"Okay, here we go," he said under his breath as Nell McCabe's voice filled his loft, as she introduced this morning's show. She had a nice voice, he'd give her that, full of warmth and promise, just the sort of person you'd want to call up and confide in. She sounded smart, but kind and funny, too, as if your love life and your secrets would be in good hands if you turned them over to Nell.

Griffin found himself smiling just thinking about it. Surely this would work. Surely lonely-hearted listeners from all over Chicago were even now reaching for their phones.

"I hope you're all as excited as I am that the day is finally here," Nell said sweetly. "If you don't have a date for Valentine's Day, you're not alone, friends. And that's why we're here to make it easy for you, to give you the romantic adventure of a lifetime for V-Day 2000. You just call me up and tell me who it is you're looking for, and we'll see if your dream date doesn't phone in, too."

Silence.

"I can't wait to see who our first caller is," Nell enthused, repeating the phone numbers.

Silence.

Okay, so maybe it was taking people a few minutes to get in through the jammed switchboard. Griffin hunched forward, closer to the radio, waiting for the inevitable flood of calls, as Nell continued to fill the dead air, talking about dates with destiny and how much fun one little call could generate. But no calls came.

She began to backpedal. He could hear a hint of desperation in her voice.

"I know it's hard to be first up," Nell assured her listeners, "but surely one of our regular callers is brave enough. Just last Friday, we talked to, uh, Pete, who had been experiencing difficulty asking out women he worked with, and Clare, who had just left her cheating lover. Pete or Clare? If you're out there, why don't you call us back, so we can find a Valentine for you.''

No dice.

Griffin stood, jammed his hands in his pockets and paced back and forth. "How stupid are these people?" he demanded out loud. "They're all out there, alone and feeling sorry for themselves, and none of them will call? I can't believe it! What are they afraid of?"

A terrible thought suddenly took root in his mind. *They're afraid of looking like losers to the rest of the world.*

"Oh, hell. Don't tell me Spencer was right. I hate it when that happens."

Back on the radio, Nell began to sound more frantic. "Okay, then, time for a quick commercial break. Remember, all of our sponsors this week are also offering prizes and giveaways at the Fantasy Bash on Valentine's Day. You won't want to miss that."

And then some prerecorded celebrity broke in to talk about her favorite brand of lingerie. Griffin tuned it out. Listening to Nell go down in flames was excruciating.

"Desperate times, desperate measures," he muttered, trying to figure out what to do. First, it was clear she needed callers. Could he rustle up some cash, grab people off the street and pay them to phone in?

"Naaah. No time for that," he decided. "And it's too bad. Because I could tell them exactly what to say."

If he had the time, he would pick a guy, any guy, and give him the lowdown. He would instruct his patsy to say he was rich but caring, good-looking but modest, wounded but willing to try again...

And then it hit him. Why not? If it was that easy, why didn't he just do it himself? He knew the drill, he wasn't above making up a good story, and he felt sure women would be calling in like crazy to get a date with his version of Mr. Right.

Griffin knew what he had to do. First he turned down the radio. And then he flipped open his cell phone.

"HELLO? IS THIS Nell at *The Hot Zone*?"

It was a male voice. A very nice male voice, confident without sounding arrogant, low-pitched in a soft-spoken, gruffly masculine way. You could tell a lot from a voice and this one was the real deal. Of course, at that moment, she wouldn't have cared if he sounded like fingernails on a blackboard. He was a caller. And he was saving her life.

At the first flicker of the little light that indicated an incoming call, Amy had rushed him on the air. Usually she would've checked him out first, asked his name and where he was from, and then typed it all into the monitor for Nell to see before she talked to him. But this one was coming in without any preliminaries.

"Yes, this is Nell," she said quickly. "Are you calling for a match?"

"Well, I guess so," he admitted, with a trace of hesitation. "I'm not the kind of person who goes for blind dates, though, so I'm not exactly sure about this. But it sounded kind of fun, you know, to have something to do on Valentine's Day."

"Well, good, that's the spirit!" She smiled into her microphone, trying to conjure up the proper warmth and welcome. "You know, we neglected to get your name and I'm sure it would really help our listeners picture you better if they had a name to go with that wonderful voice. Do you mind?"

"No, of course not." But there was a long pause. "How about John? I mean, it's John."

Nell was used to callers protecting their real identities, so she didn't mind too much if this guy was adopting a phony moniker on the spur of the moment, although John was hardly the most original choice. "And how would you describe yourself, John?"

"Physically, you mean?"

Actually, she hadn't meant that—she was going more for internal than external details, but she let him go on. Potential partners *would* want to know whether he was a Baldwin or a beast, after all.

"I guess I'm okay," he offered casually. "People always tell me—I think they're nuts, but this is what they say—that I look like Tom Cruise, only taller. I'm six-two, dark hair, blue eyes, thirty-one years old. I used to swim competitively when I was in college so I have kind of a swimmer's body, if you know what I mean."

"Well, sort of, I guess." Nell blinked, trying to process his information.

As far as she could tell, he'd just painted a portrait of himself as a god among men. Tom Cruise, only taller? An athlete's body, as in an athlete who spent his life in tiny swim trunks showing off all his assets? Could he be serious? Her experience told her that someone who claimed to look like a movie star was probably a pompous ass. A delusional pompous ass. But the way he'd said it—sort of matter-of-factly—

made her think it might really be true. *Sheesh.* If Tom-Cruise-only-taller didn't generate calls, then no one was going to.

"Okay, so we know what you look like, and that sounds, uh, pretty great. So what do you do for a living, John?"

The answer came shooting back at her, no hesitation. "I'm a brain surgeon. Too bad, huh? If I was a heart surgeon, maybe I could've fixed my own broken heart before this."

"Did you say you were a...?" Nell stopped, stunned. He looked like Tom Cruise only taller and he was a *brain surgeon?* Now she knew he was making it up. "So, it's *Dr.* John, then?" she asked dryly.

"Sure, if you want to call me that. Some of my patients do. Being a doctor, though, it almost makes it harder to meet the right women. I guess it's because, well, I've achieved a certain financial security, and that makes me a little wary. Don't get me wrong—I'm not ashamed of my money—it gives me the chance to really give back, to do some good in this world, and I love that."

"I see," Nell murmured, jotting down "JOHN: handsome, athletic, tall, neurosurgeon, rich," and "generous" in her notebook, with several question marks at the end. She frowned. Either he was the perfect man or he had no shame whatsoever when it came to spinning lies. She probed further. "How about your family? Are you close to your parents? Siblings?"

"I'm afraid there really isn't anyone. Both my parents are gone, and I'm an only child."

Well, that was convenient, wasn't it? No parents, no siblings, no one to call up and say, "That's my son and he's making that up!" Moving on, she inquired, "And what can you tell me about your last romantic relationship?"

Silence hung on the wire for several seconds. "I'd really rather not," he said finally. "Not unless I have to. It's a...a difficult subject for me."

"Oh, come on, Dr. John. That's what I'm here for." She couldn't help it if she wasn't as sympathetic as she should've been. But she didn't like the feeling that she was the victim of an elaborate put-on. "We'll know just what sort of person to match you up with if we know what went wrong the last time," she said brightly. "On *The Hot Zone* we confess all our steamiest secrets, remember? Go for it."

"It's kind of sad," he said hesitantly. "I don't want to bring anyone down."

Why did she have the feeling it wasn't the fact that his story was sad that was stalling him, but that he hadn't finished composing it yet? "Try me."

"All right. If you think it's best," he said reluctantly. His voice dropped into a deeper range, and it sounded rougher, more uneven. "Her name was Grace," he began, "and she was beautiful. Too beautiful, I guess. I know that now. But then, I was just swept away. I thought what we had together was heaven, but maybe that's why it couldn't last. We were engaged. We were in love. It was just too perfect."

Wow. Nell blinked. He sounded really wounded there. She'd heard the heartfelt sigh, detected a note of vulnerability... She couldn't help it—she was starting to believe him, and definitely getting curious. "So what happened, John?" she asked softly. "What happened between you and Grace?"

This time, the empty air stretched between them like a chasm. Just when Nell was thinking of jumping in, he finally spoke. "She died," he said slowly. "I lost her."

Died? *Oh, no.* Her heart did a funny little flip-flop. Of course he could be handsome and wealthy and kind yet still alone, if his fiancée had *died.*

Slowly, she whispered, "I'm so sorry, John. How long ago was this?"

"Two years. But it feels like yesterday."

"Would it make you feel any better if you told us about it?"

In the control booth, Amy was waving her hands furiously, making exaggerated gestures at the console and the monitor. Nell glanced down, noting the blinking lights that meant multiple calls were waiting, and scanned the glowing green lines on the computer that rapidly added to the list of contenders. Ginger, twenty-eight, from Evergreen Park on line two. Leslie, nineteen, from Lisle on three. Audrey, seventeen, from Oak Lawn on four...

Amy flashed her hands on the other side of the glass, both hands, twice, as if to telegraph that there were twenty more callers waiting.

Twenty callers, backed up? Nell stared, disbelieving. They'd never had more than five or six before. She didn't even know the station could handle twenty calls at once.

"Break in, break in," Amy mouthed. "Tell them, if lines are busy, call back."

But she was too busy listening to John tell his tale of woe, drinking in his story of walks in the moonlight, kisses in the rain, and an ultraromantic Valentine's Day past with poor, doomed Grace. She had no time to worry about the overloaded phone circuits. Her eyes were blurred with tears by the time he was finished. For this wonderful, dear, caring man to find

the love of his life only to lose her, why, it was unthinkable, impossible, unjust! Nell pulled herself together and wiped her eyes, even as she vowed to find
him the perfect Valentine.

Amy tried to tell her something else, but she
couldn't quite make it out. "This is a…" Flower? No,
power. No, it was "downer." Oh, his call was a
downer? Amy launched into a pantomime of weeping
and wailing and breast-beating, followed by picking
up a phone receiver and smiling and laughing into it.

Nell got the idea. She needed to talk to a few of
the ladies who were on hold, bring up the happy quo-
tient, and get the program back on to love and romance instead of pain and suffering. She was in
charge here, and she shouldn't be looking a gift horse
in the mouth. It wasn't every day a rich, gorgeous,
single brain surgeon called in and offered ratings on
a platter.

Nell sat up straighter. "Dr. John, I think we've all
been touched by your tragic story. I know I have. But
there are a lot of women out there who are very anxious to get a chance to show you a few hours of happiness, and maybe even to mend your broken heart.
So if you'll stay on the line, first we'll talk to Ginger,
a twenty-eight-year-old from Evergreen Park. Ginger,
are you there? Tell us a little about yourself."

"Oh, that poor man!" Ginger gushed. "That is just
so sad. I'm kind of married, but my husband is a total
slug, so I think I'd rather step out, if you know what
I mean." She giggled. "I'd love to play doctor with
Dr. John."

Ooooh, this one was *so* wrong. Nell made a slashing motion across her throat to Amy, signaling that
Ginger was out. "Thanks for calling, Ginger. But let's
try to concentrate on women without husbands or

even boyfriends—ladies who are single, with no strings, ready to find a place in their hearts for someone as special as Dr. John.''

Leslie and Audrey were both much too young, but Rita, twenty-six, from Aurora, wasn't bad. And then there was Betty—hyperactive was an understatement, Joan—so laid-back she might have been catatonic and Nanette—who admitted to being over seventy, but insisted she was young for her age. And the calls kept coming. Just as soon as they weeded out four or five, another flood of potential mates came spilling in. Each was absolutely positive that she alone was meant for the desolate doctor.

They also heard from Ginger's irate husband, a few men who were interested in specific rejected women, and at least four others who were irate that everyone wanted to meet a wimpy brain surgeon, when they felt sure their own charms were much more alluring.

All in all, Operation Strike-a-Match was turning into a staggering success with more wanna-be fix-ups than anyone could have imagined. Finally, when Nell was beginning to droop from exhaustion, Amy gave her the "wrap up" signal, and she was happy to comply.

"Okay, callers, that's all the time we have for today. We know there were a lot of you waiting who didn't get a chance to make your pitch for Dr. John, but my producer Amy assures me that the switchboard here at W-109 will take all your names and vital statistics—we're talking age, marital status and phone numbers, please—and we'll try to get back to as many as we can who fit the bill. Never fear—we will figure out a way to pick some finalists for the good doctor's V-Day date, okay? If you're interested in another one of our callers, please make sure you tell the operator that so you don't get tossed in Dr. John's pile. And, remember, I'll be back tomorrow at eleven, and every day this week, striking more matches here in *The Hot Zone*. So if you didn't get through today, try again tomorrow. We may just find the perfect valentine for you."

She had never been so ready to turn over her chair to Lucky Garnett and the noontime news. Lucky was a creep and always tried to pinch her on her way out the door, but she didn't have the energy to smack him today.

"Whew," she said to Amy, collapsing into a chair outside the studio. "I thought we were dead. And then we were so swamped I felt like a Ping-Pong ball, getting paddled from one person to the next."

"Okay, well, don't get too relaxed." Amy looked like she'd wilted a while ago, with her hair every which way and several of her nails bitten to the quick. She attempted to drag Nell out of her chair by the arm. "You still have to talk to Mr. Wonderful, you know."

"Oh, no. Dr. John." Nell shot up. "He's not still on the phone, is he? I forgot I told him to hold on after I got buried in that avalanche of love-hungry women."

"No, he's not still hanging on. I have some sense, even if you don't." Amy sighed, pressing a slip of yellow paper into Nell's palm. "I took his name and number and I told him to keep listening, to write down the name of anyone he thought sounded good, and that you'd call him back as soon as the show was over."

Over. Nell put the hand with the note in it up to her forehead, trying not to think about how close her whole career had come to being over. Lowering her voice, she whispered to Amy, ''He really saved us in the nick of time. If he hadn't called when he did, I'm not sure we'd still be working here.''

Her producer frowned. ''I know. But, hey, he threw us a lifeline and we jumped on it, and that's the end of it.'' She fixed a thoughtful gaze on her friend. ''The real question is, do you think he made it all up?''

Nell had just started to formulate her opinion on that issue when she happened to glance down at the name and number scribbled on the small yellow paper clutched in her hand. She narrowed her eyes. ''Jones? Dr. John *Jones?* Like we haven't heard that one before. Well, if I didn't think it was a scam before, I do now.''

''I know it sounds hokey—I thought so, too,'' Amy told her. ''But when I asked him his last name, he said Jones without even thinking. It sounded really natural.''

Nell shook her head. ''Only because he'd had time to practice by then. Every man who calls in expects us to believe he's a Jones, a Smith or a Johnson. You'd think they'd get a clue after a while.''

''Maybe. I don't know. But I do know you'd better get back to him pronto, before he gets away. Even if he's as phony as a three-dollar bill, we still need him to lead the way to the Fantasy Bash.'' Amy shuddered. ''I don't know about you, but I don't want to have to tell all those women that the amazing Dr. J. slipped through our fingers and nobody gets to date him.''

Nell considered. ''You have a point.''

''Good. So call him, say whatever you have to say to make sure he'll go through with this date, and then we have to start on the list from the switchboard so

we can find his one true love." As she held open the
door for Nell, Amy offered a cynical smile. "Come
on, McCabe. We've got a lot of names to go
through."

"How many do you think?" Nell asked, dreading
the answer.

"Maybe a thousand..."

That was all it took. "Before I call him, I think we
should pay marketing a visit," Nell decided. "This
was their brilliant idea, after all. Let the telemarketers
get on the horn to every single one of these people
and quiz them on what they like and dislike and why
they think they should win the date with Mr. Right. I
want whole profiles."

"Brilliant idea." Amy steered her friend back
down the hall. "So I'll talk to marketing, and you
quit stalling and go call Mr. Right. See if you can't
figure out if he's a fake, will you? I'll feel a whole
lot better if we solve that mystery."

Amy's logic was inescapable. Although she was
still a bit reluctant, Nell returned to her small, cluttered office and reached for the phone.

As soon as he said hello she jumped, and her palm
felt sweaty wrapped around the receiver. She talked
to people every day for a living. What was it with
this guy? Why did he knock her off her pins this way?

"Dr. Jones?" she asked rather tersely. "Is that
you?"

She'd thought she might trip him up right off the
bat when she addressed him by a name she was sure
wasn't his. But he was smooth as silk.

"Nell?" he asked, as if he were genuinely pleased
to hear from her. "I recognize your voice, of course.
I listen to your show all the time. You always sound
so warm and inviting."

"I—I do?" Warm and inviting, huh? She knew she had a good radio voice—it was the reason she was still on the air after seven years—but it was nice to hear.

"Oh, absolutely. Listen, I've been waiting for your call." He paused. "I enjoyed talking to you today, really I did. I think it was very therapeutic for me, you know, pushing me toward moving on, reaching closure. And it was very gratifying when so many women called in." Modestly, he confided, "I had no idea the response would be like that."

"It was pretty overwhelming, wasn't it?"

"Yes, it was. Overwhelming." He paused again before continuing. "The thing is, I'm not sure I can go through with this. With the Fantasy Bash, I mean. I'm still feeling a little gun-shy about the whole dating thing."

"Oh, no. No, no," she cut in, as alarm bells rang in her brain. "You can't back out! Think of how many women would be disappointed. You don't want that, do you?"

"Well, no, but—"

"You need to do this," she insisted. "It's for your own good. You have to reenter the dating world sometime, and this is a totally painless way to do it, all arranged and paid for by W-109. We'll be very careful to find you just the right match and to take your preferences into account."

"I don't know," he said, and there was silence on the line.

"I have to admit, John, I don't really understand your reticence." *Unless, of course, you're a three-foot troll with warts bigger than you are and this whole thing has been a con game.* Thinking out loud, she added, "You shouldn't have any problem with it. If you really are who you say you are, that is."

"What do you mean?" he demanded, with a definite edge to his voice.

Stuck, Nell finished the thought. "Well, I have to admit that a couple of us were wondering about your story. I mean, you said your name was Jones. John Jones! And there aren't too many neurosurgeons out there who look like Tom Cruise, you know."

"I said I was taller."

"I remember. The point is, if you were just having some fun at my show's expense, then I will understand why you're backing out now." She adopted her most persuasive tone. "But if you really are the vulnerable man who talked to me today, the one who loved and lost, who is ready to start again, then there is no reason in the world for you not to move on to the next step."

"And if I'm moving on," he asked, sounding just a little peeved, "what is the next step?"

Hmm… Good question. It should be picking a suitable female to accompany him to the Fantasy Bash. But for some reason, Nell just couldn't do that. There were too many doubts nibbling at the corners of her mind.

Good-looking, rich, generous, modest, a doctor… He was just too darn perfect. And his name was John Jones. She was not a suspicious person by nature, but neither was she a sap. Naaah, she couldn't in good conscience match him up with anyone. Not yet. For all she knew, he was a homicidal lunatic.

A plan formed in her fertile brain, and she grabbed it. It would certainly answer, once and for all, whether he looked like Tom Cruise.

"I want to meet you," she said quickly.

It was the oddest thing, but her heart was suddenly thumping in her chest, and she was experiencing trouble breathing.

In a choked sort of voice, he echoed, "Meet? In person?"

"That's the basic idea."

"I don't think I can do that."

"Why not?" she argued. "You were going to have to meet whoever you got for the Fantasy Bash, anyway. I mean, that was the whole idea, wasn't it? I just want to meet you first, have a nice conversation, make sure I know what kind of woman would fit you best, and then take it from there."

"I—I suppose. It's just..." He broke off and began again. "I'm painfully shy."

"Don't be absurd. I talked to you for half an hour on my show, and I can say with absolute certainty that you are not that shy." Nell couldn't believe how pushy she was being. But once she got her teeth into something, she had a hard time letting go. And now that she'd started, she was determined to meet Dr. John Jones, face to face, to find out whether he was Adonis in a bathing suit or a Billy Goat Gruff.

"Okay," he said finally, in a clipped, cold voice. "I'll meet you. Dinner, tonight."

It was as if a gauntlet had been hurled down in front of her. "Dinner. Fine." She named a restaurant, the first one that popped into her head, somewhere that was always in the paper as a place to be seen, and then she dropped the receiver into the cradle before she had a chance to think better of what she'd done.

"Oh, brother," she whispered. She put a shaky hand to her throat. "I may be having dinner with Dr. John the Ripper."

4

AFTER SLAPPING it shut, Griffin threw his cell phone across the loft.

"Damn it, damn it, damn it," he snarled. "I was supposed to create some excitement and then get out of there. Who does she think she is, not believing me? My name *is* Jones. So what if I made up the John part?" He elbowed aside the cardboard cutout of John Wayne. "It's a reasonable name. And the Tom Cruise thing—it's not my fault if people say that's who I look like. In fact, that's a direct quote from *People* magazine."

He ought to know—Spence had kidded him about it incessantly, until the words were imprinted on his brain. *With his* Top Gun *good looks and merciless wit, older brother Griffin Jones is known as an intimidator, but younger brother Spencer and his easy charm are welcome everywhere.*

Translated, that meant that Griffin frequently grew impatient with fools and bimbos, while Spencer felt right at home in such company.

What a bunch of hooey. "Okay, so I went too far when I decided to go for the surgeon thing. But it created a buzz, didn't it?" Griff ran a hasty hand through his hair as he stalked over to get his phone back, but he was still talking to himself as he hit the speed dial. "And she has the nerve to say she doesn't believe me. Me! Yeah, well, I'll show her a Mr. Right, er, Dr. Right who will knock her socks off."

"G&S," the cool voice answered. "May I help you?"

"Hildy, it's me. Did you listen to *The Hot Zone?*"

"Uh-huh." He could hear her smile. "I guess you had some fun this morning, *Dr.* Jones."

He should've realized he couldn't fool Hildy. "How long did it take you to figure out it was me?"

"Oh, about a second and a half. Pretty good job, all things considered. The dead fiancée was a nice touch," she noted. "Where'd you get that?"

"Some old movie," he said sheepishly. "It worked like a charm."

"Pretty low, boss, even for you." She continued, "So I suppose you're calling to find out if I think your little impersonation killed the bet you asked me to monitor. I did think about it. I mean, it *is* deceitful and manipulative, but when have you ever been anything else? It's not like your brother isn't on notice. Besides, no one specifically disallowed direct contact. So I think you're okay. I'll wait till the end of the two-week period to make my report, but so far, it sounds like phase one, the on-air dating service, is a winner. Congrats, Mr. G."

"Thanks." He clenched his jaw. "But that's not what I need from you."

"Oh? Oh, is this about the Seaboard project? I'm getting bad vibes on that one, boss. Seems Miss Brody and her girls have some muscle."

"I can't believe Spence is still fooling around with that," he muttered. "Jeez—we've wiped out a hundred better sites than that one. What *is* the deal?" He still thought it would take about five minutes to clear up if he were handling it himself. But that would have to wait. "Listen, put Seaboard on hold. That's not why I called—"

"Oh, I get it. This is about your brother. Don't worry, I won't tell him about your whirl on *The Dating Game*. But if he asks me right out, I can't lie."

"No, no, that's not it, either. I don't care if Spence knows." He waved his free hand in the air, as if to take that statement back. "I mean, I do care—I'd rather he didn't know—but that's not why I called."

"Don't tell me," Hildy said wearily, "you want me to call in tomorrow and pretend to be a lovelorn movie star looking for a boy toy. No way—"

"No, no. You're on the wrong track entirely. What I want…" He broke off. "Do you have a pencil handy, Hildy? Maybe you should start a list. Here's the thing. I need some new ID, whatever you can whip up by seven o'clock tonight. Better make it six-thirty. The name on the ID should be John Jones. Wait, let's give him a middle name. You can pick something that sounds good."

"Mmm-hmm," Hildy murmured. How she managed to put so much sarcasm into two syllables he didn't know. He ignored it.

"Make it a hospital badge of some sort. For a doctor. You know, something that looks plausible. That shouldn't be too tough. I'll also need some clothes." He rubbed his clean-shaven chin absently, trying to remember whether he'd had the beard when Nell McCabe saw him for the first and only time. He thought so. That at least was different. His hair was cut a bit longer now, too. But what about clothes? He chewed his lip, casting around in his mind for possible prototypes. "Remember that accountant we had in Zurich? Hans somebody. Get me what you think he would wear. Oh, and a pair of glasses. The lady has met me before so I need to look as different as possible."

"Can I offer a suggestion, sir?" his assistant interjected politely.

"Shoot."

"Stop now, while you still have a chance." Her tone was quite stern. "Pretending to be someone else on the phone is one thing, but trying to pull off a whole disguise in person is going too far."

"Thank you for your opinion. Can you get me what I need?"

"No way to talk you out of this?"

"Nope."

"All right then." He heard the rustle of paper on the other end of the phone. "The ID is a cinch, but the clothes will take a little longer. Six-thirty, you said? I think I can make that. Do you want a prescription in the specs, or plain glass?"

"Tint them, but no prescription. Oh, and you'd better get socks and shoes, too—the whole works." He frowned as he looked down at the sleeve of his Hugo Boss jacket and the antique Cartier watch on his wrist. Nothing he owned was right for this new persona. "The works."

"She going to be stripping you down to your undies, is she?" Hildy asked acidly. "Don't answer that. Okay, I've got the list. I'll get right on it. Oh, and boss?"

"Yeah?"

There was an audible pause. "Good luck."

INSIDE THE DIMLY lit Graystone Grill, Nell looked around for anyone who remotely resembled Tom Cruise. No such luck.

"Hmph," she said. "I thought so."

The place was stuffed to the gills with balding, middle-aged, businessman types. Which meant the mysterious Dr. John didn't look remotely like he'd said he did.

All ready to be righteously indignant, Nell wavered. Maybe it just meant that he wasn't here yet.

"May I help you?" the maître d' asked coolly. "Do you have a reservation?"

Thank goodness she'd asked Drake the Snake to arrange a table for her. The Graystone Grill, where the city's biggest movers and shakers guzzled fine scotch, smoked long cigars and dined on big planks of rare meat, would probably have turned her away at the door otherwise. Casting an eye around the place, she wished she'd chosen somewhere else. It was all so masculine somehow, clubby and dark and severe, with decorations that looked like they'd been brought directly from a rock quarry. There was a bustle of conversation, a haze of cigar smoke, and a shadowy atmosphere of deals being made under the table.

No, this was not her style. It seemed much more conducive to keeping secrets than uncovering them.

"Reservation?" the snooty man at the door asked again.

"Yes. I'm Nell McCabe," she said quietly, trying not to attract attention as he searched for her in the book. "I think someone from Drake Witley's office called to make a reservation for me, so it might be under his name. Or maybe the station. W-109?"

No response. Surreptitiously, she adjusted the V-neck of her pale blue sweater, wondering if she should've taken the time to go back to her suburban home and change clothes before her dinner with the mysterious Dr. Jones. She reminded herself that this was business, not a blind date, but it didn't help much.

She still felt as awkward and apprehensive as if she were the one gunning for a fix-up with an unknown Romeo.

Speaking of which... "I'm supposed to meet a Dr. Jones. Do you know if he's waiting?"

"Not yet, ma'am. But we were expecting you. Right this way." The maître d' actually had a smirk on his face as he swept through the dining room, waving her to a table right smack in the center of things. Conversation stopped and heads turned as a waiter quickly jumped in to pull out her chair and whisk away her coat.

Nell took her seat with as much grace as she could muster, sliding her briefcase full of profiles under the table. Why did she get the idea they didn't get a whole lot of women dining alone at the Graystone Grill? Was there any other reason for them all to find her so much more interesting than their oversize steaks? Whatever the explanation, it made her very uncomfortable to be the subject of so much scrutiny.

With a flourish, the waiter dropped a cloth napkin into her lap and presented the menu, a monstrosity of a thing encased in thick leather. Nell kept a discreet eye on the door as she hunkered down behind the fortress of her menu.

"Well, Dr. Jones," she murmured, casting an indifferent eye down the list of entrées, "you're late. At least two minutes late. Already a black mark against you."

She concentrated on the descriptions of porterhouses and New York strips larger than she was, trying not to notice that she still seemed to be the center of attention. What were they staring at? She was fully clothed and from the planet Earth, wasn't she? No tentacles, no second head, no fangs or horns. What was so exciting?

"Nell?" a very nice male voice at her elbow inquired. Even that one word was confident without sounding arrogant, low-pitched in a soft-spoken, gruffly masculine way.

Him.

Caught off guard, she snapped together the massive halves of her menu and fumbled it sideways into her lap, only then turning to catch her first glimpse of Dr. John, the man every woman in Chicago wanted to date.

"Uh-oh," she said out loud. Her heart did a funny little leap into her throat. He *did* look like Tom Cruise only taller.

Well, Tom Cruise if he were playing the role of an absent-minded professor. Dr. John, Mr. Right, Mr. Wonderful—whatever she called him—wore smallish tortoiseshell glasses, tinted enough that she couldn't make out whether his eyes were green or blue. But he had that interesting configuration of a straight, strong nose and high cheekbones that did so well by Mr. Cruise. Good jawline, too, very classic, with expressive lips that curved in the corners even when he wasn't smiling.

He had a large, laminated tag—a hospital ID, maybe—clipped to his lapel, and it said JOHN CHRISTOPHER JONES in big black letters. So that *was* his real name. Somehow it didn't sound nearly as phony with that "Christopher" in the middle.

As Nell continue to survey him, she noticed that his dark hair seemed too long for the way he had styled it—all sort of rumpled and tipping over his forehead without benefit of gels or sprays. Odd haircut for someone who wore it that way. But maybe he didn't know any better. Nell felt a pang for the departed fiancée who might have instructed him on hair-styling aids.

His broad shoulders were encased in a rather hideous rust-colored corduroy jacket, the kind with suede patches on the elbows, worn over a baggy beige sweater and a pair of starkly creased pants that looked as if they'd come directly from a clearance table in Filene's basement. Well, he might have excellent raw material, but he had terrible taste in clothes.

With his hands jammed in his pockets, he waited there with an odd look on his face. Was that amusement? Or embarrassment?

He cleared his throat, but his voice still sounded muffled when he asked, "Do I pass muster?"

Flustered, Nell realized she had been gaping at the poor man for far too long. She half rose, almost dumping the nine hundred-pound menu on the floor. But he jumped in to catch it for her, offering an apologetic smile as he handed back the leather-bound folder, his hand just brushing hers. That simple touch sent little ripples of excitement down her arm, melting her where she stood.

Panicking just a little, she yanked back her menu, falling into her chair with a thump. She felt like a klutz and a dimwit and a total fool. Things weren't getting off to a really great start, were they?

"Why don't I sit down?" he asked kindly.

"Please," she said gratefully. "Please sit down."

He took up his own menu, which looked much less ridiculous in his larger hands, slid into the seat across from her, and murmured something about being so happy to meet her at long last.

"I'm, uh, very happy to meet you, too." Nell gazed at him across the table, so large and strong and ter-

ribly sweet. Everything he'd divulged on her show—
about who he was and why he'd called and what happiness and sorrow had brought him to this point—
came sweeping back over her, and she couldn't help
the warmth that filled her. Warmth, empathy and ex-
pectation, as if she'd been waiting for this moment
forever. Considering she'd never heard of John Jones
until this morning, this rush of feelings was very odd.

Yet she realized that what she'd said was absolutely
true. She *was* glad to meet him.

A little too glad when you considered she was only
here to decide which one of a hundred hot-to-trot
women to fix him up with. He smiled over his wineglass, reached across the table, pulled her hand into
his and clasped it gently. "I really am happy to meet
you, Nell," he said simply.

Her hand was tingling in a most peculiar way. She
snatched it back and stuck it in her lap. But, oh my
heavens, he was adorable over there. Cute and big and
warm and...sexy. Quite sexy.

It promised to be a very long night.

"MEDICINE IS SO DULL," he told her, waving off her
question with one hand. "I live it every day—I'd really rather talk about something else." He brightened.
"Like you, for instance."

God, this was turning out to be a lot more difficult
than he'd thought. He hadn't realized he would have
to concentrate so damn hard. Why had he made himself a doctor, anyway? He knew nothing about medicine.

So far he'd managed to keep the conversation on
the good deeds and charities that supposedly filled the
doctor's life. That much was easy—he just stole from
his real life, adjusting here and there where he had to.

After all, he'd lent his name to a ski weekend to benefit the Boys' Club, hadn't he? So he made it a bike race, upped his own involvement and moved it from Aspen to New Jersey when he told Nell about it. And he'd pounded nails for Habitat For Humanity, too. Right next to Cindy Crawford and Naomi Campbell. So he just took out Cindy and Naomi and told the rest of the story.

But this doctor thing…

"I would think brain surgery would be fascinating," she persisted.

"Seen one brain, seem 'em all," he said glibly. "But you—how did you get to be a radio star?"

"I'm hardly a star." But he could see the faint flush on her cheeks, and he knew she appreciated the sentiment.

All in all, she seemed a lot less suspicious of his story than she had been on the phone, so his act must be working okay. No more fussing about whether his résumé or his name strained credulity. Of course, the fake ID probably helped on that score.

Now if he could only remember to answer right away when Nell called him "John." He was down to about a three-second reaction time, but he was going to have to do better than that.

Hildy had also done well with the clothes—maybe too well, given how ugly the jacket was—and so far Nell had shown no hint that she recognized him. He was actually a tad miffed on that score. He would've thought he'd made more of an impression, even if she had had her back to him for most of that very short meeting last July.

Griffin narrowed his gaze at her. Was she buying this whole nerdy doctor routine? Hard to tell. She hadn't said anything to make him think she was sus-

picious, but she did seem a little edgy. She'd cut up
her steak, and she was pushing it around the plate,
but he doubted she'd eaten any of it. Maybe she just
didn't like the food at Graystone's, with its concen-
tration on aged scotch and marbled beef.

He smiled to himself, watching Nell diligently apply herself to the process of hiding bits of beef under
a few sprigs of parsley. He'd been here once or twice
with Spence, who had a fondness for their cigars, but
he never would've picked this place for Nell. Unless
he missed his guess, she was more comfortable with
tearooms and salad bars.

So why had she chosen the Graystone Grill? Was
it a test of some sort? And if it was, had he passed?

His gut told him that he had, that he was safe, that
she believed in his disguise. And wasn't that what he
was doing here? To win this little "convince-me"
game she'd started?

In the meantime, he was actually enjoying her company, which was something he hadn't expected. She
was smart and funny and a breath of fresh air. And
Lord knew every other man in the place was certainly
staring, and that said something for how attractive she
was. He gazed at her wide-set hazel eyes, so guileless
and open, at her honey blond hair, softly grazing her
shoulders, at her curving pink lips, which held just a
hint of mischief.

The total package was very different from that sexy
bus poster of hers. Yeah, and the real, live Nell was
a whole lot more appealing.

Griffin tried to reel himself in. He was definitely
getting into this escapade for reasons that had nothing
to do with the success of W-109. But as long as he
was here, he figured he might as well enjoy the ride.

"So, tell me," he said, remembering to tone down

the Griff Jones guaranteed-to-charm grin, "how did you become a radio host?"

"Well, if you're sure you want to hear…" He nodded, and she went on, reluctantly at first, but warming to the subject. "It's kind of funny, actually," she said, "since it was mostly by accident. I was a sophomore in college, in a journalism program, and I walked into the office of the school paper the day their advice columnist quit. Dating and roommate advice are very hot topics on campus, so they needed someone right away, and they hired me on the spot. I'd only done about three weeks of columns when a DJ at the campus radio station asked if I wanted to try something similar on the air, and I did." She shrugged. "It really took off, which was a complete surprise to everyone. When the station manager graduated and came up to Chicago, to W-109, he asked me if I wanted to come along and bring my show. So I did."

"And you've been at W-109 ever since?"

"Never looked back."

"Never finished college?" That was a surprise. He'd assumed she had degrees and credentials in spades, given how assertive she was with advice.

"Nope." She frowned. "My parents are both in education, and they weren't very happy with my decision to leave school." Leaning in a little closer, she confided, "But sometimes I think you just know in your heart what path is meant for you, and you have to take it. I feel that very strongly."

Caught by her enthusiasm, he didn't even think about a measured response. "I agree," he returned, showing more of Griffin Jones's bold confidence than Dr. Jones's reticence. "Life is just too short to fool around. I believe that once you know what you want, you go for it, and you don't let anybody get in your way.''

As the words left his mouth, he realized it was the first totally truthful statement he'd made all night. Lying was nothing new for him—shading the truth was business as usual in his world of high finance deception and manipulation. So why, gazing into Nell McCabe's soft, hazel green eyes, did he feel the need to be honest?

"I think what you do is terrific," he said softly. "You should be very proud."

Her eyes widened, and he could see the sparkle of pleasure there. "Thank you. But you, I mean, a brain surgeon... If anyone should be proud of helping people, it should be you."

"No, not really. It's no big deal," he muttered. "Can we talk about something else, please?"

"You're so modest, John." Nell tipped her head to one side, sending him a look of compassion and admiration. "That's a wonderful trait for someone in your position. And I think that's why your call elicited such an amazing outpouring of interest. Women really responded to your sincerity."

"Right." Sincerity. When he'd made up every single detail.

Maybe he should cut this short and tell her who he really was. But the *Truelove* was at stake, also Nell's job...

She broke into his mental gymnastics before he'd made up his mind. "I loved what you said about, you know, life being too short, and going after what you want." And then she hesitated, and he saw shiny, dewy sympathy glowing in her eyes. *Uh-oh.* "John, I hate to ask, but... I mean, was it losing Grace that brought you to that realization?"

"Oh." He sat up in his chair. "Grace. Right." Thank goodness she'd used the name first or he might have forgotten what he'd called his mythical dead fiancée. "Grace. Well, no. I mean, yes. I mean, it was all part of my evolution, so to speak. I believe that people are the sum of all their experiences, not just one, that we have to go forward from where we are, wherever that is, and not look back. So, as meaningful…" He searched for another word. "As *momentous* as Grace's death was, still, I know I can't let it affect everything in my life."

"John, that is so brave."

"Not really." Mostly it was gobbledygook. He gave her a tight smile. "We all just get by the best we can, one day at a time, right? Nell, I…"

He searched his brain for a way to get out of this. He had to think of something because he was very uncomfortable with this whole charade. Was this an attack of guilty conscience? What a shock. Who knew he *had* a conscience?

Meanwhile, Nell seemed to have bought every word he'd said, even though he had no idea whether he'd even made sense, spouting platitudes right and left and sideways. But not only did she seem to believe it, she seemed to be *touched* by it. *Oh, brother.*

"So, John, were you with her, at the end?" This time, she was the one who reached across the table to take *his* hand. "You didn't say whether it was something sudden, or if you had time, you know, to prepare."

He wracked his brain. What story had he come up with on the fly when he was talking on the radio? He didn't remember offering a cause of death. Better to make something quick and painless that wouldn't require supporting medical details. "It was very sudden," he improvised. "A car accident."

Nell blinked. "Oh. I don't know why, but I thought you said she'd been ill."

"No, perfectly healthy. That almost made it harder in a way, you know, cut down in the bloom of youth and beauty." Oh, god, he was going to be punished for this, he just knew it. At the time, adding a dead fiancée and a broken heart to his story had seemed like the perfect way to appeal to lots of women. Now he just felt like pond scum.

Even worse, Nell looked like she was getting teary. *Please, no tears.* He couldn't take tears. Her hand felt soft and small inside his, and he gave it a comforting squeeze.

"I don't want you to think it was perfect between us," he murmured, trying to think of a way to make himself sound less virtuous. "I wasn't the easiest guy to live with, you know." He had a sudden inspiration. "Maybe if I had been a better person, she wouldn't have had the affair. I found the note, that she had left me for my brother, but it was too late. She was already gone. And that's when it happened, when she was driving to meet—"

"What?" Nell cried. "You're saying she left you for your brother?"

Griffin had assumed that to be the dumpee would make him sound like a jerk, or at least a loser. Guess not. Nell looked outraged on his behalf. "It was mostly my fault," he said.

"I can't believe how forgiving you are! And now, mourning her still, when she…" She broke off, as confusion settled on her brow. "Wait a minute. I thought for sure, when we were talking on my show, you said that—"

Griffin didn't have a clue what he'd said on her show, but he had a pretty good idea it didn't match something in his new tale of Grace and woe. But before Nell was able to let him know what it was he had screwed up, a forty-something man in an expensive chalk-stripe suit popped up at their table.

"I knew it was you!" he shouted, and they both turned to him in surprise.

"Excuse me?" Nell sputtered.

"It's her, all right," the man called back to the guys at his table, who snickered and raised their glasses in his honor. He slapped a cloth napkin and a pen down in front of her. "Here, hon. Sign this to Ted Hanover, with love and lots of kisses, something like that."

"Listen, pal," Griffin began, rising from his chair. He was a head taller and ten years younger than the idiot with the napkin, and he knew he could take him easily. And even if his doctor persona was supposed to be a bit of a wimp, surely he could still protect the lady he was with. He pressed a hand into the guy's chest, propelling him backward a step. "I think you need to apologize to Ms. McCabe. And then go sit down."

"Aw, come on, I'm not hurting anything. She'll give me an autograph, won't you, hon?"

"Who exactly do you think I am?" Nell asked, looking mostly stunned.

"You're the one on the side of the bus. Call me anytime, right? Aren't you the Hotsy Girl?"

"The *what?*"

"The Hotsy Girl. I don't know. You need oven mitts to handle you or something like that."

"I knew I should never have done those pictures," Nell whispered, as rosy color rushed to her cheeks.

Griffin growled, "The lady hosts a radio show, okay? It's called *The Hot Zone*. She's very good at what she does, but she's no hotsy." He glanced down at Nell, but she was busy acting mortified. "Well, maybe she is a hotsy, but not in the way you think."

"Come on, buddy," a man from another table called out. "We've all seen the buses. The least she can do is give an autograph."

For a high-toned crowd, these people were pretty boorish. At least this explained all the stares directed at their table—they'd recognized Nell from those damn posters.

"All of you be quiet and pay attention to what's happening at your own tables," Griffin ordered angrily. "She doesn't have to give autographs or do anything else she doesn't want to. You people sit down and be quiet."

"John?"

It took him a while to remember that was the name he was answering to at the moment. The fact that she was tugging on his sleeve helped.

"What is it, sweetheart?" he asked solicitously, bending closer. "Would you like to leave? Is that it?" He shoved a hand in his pocket for his wallet, ready to toss down some cash and scoop her out of there if that's what she wanted.

She peered up at him. "John, are you all right? You're not acting like yourself at all."

"I'm...not?"

"No. A few minutes ago, you seemed like a nice, normal guy, maybe a little more sedate than most. And now you're acting like The Terminator or something." She bit her lip. "This mood swing worries me."

Yeah, well, a whole restaurant full of creeps com-

ing on to you worries me. He took a deep breath and tried to think this through. How would Dr. John the Milquetoast act under these circumstances?

"I'm sorry, Nell," he murmured. "I didn't mean to frighten you. Do I take it then that you don't want to leave?"

"No, I don't think so. I'm fine, really. A little embarrassed, but I'll get over it." As Griffin glowered, she grabbed the napkin, slashed her name across it and gave it back. "Here you go, uh, Ted. No problem. You try to tune in to *The Hot Zone,* okay? Weekday mornings at eleven on W-109."

Reluctantly, Griffin returned to his seat. "I still don't think it's right for your dinner to be interrupted. You shouldn't have to put up with that just because some ad wizard put your picture on a bus."

"Listen, I'm with you on that one," she agreed heartily. "Ever since those horrible Jones Boys—no offense, your name being Jones and all—took over my station, it's been like this. It's their trademark, I guess—to buy up marginal businesses and then make them profitable by playing to the lowest common denominator. So for my show, that means anyone likely to drool over a picture of a half-dressed blonde. Unfortunately, they chose me to be the half-dressed blonde."

Griffin set his jaw. Horrible Jones Boys, huh? What was that all about? "Why would you think the ad campaign had anything to do with them? Surely they don't have time to oversee every little detail of every little ad campaign."

"It just fits the pattern," she said darkly. "My producer says I'm paranoid, but I don't think so. Have you heard of some of the stunts they've pulled? I saw over the wire that they're in L.A. right now, embroiled in some controversy."

"Oh, really?"

"Uh-huh. Trying to force nuns and orphans out onto the street so they can build a casino or something."

"Nuns and orphans?" He knew he had to tread carefully, but this was ridiculous. "The way I heard it, it was a posh school for little rich girls, and it wasn't a casino, but a beautiful resort hotel with jobs and revenue that could benefit a lot of people."

"Benefit the Jones Boys, you mean." Nell shook her head. "When it comes to progress over common sense, nuns and orphans out on the street—"

"I told you, there aren't any nuns or orphans involved."

"Still," she said tartly, "I blame the Jones Boys."

Which made it a very awkward time for him to tell her that she was having dinner with one of them. "Listen, I really think you're being too hard—"

But she stopped him cold. "Oh, my God," she whispered, "don't look now, but there's one of them."

5

"IS THAT FREAKY or what?" Nell went on. "They're like evil spirits. You mention their names and up they pop."

Griff began to get a weird feeling. "Up *who* pops?"

"The Jones Boys." She waggled her eyebrows to indicate that whoever she was talking about was over by the entrance. Griffin knew it wasn't him, so that only left Spence or some impostor. But Spence was supposed to be in California, pulling Seaboard Development's fat out of the fire.

As casually as he could, he shifted around in his chair far enough to check out the door. It was Spencer, all right. With some bimbo date and a gaggle of friends. Damn him. What was he doing back from L.A. already? And at this restaurant?

Griffin slumped inside his grotesque corduroy jacket, trusting that his brother wouldn't recognize him from the back in this getup.

"I think he sees us," Nell remarked in a vexed tone. "I've only met him once. I can't believe he remembers me. He and his infantile brother played some silly game through the whole meeting. Darts, I think it was. Can you imagine anything so rude as to play darts while a meeting is going on? The nerve of those odious Jones Boys!"

"Imagine that." Griffin applied himself to his glass

of wine, making sure he held it in front of his face. There was no way that would fool his brother for any length of time, but if Spencer didn't glance this way, he might not even notice the oddly dressed person who so closely resembled his brother.

"He's coming this way," Nell hissed. "Act natural."

Not a chance.

"What are you doing here?" Spence demanded. "And why are you dressed like that?"

"I have every right to eat dinner anywhere I want," Nell returned, clearly assuming Spencer was talking to her. "As for the way I'm dressed—well, what did you think? I may be willing to go along with your hotsy campaign for the sake of my job, but I draw the line at wearing slutty clothes on my own time!"

"Huh?" Griffin could tell that the words "Who are you?" were just about to drop from his brother's lips.

Griff pointed a warning finger. "You keep your mouth shut, do you hear me? We're leaving." Spilling bills onto the table, he reached for Nell's hand. As she scrambled to locate her briefcase, he muttered, "I'll deal with you later," under his breath to his brother.

Mystified, Spence asked, "What did I do?"

But Griff didn't answer, just made a beeline for the door, holding Nell tight and clearing the way. He knew he'd have to pay the price for this later, but he preferred to delay the reckoning as long as possible. All he was looking for tonight was to get out without losing any teeth or body parts.

Because if either virtuous Nell McCabe or his intensely competitive brother figured out what he was up to, he was dead meat.

BY THE TIME they reached the foyer, Nell found herself unable to hold back a smile. And it was all because of John. She'd never been rescued like that in her life. It was kind of cool. For a man with enough self-esteem issues to have to call *The Hot Zone* for a date, John Jones certainly knew how to make an exit.

As the young lady behind the counter turned over her coat, Nell commented, "I doubt anyone has ever told a Jones Boy to shut up and go away."

She thought John murmured, "You might be surprised," but she wasn't sure.

"Wow!" she enthused. "That was so great."

"Come on, Nell, don't make too much of it. I didn't do anything." Looking sheepish, he held her winter coat as she shrugged into it.

"Excuse me," the coat check girl said diffidently. She was a pretty, waifish thing of maybe seventeen or eighteen, so thin she looked as if any light breeze from the front door would blow her back to the kitchen. Right now, she had John's coat, but she was holding it just out of reach. "I couldn't help overhearing that he called you Nell."

Here we go again, Nell thought. *Another fan.*

"And, well," the girl continued, "the maître d' told us that Nell McCabe, from that radio show, was going to be here tonight."

"That's me," Nell responded. "Did you want an...?" She squiggled her hand in the air, in the international symbol for autograph.

"Oh, no." Completely ignoring Nell and hugging Griff's coat to her slender front, the little waif turned to him instead. "I saw your name tag," she ventured. "So if she's Nell, does that make you Dr. John, the one from today's show?"

"Well, yes," Griff admitted. He smiled. "Did you hear me on the show?"

"Yes. Yes. Oh, *yes,*" she whispered, looking like she might faint. She was such a tiny thing that seemed a distinct possibility. Instead, she threw back her head and let out a shriek. "I can't believe this!" she screeched. Craning her neck toward the racks, she shouted, "Amanda, Amanda, didn't I tell you it was him?"

"Miss?" Nell pleaded. "Miss? Can he have his coat, please?"

"It's him, Amanda!" she belted out. "Dr. John! The one who lost his girlfriend and needs a date for Valentine's!"

Beaming, she turned back to him, tipping herself closer, gazing up at him with complete devotion, clutching his coat in a death grip. "It's him, it's him, it's him. I can't believe it." Nell had to hold herself back from shaking the tiny twit.

John, however, did not appear to be upset. In fact, he seemed flattered and amused by the deluded child's display of ardor.

"I want to be in on the lottery for the date," the girl said breathlessly. "Can I put my name in? I think you're adorable, and I would love to go to the dance with you."

"Thank you," he told her. "I really appreciate that."

"Hold on." Nell fought her way into the recesses of her briefcase, emerging with one of the forms the marketing department had been using to assess potential dates. "You fill this out, you send it in and you'll be right in there, okay?"

"Terrif." As the Poor Little Coat Check Girl tried to snatch the paper from Nell's hand, Nell wedged herself firmly in front of Dr. John, far enough to catch the edge of the hostage coat. Finally, the girl had to let it go to glom on to the form. "Can I make copies?" she asked desperately. "You know, like for extra chances?"

"Knock yourself out."

The girl called out, "How about *your* autograph, Dr. John? I have a pen, and you can sign my arm. Or my neck. Or my…"

But Nell was already shepherding the adorable doctor John out the door. Once they were safe on the sidewalk, she turned up her collar and gave him a thin smile. "Now we're even—rescue for rescue."

He laughed at her. "I don't think I needed to be rescued from her."

"Well," Nell said with spirit. "*I* did."

He regarded her with a mocking expression. "Nell McCabe, were you jealous of that sweet little coat check girl?"

"Jealous? I hardly think so."

"I think so."

"I was not!" Just because the child was barely old enough to tie her shoes and weighed less than the average cantaloupe didn't mean that Nell cared in the least…

Oh, hell. She *was* jealous.

"I wasn't jealous," she insisted, lying through her teeth. "Unless, of course, *you* were jealous when you tried to bully the man who wanted my autograph, or stood up for me against Spencer Jones."

"Jealous? Uh, no," he said quickly. "I was going for chivalrous."

Clearly working under that same theory, he wordlessly hoisted her bulging briefcase into his left hand and guided her down the icy sidewalk with his right.

Nell let him take her bag and her arm, but she gave him a speculative gaze. "You know, you keep surprising me."

And she didn't like it. Just when she thought she had him pegged, he acted like The Terminator or Sir Galahad or somebody else she didn't expect.

"I do?" He seemed taken aback. "Well, I told you, I haven't dated in a while. I'm sure my, uh, self-consciousness is what you're picking up on. My social skills are rusty."

Uh-huh. Which was why he had been so flustered and upset by all the attention from the coat check girl. *Not.*

She continued to ponder who and what Dr. John Jones really was, when he changed the subject, completely distracting her. "Nell, listen, about the Jones brothers…"

"What about them?"

He had the oddest expression on his face, one she couldn't figure out at all. "They own your station, right? Did you ever think that maybe it would be smarter to try to see the good in people like that, rather than disliking them so much?"

"But they're terrible people," she said immediately. "Corporate gobblers, womanizers, pirates. I told you about the nuns and the orphans. It's typical. And terrible. If I didn't dislike them, it would be dishonest."

His features tightened. "And I told you that the nuns and orphans thing is overblown and unfair. So maybe the Jones brothers aren't so bad after all."

"You don't know them like I know them. Don't worry," she hastened to assure him, deciding it was awfully sweet of him to be concerned for her job, "Spencer Jones can't turn around and fire me just because I wasn't nice to him at the restaurant tonight. At least I don't think he can. For one thing, I have a contract that gives me thirty days notice, and for another, there was some kind of deal that made my job secure until Valentine's Day."

"What do you mean?"

"Oh, I overheard a conversation months ago. Actually, I eavesdropped from the hall, but that doesn't matter." She frowned, remembering. "The Jones brothers, plus the marketing manager at W-109, agreed to wait until Valentine's Day to see if the ratings for my show went up. And if they don't—poof! I disappear. With, I assume, thirty days of severance pay."

"But, Nell, Valentine's Day is just two weeks away."

"I've known about this forever, so I'm kind of resigned to it by now." She gave him a reckless smile. "Besides, there's you."

"Me?"

"I think you might be able to save it all, including my show and my job." She hoped she wasn't scaring him. Someone in his precarious dating condition didn't need extra pressure. But on the other hand, she needed *him.* She turned into his path, walking backward so she could be more persuasive, face-to-face. "There was such a huge response to you on my show. So I'm hoping we can draw this out, purposely not match you up a few days longer, heighten the suspense, you see? And get more calls on the side and make some more matches, now that the ball's rolling, and really ride this wave of incredible PR and excitement all the way to the Fantasy Bash."

"And all this hinges on me?" he asked doubtfully.

"Yes. I'm not going to lie to you. It definitely hinges

on you." She fixed him with a hopeful look, even though it felt rotten to use him this way. "We still need to go over the profiles marketing completed, of women who called in wanting to go to the Fantasy Bash with you. In all the excitement, I never did get around to finding out, um, what you want in a woman."

So why did his expression and her heart seem to be telling her that what he wanted in a woman was *her*?

Nell, stop that right now. You don't know what he's really thinking, you keep picking up inconsistencies in his statements, and you have to match him up with someone else, anyway.

Inconsistencies. *Hmm...* The idea pricked at her memory. What was it she'd thought earlier, about something he'd said that didn't seem right?

As she concentrated on the vague recollection, her foot caught a patch of ice, and John reached to steady her. She felt his hand on her waist and she smiled to herself. Whatever it was she'd been trying to think of, it couldn't have been important. Probably just her mistake. From what she had observed so far, John was just too kind and compassionate to be lying to her. Hadn't he leapt to her rescue, totally out of character, when he'd thought she was bothered by the man who wanted the autograph? And hadn't he told Spencer Jones to stuff it, and then swept her out of the Graystone Grill like nobody's business?

Nell let herself edge in a little closer next to him, enjoying the mental image of mild-mannered Dr. John Jones leaping to her defense.

"Nell?" he asked, and she perked up.

"Hmm?"

"Where are we headed?"

"Oh, I don't know." She hesitated, glancing around at the empty street, shamelessly using his big, strong body as a wind block. "We didn't discuss that, and I guess I just assumed…" Now that she thought about it, she didn't know what she'd assumed. "We still have quite a few things to go over. Is there someplace we can go? Someplace not too noisy, so we can talk?"

She hadn't realized it was snowing, but as she spoke, a few stray flakes drifted on to the top of her head and another landed below her eye. She reached to flick it away, but John got there first.

With his bare, cold thumb, he slowly brushed the snowflake off the curve of her cheek, his gaze holding her fast as his touch lingered.

He whispered, "I don't want to talk."

"I don't underst—" But she did understand. The currents sparking between them all night had not been her imagination. She could feel it now, as tangible as the snowflakes dancing around them.

He raised his hands to frame her face. He stared down at her. Her heart seemed to stop in her chest. And he lowered his lips to hers, so sweetly, so perfectly, she thought she would die, right there in the cold January night.

When he spoke again, his voice was lower, huskier, more urgent. "How about your place?"

Her whole body was trying to fold itself into his heat, to wrap itself around him. It was very cold out here on the windy Chicago street, and Dr. Jones was like a cozy, toasty haven of warmth. Not *her* toasty haven, mind you.

But he'd kissed her. She'd wanted him to kiss her and he did and now she wanted him to do it again.

Whoa! None of this was supposed to be happening.

Especially not with a vulnerable, lovelorn man who had a dead fiancée complex.

"Um, th-thank you," she managed to stammer. "That was very nice. But we can't do that."

"Why not?" he asked gently, looking every bit as if he planned to swoop right down and do it again.

"Well, for one thing," she told him shakily, holding him off with one mitten against his chest, "because I have to find you a date on my show. If I took you myself, it would screw up the whole thing, and all my callers would have a fit and I wouldn't blame them."

"But you can kiss me now and I can still take one of them to the Fantasy Bash later," he said sensibly, dipping his head and barely touching his mouth to hers, only grazing her, lip to lip, but making her want a lot more.

"I can't. It's in the rules—at least I think it's in the rules—that I can't date you."

His lips brushed her chin and then her ear, and she couldn't remember her own name, let alone what the rules of the stupid contest were. "So break a few rules," he whispered. "Who cares?"

"I care." She had to make herself behave. She had to. "Besides, you're still emotionally connected to Grace. It's like a rebound thing."

"You're the one who said it was time for me to move on and make new beginnings."

No arguing with that. She tried something more concrete. "We can't stand around kissing because…it's freezing out here. And that stupid Spencer Jones could come out at any minute and beat you up."

He smiled. "I think I can handle myself."

"You know, this combative side of you doesn't really fit the image I had."

He moved closer, sliding his arms around her. "So maybe you need to redo your image."

Nell wavered. Maybe she did need to adjust her focus. He was certainly not the timid, socially inept schlemiel she'd expected. But not the slick, manipulative babe cruiser who would've made up a silly story on the air, either. She needed time to think and mull and brood over every detail of their conversation...

But he didn't give her a chance. He dropped a tiny kiss onto the curve of her neck and nudged her to move down the sidewalk. "Let's go to your place, then."

"We can't." Nell backed away from him, ready to do just about anything but that. "I live way out in Geneva. Do you know where that is? No? It's far. It'll take a good hour to get there. I live in my grandmother's old house. My parents live just down the street. The minute we drive up, they'd be on us like CNN on a forest fire."

"Well, that's no good." He blew on his hands and rubbed them together. "Where's your car?"

Oops. "I commute. My car is parked at the train station out in West Chicago." She was so used to being a suburb dweller, she never thought about these logistical problems anymore.

"It's starting to snow harder. We have to go somewhere."

"What about your car?"

"I don't..." But he bit his lip, not finishing the thought.

"What? What?" Nell asked, shivering with cold.

"Okay, fine." He took a few steps toward the curb

and then stopped. His whole expression changed when he said, "Don't make any conclusions based on my car, okay?"

That was an odd thing to say. Why would she care what kind of car he drove?

But as Nell followed him straight across the street, her mouth dropped open. Why should she care? Because it was a jazzy, low-slung, foreign thing, black as night, and he opened the doors by pointing at it and clicking. The license plate read JONES 2.

Once again, her mental image had to be adjusted. It was details like that that kept making her wonder whether she should really trust him. Why would a nebbishy doctor with no dates drive this little seduction special?

Well, he'd never claimed to be poor. And in a way, the fact that he had this amazing car kind of proved his story, didn't it? Who else but a brain surgeon could afford it? Besides, the license plate matched the name on his ID, the very name that had made her suspicious from the start. He'd said he looked like a movie star, and he almost did. In fact, he'd be right there if he got better clothes and combed his hair. He'd said his name was Jones, and his ID and his license plate both confirmed that. It all pointed to the conclusion that he was exactly who he'd said he was from the beginning. He might be mercurial, he might be hung up on a dead woman who had betrayed him and he might even be the world's worst dresser, but he was still Dr. John Jones, the man every woman in Chicago wanted to date.

Nell slid into his car and buckled herself up, letting him drive her away into the winter night. Leaning forward to catch the welcome heat from the vent, she asked, "Where did we decide to go?"

"We didn't. I did." He let out a tense breath. "We're going to my apartment. I mean, my loft."

"Your loft? Sounds, uh, great."

A loft, alone with the mysterious doctor? Actually, it sounded pretty darn scary, and she hoped her knees weren't knocking together all the way there.

HE HOPED THIS wasn't a big mistake. For one thing, stealing his brother's car wasn't too smart, and Spence was going to be royally ticked off when he came back and found it gone. Ah well. Little Bro would get over it. Besides, the brothers were accustomed to borrowing each other's cars when the need arose—that's why they kept extra sets of keys. It was surprising how many times that came in handy.

He hazarded a glance at Nell, who seemed to be talking to herself. What was that all about? When he looked over, she offered a smile that was slightly wobbly, and he felt his own lips curve, too. He couldn't help it. He liked her. He especially liked her smile.

And then there was the way she kissed, all warm and sweet and full of promise. He had the urge to pull over and see how she felt about going for a romp in the back seat.

Except for the fact that Spencer's Porsche didn't have a back seat.

What a sap he was turning into, mooning over Nell McCabe, acting as doofy as a teenager, as inept as his nerd-boy alter ego.

Griffin gripped the steering wheel and stared into the darkness. So how swift was it to take her up to the loft? He already knew he was going to want to kiss her again. What a complication this was turning into. He liked her, he liked the idea of kissing her—

a lot—and yet for several really stupid reasons he couldn't make a serious move on her. There was the idiotic bet, the even more idiotic secret identity, and an incredible amount of fallout if she found out. He'd lose her, he'd lose his bet, she'd lose her job...

And it would all be his fault.

Yet still he drove on, getting ever closer to the loft, like a spider with a juicy fly riding in the front seat. If the spider knew the fly was poison, would he still lure her into his web? Probably.

Why? Because it was his nature.

Besides, what fun was life if you sat back and looked at all the reasons not to make a move? He was a doer, a risk-taker and he knew what he wanted. He wanted her. Tonight. So he was going for it.

Griffin sent her another glance and Nell caught it. Her sunny smile was brighter this time, and he felt himself melt from the heat. Yep, wanting Nell definitely felt like second nature.

At least at his loft, they could be alone. No other men would be drooling over Nell, no other women would be vying for his Valentine's Day favors and Spence was unlikely to drop in anytime soon. Griffin knew his brother—he'd be smoking cigars and tossing back scotch for hours, and after that, he should be occupied with the young lady who had been on his arm. If there was one thing Spence hated, it was spending the night in his own bed.

Besides, Spencer didn't have a car. Griffin grinned into the darkness. It was going to take his little bro a few minutes to get around that problem.

He put Spencer out of his mind and tried to remember to tune in to his meek "John" persona as he parked in the ramp under his building. Playing a nerd-boy wasn't easy, but so far he thought he was doing a damn fine job. Feeling a little cocky, he switched off the car, picked up Nell's briefcase and led her to the private elevator.

Introducing Nell to the Loft From Hell ought to be interesting. But since she'd already accepted his awful rust-colored jacket, Spencer's Porsche, and his desire to throttle any competition and make out with her, Griffin had no trouble believing she'd find some way to make the nutty loft fit the picture, too.

He threw open the door. "After you."

Nell blinked and looked around. "Wow. I never would've guessed... I mean, it's different, isn't it?"

She seemed to be taking a survey of the place, and he followed her, hoping nothing incriminating was hanging around. He sure didn't see anything. It helped that he'd only been here a few days, and also that he traveled light. Of course, the crackerjack housekeeping service arranged by Hildy didn't hurt. Even if he had thrown socks on the floor or left notes and letters lying around, the maid would've picked them up.

Uh-oh. Outrageously expensive black leather jacket direct from Milan hanging on rack at two o'clock.

"Can I take your coat?" he asked, quickly shedding his own overcoat and draping it over the leather jacket before she noticed anything. For good measure, he took off the nasty corduroy jacket he'd been stuck in all night and put that on the back side of the rack.

Nell handed over her coat absentmindedly, clearly more interested in her surroundings. "Do you play the piano?" she inquired, prowling around as if she were determined to put a complete profile together based on the objets d'art in the loft. She peered at the cowboy cutout. "Are you a fan of John Wayne?"

"It came furnished," he said, still jingling the keys. "So none of that is mine. Nell, listen, why don't you go ahead and sit down? There's a sofa over by the TV.''

But she ignored him, too busy poking into every nook and cranny of the crowded loft. ''While all of these knickknacks are very interesting, I can't help but notice there's nothing personal here,'' she mused, holding up a small Mickey Mouse clock. ''No photo albums or books or mementos. Not even a postcard.''

''I haven't lived here long.''

But he heard her whisper, ''Poor John,'' as she turned her head away. ''The memories must be too painful.''

Oh, lord. She was on the Grace kick again. If there was one thing that drove him nuts, it was Nell in full-blown pity mode, when she tipped her head to the side and gave him one of those moist, soulful gazes.

''Nell, come and sit on the sofa, okay? It's the only decent seat in the place.'' He couldn't resist the impulse to add, in his most innocent tone, ''Except for the bed. I suppose we could sit on the bed if you'd rather.''

Nell made tracks for the entertainment nook, exactly as he'd known she would as soon as the word ''bed'' was mentioned. He had her pegged, all right.

So he sat down next to her on the couch, a little closer than absolutely necessary, close enough to breathe on her, close enough to see her swallow, to watch the flush of rosy color stain her cheeks, to inhale her delicate fragrance, to see how her nostrils flared slightly as she struggled to take in enough air. For a long moment, he just looked at her, breathed with her, enjoyed the sensation of her hip pressed next to his, her soft sweater teasing his hand. Absently, he rubbed his thumb down her sleeve. Cashmere? Very, very soft.

"J-John?" she ventured.

Damn it. He wanted to hear his own name on her lips, not some pseudonym. Once again, he forgot to answer to his adopted name. "Yes, Nell?" he murmured when he remembered.

"We can't do this."

"We're not doing anything." He angled around to find her lips. "Are we?"

Closing her eyes, leaning into his kiss, Nell whispered, "I don't know. Are we?"

And then his lips met hers, and she tasted like wine and winter and delicious woman. He heard her make some sweet, cute little moan, just a tiny thing, and he knew she was as turned-on as he was.

6

HE EASED HER carefully into the sofa, brushing kisses into the nape of her neck and around the V of her sweater. Unsure of whether she'd slap him or help him, he didn't rush things. She helped. Circling her arms around his neck, she started kissing him back in earnest, opening her mouth to him, letting him probe deeper, warmer, wetter, making it a whole lot harder to remember why he wasn't supposed to be doing this.

Aw, what was the harm? "Nell, you taste incredible," he murmured into her ear. "You feel incredible."

"You, too. I can't believe we're..."

He didn't know what stopped her, what changed her mind, what changed the mood. But he felt it as soon as she stiffened under his hands.

"Nell?"

With a muttered oath, she sat up and scooted out from under him. "I can't believe this. You promised this wouldn't happen."

Huh? "I did not."

"Yes, you did." She paused. "Well, maybe you didn't. But I did! I promised myself. You're on the rebound, I'm like your counselor, and you need to date someone else."

"Why can't I date you?" he asked sensibly. With his thumb, he sketched a tiny figure eight on her cheek. "It's nobody's fault if we just connected, if there's some force pushing us together that we can't deny.''

"We can deny it. We have to.'' Scampering off the sofa, she retrieved her briefcase and started to pull out sheaves of paper. "Look at all these women who want to go to the Fantasy Bash with you. How can you disappoint them?''

"I can only take one. So the other nine hundred and ninety-nine will be disappointed, anyway.''

"That is *not* a good attitude. Let's just go through them, all right?'' She sat on the floor at the far end of the sectional, with as much space between them as she could manage. Adopting a very serious expression, she brought out a legal pad and a pen, and began to stack various folders and papers around her on the hardwood floor, creating a physical barrier between them. "We should have done this from the beginning. We should've met, laid out the papers—gotten to work. Dinner was a terrible idea. And then we wasted all that time talking about this and that and those stupid Jones Boys...'' She glared at him. "What age limits do you want to set?''

"I don't care.''

"Yes, you do care. We had calls from women in their teens and women in their nineties. You don't want to date either of those,'' she snapped.

"I don't care.''

"All right then I'll do it.'' She turned to her pad. "No one under twenty, and no one over forty. That ought to cut down the numbers. Divorced women okay? Women with children?''

"Sure. Why not?'' Griffin wished there was a magazine handy he could leaf through, just to show her how *not* interested he was in these silly questions. He wanted her back underneath him on the couch. He wanted his hands and his mouth on her skin. He wanted her to make that little moaning noise again. Again and again...

"Okay, so the over sixty pile is out. Ditto for the forty to fifty and fifty to sixty crowds. And here go all the teens." She tossed those stacks aside. "Now, any other disqualifying factors you can think of? Household income, number of children, ethnic background, occupation, hair color, eye color, shoe size, sign of the zodiac, height, weight, favorite color, level of education..." She looked up, manufacturing a strained smile. "Did I leave anything out?"

"Nope." Griffin leaned forward, fixing her with a direct stare. "Here's what I want—take this down. She has to be smart, with a good sense of humor. Sweet, genuine, kind of spunky. She should be blond, around five-four, 110 pounds. Hazel eyes. Hazel *green*. No substitutes."

Nell blinked.

"Favorite color is probably blue," he decided, taking his cue from her sweater. "Sign of the zodiac and shoe size? I don't know—something uptight, like a Virgo, and she wears around a size six. Occupation? Something in the media would be good. Ethnic heritage? Scotch or Irish, at least on one side. No children. Never married. Level of education? Maybe a year or two of college, preferably in journalism, but a degree isn't mandatory. Lives in the suburbs and commutes into the city to work. Maybe she lives in her grandmother's house, a few houses from her parents. A real family girl. Doesn't date much. She's been too busy with her job, I think, although maybe that's just an excuse." He paused. "Did I leave anything out?"

Color rose to her cheeks. "For your information, I am five foot five. My favorite color is yellow. My shoes are a seven, I am a Taurus and I date a lot. Constantly.''

''Nell, I was just trying to make a—''

''I know what you were trying to do, and it was very clever. Very smooth. Just the way to impress a woman.'' She began to stuff all the various profiles and surveys into her briefcase. ''I think I have a very good idea of your taste now, Dr. Jones, so it should be a cinch to get to work on a date for you.''

''Nell, I...''

With her briefcase in tow, she scrambled to her feet and turned on him. ''You know, I thought that if you were who you said you were, you would need some serious effort before you were in shape for something like the Fantasy Bash.''

''Oh, I do, I do,'' he told her. ''I throw myself on your mercy. I'm a mess. I'm pitiful.''

''No,'' Nell said plainly, ''you're not. It's taken me a few minutes to put this all together, but I've got it now.''

Griffin kept his mouth shut. He knew when discretion was the better part of valor. As long as she didn't look like she was going to throw things, he figured he wouldn't offer ammo.

''At first I thought, wow, he doesn't kiss like a man in mourning for his lost fiancée,'' she continued. ''And then I thought, he's awfully smooth at putting a move on me for someone who hasn't had a date in two years.''

This didn't sound good. He braced himself.

''And then, you pull off this flattering display of memory—you actually remember every detail I tell you about myself and recite them all back. Very impressive. And not at all like someone who needs dating help.'' Nell shook her head. ''This is more like a man who knows his way around women and then some. This is more like a man who's always thought he was a major operator, who had his pick of women, tons of women.''

Major operator. Pick of women. Tons of women. Yeah, that pretty much described Griffin Jones, the Early Years.

"But," she went on, "then you loved and lost. So it all comes back to Grace, doesn't it?''

Huh?

"It's okay, John. I understand. When she left you and then she died, you fell apart.'' Her voice softened, but she was picking up speed. "I guess you just didn't trust yourself as a man anymore. She left you for your brother. She died. That would knock the wind out of any Casanova. And you had further to fall, didn't you, since you had always been so good at the game of love before that?''

"I did? I was?'' She was confusing him so completely he couldn't distinguish his fictional bio from his real one.

"It all fits," she said serenely. "So now, with me, you begin to feel comfortable again, and your old patterns, the Romeo you were before Grace, surfaces again. But it isn't really about me, is it?''

"No?''

"No. It's about your pride and your masculine impulses.''

Now she really had lost him. "I don't think I—''

"Yes, you do. And it's okay, John, really it is. I understand.'' She offered a rueful smile. "While I'm very sympathetic to everything you've gone through, I'm also not really willing to be your guinea pig— you know, that first seduction on the comeback trail. Sorry, I don't mean to dent your renewed confidence or anything, but it just isn't me. So, under the circumstances, I think we'd better call it a night, don't you?''

He was too perplexed to fight back. Should he be insulted that she thought he was a Romeo on the rebound, which he sort of was, without the rebound? Or go for the compliment hidden in there somewhere, about how his kiss and his moves were smoother than she'd expected?

Sheesh. He'd never had this much trouble with a woman. But maybe there was a way to salvage this yet.

''Are you sure I don't need help?'' he asked hopefully.

''Well, maybe your clothes.'' She gave him a once-over. ''And your hair. I guess I could help you spiff up the outer man to better reflect the inner one.''

Once again, he wasn't sure whether to be insulted. Under his breath, he muttered, ''Fine, let's spiff me up by all means.''

She patted his arm helpfully. ''It's okay, John. We'll get you back up to full speed in time for Valentine's Day, you'll see.''

''Oh, I have no doubt about that.'' As she made a move for the door, he added, ''Will you at least let me drive you home?''

''I live in Geneva,'' she reminded him. ''You don't want to go that far. But I'll tell you what. You can take me to the station and I can grab a train home from there.''

''No,'' he said flatly. ''I'll drive you home.''

Nell hesitated. As she stood there, deciding whether to give in on the ride issue, he suddenly understood what was going on here.

For whatever reason, she had remembered that she

was Nell McCabe, host, and he was only another caller. She wanted to figure him out, like she did all the other disembodied voices on her show—from a safe distance. Up close and personal was a little too close and a lot too personal for Nell McCabe.

In her eyes, he figured he was something like a Ken doll, someone she could fit into a neat box labeled "Mr. Right"—not for her to take out and play with, but to hold at arm's length, dress up, analyze, examine. And, oh, while she was at it, she could match him up with some hapless Barbie who called into her show. Sure, *she* didn't want to be the first seduction on his alleged comeback trail, but she didn't mind sacrificing some Barbie from Crystal Lake or Carpentersville.

Meanwhile, if he reverted to his real identity and let her know he was no mere caller, she would really have a fit. Damned if he did, damned if he didn't.

But he was nobody's Ken doll. And he had plans to share that fact with Nell McCabe. Maybe not tonight. Maybe he would have to plan a strategic retreat and rethink his options. But he would win. Sooner or later, he'd win, and Nell would be putty in his hands.

Cynically, he pulled out his brother's car keys. "I'll drive you."

"It's a long drive," she said stubbornly. "I can take the train."

He abandoned any pretense of being mild-mannered Dr. John Jones. "No way. No woman I know is taking a train home this late at night. Not while I can help it." Griffin hit the button for the elevator, letting his gaze flicker over her, top to bottom, just to annoy her. "Don't worry. I don't bite."

Tuesday, February 1
13 days till V-Day 2000

THE PHONE RANG at six-thirty.

Nell propped herself up on one elbow and dived for it. "Mmph?"

"Hi, Nellie, it's Mom. What was that black car doing in your driveway so late last night? Where's your car?"

She collapsed back into the bed. "I got stuck downtown and a guy from work drove me home. Can you take me to the train in about an hour and a half?"

"Sweetie, I have to be at school at seven-thirty, but maybe Dad can give you a ride." Nell could tell her mother had put a hand over the phone before she yelled, "Fred? Nellie needs a ride to the train at eight. Can you take her?" Back at full volume, she said, "Yeah, he's fine. His first class isn't till one. Why don't you get dressed and come down here for breakfast and then your dad can drive you?"

"Thanks, Mom." She smiled sleepily. There were some benefits to having parents who lived so close. Like breakfast and rides. Burdens, too, of course. Like checkup calls. "Can I go back to sleep now?"

"If you tell me who the man in the black car really was," her mother said slyly.

Nell sighed, loud enough for her mom to be sure to hear. "I told you—a guy I work with. We had a meeting to discuss the whole Valentine's Day campaign they're doing for my show. It got late, he didn't think I should take the train, so he insisted on driving me."

"How very thoughtful of him. Is he handsome?"

"Remotely. Okay, very. Terrible dresser though."

"So was your father. I got over it."

"Mom!" Nell exclaimed. "This is not a boyfriend prospect, just a guy from work."

There was a pause. "You sat in the driveway kind of a long time for just some guy from work."

"What were you doing, keeping a stopwatch on us?" Nell demanded.

"I couldn't help but notice," her mother said cheerfully. "It's not often there are strange Porsches in your driveway."

"How do you know what kind of car it was?"

"I'm not blind."

"Please tell me you weren't using binoculars," Nell groaned.

"Binoculars? I just wanted to check and make sure you got in okay. Is that a crime?" her mom argued.

"No, but being a Peeping Tom is." Nell paused. "So? What did you think of him?"

"It was too dark to tell. Bring him around some time when I can see him in the light." Her mother dropped into a more conspiratorial tone. "So he isn't just some guy from work, huh?"

"Yes," Nell said firmly, "he is. Have a good day at school, Mom. Tell Dad I'll be down in about forty-five minutes."

"Oh, Nellie, you are no fun at all."

"And you," Nell returned, pushing back her covers, "are a very nosy lady. Remind me to look for a new place to live, like ten or twelve miles away, will you?"

"You never know," her mother declared. "Maybe your father and I would like to have our freedom, too. Maybe we could get up to all kinds of mischief without you right down the block cramping our style."

"Go for it, Mom," she said with a laugh.

"Hey, I heard the tail end of your show yesterday, the one with the doctor looking for love. They had it on in the teachers' lounge. You sounded great."

"It went pretty well," Nell admitted. "I'm glad you didn't hear the beginning, though. It was nerve-wracking there for a while, when we were wondering if anyone would call at all."

"Oh, I knew it would turn out, honey. You work so hard, and you deserve it. And that doctor who called, he was too good to be true." Her mother made an audible gasp. "Wait a second! He was the one in your driveway last night, wasn't he?"

"Why would you think that?" Nell asked hastily.

"Because if there was someone else at work, you would've said something before this. But that doctor..." Nell could almost hear the gears turning in her mother's head on the other end of the phone line.

"Okay, okay, I admit it—it was him."

"I knew it! So, what was he like? As impressive as he sounded on the radio?"

What a loaded question. In how many ways could she answer that one? *He's gorgeous, he's hard to figure out, he sends me these looks... He's definitely smart, he has compassion and charm, he kisses like nobody's business...*

She had to break away from the mental images. John Jones might seem like a mild-mannered neurosurgeon, but there was something there, lurking just below the surface, that whispered dark words about muscle and moonlight and sultry nights tangled in sweat-soaked sheets.

Nell lifted a limp hand to her forehead. All she had to do was think of him and her senses jumped to life. And her mind filled with pictures of him in various states of undress.

Oh, jeez. Where was her brain coming up with this stuff? What was it about him that affected her this way?

"Nell?" her mother prompted. "Was he as cute and nice as he sounded?"

"Yes, Mom," she returned quickly, "he's actually very cute and nice. But he's also off-limits."

"Don't be such a pill, Nellie! Catch on to that one. Eligible doctors don't grow on trees."

"Thanks for the sage advice, Mom," Nell said dryly. "I have to go now and so do you. I'll talk to you later…"

As she hung up the phone, she thanked her lucky stars she hadn't invited him in last night. Not only was he much too overpowering to fit inside her small home, he would've been right there under the streetlight, right there in the middle of her living room, framed in the picture window, for her mom to drink in every detail. She never would've heard the end of it.

As if Dr. John Jones, heartthrob of the masses, was the kind of man you brought home to mother. Well, actually, he kind of was. And then he definitely wasn't. Which was exactly why he had Nell in such a tizzy.

After she was safely in his car on the endless drive to the suburbs last night, with a big old gearshift between them, she'd relaxed, he had, too, and they'd talked about sports and music and movies and laughed and argued the whole way. He liked basketball, U2 and bad Kung Fu movies, and seemed to have avoided every single chick flick ever made. As a companion, he was terrific. If that was how socially inept guys behaved, she should've started hanging out with them years ago. She had been seconds away from inviting him in for coffee when she looked at the time and remembered it was a Monday night and way too late and way too scary.

Eligible doctors don't grow on trees...

And ineligible doctors had to be nipped in the bud. Okay, so she needed a date for the same Valentine's Day dance he did. That was no reason to get so mopey and mushy and vulnerable that she completely turned off her common sense. How many times had she counseled a listener not to leap after the first man who crossed her path?

"He isn't right for me," she said out loud. He was a lonely, mixed-up man who had put his romantic life in her hands when he contacted her show, and it would be like betraying a trust to him and all her devoted callers to turn around and date him herself.

Not to mention the fact that it was very probably against the rules of the contest to go anywhere near him.

Not to mention the fact that she had no idea whether he really liked her, or was just smitten by her know-it-all voice on the radio, or even by her hotsy-totsy picture on the side of a bus.

Not to mention the fact that he had a very pushy, masculine side that surfaced just when she didn't want it to. Controlling men were not a group Nell willingly tangled with. Not even gorgeous, lovelorn controlling men.

"Definitely not right for me," she said with more conviction.

So she was going to go to work, pore over the call-in surveys from the right age group and boil it down to some finalists. Time to get him paired up and off the market. Past time.

Nell headed for the shower, doing a fast rewind of their conversations last night, from his contention that Springsteen was better than Elvis to his belief that the world would be a better place if people could drop everything and take a drive in the country the first nice day of spring. He really was terrific.

Damn it.

W-109 WAS A madhouse.

A sea of women, all clamoring for a date with Dr. John, clogged the front entrance, the lobby and the hallways. And the crowds just kept getting bigger and crankier.

After fighting her way back and forth through the lobby a few times, taking her office phone off the hook to make it stop ringing and drowning under piles of piles of papers from marketing, Nell managed to get to the microphone for the second day of the great on-air fix-up extravaganza.

She had to announce right up-front that Dr. John was out of the action and she wouldn't even discuss him today, except to remind everyone that they would announce the winner in the Dr. John sweepstakes this week, so to remember to tune in.

It was a major relief when things went swimmingly—she made matches right and left, lining up five fun couples for the Fantasy Bash before she had time to think about how well it was going.

As the show wound down, she pondered the possibilities for couple number six. "Okay, we've been talking to Sheila, who is thirty and divorced and lives in Elk Grove Village. Sheila, from the men who've called in for you, I think Danny, also thirty and from Bensenville, will make a great date for you. Stay on the line, Sheila and Danny—you've won tickets to the Fantasy Bash courtesy of W-109 and the beautiful Arcadia Hotel."

And that was that. *Whew.*

Amy called something to her as Nell left the studio,

but she couldn't hear. There were women in the hallway, women of every shape and size, not to mention TV cameras and reporters creating enough uproar to drown out an exploding bomb. Pushing her way through the mob, Nell sought retreat in the conference room where she had taken the extra survey forms when there got to be too many for her office.

She had brought a copy of the rules, which was sort of an afterthought, but ended up being the first thing she looked at. And there it was, in black and white. *No employee of station W-109 or any of its affiliates is eligible to participate as a date in the on-air matchmaking program called Operation Strike-a-Match...*

So even if she'd had second thoughts—which she hadn't—her hands were tied. She couldn't match herself up with Dr. John no matter how well he kissed or how broad his shoulders were or how perfect his arms felt around her...

Determined to think about something else, Nell glanced at the clock. It was already well past time for lunch, and yet she was no closer to finding a date for Dr. John than when she'd started that morning. So much for her plans to pore over the possibilities and get a list of possible winners together on the double. But she'd had a show to do. And there were just too many contenders!

"Nell, are you ready to start seeing some of these women?" Amy asked, looking harried as she ducked in behind her boss. "The receptionist has been handing out numbers, but they're getting kind of antsy."

"These are the ones we weeded out, right? The telemarketers called and told them to come in so we could look at them?"

Amy nodded. "They've identified about a hundred

and fifty so far who are twenty-one to thirty-five, un-attached, live within a hundred miles and have no criminal convictions. They're inviting them all in. Drake the Snake has called TV and newspapers to shoot pictures of them all lined up to hype the story even more. Looks like this one is a marketing bonanza.''

Nell's eyes widened. ''A hundred and fifty already? And I haven't even been through these.'' She waved a hand at the overflowing conference table.

''Here's a plan.'' With a grim smile, Amy grabbed a wastebasket and started shoving in stacks of paper. ''If they didn't get in by ten this morning, then they don't get in.''

''No, stop!'' Nell cried, rushing to rescue the people who had been so summarily dismissed. ''What if the perfect woman is in there somewhere?''

''Oh, Nell.'' Amy just stood there, her hands on her hips, with a pitying look on her face. ''Are you doing this because you're a perfectionist, or because you're a romantic and you really think there's one perfect Ms. Right to go with Mr. Right?''

''Dr. Right,'' Nell corrected absently. She was a perfectionist, no question about it, especially when it came to her job. Romantic? No one had ever accused her of that before. But she did think, somewhere in her heart, that Dr. John deserved a really wonderful date for Valentine's Day. Someone smart and funny and sweet and genuine and maybe even spunky...

It took a second before she remembered where she'd heard that description before. From him. About her. As if any of that really applied to her. As if *he* were in any position to know.

Quickly, she told Amy, ''I don't know why I feel

like they all deserve a chance. Anything else offends my sense of fairness, that's all.''

''That's dandy, but what about the ones who are already here, lining up in the hall? We have to do something with them.''

Nell scrounged around under the piles of paper until she found a legal pad and a pen. She numbered all the way down the left side, and then scooted her chair around so that she was facing the door. She was beginning to feel like a judge at the Miss America contest. ''Okay, bring them on. One at a time.''

''Expecting to know Ms. Right if you see her, huh?'' Amy asked sarcastically.

''Well, maybe.''

Amy muttered something under her breath that sounded like, ''If you ask me, you won't like any of them,'' but Nell refused to rise to the bait. Still, she got the idea. Everyone seemed to think she was interested in Dr. John herself. Which was ridiculous. There was no way she was going to make a play for him. Never, ever, ever.

''Send in number one.'' Lifting her chin, Nell picked up her pen and faced the door.

7

A LOT MORE THAN a hundred and fifty women later,
Nell was exhausted and testy and not terribly happy
with the state of American womanhood. It was even
worse that Amy seemed to be enjoying this im-
mensely. Amy had come in to keep her company, and
then when she saw how few were making Nell's
grade, she started keeping a list of her own. Nell
glanced at Amy's list from time to time and was surprised to see stars and exclamation points in the mar-
gin. From this parade of losers? What was Amy thinking?

Meanwhile, the telemarketers kept adding to the
pool, until the numbers stretched well past the original
tally. By the time they closed the doors for the day,
Nell's vision had begun to blur and she couldn't read
her own handwriting.

"Who've you got?" Amy asked. "I've got my top
five, plus three more I can live with."

"I've got none."

"None?" Amy looked confused. "So do you just
want to pick the one you like best from my list?"

Too tired to sit up, Nell laid her head down on the
conference table. Her voice was muffled when she
said, "Come on, Amy, they all reeked. I don't want
any of them."

"Oh, they did not *reek*. Penny, number seventy-one, was very cute and bubbly, and one hundred ninety-seven, Venus, was a hoot.''

''She was the worst,'' Nell returned, wincing as she recalled Venus's particulars. ''She had an IQ of about six, a laugh like a hyena, and those *pants*... Sheesh. Glow-green Spandex capri pants—in the winter! All she needs is a bowl of fruit on her head and she can lead a conga line.''''

''I notice you didn't mention the fact that she also had a body like a Barbie doll. Besides, the way you described Mr. Right's clothes, she sounds perfect for him.''

''Dr. Right. And his clothes were ugly, but not trampy.''

Amy let out an aggrieved noise. ''You're too picky. What about number one hundred and eight? She seemed very nice.''

''Was one hundred and eight the blond office manager with the overbite or the six-foot-four professional volleyball player?'' Nell asked wearily, peering at her notes.

''Volleyball.''

''She's taller than he is. Boot her.''

''Nell, we won't have anyone left,'' Amy persisted. ''We will have gone through close to three hundred women and found none that suit you. Doesn't that strike you as odd?''

''No,'' Nell said defensively.

Amy crossed her arms over her chest. ''It strikes me that maybe someone doesn't want to find to find a match for sweetie pie Dr. John.''

''Not when they're as bad as this bunch. It's not my fault if he deserves better.'' She lifted her head. ''Did marketing have any more to go through?''

''Nope. They said we've seen every single woman

in the twenty-five to thirty-five category who went to the trouble to come down here.'' Amy shoved back her chair, flipped pages on her pad and scribbled numbers on to a fresh sheet. "Come on, Nell—choose! Here's a list of eight finalists. They're all nice, smiley ladies who will look great in the publicity pictures. And isn't that what counts?''

"No!'' Nell said with more energy. "Dr. John needs just the right woman. Not because she's Miss Photogenic, but because she'll fit. With him.''

"And Sheila and Danny got matched up sight unseen in approximately three minutes of airtime because they don't deserve such care and consideration?'' Amy inquired, lifting an eyebrow.

"Oh, Amy, you just don't get it, do you?''

"I think I get it a little too well.''

"Wait.'' Nell sat up straighter. "I have a great idea. We can let him pick his own valentine. I'll call him and tell him. You notify the finalists—the ones you've got there are as good as any—while I call John. Then we bring in all the women, he can see and hear them for himself, and he can choose. Let's set it up for tomorrow night, okay?''

"Uh-huh.''

Nell shot her producer a look. "What does that mean?''

Amy rose, list in hand. "Let's see, *I* call the finalists and *you* call Dr. John. Hmm… Nice how that works.''

"What?''

"Don't give me that innocent face, Nell. You just want to talk to him again and you don't want to admit it,'' Amy said with a certain edge. "Maybe you can even hold his hand while he looks over the contenders, huh?''

"Amy!" Nell protested. "That is so uncalled-for."

"Sorry," her producer said, but she didn't look sorry. "Nell, the real point is that I think you have a crush on Dr. John, paragon of virtue."

"A crush?" Nell echoed, horrified. "A crush? Please!"

"Okay, okay, let's just say, all things considered, you'd rather keep him for yourself. You need a date for Valentine's Day, he needs a date for Valentine's Day..." Amy threw up her hands. "So why not just admit it and go for it instead of all this shilly-shallying and fooling around?"

"Look, even if it were true that I had, um, feelings for him, which I don't—" She broke off, frowning. "I can't take him to the Fantasy Bash, Amy. I checked the rules of the contest."

"You did, huh?" Her producer raised an eyebrow. "And you felt the need to check the rules because you *don't* have a crush on him, right?"

"I just wanted to see what the rules were."

Amy shrugged. "Suit yourself. But if you can't take him to the Bash, someone has to. Nell, we need him. He's a marketing miracle and the only shot we have to keep this show on the air. Your idea of a cattle call sounds like it will work as well as any other scheme. Where do you suggest we do this roundup?"

"It's not a cattle call," Nell insisted. "Do you remember when Channel 7 did that investigative series on job interviews, to show all the ways people screw up? They used that new bookstore on Michigan Avenue. We could do it just the way they did—with you interviewing the women down at the coffee bar with a hidden microphone, while Dr. John and I go up a level, to the gallery, where we can stay out of sight but watch and listen to the whole thing. It worked great for them.''

''Or we could just let him talk to them himself,'' Amy offered. ''Plain view, a conference room, one-on-one, him and the girls. Maybe throw in a box of doughnuts. You know, the easy way?''

''I think he's too shy for that. I don't think he'd do it.''

Amy shook her head. ''So instead *I* talk to them, while you and Dr. John get nice and cozy, out of sight, all by yourselves. Sure, I get it.''

''Amy, please stop being so suspicious. I'm too tired to deal with it right now.''

''Listen, as long as we actually come out of this with a match for this guy, I don't care whether you sit on his lap the whole time he chooses,'' Amy told her. She was halfway out the door with her list of finalists. ''Besides, if we do this undercover operation, I get paid overtime. And I get to see the mysterious doctor for myself.'' She smiled mischievously. ''Maybe I can figure out what the fascination is.''

''There's no—''

''You can be fascinated all you want—I don't care,'' Amy interrupted. ''But keep in mind that he has to get matched up with someone else. *Not* you. *The Hot Zone* is on the line.''

Wednesday, February 2
12 days till V-Day 2000

''WHAT THE HELL are you dressed like that for?''

Caught outside the door of his loft, Griffin didn't know what to say. Especially given the look of horror on his brother's face.

''What are you supposed to be?'' Spencer asked,

backing up for a better view. "Those clothes... And your hair? When I saw you the other night, I almost didn't believe it was you. And who was that woman and why was she yelling at me?"

"Spence, it's a long story and I have a date and I can't—"

"Oh, yes, you can." His brother pushed him back into the loft. "I have to hear this."

Griffin was mentally sifting details to spin a coherent cover story. "She's someone I met at the gym," he made up on the spot. "She doesn't trust people with money—grew up poor but honest—you know the drill."

"She sounded like she was off her rocker."

Not off her rocker. Just not on the same page as the Jones Boys. "Rich people give her hives."

"So the clothes are supposed to make you look poor?" Dubious, Spence gave him the once-over, taking in the jeans, flannel shirt and nubby tweed jacket. "I guess they do the trick. They're low rent all right."

"Yeah, well, small price to pay for the right woman," Griffin said with a tight smile.

"Whoa!" Spencer's eyes widened. "Did you just say the right woman?"

"I didn't mean it like that."

"Oh, yeah? Then how did you mean it? I can't remember those words ever coming out of your mouth before." Spence scratched his chin thoughtfully. "In fact, I would've said you'd take poison before you'd settle on one chick."

"Don't call her a chick."

"Hold the phone. Changing your clothes, changing your attitude..." He grinned. "Don't tell me my big bro's in love?"

"No, I am not in love." Why the hell was he defensive about this? "Not that I couldn't be. I mean, I lived with Mimi for almost a year. And Linda and I were together for three years. Did I take poison then?"

"No, you just got bored and dumped them." Still looking smug, Spence ambled nearer, eyeing his brother suspiciously. "I seem to remember both Mimi and Linda pushing you toward the altar. When the going got tough, you got out of town, bro. That's always been your style."

"Aw, come on. I didn't want to get married. That doesn't mean the going got tough *or* I got out of town," Griffin protested.

"No? Well, you watch—the lady gets too close and you'll find a reason to go skiing." Spencer laughed out loud. "You always were a dog. You are a dog. Same as me."

"Yeah, well, this dog has a date." Griffin edged around his brother and pushed the button for the elevator. "And I plan to keep it."

Spencer hooted. "Worrying about keeping a woman waiting? Griff, my man, this is *so* not like you."

Griffin got in the elevator and waved goodbye as the doors closed, more than ready to change the subject. "See you, little bro," he called out. "Only a week and a half till you lose that bet we made. Be sure you have the Learjet plane warmed up and ready for me, okay?"

"You're not going to win!" Spence shouted down the elevator shaft. Griffin just shook his head.

GRIFFIN WAS NOT in the world's best mood. On one hand, it had been gratifying to pick up the phone and hear Nell begging him to come and meet her at this bookstore. On the other hand, it was less than flattering to find out she was doing her damnedest to fix him up with someone else. Someone else? Did she really think she was going to get rid of Griffin Jones, er, Dr. John Jones, that easily?

Still, when he spotted Nell at the bookstore, he found himself very glad to see her. It was a big place, but somehow she stood out, even with her nose buried in a coffee table art book.

He leaned in over her shoulder. ''You like Maxfield Parrish?'' he asked softly, startling her enough that she fumbled with the book, letting it fall from her hands and clatter to the floor.

Every time he came up on her, she seemed to drop things. Which was actually kind of fun. It meant he was getting under her skin, and that was just where he wanted to be. With a sly smile, he retrieved the book for her.

''I, uh, like the vivid colors,'' she mumbled, grabbing the book back without touching him and setting it carefully on the nearest shelf. ''And the light. There's a lot of, um, passion there.''

That he understood. Parrish was full of nude nymphs cavorting in front of spectacular backdrops. Passion. Yeah, that he understood.

''I don't really know anything about art,'' Nell went on, ''but these are so lush and...romantic. The only art in the world I really covet, if you know what I mean.''

Probably wiser not to tell her that he owned one, or that she would love it even more in person than on the page.

''You look great tonight,'' he said warmly, eyeing her pale sweater and skirt. ''Blue is your color.''

''Th-thank you.'' Clearly feeling awkward, she

picked up her briefcase and fiddled with the handle. "You, too. I mean, you would look nice in blue, if you wore it, which you're not, of course, at the moment. But you would, if you did, because your eyes are such an amazing shade. Of blue, I mean." She stopped abruptly, as she gazed up into his face. "I didn't notice you had blue eyes before. You had glasses. Tinted ones. Where are your glasses?"

Damn. He was really going to have to be more careful. The glasses were sitting back at the loft, forgotten.

"Contacts," he improvised. "They're new." Nell was still giving him a funny, measuring look, as if she were trying to put him in focus, but she didn't say anything.

Griffin had always believed that people latched on to first impressions with a death grip. So surely Nell had already compartmentalized the nerdy, needy Dr. John persona, and it had superseded any memory she retained of the real Griffin Jones. Heck, for all he knew she had no recollection of Griffin Jones whatsoever, and nothing that even needed to be blocked out.

But she was still gazing at him, her head tipped to one side and then the other, as if she couldn't quite figure him out. Just to be on the safe side, he decided he'd better get her off track.

Dropping his voice, he asked, "Listen, Nell, do we really have to go through with this matchmaking stuff?"

"What do you mean?"

"It seems kind of silly, don't you think? Given that we already know that we—you and I—are an incredible match. So why…" He paused, noting the flush already starting on her cheeks. "Why can't I take you?"

"Take me?" she choked.

He smiled. "Just to the Fantasy Bash."

"Oh, I…" She bit her lip, backed away, and started again. "I can't go with you, John. Even if I wanted to. It's in the contest rules that winners, that is, people matched up for the Fantasy Bash, cannot be employees of the station. I double-checked."

Should he be glad she'd felt the need to check? Or annoyed at the result? "Nell, come on, surely we can bend the rules. You're in charge."

"Even if I were in charge, which I'm not," she persisted, "I could get the station into legal trouble. I have to abide by the rules, so we are not going to discuss this anymore. I firmly believe in doing the right thing. And this is the right thing. Think of me as your mentor. Or…" She faltered. "Or your therapist. Whatever works. Off-limits, okay?"

He waited as long as he could. "Okay," he said reluctantly. Even if he had no intention of actually giving in. "So how is this matchmaking thing supposed to work?"

Nell, clearly relieved to be off the hook, grabbed up her briefcase and nudged him around behind the rack of books. "Amy, my producer, is setting up in the café area, near the coffee bar," she explained. "Right over there. Amy will sit at that table with each of the eight finalists and do a little interview, hopefully get them talking about themselves. There's a microphone in the vase of flowers. Meanwhile, you and I will be upstairs." She pointed to the gallery that overlooked the first floor. "That way we can watch and listen, but they can't see us."

Griffin was beginning to like the sound of this. "Just us two?"

"Well, yes, but we can hear them. And see them if we want to, you know, check them out." She hesitated. "I thought it would be easier for you if you had a little distance from the contenders. And if I sat with you while you choose the right one." She fastened those sincere hazel green eyes on him. "I thought you might need my help."

Yes, he definitely liked the sound of this. "Ready to get into stakeout position?" he teased, offering his arm.

"Go upstairs, you mean? I guess so." Ignoring his arm, adopting a very businesslike attitude, Nell hauled herself and her briefcase up the stairs ahead of him. She led the way to the second floor, back into the intimate aisles of the Romance and Erotica sections.

Glancing at a few of the titles, Griffin couldn't help but wonder if she'd chosen this area on purpose. *Good grief.* It was hardly his fault if books like *Wild, Wanton Love* and *How to Bring Your Man to His Knees* gave him ideas.

Hidden among the tall bookstacks, someone—presumably Nell—had carved out a small enclave flanked by two of the bookstore's oversize wing chairs with a wooden end table wedged between them. One of the chairs had a matching ottoman, inviting you to lean back and put your feet up. Very cozy. Although the nook was private, tucked back into the shadows, the railing overlooking the coffee bar was just a few feet away, offering a perfect view of the would-be dates.

A couple of technicians were already there, fussing with wires and receivers and switch boxes on the end table, and they handed over a pair of headphones as Nell perched on the edge of one of the wing chairs.

"Have a seat," she instructed him, holding the headset up to one ear. "Amy says our first candidate is standing by, ready to go."

But Griffin didn't sit down. Instead, he ambled over nearer the railing, taking a lazy look in the direction of the table downstairs, where he could see the woman who must be Amy talking into the flower vase. That looked pretty silly. She glanced up toward them, screwing up her eyes to peer at him more closely. And then an expression of major alarm crossed her face and she spoke more animatedly into the flowers.

He turned back to Nell. "What is she saying?"

Nell's face had turned a most becoming shade of pink. "He *is* not," she said frantically into her mouthpiece. "Well, okay, he is, but... I can control myself, you know. No, Amy. No. No way!"

Griffin raised an eyebrow. This sounded promising.

Nell scooted around in her chair so he couldn't see her face. She muttered fiercely, "I know what he looks like, Amy. No, I have no intention of... Let's just bring on the first one, shall we?"

She spun back to gesture furiously at Griffin to get away from the railing where he could be seen.

He shrugged, stuck his hands in his jeans pockets and strolled back. One of the techies handed him a headset, and then the two of them disappeared to monitor the equipment elsewhere, leaving Griff alone with Nell. She pointed to the other wing chair, her somber expression brooking no objections. All right, if she was determined to play this game, he'd see it through. It wouldn't be long before he had her right where he wanted her—begging him not to date another woman, falling into his arms and his bed with carefree abandon.

Adjusting his earphones, Griffin dropped onto the ottoman, listening in to the transmission from downstairs.

He could see the first woman fairly well as she hovered at the table. Her name was Sherry, and she was pretty enough, with big brown eyes and a cute figure, but she had a desperate, stressed-out air about her.

"Sherry, tell us about yourself," Amy encouraged in his ear.

He got the idea quickly enough. Rising young exec in a downtown firm. Busy, busy, busy. Scheduled tighter than a drum, rushing from breakfast meetings to spinning classes to financial planning seminars. Felt success and money were the most potent aphrodisiacs. Already nipping into her third cup of double espresso and lighting up her fourth cigarette.

Nell chewed her lip. "What do you think?"

What he thought was that Sherry was a maniac and couldn't hold a candle to Nell. But whomever they brought in down there, he didn't much care. He just wanted to sit close to Nell and see how long it took her to cave in. Carelessly pitching away his headset, he edged his footstool closer. "My headphones aren't working very well. There's a lot of static. Can I listen in with you?"

Nell swallowed. "It's, uh, more important for you to hear than me. Here." Primly, she handed over her set, which was not what he was aiming for at all.

Momentarily stumped, Griffin frowned. But he wasn't beaten yet. With a hard shove, he pulled his ottoman up against her chair, effectively trapping her there between his knees. Nell gulped. Adopting an innocent expression, he bent in right next to her, with only the width of the earpiece separating them. "I think we can both listen," he murmured, tipping his head into hers, cozying up closer just to make his point. *Try to foist me off on somebody else, will you?* He smiled deviously. "Well, Sherry certainly is up-tempo. That's good, don't you think?"

"Sure. Up-tempo. That's one way to put it." Nell seemed to be having trouble breathing. "Maybe she should try decaf."

"Oh, so you don't like her?"

"John, she's not your type," she said fiercely. "Not at all."

This was more like it. With every breath, Nell's breasts rose and fell unsteadily under her baby blue sweater. He hated to tear his eyes away from that delectable sight, but he didn't want to drool on her, either. Not quite yet.

"Okay," he whispered, gazing right into her eyes. "Let's forget Sherry and see the next one."

This one was Irene, a successful actress who began to describe some of her favorite roles. "A little too high on herself, I think," Nell said quickly. Her lips were only inches from his, and he watched her tongue dart out to moisten them. "Let's move on."

Griff let his gaze linger on her tongue and her mouth. *Oh, yeah.* "By all means," he said in a husky tone. "Let's move on."

"What are you two doing up there?" Amy demanded. "I can barely hear you. Are you asleep or what?"

Asleep? Not even close. His body thrummed with tension, and sleep was the farthest thing from his mind.

Nell cleared her throat and did her best to give a

sharp, clear response right into the microphone, but Griff kept quiet. He was occupied with his own thoughts, his own timetable. About two more interviews and he would have her stoked high enough to move in for the kill. As Amy and the other women droned on down there, he and Nell would be all tied up in the confines of the wing chair...

Next up was Dinah, a surfer girl from Australia whose white blond hair drifted all the way down past her hips. A very pretty lady.

"Nice hair," he noted, giving her a glance.

"She could use a trim. And that color isn't found in nature," Nell snapped.

He smiled, holding back, purposely ruffling Nell's nerves, driving her crazy with the briefest of touches, the tiniest of caresses, shifting her ever closer, one centimeter at a time, until she was dangerously close to toppling off her chair and into his lap.

Dinah was followed by Penny, a perky fitness trainer who bracketed three or four mindless giggles around every word. While she bubbled over, Griffin managed to maneuver his free hand on to Nell's knee, making it seem like he needed it for balance. He didn't. But her silky skirt crept up on her thigh, and he rubbed his thumb along the hem.

Nell shivered. He bided his time. As they listened to Jo, a tall, sporty woman, go on at length about how much fun it was to pound volleyballs into opponents' faces, he moved his hand to Nell's hip, carefully nudging her deeper into the V of his knees.

"That woman was too, uh, hard," Nell murmured. "Next."

He could see it in her eyes. There she was, ripe for the plucking, and he didn't mean to let his opportunity pass. Letting the second set of headphones drop harmlessly into the depths of the wing chair, cutting off the incessant chatter from the coffee bar, he circled both arms around her, hoisting her into his lap, dipping his head to find her lips.

"John," she whispered, hanging back an inch or two, "we're supposed to be—"

"I know what we're supposed to be. Who cares?"

"Uh-oh," she breathed, but it was too late. He pressed her up against him, taking her mouth with every bit of Jones Boy bravado he'd been hiding, wrapping her around him and lifting them both up into her chair.

Nell responded hungrily, nipping at his mouth as he delved deeper. He was filled with triumph. He knew it. She couldn't resist any more than he could. Her fingers threaded through the hair at the back of his neck, cool and tingly against his hot skin, urging him on. At some level of his brain, Griffin knew he had moved beyond the game into something far more instinctive, more important, more urgent. He slid his hand up under the edge of her skirt, pulling her closer, pushing her deep into the wing chair.

It was madness. A public place, the wrong woman, the wrong man, the wrong everything. And he didn't care.

Until scratchy, sputtering noises erupted from somewhere underneath Nell, hissing and squawking and totally wrecking the mood. She jumped about a foot, while he snatched up the headset wedged down in the cushions.

"Hey!" Amy's voice called out, faint but audible through the static. "I haven't heard word one from you guys on either Alyce or Yolanda. What's going on up there?"

"Amy wants to know what's going on," he relayed darkly.

"Nothing!" Nell cried, but she was nowhere near the microphone since it was attached to the headset in Griffin's hand. She scrambled for the other one, the one he'd abandoned at the very beginning, flipping switches and blowing into the mouthpiece. "Amy? Can you hear me?"

"I can hear you fine. Quit shouting, will you? Where've you been?"

"Well, uh…" Bless her honest little soul, Nell clearly couldn't come up with anything on the spur of the moment. She looked at him helplessly.

Griffin held the microphone up to his mouth. "We lost the transmission there for a while, that's all. Technical problems."

"So why didn't you signal me?" Amy demanded. "Did you completely miss Alyce and Yolanda? Alyce is a great choice if you like wispy girls in Laura Ashley dresses, and Yolanda, well… She's a knockout. A smart knockout. Historical society librarian by day, stripper by night. What more could you want?"

Whoa. He was almost sorry he'd missed that.

"We saw them and he didn't like either of them," Nell said hastily. "Alyce is too vague and Yolanda's stripper thing is a major turnoff."

"For whom?" Amy asked pertly. "For you, or for the good doctor?"

"Him, of course."

"Right. Listen, Nell, there's only one more. Venus. You remember how much you liked Venus? Not. So when are you going to admit you have no intention—"

Nell cut her off. "Just get Venus in there and get

this moving," she ordered. "We need this to be over."

She cast a troubled glance at Griffin, who wondered exactly what she meant by that. He also wondered how long he should give her before he insisted on an answer to Amy's question himself. How long could Nell go on letting herself get tangled up with him, and still pretend she had no qualms about sending him out on a dream date with someone else?

But there was no time to push her into an answer.

"Well, well, well, isn't this cozy?" The sound came from behind them, and they both turned in time to see a tall, broad-shouldered, slickly handsome man in an expensive suit emerge from behind the Erotica bookcase. He tipped up his sunglasses. "What have we here?" He indicated the headphones and equipment. "Don't tell me—you're learning French the easy way."

Spencer. *Hell.* His little brother must've followed him. But how much did he see?

Spence grinned, leaning negligently against a stack of volumes entitled "Stories of the Big O." "Well, whatever you were doing, it looks like you two were enjoying yourselves."

Hovering protectively behind Nell, Griffin sent his brother every subliminal message he could think of, mouthing *Keep your mouth shut* over her head. Spence gave a curt nod, but he moved nearer just the same.

"I know you, don't I?" he asked. Griff could see his brother begin to turn on the charm, and Nell react, first with confusion, and then with a kind of grudging appreciation. Griffin, however, was far from appreciative, even if he recognized his own moves in action.

Everything Spence knew about women Griff had taught him.

"I remember now," Spence mused. "I didn't recognize you, the other night at the restaurant. But now I've got it. Nell McKee. From the radio station."

"McCabe," she corrected automatically. Flustered under his scrutiny, she added, "I'm sorry—I don't mean to be rude, but—would you mind? We're in the middle of something."

"I'll bet you are."

"This has nothing to do with you," Griffin interceded, warning his brother off, sliding in between him and Nell.

"Oh, but I think it does." He winked at Griffin, indicating he was going along with the masquerade. "Y'see, Mr. Whoever-you-are, I own the station where she works. Well, my older brother and I do. Maybe you've heard of him? The famous, or maybe I should say *infamous* Griffin Jones. But seeing as how Griff isn't here right now…"

Spence's lips quivered, as if he were trying very hard not to laugh. Griff glared at him, pondering precisely how long it would take to knock his brother out cold.

8

WITH A SELF-SATISFIED grin, Spence finished his thought. "Since Griff isn't here, I guess I'm in charge."

"You? In charge?" Griffin echoed in a dangerous tone.

His baby brother went on affably, "Well, someone has to look out for the radio station. And I'm getting the definite idea this little rendezvous concerns W-109. Am I right?"

"Oh. Well, yes, actually." Nell blushed. "I can explain."

"You don't have to," Griffin protested.

But she whispered, "You're the one who told me to be nice to him. He *is* my boss."

"Nice to him? Nice to *him?*"

But she had already sidestepped Griffin in order to talk to Spencer. "This is part of the Fantasy Bash promotion," she began. "It came up at the marketing meeting, where Drake the Sn—I mean, Mr. Witley outlined the campaign. This…" She touched Griffin lightly on the shoulder and then said proudly, "This is the first person who called in to be matched up to go to the Fantasy Bash. Dr. Jones. Dr. John Jones."

"Oh, really?" Spencer stepped back and eyeballed his brother. "Funny, he doesn't look like a doctor to me."

"Oh, he is," Nell assured him, while Griffin reconsidered the use of a sucker punch. Anything to shut up his idiot brother. "Dr. John has pretty much taken Chicago by storm. We had so many women calling in wanting to go to the Fantasy Bash with him, that we were just swamped. It's terrific. And he's been a promotional gold mine." She gazed up at Griff and gave him a hopeful smile. She might as well have pinched his cheek. "You could say that this man has single-handedly insured the success of the Fantasy Bash."

"Oh, really?" Spence asked again, narrowing his eyes. "I think I'm beginning to figure this out."

"Oh, no, you're not," Griffin returned.

"Maybe he is," Nell put in.

"No, he's not."

"Yes, he is." The younger Jones brother draped an arm around Nell. "So, listen, pretty lady, as I recall, part of this campaign calls for you to host the Fantasy Bash yourself. Am I right?"

"Um, yes."

"And do you have a date lined up?"

"Well, no, actually, now that you mention it…"

"You know, Nell," Spencer said, in a honeyed and persuasive tone, "I would be honored to escort you. As the owner of the station, and well, a bit of a celebrity, it seems like a great idea to me."

"Y-you?" she stuttered.

Okay, now he *was* going to kill him. Griff cut in, "I don't think you're in any position to take her to the Bash."

Spence arched an eyebrow. "And you are?"

"Yes."

"No!" Nell insisted. "He has to go with one of the women who called in." As Griffin opened his mouth to disagree, Nell stopped him cold. "I told you—it's in the rules. And you, Mr. Jones..." They both turned. "Um, I mean, *Spencer*, thank you for asking, but I don't think so."

He lifted his wide shoulders in a careless shrug. "Take your time. Consider my offer. I think you'll decide I'm the perfect choice." Before anyone could refute that, Spence inquired, "So what were you two doing up here, anyway?"

"You might say we were eavesdropping on the finalists," Nell responded. "For the date with Dr. John, I mean. The last one, Venus, is being interviewed right now."

"Venus?" Spencer guffawed. "One of your date possibilities is named Venus? This I gotta see."

"Down there." Griff inclined a thumb over his shoulder, and Spence went to spy over the railing.

"Whoa. Looks like a winner to me. That girl has curves that won't quit."

"Yeah, well, at this very moment," Griff said, tapping his earphone, "she's talking about her favorite things—lightbulb jokes, disco gymnastics and making clothes for her Chihuahua. Interesting mix. Still think she's a winner?"

"Oh, yeah. You gotta see this. This must be disco gymnastics."

Curious, Griff turned around and took a gander, too. *Good grief.*

Behind him, he heard Nell whisper, "Good lord. She isn't."

But she was. Eager to impress, Venus was demonstrating her favorite handstand, right there on the floor of the coffee bar. And her handstand showcased certain other bountiful attributes, attributes that were going to slide right out of her clingy halter dress and strangle her, if she wasn't careful.

"Those can't be real," Griffin murmured.

As he pondered that issue, Venus jumped back to her feet with a cry of "Voilà!", rearranged her clothes and slid back into her seat opposite a bug-eyed Amy.

"That really gets the blood circulating!" Venus shouted happily. And then she laughed directly into the vase of flowers, a calling-the-hogs, honking whoop that made Griff's hair stand on end. He staggered, as Nell winced and held the headphone away from her ear.

"God, that's awful," Griffin said out loud.

Even Spencer could hear it, without a headset. "I guess Venus has a good sense of humor. And a healthy set of lungs. Oh, too bad. She's leaving. I can't wait to see who's up next. Sheena, Queen of the Jungle?"

"Sorry to disappoint you, but Venus is the last one," Nell said briskly. "Maybe one of the first seven was more to Dr. Jones's liking."

"You know what's to my liking," he muttered.

"Listen, uh, Dr. Jones," Spencer put in. "If Venus is the last one and you're done here, can I offer you a lift? Now that I know you're the man who is single-handedly insuring the success of the Fantasy Bash, I think you and I have some things to discuss."

"I don't think Ms. McCabe and I are finished," Griffin returned curtly.

"Oh, yes, we are."

His gaze drifted over her as she removed her earphones and started to wind up the cord with swift, savage strokes. Her jaw was clenched, her shoulders tense, her eyes focused on anything but him. With that attitude, he didn't stand a chance of coaxing her back into his arms. Not tonight. "Are you sure? You really want to leave it this way?"

"I'm positive."

"See? The lady's positive." Spence clapped his brother on the shoulder. "Come on. My car's right outside on the street. I have a feeling you'll feel right at home in it."

Oh, God, the car. Better to get Spencer and his black Porsche out of there before Nell spotted the car.

"Yeah, let's go." He dumped his headset and wheeled toward the stairs. He turned back. "Nell, I'll call you."

"Of course. You need to let me know who you've chosen. As your lucky date," she said with determined brightness.

"My lucky date?" Griffin shook his head. "We both know who I'll be spending Valentine's Day with, don't we, Nell?"

But she refused to meet his eyes. Still, Griffin wasn't ready to throw in the towel. If she thought she was dumping him this easily, she was very wrong.

Grim but resolute, he trailed his brother to the Porsche. Damn Spence, anyway, for following him and screwing up everything.

"Man, you have really stepped in it this time," Spence howled. "I should be madder than hell that you're pulling this scam just to win the bet, but it's too damn funny for me to care."

"Yeah, whatever."

Spencer didn't stop laughing all the way to the loft. It was getting on Griffin's nerves.

"Oh, come on, big bro," Spence teased. "It's obvious you have a thing for Nell McKee. I saw how you reacted when I asked her out."

Griffin growled, "It's Nell McCabe. And I don't have a thing for anyone. You know me better than that."

"Yeah, well, I never would've expected to see you wearing Joe six-pack clothes and AV nerd headphones, playing footsie with some radio chick, either." Spence pulled the Porsche into its parking space. "So how do you explain all that?"

"It's a scam, okay?" Griff slammed the door a little more sharply than necessary. "The call-in matchmaking wasn't going very well, so I gave it a boost. No big deal. You would've done the same thing if you were on my side of the bet."

"Doubtful."

"Okay, I admit it—you probably wouldn't have, just because you're not smart enough to think of it." Griff offered a sardonic smile. "Right, baby bro?"

"Wrong. I wouldn't have, because it's beyond lame and makes you look like a flaming lunatic."

"Too late now." Griffin pounded the elevator button. "I did it to get Operation Strike-a-Match going, and it got going. Through the roof. So what if I took it a little further than I should've? It's all in good fun."

"Yeah, and when your girlfriend figures out you're really the infamous Griffin Jones, what then?"

Griffin regarded his brother with cold eyes. "She's not my girlfriend, and who says she has to figure it out?"

"Hey, don't look at me. I'm not going to tell her." Spence chuckled. "You're in enough trouble without me saying a word. I'm enjoying the show."

"And you can enjoy it all the way to the end, when you're turning over the Learjet, the house in Palm Beach and your share of W-109." Griff stalked off the elevator and opened the door to his loft. "Since you're pretty much conceding, that is."

His brother followed him and stood, blocking the

doorway. "Who's conceding? Maybe I have plans of my own."

"Yeah, right."

Spencer shook his head. "You're so hooked on the girl, you're not thinking straight. Perfect time for me to step in and run interference."

Setting his jaw, Griffin asked, "What kind of interference?"

"It's a surprise."

"Like moving in on Nell?"

Spencer laughed out loud. "You *are* whipped, aren't you?"

"No way." Whipped? Him? It was ludicrous. "I just don't like you horning in on my, uh, turf." Or something like that.

"I'd keep an eye on that turf, if I were you." Spence narrowed his eyes. "For one thing, I'm wondering exactly where you're headed with this. A clinch or two at the bookstore while you're in your flannel-boy outfit, sure. But I don't think that's what you have in mind."

Griffin wasn't really sure what he had in mind, either. So far he'd been playing it by ear. Or maybe by another part of his anatomy.

"So what about when you take things to the next level?" his brother mused. "Face it—the lady's not stupid. I don't know why she hasn't cottoned on to your ridiculous disguise yet, but you go much further, take off the dopey clothes, take her to bed, and it'll be all over. She's got to know you aren't who you say you are. And I have a feeling she's not the forgiving type."

Griff really, really hated it when his brother had a point.

"Yep," Spence continued, "I'm planning to just

sit back and watch the fireworks. Will the Bash be a success and you win the bet? You may not live that long, not if Ms. McCabe finds out about your secret identity.''

"I can handle Nell," he said grimly. "And I will win. I always do."

But the question had become what exactly he wanted to win. And what prize he wanted to walk away with when this was all over.

What did he want? To win a Learjet? Or to win Nell McCabe?

With a muttered oath, he brushed past his brother and headed back toward the elevator.

"Uh-oh," Spencer called after him. "I know that look. It's the one you get when your love life gets tough and you get out of town..."

Friday, February 4
Ten days till V-Day 2000

EVERY TIME THE phone rang, Nell thought it might be him. It wasn't.

"I promised myself I would never sit around and wait for a guy to call," she grumbled. "This man isn't even mine, and here I am, mooning over the phone."

Brrrringggg.

She jumped, catching it on the second ring. But it was just Penny, the perky fitness trainer, dying to know if there had been a decision yet.

"Nope, nothing yet. He said he thought you were all great, so it's hard to choose. We'll let you know as soon as we hear," Nell assured her.

Pushy bunch of women, anyway. A couple of them had called three or four times, while Venus with the hyena laugh—her whole name was Venus DiMaio, which was even sillier than John Jones—had left six messages and gotten through to Nell for three asinine conversations. If Venus phoned one more time, Nell swore she was going to tell her she was out of the running just for being annoying. Or maybe for tempting all the men to drape themselves over railings just to ogle her and her outrageous bosom.

It was bad enough that Spencer Jones had asked her out with one breath and gasped over Venus with the next, but kind and conscientious Dr. John Jones had done practically the same thing. *Men.* "Worthless piles of testosterone, anyway," she muttered.

That was so unkind she couldn't believe she'd said it. But in her current grumpy mood, anything was possible. Even her mom had noticed. At breakfast that morning, Adele McCabe had snapped at Nell to straighten up and fly right, to shape up or ship out. Nell hadn't heard either phrase since she was a surly teenager.

But in her heart of hearts, she knew what was wrong.

Blast her stupid, sentimental hide, she missed him. *Him.* Dr. John Jones, Chicagoland's most eligible bachelor. Besides the fact that she couldn't seem to be around him for five seconds without wanting to throw him on the ground and ravish him, she had also come to the unsettling realization that she actually enjoyed his company. When he wasn't ignoring her to gape at Venus DiMaio.

The jerk.

Speaking of jerks... A low-level marketing department minion had been trying to catch her attention for several minutes. He was hovering just beyond her doorway waving a sheet of paper.

"Yes?" Nell called. "What is it?"

"Memo from Mr. Witley." He marched in and slapped it down in front of her.

"Okay. Thanks. You're excused."

"No, I'm supposed to wait," he said smartly.

Sheesh. W-109 was turning into an army base or something, with Drake Witley and the almighty marketing department commanding the fort. Quickly, Nell scanned the lines. *Witley's office, immediately, several items to discuss...*

"A summons, huh? How nice." But at least if she complied, she wouldn't be in *her* office, staring at the phone or fielding calls from the Eager Eight. She rose. "Okay, I'm coming."

She was afraid Drake the Snake would be pacing as he waited for her in his palatial office. Instead, he was crouched over a small golf club and a bucket of balls. When your office was big enough for a full-sized putting green, you could do that.

"Hello, Mr. Witley," Nell said with only a hint of temper. "Thanks so much for asking me in."

"Sit," he barked.

She found a steely metal chair parked out away from the steely metal desk and took it, crossing her legs, trying in vain to get comfortable. "And what can I do for you, Mr. Witley?"

"I'll make it brief." He glanced up from his putting stance and glared at her. "That guy, that Dr. Jones, needs a woman pronto. This has been going on too long."

"Yes, but—"

"I'm not finished. Get him to pick a date, and I don't mean you."

Nell inhaled sharply. "M-me? Who said anything about me?"

"Spencer Jones. You know, the owner. He says he

saw the two of you together for some strategy session the other night and it looked like you were getting along a little too well." Nell tried to interrupt, but Witley held up his golf club to wave her off. "Spencer Jones also told me he offered to take you to the V-Day 2000 Fantasy Bash himself."

"Yes, but—"

"No buts." Drake the Snake fixed her with his beady eyes. "I'm not asking you to marry the guy, not even to sleep with him, although I don't know why you wouldn't want to. He's filthy rich and looks like a movie star. What's not to like? So let's just say if you know what's good for you and W-109, you will say yes, and you'll start getting yourself and Spencer Jones in the paper to push the Bash, to make it a rousing success—it's what we all want, am I right?"

"Yes, but..." Even if it meant her job, she really had no intention of taking one of the odious Jones Boys to the Fantasy Bash, to waste her Valentine's Day on an arrogant, overpowering pirate. Especially not after Spencer Jones had phoned the W-109 brass to rat on her. What a scummy thing to do! And typical unscrupulous Jones Boy behavior, right up there with pushing nuns and orphans onto the street, buying up people's radio stations, threatening their jobs...

"Nell? Get in touch with Spencer Jones and accept his offer. Now."

"I'll think about it."

"Just do it." Frowning, he ordered, "And while you're at it, make sure you address all these rumors going around, that the Bash is canceled, that the hotel is a mess, whatever. We're trying to trace where this stuff is coming from. Probably a competitor. But in the meantime, make sure you announce on the air that the Bash will proceed as advertised.''

Rumors? This was the first she'd heard. Who would care enough to try to sabotage a silly Valentine's Day party?

Witley smiled at her, that peculiar grimace thing he did, and Nell really wished he hadn't. It made her feel as if she needed a shower. ''Is that all of it?'' she inquired.

''That's it.'' He was already concentrating on tapping the little white ball into the cup as Nell scooted out of his office.

She hated this. She really hated this.

Back in her office, she picked up the phone, intending to call a friend or maybe even her mother, just to vent over Drake Witley's demands and this whole unpleasant mess. Valentine's Day with Spencer Jones? Choosing one from among a bumper crop of bimbos just to get the poor doctor safely matched up?

Whoever would have thought her life would come to this?

The more she thought about it, the more strongly she felt that it was unethical, absolutely unconscionable, to send John off to the lovefest of the century with any one of those eight unsuitable women. Outrageous!

Even as she steamed, she found herself flipping her Rolodex to the brand-new Dr. John Jones card. Her fingers dialed his number before she realized what she'd done.

Uh-oh. It rang once, and her heart began to beat faster. Nell licked suddenly dry lips. What was she going to say to him? What did she expect him to say in return?

It rang a second time, and her anxiety only increased. "What can he do?" she asked out loud. She needed a miracle, not a nice, schlubby neurosurgeon who wasn't competent to pick out his own jackets or find his own dates.

"Oh well," she whispered miserably. "At least I'll hear his voice." And if that wasn't a pathetic sentiment, she didn't know what was. Nell silently vowed to get a grip.

But it was a woman's voice, not Dr. John's she heard. Inexplicably, the voice answered, "G&S, may I help you?"

"G&S?" Nell hesitated. "I think I may have a wrong number. I was calling for Dr. John Jones."

"Dr. John...?" There was a long pause. "Oh, excuse me. Of course. Dr. Jones. This is his answering service. I'm afraid he's in, uh, surgery. May I take a message?"

In surgery. She should've realized he wouldn't be hanging around waiting for her call. "No, no message. Well, you can tell him that Nell McCabe called. No, wait. On second thought, *don't* tell him that Nell McCabe called."

"Okay," the woman said doubtfully.

Nell replaced the receiver with a heavy heart. "I guess it's the end of the line for Dr. Jones." Drake the Snake's words kept echoing inside her head. *That guy needs a woman pronto. Get him to pick a date and I don't mean you.*

Nell sighed. She had no choice, did she? She had already decided—and told him in no uncertain terms—that he had to pick one of them. All this stalling and righteous indignation was just postponing the inevitable. In a rush she located the photos brought in by each of the women, stapled them to copies of their forms and fact sheets, shoved the lot into a big envelope and carefully wrote his name and address on the outside.

She added a note—"Choose one by Monday, please!"—and called the mail room. "I need a messenger to deliver this ASAP," she instructed them. then she mumbled, "I need it out of my hands before I change my mind."

Okay, so she had taken a definite step toward what the Snake had ordered. Surely she could put off the rest of it, especially getting in touch with Spencer Jones, for a little while. "I'll do it later," she said out loud. "Maybe tomorrow."

With that off the front burner, she managed to manufacture enough other things to occupy herself until it was time to go on the air.

She launched the show in her most cheerful, upbeat voice as she related how well plans for the Fantasy Bash were going. Everything was on schedule and looking good, she stressed.

"That night, we're even going to draw names, with one lucky couple winning an overnight stay in a fabulous honeymoon suite, right there at the gorgeous, newly renovated Arcadia Hotel. Complete with champagne, chocolates and a whirlpool bath right out your fantasies. It will be romantic, luxurious and simply *amazing.*"

Too bad she couldn't win it herself. She could just imagine John dropping his towel and folding his sculpted frame into that hot, steamy, bubbling water...

"Stop it, Nell," she said out loud. *Oh, lord.* She was on the air!

Hastily, she told her listeners, "Whatever rumors are swirling out there about the Fantasy Bash, just disregard them. All it means is that we're the hottest topic in town. The Bash is on, and it will be awesome. I'll be there and I hope you will, too. Remember— we'll be giving away tickets on the air all next week, too, all the way up to V-Day 2000 itself.''

Then she announced, ''And remember—don't be shy. Call in if you need a valentine. We've made twenty-one matches so far this week, and it's not too late to jump on the Fantasy Bash train for your most exciting Valentine's Day ever.''

With that out of the way, she turned to a trickier task. ''A lot of you are still calling about the popular Dr. John, our very first valentine candidate, so here's the scoop, folks. We've narrowed it down to eight finalists, and he's still in the process of choosing that one special woman. I know we promised you that today was the day we'd reveal his match. Unfortunately—fortunately for Dr. John—the eight finalists were all so tempting that he's having a really hard time making up his mind. So we're allowing him a few extra days. I feel confident we will be able to announce his choice on Monday.''

After a deep breath, Nell added, ''For the latest on the continuing saga of Dr. John and his date to the Fantasy Bash, stay tuned to *The Hot Zone*...''

Monday, February 7
One week till V-Day 2000

''GOOD MORNING, BOSS,'' Hildy greeted him. With her usual quiet efficiency, she lined up a steaming cup of black coffee; a neat stack of mail, all opened and annotated; several pink message slips; a printout of his e-mail; a copy of the latest ratings for the radio station; and three newspapers, already folded to the relevant pages.

Griffin took the ratings first. "Hovering at seventeen and a half percent," he mused. "It could still make it to twenty, but I'd better not count on it."

"Unwise," Hildy agreed.

"But even if the ratings go to Spence, I'd say Operation Strike-a-Match has to be considered a success, and that's one for me. One to one, with the Fantasy Bash left to go." He glanced at Hildy. "Do you have your ticket to the Bash? Everything set?"

"Yes, sir." There was hint of mischief in her smile. "I have a date and everything."

Hildy? With a date? "How did you manage that when you've only been in Chicago a week?"

Her grin widened. "I called *The Hot Zone* like everyone else. I'm going with..." Scrutinizing an index card on her desk, she said, "My date is Jerry Travers, a forty-year-old accountant from Wicker Park."

"Sounds like a real catch." Griffin shook his head, reaching for his messages. Hildy calling *The Hot Zone*. What next? He narrowed his eyes. "Nell McCabe called on Friday? And then said to say she didn't call? Why didn't you tell me right away?"

"Because it was the weekend?" Hildy asked calmly. "Because the schedule I had for you said you were incommunicado all weekend, maybe in Aspen, maybe in Gstaad, you weren't sure, and how am I supposed to tell you right away if I don't even know where you are?"

"You know you can always find me," he grumbled. "I didn't mean I was incommunicado from *her*."

"Then you should have specified that, shouldn't you?" Hildy returned easily. "And by the way, I want you to know that you didn't warn me you'd forwarded your cell phone over here and you might want to take the forwarding off now that you're back. When she called, she asked for Dr. John Jones, and it threw me for a sec. But I covered—I told her you were in surgery. You're supposed to be a surgeon, aren't you? If you're a GP, you may be in trouble.''

''Dr. John is a, uh, neurosurgeon,'' he said self-consciously. He flipped through the rest of the messages, frowning over information about the continuing muddle in California. It looked like he was going to have to take it away from Spence and handle it himself. But he just didn't have the heart to go out there and squash Miss Brody and her academy the way they deserved to be squashed. Not right now. His mind was occupied with other things.

''Did you have fun on the slopes, sir?'' Hildy inquired.

He shrugged. ''Not really. I just thought if I got away, did a little skiing, it might clear my head.''

''And did it?''

''No.'' In fact, he was more confused than ever. Neither the icy wind in his face nor the reckless speed at which he'd rocketed down the mountains had helped at all. And he wasn't happy about it. Confused? Him? It was a joke. Without his cold, decisive, ruthless streak, he didn't know who he was.

''Sorry to hear that.'' She coughed politely. ''I am, uh, somewhat surprised to see you back so soon, boss.''

He arched an eyebrow. ''Why?''

''Well,'' she hedged, ''usually when you have romantic troubles and you head for the slopes, you don't come back until the woman has packed up and left. Last I heard, Ms. McCabe was still in town.''

He was not amused.

"As long as we're discussing Ms. McCabe, are you interested in looking at the envelope from her?" Hildy asked delicately.

"There's an envelope from her?"

"The big one. She sent dossiers on the women you're supposed to choose from, in your Dr. Jones persona, that is." Hildy paused. "I took the liberty of ranking them for you, boss, in case you didn't want to. You will note that it does say you were to make your selection by today."

A phone call to say she hadn't called. An envelope packed with other women she wanted him to date. He felt like choking Nell McCabe with his bare hands. "Thanks, Hildy," he said grimly, "but I'm not going anywhere with any of these women."

"Whatever you say, boss." Hildy nudged his coffee closer, apparently hoping that would improve his mood. "So what do you want to do about the Monday deadline?"

"Ignore it." He didn't know why he even glanced at them, but after taking a quick look at Hildy's rankings, Griffin was really steamed. "For first place, you picked the disco gymnast with a laugh that shatters glass? Is this a joke?"

She shrugged. "She sounded like fun."

"Second place is the jock who gets her kicks rattling people's teeth? And third is the caffeine/nicotine addict?"

"That kind of stuff isn't actually in the reports," Hildy said helpfully.

"I'm not picking any of them—I want you to understand that. But I'm disappointed you don't know my taste any better than that." For some reason, he was highly outraged, and felt the need to set the record straight. "If I absolutely had to, I'd go with…

No, even if I absolutely had to, I couldn't pick any of these woman. And especially not..." He shuddered. "Especially not Venus DiMaio."

Hildy blinked. "Want me to write that down?"

"No, I don't want you to write it down!" With a savage oath, Griffin threw the whole envelope across the room, aiming for the trash can. But most of the papers fell out on the way, and Hildy rose immediately to tidy up. Now he felt like a bad-tempered jerk *and* a mean boss.

From her place on the floor where she was recompiling the files, Hildy suggested, "Why don't you take the newspapers into the other room, boss? There are some things in there you're not going to like, either, and I'd rather not be in the line of fire when you read them."

What could there be in the newspaper that was so unpleasant? Not heeding her advice to vacate the room, Griffin reached for the papers. "One report that the Fantasy Bash hasn't sold enough tickets and may be canceled and another that it's sold out, so don't bother to try? And this one says the party may be picketed by people who think Valentine's Day is a pagan holiday." Griff's mouth dropped open. "And here's a quote from an unnamed inside source who says that the renovations aren't finished at the hotel and the roof may fall in..."

He swore under his breath and ran a hand through his hair. "Well, I guess we know where all the misinformation is coming from, don't we?"

Hildy looked up from the floor. "Your brother, sir?"

"My brother."

"Would you like me to have him bound and

gagged and thrown on a slow boat to Costa Rica like the last time?'' Hildy asked in a hopeful tone.

''No.'' Griffin jammed his hands in his pockets. ''Let's go a different route. I'll need you to call the editors of every newspaper and magazine in town. Offer them Bash tickets, Bulls tickets, Blackhawks tickets, whatever it takes to get them to print something good about this shindig.''

She was already reaching for the phone.

''Oh, and Hildy?''

''Yes, boss?''

''Better beef up security at the hotel.'' He set his jaw into a rigid line. ''You never know what else my little brother has up his sleeve.''

Firecrackers. Killer bees. Food poisoning in the punch.

When it came to Spencer, it could be anything.

9

Tuesday, February 8
Six days till V-Day 2000

NELL POUNDED ON the door of the loft. "John? John? I know you're in there. Let me in!"

Damn the man, anyway. She had promised her listeners an answer on Monday and she couldn't find him to pry one out of him. Every time she dialed, she got the message that his cell phone was turned off. No cell phone. No answer. No date. No good.

She was going to kill him. Or at least strangle a choice out of him before today's show.

She couldn't face another day like yesterday, trying in vain to reach him while all eight of the finalists and a flock of irate callers hounded her; while Amy hung around with suspicious comments and reminders that their careers were on the line; while Drake Witley bombarded her with ominous memos about Spencer Jones and his Fantasy Bash invitation. With only six lousy days left and her job and her sanity hanging in the balance, everything was a mess.

She pounded harder. "John? Will you please let me in?"

Pressing her ear to the door, she thought she heard a muffled response. Something like, "'s open." But why would his door be open?

Frowning, Nell tried the handle. Sure enough, it

turned with no resistance. Moving slowly, she eased into the loft, peering around the corner for a glimpse of John Jones.

Well, there he was, sprawled across the bed, holding a pillow over his head. She stopped dead in her tracks. That *was* him, wasn't it? All she could see was a naked torso—firmly muscled, all tanned skin and hard man—draped just to the point of decency by rumpled bed linens. *Wow.* Nell swallowed, took a step back and tried to remember to keep breathing.

She forced herself to look away but it was no use. That body was a real magnet. It took about three seconds for her gaze to zoom right back to the bed. Her eyes drank in the sculpted strength of his outstretched arm, drifted past his sinewy chest and flat stomach, and lingered over the junction of sheet and hip, where the creamy linen pooled just under his belly button.

This was a sight any woman would pay money to wake up to for the rest of her life.

"J-John?" she tried again. "Are you awake?"

No response from the bed. She sure hoped this was him, and not some pal he was offering a place to stay. She edged nearer, wincing, pressing her eyes closed as she reached out one finger to poke him in the ribs.

"Huh?" He whipped the pillow off his head, snaking out his arm and catching her hand in the same motion. He yanked, and she pitched down onto the bed, hard. Sitting up about halfway, still holding her hand, he faced her with tousled hair and sleepy, confused eyes.

It was him all right, no doubt about that. There was no mistaking those blue, blue eyes, the dark brows slashing together above the straight nose, or that quirky, perfect mouth and elegant jaw. "Nell?"

She cleared her throat, wishing she were a lot farther away. Far enough not to notice the warmth of his skin where his fingers curled around her wrist pressing against her jumpy pulse. Far enough not to feel the heat emanating from his just-awakened body and his just slept-in bed. How easy would it be to grab him, crawl in and worry about the consequences later?

She bit down on her lip hard enough to cause pain and send a message to her brain. "Sorry to wake you," she ventured. "You told me to come in. At least I think you did. And the door was open." She narrowed her eyes. "Why *was* the door open?"

"Door open?" He blinked a few times and shook his head rapidly, as if he were trying to wake up sufficiently to form a coherent thought. He mumbled, "Oh, I, uh, think my brother was supposed to drop off some stuff. He lives upstairs."

"Really?" This was news. Curious, Nell let herself lean in a bit closer. "Your brother? The one who stole Grace away from you? So the two of you are reconciled?"

"Huh?" Now he really looked bewildered. "Grace? Grace who?" And then he seemed to come fully awake all at once, shooting upright, releasing her hand, shaking his head hard. "Oh, *Grace!* Grace, of course. Same brother? Yeah. Sure. I don't hold a grudge."

She tucked her hand under her leg, but it still felt tingly and overheated. "And your brother lives upstairs?"

"Uh-huh," he said warily. "He's gone now, though. Out of town. Yeah, that's right—to, uh, Canada. He dropped off some stuff on his way out of town, which is why the door was open."

"I see." Although she didn't see. "So, listen, are

you awake enough now to, I don't know, get dressed or something?''

He glanced down at his lap and back at her face, and then adjusted his sheet more securely. "What are you doing here?" he asked in a more alert tone. "What time is it?"

"It's about seven-thirty. I'm sorry to come by so early, but it *is* your fault since you didn't call me with your answer yesterday, so I felt I had to see you first thing, before I went in to work.'' Nell regarded him sternly, trying to project a no-nonsense image. It wasn't easy when she was crouched on a bed with a half-naked man. "I promised my listeners that I would announce your decision yesterday. It really left me high and dry when you didn't call and turned off your phone.''

He gave her a cold look. "I told you, I refuse to go out with any of them.''

"John, please don't be like this.'' She attempted to create a convincing, persuasive tone, as she stared right into his glowing bronze chest. Bad move. She lifted her gaze to those amazing blue eyes of his. Worse move. She dropped it. Right into his lap. Worst move.

Fixing on a point over his shoulder, Nell tried again. "I know that you think you're attracted to me, and I, well, I admit it. I'm attracted to you, too. But my job is in jeopardy here. I can't go to the Bash with you. You have to go with someone else. If both of those things don't happen, I will be out on the streets with my résumé before February fifteenth.''

"Nell,'' he said softly, "look at me. My face, please.''

She knew it wasn't wise, but she did it. How did those eyes get to be so blue? And those thick, dark lashes... She was turning this guy down? She felt like throwing herself headlong on top of him.

She concentrated, applying every bit of focus she had. *Listen to his words. Pay no attention to his eyes or his pecs or his washboard abs...*

"Nell," he went on, "I'm not just attracted to you. I have definite feelings for you. Romantic feelings. Like you and I belong together."

"John, no," she tried, but he wasn't giving in.

His gaze held her steady as he said, "I deliberately stayed away from you this weekend—to give me time to think, to sort things out. The only conclusion I came to was that I didn't want to stay away from you. Then I got your envelope and I got a little ticked that you still wanted me to pick someone else, so I didn't call. But now, seeing you... I can honestly say I've never felt like this before, not with any woman I've ever known. Not even close."

He seemed so sincere. *Wow.* If you were going to concentrate on words, these were pretty nifty ones. So maybe listening but not looking wasn't such a great idea, either.

"You've never felt like this? Not even with Grace?" she asked, searching his face.

"Definitely not with Grace." He said it so fast and with such conviction, Nell believed him with all her heart. *He pined over Grace for two years and now he's over her because of a week with me...* She felt so important, so...loved. Nell closed her eyes, begging herself not to even think that word again.

"Nell, please," he commanded. "I need you to hear this. A part of me thinks I should just say, yes, fine, I'll take one of those women to the Fantasy Bash on Valentine's Day, so what, who cares? Why not say that Sherry or Yolanda can have Valentine's Day, but I get you every other minute of every other day?''

''Maybe that could work,'' Nell whispered, as hope began to flicker inside her heart.

''No, it couldn't work. You're too honest. You would hate it.'' He reached for her hand, threading his fingers through hers. ''Besides, I don't want the woman I'm in love with spending that evening with someone else.''

Her heart pounded. She felt like her throat had constricted. *He said the L word! Now what do I do?*

As serenely as if he hadn't even noticed the bomb he'd dropped, John continued. ''We're talking about Valentine's Day 2000 here. Call me crazy, but I feel like it may set the tone for my love life for the rest of the century. The bottom line is that I don't want to spend this momentous, portentous Valentine's Day faking it, and I don't want to spend it with someone else. I want to be with you, Nell—2000, 2001, 2002. And I want to know that you feel the same.''

We're talking about Valentine's Day 2000 here. Call me crazy, but I feel like it may set the tone for my love life for the rest of the century.

Her head was spinning. Hadn't she expressed that very sentiment to Amy, just about a week ago? How did John know exactly what to say to reach her, like Cupid's arrow through her heart?

''Would it help if I promised you wouldn't lose your job?'' he asked gently, lifting her hand to his lips for a brief kiss.

''You can't promise that.'' If she made a stand and took him to the Bash, it was all over. Drake Witley would be irate, Spencer Jones would be irate and the two hundred fifty plus women who'd lost out in the

"Dr. John" sweepstakes would be the most irate of all.

"I could buy you a new radio station," he said with a crooked smile.

"Even if you are just teasing me, I appreciate the effort."

With a small groan of frustration, he dropped his head back into the pillows.

"The thing is…" She wasn't exactly sure how to put this. "What I'm grappling with here is whether I should just take a stand and let the chips fall where they may. That seems like the brave, honorable thing to do. But throwing away my job isn't easy, especially when you and I…we… Well, we haven't known each other very long, have we? This doesn't strike me as terribly practical or smart. If one of my callers asked me what to do in a similar situation, I'd tell her she was nuts to risk her career for a man she'd known for a week, a man she doesn't really know at all, when it comes right down to it."

"So come in here with me now and you can learn everything you ever wanted to know about me," he said in a rough, husky voice that spun around her like a web. He leaned back, tugging on her hand. "Stay with me now. We'll figure out Valentine's Day later."

She wanted to, but… But her brain was whirling and her body was whizzing with unsettling sensations, both conditions that seemed to occur every time she was around Dr. Jones. She knew she had to be away from him and his big, warm, strong, naked body for a few minutes or she would never be able to think. Reluctantly, she disentangled herself. "I can't stay. My show's at eleven and I have to be in the office by nine."

"Nell…" he coaxed, but she was already backing away. She had some scrap of sanity left. Not much, but some. He persisted, "At least tell me you'll announce on your show today that this farce is over, and you're going to the Bash with me."

She smiled, hoping to look mysterious and sultry. "Maybe. I guess you'll just have to tune in like everyone else to find out."

As she hurried toward the door before she changed her mind, she softened enough to blow him a kiss. John held out a hand to her, giving her one last chance to stay, but she couldn't, wouldn't take it. Not yet.

As she rode the elevator away from wonderful, maddening Dr. John, Nell was lost in thought, weighing this against that, adding two and two, examining every angle of this new and wonderful dilemma. So she barely noticed when the doors opened onto the underground garage, one floor down from where she'd intended.

"I don't think I have a choice. I have to take a chance on him," she mused aloud, stepping out. She could feel herself really starting to gain courage as the elevator doors closed behind her. She was looking at concrete walls, but she was thinking about John wrapped in that sheet, and it made her knees weak. "Every time I try to clear my mind, all I think about is him. I can't deny that. And why should I? He says he's in love with me, and if I'm honest, I'm in love with him, too."

She could hardly contain the flutter of excitement deep inside her. "How many times does someone like him drop into your lap?" she demanded of no one in particular. "He's perfect. Or at least he's perfect for me. If I don't go for it, I'll always wonder if I passed up on The One."

She smiled. "After all, what's the worst that can happen? At least I'll always have this one Valentine's

Day to remember..."

But she stopped in midsentence, stepping back against the wall to safety as a low-slung black Porsche with the license plate JONES 2 screeched across the parking garage. It spun into a space, and the driver's door shot open.

John's car. Except *Spencer* Jones popped out.

Wearing what had to be last night's suit, the younger half of the odious Jones Boys wobbled out of the car looking like he hadn't slept in a week. He took a moment to straighten himself, not bothering to tie his tie. Rubbing a hand absently over his stubbled jaw, he ambled past her on his way to the elevator.

"What in the world was *he* doing in John's car, in John's building?" Nell murmured. How odd that the car seemed to reflect Spencer Jones's personality quite nicely, whereas it had never seemed right for Dr. John at all.

Spencer Jones. JONES 2. John Jones.

It was as if there were strobe lights flashing behind her eyes. Nell couldn't seem to focus, but her ears roared, her brain kicked into overdrive, and the jagged pieces of the truth fell into place.

Spencer Jones. Coming over to their table at the Graystone Grill.

Why are you dressed like that? But he was asking *John,* not her.

Spencer Jones. Parking a black Porsche, license JONES 2, underneath John Jones's building.

My brother lives upstairs.

The brother who stole Grace away from you?

Grace? Grace who?

"Oh, God." She slid down the wall to a sitting position, barely noticing the cold concrete underneath her. "There is no Grace. There never was a Grace. How could I have been so stupid?"

She'd thought from the beginning that the gorgeous, wealthy neurosurgeon with a broken heart was too good to be true. *If it seems too good to be true, it is too good to be true.* She'd given that advice a thousand times. So why hadn't she believed it?

And then she remembered what it was about his story, that night at the Grill, that had bothered her. He'd said Grace had run away with his brother. Yet, the day before, on her show, he'd claimed to be an only child.

No brother one day, brother the next. Brothers.

"Damn it. Why didn't I listen?"

Everyone knew that the Jones Boys were always together. Yet Spencer Jones kept surfacing all by himself. Why had it never occurred to her to wonder where the other one was, the one with the blue eyes and the goatee?

"So he shaved off the beard and he wore tinted glasses and he thought I wouldn't notice." Nell put hand over her mouth. "And I didn't. Even when he forgot the glasses and I stared right into those beautiful blue eyes, I still didn't notice. Which makes me the world's biggest idiot."

Her hands balled into fists, she stood up. "All that crapola about honesty and integrity and wanting to start the new century out right. What a big, fat liar!"

She shouted out her anger into the almost empty garage, not even noticing how her voice echoed and reverberated. "Griffin Jones is going to pay!"

Wednesday, February 9
Five days till V-Day 2000

Zzzzing.

Her dart stuck in the wall, a good three feet to the left of the dartboard. Nell frowned, concentrating harder as she aimed right at Griffin's smiling face, taped over the bull's-eye on the target.

Zzzzing.

"Oh, blast!" This time she was way too low. On the other hand, if she mentally sketched in the rest of his body, the dart would be lodged somewhere between his heart and his crotch. Nothing wrong with hitting either of those.

"Uh, Nell?"

She whipped around, her pulse pounding. But it was only Amy. "Sheesh. You scared me."

"Nell, what are you doing in here?"

"Isn't it obvious?" She gestured to the dartboard and the magazine photo of Griffin, and squinted as she aimed her last dart. She was closer, but it still barely nicked his chin.

"Listen," Amy said gently, coming all the way into the conference room, "I know you're upset about this and you have every right to be, but you're starting to scare me. So, what exactly are you doing, hiding out in here throwing darts? And why are there armed guards all over the building?"

Nell shrugged. "I lied. I told Witley I had a stalker."

"You *what?*"

"It was just to buy me time until I figured out what to do with Griffin Jones." She was only too aware of the snarl that crept out when she said his name. She couldn't help it. "But he's not going to sit back and take this. I know he had to be listening to my show yesterday, expecting me to announce that he and I would go to the Bash together. But when I told the world he'd picked Venus..." She smiled smugly. "Oh, yeah. That had to hurt. He's tried to call, what, five times?''

"On the air? Seven," Amy told her. "Three yesterday and four today. Of course, as soon as the show was off, I stopped answering, so who knows how many more times he's tried?"

"Yeah, well, I know him. He's not going to stick to phone calls for long. Which is why I upped the ante with the guards." She chewed her lip thoughtfully. "Actually, I'm kind of surprised he hasn't already tried to storm the barricades. But even if he gets past them, they should create enough of a ruckus to provide an early warning system. Meanwhile, my mom and dad are keeping an eye on my house. I stayed in town with my sister last night and I may again tonight."

Heaving a big sigh, Amy dropped into a chair at the table. "We're dead." She glanced over as Nell began prying darts out of the wall for a fresh round. "Did it ever occur to you that he owns this station and he can come in here anytime he wants? That he is a very rich man who can send other people to stalk you for real if he wants to?"

"Oh, pooh!" Nell returned. "First of all, he won't do anything until he's sure I know. About him, I mean. If he thinks I'm still in the dark, he can't show his face around here—his real, Griffin Jones, womanizing, lying pirate face—because I might see him and figure it out. As Dr. John, he can't show his face, because Drake the Snake might see him and figure it out. No, he's stuck. Unless he comes up with a third disguise," she mused. "I hadn't thought of that."

"Nell, I don't understand any of this," Amy said in confusion.

"It doesn't matter," Nell assured her, waving a hand. "The important thing is that he can't get to me for the next five days, until the Fantasy Bash itself. It's all part of my plan."

"Your plan?" Amy asked with obvious apprehension. "What kind of plan?"

"It took me awhile to get this all sorted out, but now I think I really have it." Caught up in the details of her scheme, Nell joined Amy at the conference table, still clutching darts in one hand. She used one of them to point to a legal pad she'd been scribbling on most of the day. "Step one was announcing on the air that I chose Venus for him. She's by far the worst, don't you think?"

"Oh, yeah, she's terrible. In fact, Venus alone is plenty of revenge," Amy said loyally.

"Nice try, but I don't think so. No, Venus is just the beginning." Her smile widened. "Step two is Spencer Jones. I already called him and accepted his invitation to the Bash. I figure it will take all of five seconds to get back to Griffin that I have a date with his brother."

"So, first you humiliate him with Venus and then with his brother, and then you're done, right?"

"Oh, no. Then I move in to step three."

Amy's voice held dread when she asked, "Step three?"

"Uh-huh. First I thought murder might be good, you know, hire a hit man," Nell said breezily.

"Uh, you're not serious, are you?"

"No, not really." But she had enjoyed entertaining the notion for all of thirty seconds. "Killing him is a little final. Besides, I want him alive and kicking at the Bash, him with Venus, me with his brother—

the perfect time to really bring him to his knees. And I know very well that he—that is, Dr. John—is necessary to pull off the Bash at all, and we need to do that to save the show. So, I can't kill him. But I do want him out of the way until then.''

''Out of the way?'' Amy gave a hollow laugh. ''Well, at least you're not trolling for hit men, so let's count our blessings.''

But Nell was off and running. She flipped a page on the yellow pad, scanning her list of possibilities. ''So then I thought, hmm, how about kidnapping? You know, put him on ice till the Bash? But I can't imagine he'd stay kidnapped. He's very wily. Plus there'd be a big hue and cry and his brother would be looking for him.... No, that wouldn't work.''

''Okay,'' Amy declared, ''so murder and kidnapping are out. That's good.''

''My next idea was to have him arrested,'' Nell continued. ''While I would feel a certain satisfaction seeing him behind bars, I know he'd call up his fancy lawyers and get out the same day. Nope, not going to work.''

Amy craned her neck, trying to get a look at what was on that legal pad. ''Nell, you're really starting to frighten me.''

''Don't worry—I have it all figured out now.''

''You do?'' her producer asked nervously. ''And it doesn't involve any felonies?''

''No felonies. But if I can't kill him or kidnap him or even arrest him, I can banish him, can't I?'' Nell asked logically.

''I give up—how are you going to banish him?''

Nell leaned forward. ''The nuns and orphans!'' she said triumphantly.

her nuts. He smiled darkly. Maybe he'd turn her over his knee.

But he knew one thing for sure. He'd be spending Valentine's night with the woman he loved.

For the first time in seventy-two hours, Griffin felt a surge of excitement, the anticipation of the game of wits unfolding before him.

Aloud, he said, "Hildy, put in another call to Miss Brody. Let's see if we can't wrap this up by Monday." Under his breath, he added, "Fasten your seat belt, Nell. I'm coming back."

Saturday, February 12
Two days till V-Day 2000

NELL BACKED UP against a wall and tried not to get run over. Around her, workmen and marketing minions scurried every which way, hurrying to make sure that the ballroom walls were painted and the crystal chandeliers installed in time for the official unveiling of the newly renovated Arcadia Hotel.

Everything looked beautiful, she thought wistfully, and miracle of miracles, it was actually starting to look as if they'd finish by Monday. Nothing like squeaking in under the wire.

She was a fifth wheel around the ballroom, but at least all the hustle and bustle was distracting. Without a show to do on the weekend, left to wander from newsstand to newsstand, from cable channel to channel, desperate for reports from the West Coast just to make sure Griffin was still safely occupied elsewhere, her mind was full of all kinds of things she didn't want to think about.

Her plan had gone like clockwork so far, so why was she was on the verge of a nervous breakdown?

"Maybe he won't come back at all. It sounds a lot worse out there than I expected. Meetings and hearings and press conferences. Maybe I banished him too well."

She lifted a hand to her forehead. Whew. Trying to outmaneuver one of the Jones Boys was exhausting.

Besides, she seemed to be spending most of her days—and all of her nights—thinking about him draped so artfully, so sinfully, in that sheet, and how easy it would've been to slide right in beside him. If she had, would it have turned out any differently? If they'd slept together, would it have made things better? Or worse?

"I have to stop thinking about him," she said out loud. How odd that distance didn't seem to help, but instead only intensified her crazy longings. All she did was think about him, miss him, want him.

Him. The traitor. The jerk. The womanizing, lying, cheating... But her search for another derogatory word was interrupted by one of the men from marketing.

"Ms. McCabe?"

"Yes?"

"There's a message for you from the office." He peered down at a piece of paper in his hand. "A woman named Venus has been trying to reach you. The switchboard says she's called several times."

"Oh, no," Nell murmured. "Don't tell me Dr. John canceled on her and she's having a fit."

"Um, no. That's not it." He read the message slip. "She says, 'Thanks so much for choosing me. Dr. John's sent dozens of roses and Godiva chocolates and a bouquet of balloons so far. Can't wait to see what's next. Can't wait till Monday and my dream date.'" He looked up. "That's it."

"That's *it?*" She was aghast. "He sent her roses

and chocolates and balloons? He didn't send me anything. I was all prepared to throw it in the river if he tried and he didn't even try! No, he sent it all to Venus DiMaio. He's even more of a jerk than I thought!''

''Excuse me?''

''Nothing.'' A part of her had actually begun to take pity on him, and she had spent a few weak moments wondering if she should try to undo some of the havoc she'd wrought in California. But not anymore. Not with him cheerfully wooing Venus with flowers and candy and God knew what else.

But then it hit her. She took a step backward. ''Wait a second. He isn't doing this because he's pond scum. He's doing it because he knows I know.''

''Excuse me?''

''This is like thrust and parry, cross and double cross,'' she declared. ''He wants me to know he knows I know!''

''Excuse me?''

''Never mind.'' Nell straightened, filled with new resolve. If he was making nice with Venus, then Griffin was definitely headed back to town, just as she'd expected. And she had a dress to find, plans to lay, schemes to put into motion.

It wasn't going to be easy to make the Bash a smash, save her career and hit Griffin Jones over the head with a two-by-four, all in the space of one evening.

But, yeah, she could do that.

Sunday, February 13
One day till V-Day 2000

''GRIFF, THE TIDE is definitely turning. If we hang in a couple more days—a week tops—I think we can swing this thing."

But Griffin's tone brooked no objections. "We haven't got a couple more days. All three of us have a date back in Chicago tomorrow night. We leave first thing in the morning."

"Look, if this is because of the bet, I'm willing to let it go. Hildy gave me last week's ratings—they topped out at eighteen percent." Magnanimously, Spence threw up his hands. "So you won the first part when the matchmaking thing survived, and I won on the ratings. The Bash would've decided it all, and I admit, I had some great plans for that thing that I would've loved to see pay off." He grinned, but it faded quickly. "This Seaboard deal is too important and I'm happy to just forget about the whole radio fiasco. We need to stay here and see this through."

"We can't," Griffin said flatly. "And this isn't about the bet. Although I still want that jet if the Bash flies."

"Oh, come on! Fun is fun. But this is money we're talking. Big money," Spencer countered. "And we're so close. After she talked to you yesterday, the Brody woman was hovering on the brink, so close to folding. If you can just lean on her one more time tomorrow—"

"Not tomorrow."

"You're kidding me, right?" Spence bent so far back in his chair it was in imminent danger of toppling into the plush white carpet. "You're willing to throw in the towel on a six-billion-dollar deal, and all because of some woman?"

"She's not some woman." He was feeling a little too tightly wound to listen to his brother right now.

"Griff, please, I'm begging you. Don't do this."
Righting his chair, Spence rose, trying to meet his
brother's gaze. "I know you, bro. Down the line,
when you're tired of her, you will be so sorry you did
this."

"Shut up, Spence."

"No, listen, I don't think you're—"

"Shut up, Spence," he said again, louder this time.
"I'm only going to say this once, so you'd better pay
attention. I'm in love with her. And I have to be there,
with her, tomorrow night. Don't ask me how I know.
I don't even understand it myself. But I know that if
I don't make it back there tomorrow night, she will
walk out of my life and that will be that. I will have
missed my chance. And I am not going to let Nell
slip through my fingers."

Spence blinked and backed away. "Jeez. You're
serious."

"Absolutely."

"She's more important to you than the Seaboard
deal?"

He thought a moment. "It's not even a contest."

Spence sat back down with a thump. "I never
thought I'd see this day."

"Yeah, well, I'm pretty surprised myself."

His brother sent him a speculative glance. "So, you
think she knows about your Dr. John thing?"

Griffin frowned. "Oh, yeah. I think she knows.
And she wants my head on a platter."

"How are you going to get around that?"

"I don't know yet." He walked over to the window, to gaze out at the blinking lights of the Los
Angeles skyline. "But I'll think of something."

Monday, February 14
V-Day 2000

NELL FELT AS nervous as Venus DiMaio's Chihuahua.

Was he back yet? Was he going to show at all?

"Amy—"

"No, I haven't seen him," her producer returned shortly. "That's the twelfth time you've asked. What do you want me to do, get out my magic wand and make him appear out of thin air?"

"Sorry I asked."

With an aggrieved glance, Amy ducked out of sight to get another opinion on the heating problem they were experiencing. It wasn't very crowded yet, but it was already a little steamy in the ballroom. Even in a rather bare dress, Nell could feel herself starting to perspire.

Fanning herself with a menu card, she looked down surreptitiously, trying to decide if she should risk hoisting the bodice up into a more respectable position. It was a lovely dress—just much more revealing than she'd intended. She'd wanted red, something to knock Griffin's socks off and make the point that she was just fine without him. Although she loved the sweeping skirt, she wasn't crazy about the bare shoulders or the deep V in the heart-shaped neckline. Or all the pale skin on display.

Oh well. No one was looking at her, anyway, not with the Venus dog-and-pony show around.

Venus had arrived early, in a limo sent by the elusive "Dr. Jones." Her dress was a pink satin replica of the famous Marilyn/Madonna/Material Girl costume, all overflowing bosoms and rhinestones, with Kitty the dog in a little pink evening gown and rhinestones of her own. Venus had completed her ensemble with a purse shaped like Kitty, and the purse was wearing an even smaller version of the same dress! As soon as they entered the ballroom, there was a hubbub of attention and the real dog started yipping.

How odd that Griffin Jones, the absolute heel, had declined to arrive with his date. An hour after Venus had sashayed into the spotlight, there was still no sign of the infamous Dr. John or his alter ego.

As if Nell wasn't already anxious enough, this waiting game was driving her mad.

She fanned her face again, willing herself to calm down and cool off. Was it really so hot in here? Or was it just the tension, and not the heat at all?

After all, the temperature trouble was only the latest in a string of snafus.

First there'd been a surprise health inspection in the kitchen minutes before the Bash was to begin, which sent half a dozen illegal aliens and some improperly refrigerated hors d'oeuvres packing.

Then the florist never showed up with the dozens of red roses needed to decorate the ballroom. It seemed someone had called a week ago and canceled the order.

And then nobody could locate the band scheduled to play, either. They, too, were the victims of an apparent cancellation hoax, and they'd accepted another gig in Milwaukee, meaning they were well out of range. Luckily, a minion from the marketing department had the brilliant idea of putting in an emergency call to one of the station's disc jockeys, who grabbed a few hours of hits on tape and made a beeline for the Bash. So there *was* music, even if it wasn't live.

In the midst of all this, Nell noticed a nicely dressed, rather sedate woman who seemed to be popping up and taking notes every time there was a problem.

After watching the woman eavesdrop as the florist and the music muddles were sorted out, Nell cornered her. "Excuse me, but who are you?" she asked as politely as she could manage.

"Oh." The woman hesitated, looking a little rattled. "You must be Ms. McCabe. Mr. Jones has spoken of you often. Well, not really often, but I could tell he was thinking of you. He gets that sort of intense, I'm-going-to-kill-someone look, if you know what I mean."

"No, I don't." But Nell considered. "Which Mr. Jones are we talking about? And who are you?"

"Um, I'm Hildy. Hildy Johnson. I'm the assistant to, uh, Dr. Jones. Dr. John Jones. You and I have spoken on the phone."

Dr. John Jones? *Ha!* Nell was so edgy she started to tremble the minute she heard his name, even the fake one, but she got herself under control as quickly as she could. So this was Griffin's assistant. For some reason, the woman seemed to be judging every second of the Bash, which was totally unfair. Nell had the vague idea this figured into the question of her own continued employment somehow, but she didn't know exactly how.

When she tried to pin down with questions, Hildy mumbled something about checking on the food and raced off, leaving Nell with a lot of questions and no answers.

"Is he even coming?" she called out, but Hildy didn't respond. "And why did he send you to take notes? Is he hoping the Bash will be a bust? Or a big success?"

Every time she thought she had a handle on Griffin Jones, some new wrinkle surfaced. Damn the man, anyway.

Even if neither he nor the flowers had shown up, lots of other party goers had. The sumptuous ballroom at the Arcadia Hotel looked spectacular, with red and pink hearts festooned everywhere, shiny metallic hearts and heart-shaped balloons bouncing around as table decorations and a huge ice sculpture of Cupid shooting an arrow sideways through the numbers 2000.

For all its miscues, the Bash was so beautiful it made Nell want to cry. Somehow, when she'd imagined the most magical V-Day 2000 possible, with the pea-brained idea that this was the night her romantic life would soar to meet the new century, she'd pictured it just like this.

"Except for him." Spencer Jones, the *wrong* Jones, had arrived. As he stalked across the ballroom, his hands in his pockets, Nell had to admit that he looked good in a dinner jacket. If only he were anyone else. *Anyone.* Looking at him, all she could think of was that blasted black Porsche and his rotten brother and the whole masquerade.

Still, if she planned to use him to humiliate Griffin, she knew she had to be nice to him. Surely hanging on Spencer's arm would twist a knife in Griffin's competitive little heart. If he ever got here, of course.

As the wrong Jones brother approached, Nell summoned up a glimmer of a smile and tried to stand up straight to show off her wicked dress. It was very unlike her, but if she couldn't throw caution to the winds tonight, when would she?

Stick to the plan, she ordered herself. Step one—match him up with Venus. Step two—match herself up with his brother. Time to work on that one.

"Hi there," she said brightly. "How are you tonight?"

"Oh, I'm just dandy," he said coldly. And that was it.

Uh-oh. When she'd met him before, he'd come on like gangbusters. So what had his brother done to him in the meantime?

"I just want you to know," he said in an angry tone, "I don't want to be here. This was not my idea."

"Well, actually, you *did* ask me," Nell put in delicately. "So technically, it was your idea."

"Yeah, well... Oh, forget it." And he abandoned her for the bar, without so much as a by-your-leave.

As Nell watched with wide eyes, Spencer downed not one but two frothy pink tequila concoctions, looking as if he'd just lost his best friend and diving headfirst into the margarita pool would make him feel better. What in the world was this all about?

Still grumpy as all get out, he marched back to her side. "So, you wanna dance?"

"Well, okay."

He turned her out onto the dance floor with a decided lack of enthusiasm, and wheeled her around as if she were somebody's aged, and very fragile, grandmother.

No, she hadn't imagined herself whirling on a romantic Valentine's dance floor with the likes of Spencer Jones. She had envisioned his warmer, pushier, more amusing brother, the one who lied through his teeth instead of knocking back tequila, the one with the impossibly broad shoulders and impossibly blue eyes, the one who didn't take no for an answer, who held her in his arms as if he didn't want to let go...

But she had no time to think about that. Not with raised, furious voices right behind her, cursing a blue streak and threatening all kinds of dire things. There was the sound of glass shattering, and a balloon bursting, and then someone shouted, "You are a freakin' slob!"

Nell broke away from Spencer Jones, picked up her skirts and made a beeline for the altercation, where other curious onlookers had already started to gather in a dangerous knot.

"You creep!" the woman in the fight yelled. She was quivering with anger, making the bows on the front of her hot pink dress bounce up and down. "On the radio, you said you were thirty and single. Now I find out you're forty and a three-time loser!" She hauled off and slapped him with her purse, swinging wide and knocking over another wineglass, smashing it to smithereens against the remnants of the first one.

"You're nuts!" he barked right back. "You said *you* were thirty. And a Sandra Bullock look-alike. More like Sandra Bullock's grandmother!"

"I'm going to sue!" trumpeted his date.

"Me first! This is assault and battery, baby! I got a piece of glass in my hand.

"I'll give you assault and battery."

"Everyone, please, calm down!" Nell interceded, pushing her way to the front.

"Why should he calm down?" another angry man argued, throwing an elbow to hold Nell back. She dodged the elbow, but just barely. "She hit *him*. I saw the whole thing."

"Well, he lied to me!" the woman bellowed, turning on her new foe and giving him a shove.

He toppled sideways, right into Nell. She could see it coming, but her escape route was blocked by all the other Bash goers who were crowding around yelling, "Fight! Fight!" and "Catfight!"

She felt the impact of the man with the elbow, she

felt a rush of air as the crowd parted, then she felt a pair of very strong arms scoop her up and out of harm's way.

As she scrambled to get back on her feet, her rescuer asked, "Are you okay?"

She nodded, breathless, as his dark, harsh voice cut through the melee. "You people, back up. You, sit down. You, shut up." It was like Charlton Heston, playing Moses, parting the Red Sea.

There was a feeble protest from someone or other, but Griffin—of course, it was Griffin—quelled it quickly. Before Nell knew what had happened, he'd commandeered enough hotel staff to haul the table with the broken glass and all three combatants out of the ballroom completely. Amazing. Speedy and very useful, and amazing.

"Are you sure you're all right?" he asked again.

"Yes, I'm fine." Actually she was embarrassed and caught off guard, when *he* was supposed to be the one doing the Humiliation Shuffle, but she tried to make the best of it.

Head held high, hoping she was still mostly inside her dress, Nell gave him what she hoped was a scathing glance, up and down.

Oh, hell. He looked wonderful. He even smelled wonderful.

Not only was he neither remorseful nor contrite, but he had also not bothered to dress down as the nerdy doctor to maintain his disguise. No, tonight he was all designer edges and international tycoon gloss. She'd only seen him once as his real self, and she'd forgotten how overpowering he was in full regalia. That time he'd been hampered by a plain old suit and a dopey goatee. Tonight, he wore black tie as if it had been created for him, and his face was clean-shaven and simply gorgeous. In the right clothes, with his hair styled the way its expensive cut was intended, he could stop hearts at twenty paces.

"And I offered to help him with his clothes," she muttered under her breath.

His eyes swept over her, making her feel even more unsettled. "You look beautiful in that dress. Too bad you're wasting it on my brother."

So he knew. And it bothered him. *Good.*

Gathering her resolve, she tried to act cold and haughty, but it wasn't easy in the close, overheated air of the ballroom. She was flushed. She was melting. She'd had a prepared speech for this moment, but she couldn't for the life of her remember what it was. So she made something up on the spur of the moment.

"After what you did, I can't believe you had the guts to show up here tonight," she seethed. "I should slap you. I should get up there on the podium, and announce on the microphone in front of all these people who you really are."

"A simple thank-you would suffice," he returned calmly.

Oooh. She really hated that calm. "For believing all your nonsense? For letting you lie to me and make a fool of me?"

"Actually, I was thinking that I deserved some gratitude for saving your show two weeks ago and your pretty little butt five minutes ago."

She paused. He certainly had arrogance to spare, didn't he? "Fair enough," she allowed. "Leaving aside what you did for—or to—my show, I will say thank-you for the rescue tonight. But that doesn't change the fact that I know who and what you are, and I might just be in the mood to share it."

He arched one dark eyebrow. "You think I'm afraid of you, Nell?"

"You should be."

"I'm not." He smiled. "You did your worst." And then he leaned in closer, close enough that his warm breath puffed against her cheek. "You set the nuns and orphans on me, Nell. What else is left?"

She could feel her face flame. "Why would you think I had anything to do with it?"

"I know you. Inside and out. It had to be—"

But he didn't get a chance to finish.

"Dr. John!" a high-pitched voice cried. Crowing and squealing, Venus came flying in from the side in a blur of pink satin, threw herself headlong into Griffin's arms and rained kisses all over his face.

She'd left her little dog with Spencer, of all people, who stood unsteadily off to one side, the Chihuahua in one hand and a huge margarita in the other.

Nell fell back, catching every move as Griffin tried in vain to peel Venus away from his body. His evident discomfort might have been funny if he didn't deserve a lot worse.

"Okay," she whispered, "I banished him, and I've humiliated him with Venus and with his brother. I guess it's time for Step Four."

Dirty dancing.

11

NELL LEFT HIM wrestling with Venus as she swept back over to the head table. She had to stop before she got there, however, when another fight broke out between a couple she'd matched up on the air. Could her fix-up skills have been any worse? This one she handled on her own, quickly unmatching and then re-matching them with other people they liked better.

When she finally made it to the podium, she had lost sight of Griffin and Venus. But she could still hear those unmistakable cackles and honks. She smiled.

Nell realized she was actually starting to get into this. Revenge was kind of fun when it came right down to it.

"Everyone, if I could have your attention?" she called out over the music and noise. "It's time for a special part of our program. Dr. John and Venus, the couple who launched our whole Operation Strike-a-Match, will now lead us in dirty dancing!"

There was a hush for a second or two, before Venus hustled herself out onto the dance floor. A spotlight caught her as she stood there, a bosomy vision in pink, beckoning to Dr. John, aka Griffin, to join her.

He looked appalled, but Venus was so thrilled and excited, even he couldn't turn her down. Especially not with four hundred people clapping in unison, chanting, ''Ve-nus! Ve-nus!'' and pushing him out to her.

Was it Nell's imagination, or was the unflappable Griffin Jones blushing as he ambled out to dance with his dream date?

The DJ found some hot salsa dance tune, and it didn't take long for Venus to get Griffin into a clinch and a tangle. Other couples joined them, blocking the view on and off, but Nell couldn't miss the fact that the Material Girl had one hand firmly planted on his bottom and the other one roaming all kinds of places it shouldn't be going. Nell found herself steaming a little more as each beat passed.

Hey, this was supposed to be provoking *him,* not her!

Venus had him practically bent over backward, as Nell fumed. He wasn't enjoying himself, was he? In about one more minute, and she was going to go out there and show Venus a thing or two about dance floor decorum—pry those hands off his body once and for all.

Except that half the ballroom suddenly went black. A whole row of chandeliers blinked and then died, and there was a rush as people crowded into the still lighted areas, which happened to be most of the dance floor. Even without the extra light, the place was blazing hot. In fact, it seemed hotter than ever.

''What did they do?'' Nell muttered. ''Set the furnace to fire and brimstone?''

The temperature, the fights, the lights, the flowers, the music—what else could go wrong?

Although she knew Amy had gone to look into it hours ago, Nell decided she'd really better ask someone about fixing the heat herself. She couldn't take much more of this. One more degree and she'd be swooning.

As she threaded her way through the edge of the thumping, bumping, grinding dancers, looking for any sort of hotel personnel, Spencer appeared out of nowhere. His lids were drooping, his speech was slurred and he was still toting Kitty the dog. "Listen," he drawled, tugging on her hand, teetering nearer, obviously the worse for tequila, "d'ya wanna dance?"

Nell turned back to him, ready to firmly turn him down. But she had no sooner opened her mouth than Venus emerged from the dance floor, laughing so loud it made Nell's ears ring. Crying, "Change partners!" Venus gleefully glommed on to Spencer and hiked one leg up over his shoulder. Nell blinked, shocked. How was that physically possible?

However it was possible, Venus was doing it. Spencer seemed to have regained consciousness nicely, as Venus initiated him into her brand of wild disco voodoo, with Kitty the yipping dog somehow hoisted between them. Twirling, laughing, tripping over each other—they were clearly having the times of their lives.

"Okay, I may be a terrible matchmaker," Nell declared, watching the bizarre dancing exhibition. "But even I know a perfect match when I see one."

"Thank God." His relief was evident as Griffin caught Nell's hand, swinging her into a much more sedate sort of dance.

But not sedate enough. She could feel him there, his chest and hips and legs almost but not quite touching her, emanating heat and desire and overwhelming maleness. "Um, I don't remember saying I would dance with you," she managed to say, but her voice came out husky and funny. His arms were firm and strong around her, and she had no choice but to nestle closer on the jammed floor.

"Were you going to leave me out here all night with Venus flytrap?" he asked moodily

"As long as it took."

"For what?" And then he did this neat little turn, where he spun her around and back into his embrace, only much, much closer leaving her off balance and out of whack and over her head. Her breath seemed to get stuck in her throat, her head was swimming and she was having a whole lot of trouble remembering she was mad at him.

"Whoa..." This wasn't going the way it was supposed to!

Nell pushed away from him, jumping on to the next phase of her plan before she had a chance to let him undermine her one more time.

Running back to the podium like a scared rabbit, she grabbed the microphone and hurriedly announced, "Can you cut the music, please?"

There was an audible groan from the masses of humanity pressed together on the dance floor, but Nell persevered. "Listen, this will be worth it, I promise!"

When she'd sat in the conference room with her legal pad, concocting the perfect scheme to bring him to his knees, Step Five had seemed so right, so cosmic, so inspired. But now, when she had to put it into practice, it just seemed insane.

They were all staring up at her, waiting, and she saw Griffin among them. His expression was impossible to read, but it wasn't good. *Yeah, well, just wait, bucko. It's going to get worse.*

"Our good friend Dr. John," she began, trying to keep the quaver from her voice. She concentrated on Grace and the brain surgeon story and every single one of his outrageous lies. "Our good friend Dr. John has volunteered to auction the clothes right off his back for charity!"

A female voice cheered, "Yeeee-ha!" and people began to shove him closer to the dais.

"Let's help him up here, shall we?" Nell suggested, watching him fight the crowd. She could see the anger simmering in his eyes from where she stood.

The ballroom exploded into cries of, "Take it off, take it off!" and Griffin stopped dead. "Okay, that's enough." He shook off whoever was clutching his arm, and he stalked up to the podium right next to Nell. She knew he was furious, she knew she had skated onto ice that was perilously thin and she just didn't care anymore.

Nell plucked his sleeve. "How much of a bid for the good doctor's jacket?"

But the huge center chandelier popped and started to hiss, sending another wide section of the ballroom into darkness, and the temperature seemed to rise another ten degrees. As people screamed and tried to get out from under the smoking chandelier, Griffin took his chance.

A full-scale riot was erupting around them, but Nell saw only him. With one easy lunge, he swung her and her sinful red dress into his arms and carried her out of there.

Nell went very still, but it didn't stop the electric shocks sizzling through her overheated system, one after the other, or the dangerous tension spiraling inside her. *Damn it.* Why did his embrace have to feel so secure, so heady, so wonderful? Why did his arm against her bare back and his hand against her thigh have to be so very warm, and the silk of her dress so thin? Why did his gaze have to be directed right down the gaping front of her bodice, and why did her skin have to tingle and burn like that, everywhere he touched, everywhere he looked, everywhere he thought of looking?

She was being toted through the halls of the Arcadia Hotel by a man she hated, and she wasn't even sorry! No, she was thinking of how fast she could wiggle out of her silly dress and pull off his shirt and pants and drag him into a closet somewhere.

"Where are you taking me?" she demanded, as he twirled her around far enough to hit the button for the elevator. "When are you planning to put me down?"

"You know, Nell," he said in a testy tone, juggling her slightly and getting a different grip, "for all the thanks I get, I may just stop rescuing you."

"Thanks?" she asked dizzily.

She had to say something, anything, to get her mind off the fact that his fingers were tickling her rib cage, an inch from her breast, and that she was practically writhing with suppressed desire. She couldn't breathe, couldn't move, didn't dare try to extract herself.

"I thanked you for keeping me from bodily harm the last time, didn't I?" she went on, amazed that words kept coming when her brain seemed to have ceased to function. "That's as far as I'm going. I mean, you haven't even said you're sorry. I'm supposed to forgive you and start throwing thanks around, and you haven't even groveled a little?"

He seemed to consider that for a moment. His blazing blue eyes held her. "And if I grovel, will you?"

"Will I what?" she asked cautiously, trying not to fidget or squirm. It was impossible to maintain any dignity, riding around in his arms this way, but she was doing her best.

The elevator doors opened and closed behind them before he answered. "Will you forgive me?"

Her heart did a funny little flip-flop and she knew she had to harden her resolve. She was alone with him in a very small elevator, and that was dangerous turf. Lashing out, she asked, "Isn't what you really want to know whether I'll sleep with you?"

"Oh, I already know you'll sleep with me. But that's not what I want—not until you forgive me."

Her mouth fell open at his audacity.

The elevator doors slid open to reveal the fortieth floor. Griffin swept her out into the hall as her brain fed her information—the fortieth floor of a forty-story hotel, only one door, a brass plaque that said Honeymoon Suite.

As he fitted a key into the lock, Nell demanded, "We're going in there? The honeymoon suite? Did you do this on purpose?"

Griffin raked her with an amused gaze. "There was a big glass bowl on the podium next to you, along with a sign that said, 'Win a night in the honeymoon suite.' And there was a key taped to the sign. When I grabbed you and got the hell out of that free-for-all, I also took the key. I like to have an exit planned."

"Very convenient," she muttered, but she let him carry her in without a fuss.

Once over the threshold, he slid her down to a standing position. She glanced quickly at the door, wondering if she could make a getaway, but Griffin moved into her path. "If I were you," he said grimly, "I'd stay awhile. There are obviously things we need to talk about. You want me to grovel—I'll grovel. But you have to stay here and listen."

Gingerly, Nell retreated into the suite. It was very pretty—all pale yellow and white, with fresh flowers and trays of chocolate and champagne. Very romantic. Very depressing.

"I'll hear what you have to say," she decided. "But you can't touch me."

"I don't want to touch you." But his eyes, licking her with little trails of fire, told a different story. "I told you—I want you the right way, with everything out in the open between us."

Her voice seemed to get stuck. "Okay," she whispered, and she backed up far enough to perch, carefully, on a plush chair near the middle of the room.

"For your own safety, Nell, I also think you should stay here awhile." His expression was forbidding. "I have a feeling all the power problems downstairs were one of Spencer's bright ideas. There's no telling how it could affect the rest of the hotel. Such as the elevators."

"Power problems? The heat, you mean? And the chandeliers? Why would he do that?"

"He was trying to sabotage the Fantasy Bash. He told me he'd set plans in motion and I knew he'd try something stupid, but I never thought he'd wreck the whole hotel, all over a—" He broke off. "Okay, you might as well know all of it. But promise me, Nell, you'll give me a chance. My motives were good."

"Why do I think I'm not going to like this?" she mused. Luckily for him, she was so curious at this point, she actually wanted to hear it.

Griffin scanned the room, found a silver champagne bucket, pulled out a bottle and popped the cork with one fast shove. Bubbles and wine sprayed everywhere, ruffling Nell's already frayed nerves.

He poured two glasses of champagne, handing her one and gulping down his own.

"That good, huh?" Nell inquired. If Griffin had to

take a stiff drink to find the courage, it had to be bad indeed.

"Spence and I..." He downed another glass. "We made a bet."

"A bet?"

His voice had a sardonic edge when he continued. "We do that, you know. We bet on things. It keeps us amused. Anyway, this one had three parts—the ratings for your show, how many people called in to have matches made on the air and whether the Fantasy Bash came off. If two of the three succeeded, I won. If two of the three flopped, Spencer won."

"So that's why you called into my show," she said softly. "Not just to make a fool of me."

"Of course not." He came nearer, his blue eyes sincere and pleading. "I liked you. I wanted your show to succeed. So I bet on you. But nobody called and your show was dying. Witley and Spencer both wanted to pull the plug—the damn Valentine's promotion was all that was keeping it alive—and I did something stupid, but for a good reason." He bent in front of her, taking her hands in his. "The whole Dr. John thing just got out of hand, Nell, especially after we had dinner that night. Do you remember? You told me your show was riding on me."

"But, Griffin, you made up so many things. All that stuff about Grace and the walks in the moonlight...." She shook her head, pulling her hands away. "That was terrible. I felt so sorry for you. Everyone did! And you were just using our sympathy to win round one hundred and ninety-seven in a neverending battle with your brother!"

"You're right." Falling back, Griffin lifted his shoulders in a careless shrug. "What do you want me to say? You're absolutely, positively right. I was a dog. Spencer thinks I always will be a dog. But I think I can learn new tricks. The important thing is whether you think so, too.''

"I don't really care. I don't want to be with a dog," she said flatly. "I deserve better."

"Yes, you do." And then he turned away and she knew they were at an impasse.

"Well, okay, I heard you out. I know that you cavalierly played games with my show and my career—and my heart—because you have a pathological need to win at all costs." Nell stood up, just as angry at him as she had been five days ago. "Why in the world should I believe that anything has changed, or that you've changed? How can I know that all this drippy sincerity isn't just another game, another chance to win?"

This time, he advanced much closer, right up against her, glowering down at her from his taller vantage point. "How should you know? Damn it, Nell, I've jumped through hoops for you that I've never even approached before. I told you I was in love with you and you hung me out to dry. I let you torment me tonight—wearing that dress, dancing with my idiot brother, making me spend even one minute in the company of Venus DiMaio—not to mention the fact that I have allowed you to torch my whole Seaboard deal without turning you over my knee and spanking you!"

She glared right back at him. "You allowed me to torch it? What does that mean?"

"It means that I know very well you leaked all kinds of crap to the media out there just to keep me occupied and out of town last week. It was just as manipulative and devious as anything you've accused me of."

"But I—"

"Let me finish," he said, and there was an edge of frustration and temper there she'd never heard before. "How in the hell can you not know that I love you if I was willing to turn my back on a six-billion-dollar deal just so I could come back to spend Valentine's Day with you?"

Nell searched his eyes. "You did that? For me?"

"What the hell am I doing here?" he demanded.

"I thought you came back because you fixed it," she said slowly. "I thought you were here because you were finished."

"Oh, I'm finished all right. To the tune of six billion dollars, up in smoke." He shrugged. "But you know what? I don't care. Without you, it doesn't mean anything, anyway."

Nell's mouth formed a little round O. "Good grief, Griffin, I think you're serious."

"Of course I'm serious. What have I been telling you?"

"But this is so great!" She threw her arms around his neck and squeezed him. "Don't you see? It wasn't that you fell in love with me and became magically transformed. It was because of Dr. John!"

"Nell," he said wearily, resting his head on hers, "there is no Dr. John."

"Oh, yes, there is. The man that I fell in love with was not a womanizing pirate who lies and cheats and steals. He was a better person than that." She sighed. "When you pretended to be a better person, you discovered you *were* a better person."

"You're looking at me like you did every time the subject of Grace came up," he said suspiciously.

She ignored him. "Griffin, when you told me that you were in love with me, and you wanted to start the new century off right by spending Valentine's Day with me and no one else, were you telling the truth?''

"Yes," he said simply.

"Okay." She reached for him again, and kissed him with joy and tenderness. "Then let's do it. Let's start our millennium out right."

"Nell," he whispered, bending down to brush his mouth against hers. "I know you love me. But I would really like to hear it. With the right name."

"I love you, Griffin. I forgive you." She smiled. "I'm sorry I screwed up your deal in L.A., but there will be more nuns and orphans to throw out on the street."

"Nell, I swear there never were any—"

"I know, I know," she breathed, lifting herself up on her toes to kiss his chin and his nose and the curve of his elegant jaw. "And I'm going to make sure there never are. Somebody has to keep you on the straight and narrow."

"Do you have to?"

"It's my nature," she said sweetly. "And now that I've forgiven you, could you please make love to me? I'm about ready to die here."

He kissed her quick and hard, once more swinging her up into his arms. "Never let it be said that Griffin Jones denies a lady what she wants the most."

As he carried her into the bedroom, Nell felt an overwhelming sense of rightness, of destiny, of being swept up by forces beyond her control. Had she punished him enough, exacted the revenge she wanted? Not really. And it just didn't matter anymore.

She believed him. She loved him. That was enough.

He set her down gently on the bed, and shrugging off his shirt, reached for her.

"This is not how I thought this night would turn

out," she said with a laugh, running her hands over
the firm planes of his chest, trying to pull him down
beside her. "I mean, I thought I'd have you right
where I wanted you, but not quite like this."

"Really?" His reckless smile took her breath away.
"This is exactly how I saw us ending up. Come on—
it's Valentine's Day."

"Valentine's Night," she amended. She reached
for the top of his pants, but he caught her hands and
pressed them down into the bedclothes.

"Slow down," he murmured, sliding his lips
around the curve of her bare shoulder, tickling her,
arousing her.

She shivered. "I don't want to go this slowly. I
already feel like I've been waiting too long."

But he held her back when she tried to wriggle out
of her dress. "Nell," he chided softly. "You've only
known me for two weeks. How can you say you've
been waiting too long?"

"You're The One." She didn't know any other
way to say it. "I always knew I would meet you and
love you. I just had problems biding my time until
you finally showed up and got your act together."

"I think I know what that means," he said dubi-
ously.

"It means hurry up!" Laughing, she nipped at his
lips, trying to drive him faster.

But he wouldn't. "I always knew I would meet you
and love you," he echoed. "And that's why it has to
take forever."

First he tantalized her, kissing and stroking every
inch of her, tracing a sinfully slow path over her exposed skin with one finger, and then with his tongue.

"If you don't let me take this dress off, I'm going
to die," she whispered. She was so very hot, so very

ready to feel his skin on hers, top to bottom. The bones in the bodice were cutting off her air and she could barely breathe, barely think. Any more of this and she would be panting with desire.

Zip. His clever fingers unhooked and released her, and the red dress fell to her waist. And then his mouth and his hands slipped over her breasts, teasing her nipples into hard peaks, and she trembled and arched into him.

He slid the yards of fabric down her legs and knocked the red dress off the bed with one swift stroke. His eyes swept her from head to toe and his voice lowered into a husky, hypnotic range. "Nothing but a pair of panties and one red shoe. That's what I call erotic."

She raised herself, letting him look his fill, as she reached for those damn pants of his. This time, he let her strip him all the way down.

"Nothing but skin," she whispered, staring straight at him in all his masculine glory. "That's what I call erotic."

He moved so fast she didn't know what hit her. One second she was undressing him and the next he had rolled her underneath him, pinned, trapped, gasping, on fire.

He sat back, looking smug, and she said, "Don't you dare make me wait."

He didn't. He smiled like the pirate he was. He ripped off her panties as if they were tissue. And while she quivered underneath him, he made love to her, long and hard and gentle and sweet all at once.

She had never felt so happy and so crazed, all mixed up together in one stormy tide of passion and emotion.

It was all so easy with him, so easy to feel, to

touch, to want, to have. Her body melted into his, and his into hers, finding a rhythm like no one else's, until they plunged into ecstasy together. So easy. So right. So *amazing*.

"I love you," she whispered, exhausted, cradled in his arms as they drifted off to sleep. "I love you."

"WAKE UP, NELL." He smiled down at her.

She looked awfully cute in the morning, all tousled and drowsy, her fair hair rumpled into a halo spread out on the pillow. Griffin was feeling pretty worn-out this morning himself, so he understood her reluctance to get up and at 'em. He dropped a kiss on the tip of her nose. "The hotel left breakfast outside our door." He shifted the silver tray onto the bedside table. "Wasn't that nice?"

"Oh, no!" She bolted upright. "Where are my clothes? Do I have any clothes? We have to get out of here! Who knows whose room this is really supposed to be."

"Relax." Griffin kissed her again, on the lips this time to quiet her down. "There was a note on the tray from the hotel, apologizing for any inconvenience. And another note." He paused. He hated to admit this part, but... "From my brother. He says by the time we read this, he and Venus will have sailed off into the sunset on my favorite yacht."

"That doesn't sound good," Nell commented. She arranged the sheet around her to cover all the most interesting bits. Well, he'd have to see what he could do about that. "He stole your favorite yacht?"

"Not exactly." Griffin unfolded the card. "Spencer says, 'You lose, bro—the Bash is a certified fiasco. But I might be willing to give you the yacht and the radio station as wedding presents. Go on—ask the girl.'''

Nell didn't say anything, but her eyes got very wide.

Griffin decided he might as well force the issue. "Yeah, well, I hate the idea that my little brother won one, but I know when I'm beaten."

With a rakish grin, he tossed himself headlong into the bed beside her. Nell squealed, but she made room. She circled her arms around him and cuddled up close, which he took as a very good sign.

In his most sincere tone, he murmured, "You see, Nell, if I get to keep you, maybe I lose the bet, but I win the war." She began to giggle as his lips moved down the slope of her neck and around her bare shoulder. "I notice you haven't said anything," he said darkly.

"About what?"

"Nell, my dear..." He took her hand in his and brought it to his lips with mock formality. "Will you marry me?"

She tilted her head to one side, and he marveled again at how enchanting she was. Before he had a chance to say something sappy, she laughed. Her smile was stunning. "You better believe I'll marry you. Someone needs to straighten you out." She rolled over on top of him, pressing her hips suggestively against his. "And I'm just the woman to do it."

"I like the sound of that."

She kissed him, and he knew without a doubt she was The One. "Happy Valentine's Day," she murmured. "Although next year, maybe we should stay at home..."

CONNIE FLYNN

The Wedding Dress Mess

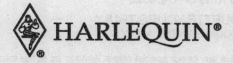

HARLEQUIN®

TORONTO • NEW YORK • LONDON
AMSTERDAM • PARIS • SYDNEY • HAMBURG
STOCKHOLM • ATHENS • TOKYO • MILAN • MADRID
PRAGUE • WARSAW • BUDAPEST • AUCKLAND

Dear Reader,

There is something truly magical about a wedding dress.
No matter the fabric—lace, satin, voile, even cotton—
once constructed, it becomes more than a dress, it
becomes a vessel for hopes and dreams. And what better
to hold these hopes and dreams than a gown worn by
generations of brides? Incredibly romantic, especially if
the gown billows with yards and yards of ancient lace.

I designed such a gown for an earlier book, but it really
didn't fit that story. With much regret, I axed it. The gown
lingered in my mind, however, demanding a story filled
with women who would cherish its romantic heritage. So
Vicky Deidrich and the Mulcahey women were born,
along with Duncan Mulcahey, a man well worth
marching down the aisle for. Of course, Vicky's original
reasons for chasing the dress had nothing to do with
marriage, but...

Well, you'll find out for yourself in *The Wedding Dress
Mess,* where I put Vicky and Duncan through a wild
romantic adventure before they finally set things to rights.

Enjoy!

Connie Flynn

Books by Connie Flynn
HARLEQUIN SUPERROMANCE
726—40 TONS OF TROUBLE

SILHOUETTE YOURS TRULY
ONLY COUPLES NEED APPLY

Don't miss any of our special offers. Write to us at the following
address for information on our newest releases.

Harlequin Reader Service
U.S.: 3010 Walden Ave., P.O. Box 1325, Buffalo, NY 14269
Canadian: P.O. Box 609, Fort Erie, Ont. L2A 5X3

To Alex Dimitri Mavrikos

Welcome to our family, little man

1

WHO IN THEIR RIGHT MIND would have offices down here? Vicky Deidrich irritably asked herself as she prowled the dark underbelly of the Horace Whitfield Museum with very uncertain credentials in search of an elusive claimant.

And feeling just a tad jumpy about it, too.

She stopped for a second to let her feet recover from the beating they were taking from the concrete floor, and looked down at the purloined list in her hand. There it was. Dr. Duncan Mulcahey, room B-33. This was the place, all right.

It figured. The upstairs of the museum was cheerful and airy, especially now with the colorful Valentine's Day display, but the man she was hunting chose to work in the dungeon. Just her luck these days.

She slipped the employee list back into the outside pocket of her briefcase and was about to move on when approaching footsteps sent her into a panic. The Guest–No Escort Required badge clipped to her lapel didn't give her license to be in the basement, so she flattened her body behind a particularly spiderwebby concrete post and peeked out. In the dim light cast by the bare overhead bulbs, she saw a man rushing toward her with his head cast down. He passed quickly, hurrying in the direction of the stairwell so fast she only caught a few quick impressions. A forward-leaning, perpetually rushed demeanor, a small half-moon-shaped birthmark on the jawline, a jutting, hawklike nose.

Then he was gone.

Vicky let out a disgusted sound. Why, that could have been the very man she'd come to see! Her boss had been right about her, after all. She lacked daring. Nerve. Guts. And whatever else it took to get a claim form signed. She might as well just leave Denver. Her days as an insurance adjuster for Global Fidelity Mutual Insurance Company were numbered. She didn't deserve that promotion to investigator anyway. Didn't deserve it at all.

Reminding herself that self-abasement wasn't helpful, and that Ida had never indicated her job was in jeopardy, she brushed a lingering web off her Evan-Picone jacket with just a minor shudder, and decided her only course of action was to keep searching for Dr. Mulcahey's office.

She marched ahead purposefully, looking left, looking right in search of an office door. Her footsteps echoed ominously off the dank walls, adding to her jitters, but also providing her with sullen satisfaction as she countered Ida's accusations in time with each angry beat of her high-heeled shoes.

Click, click. *Lacks initiative…* Grossly untrue!

Click, click, click. *And daring…* True, but grossly unfair!

Click, click, click, click. *Must take more risks.*

Her boss had followed these criticisms with some gobbledygook about Vicky being too respectful of authority and needing too much direction. Fine qualities for an adjuster, Ida had added, but not necessarily for an investigator. If Vicky wanted that promotion, she had to become more forceful, develop guile. She had to bend the rules sometimes. And the still-open Whitfield wedding dress case was an example of how she'd failed to display these traits.

Vicky liked her boss most of the time, but Ida had taken qualities she thought were assets and turned them into liabilities. Level-headed and steady—that was how Vicky viewed herself, and until this last Monday morning she'd been proud of it. But then, she'd also thought the promotion was in the bag.

Wrong. Not unless she got the Whitfield claim signed this week.

Well, she'd been by the museum so often this week that the guy at the reception desk greeted her by name even as he politely denied her access to the director. Here it was Friday already, and she still hadn't gotten in to see Dr. Mulcahey.

This unfortunate fact had driven her to a desperate act.

Poor Greg. The image of the receptionist's worried face when she'd spilled the contents of her briefcase on his desk still haunted her. If anyone discovered she'd used that staged accident to sweep up a guest identification badge and the employee name list, he'd be in big trouble.

Well, she'd shown initiative and daring, all right, and it definitely didn't seem like the real her. Instead of feeling good about it, she had a swirling sensation in her stomach, as if she'd just crossed a line and now there was no turning back.

This promotion meant everything to her. While she was reasonably certain it didn't rest on closing this single, insignificant claim, it sure seemed like it. In fact, she was almost convinced if she failed today she'd be throwing her whole career into the Dumpster.

This thought spurred her to pick up her pace. She winced each time a foot struck the floor, and tried to ignore the pain by again taking solace from the sound.

Click, click, click. *Forceful and daring.*

Click, click, click. *Daring and forceful.*

Yes, that was her. Daring and forceful, forceful and daring. Wasn't it?

Of course it was.

It had to be. She wasn't about to let some highbrow intellectual who thought he was too important to take care of business stand in the way of her hardearned promotion.

WHERE THE HELL was that letter?

Duncan Mulcahey tore through the folders in his desk file drawer yet another time, although he had no real hope of finding the document in question. A single sheet, that was all he needed, and he just knew he'd filed it in this drawer.

So why wasn't it there?

Not surprisingly, he *still* didn't find the letter. Frustrated, he slammed the drawer closed. He'd checked everywhere, even under his computer and monitor. And the stray papers jutting from the closed drawers of his filing cabinets were testimony to his hasty, but thorough search.

He found himself irrationally angry at Horace Whitfield for dying so inconveniently last summer. If the old man were still alive, Duncan wouldn't even need the letter giving his family claim to the wedding dress, nor, in fact, be experiencing any of his current misery. Horace's heirs wouldn't have sold the museum to Calwood Entertainment Ltd.— a soulless corporation if he'd ever come across one—and Duncan wouldn't have been forced to take the director position just to make sure Alistair Shields didn't get the job and destroy everything Horace had valued.

Speaking of Shields. The man had stormed in and out of Duncan's office like a dust devil, evidenced by the pink message slips scattered across his rolltop desk like giant confetti. He wearily collected them into a haphazard stack, then absently slipped them under the shrunken head he used as a paperweight. He had no need to thumb through them. The messages were identical—all twenty-something of them—and came from the same person, a Vicky Deidrich from Global Fidelity Mutual Insurance Company.

Get this claim settled, Shields had demanded, as if Duncan worked for *him* instead of the other way around. Well, he'd be damned if he'd add insurance fraud to the possible charges he might end up facing.

The missing wedding dress was causing Duncan more heartache than Shields, Calwood, this paper-pushing job and a whole tribe of headhunters put together. And now his sister, Meg, was up in arms because he refused to let her wear it during her wedding reception.

He was bone-tired, and he put his elbows on the desk, then rested his head on his hands. The almost back-to-back trips he'd taken over the last month and a half had given him a serious case of jet lag. He needed a breather, but there wasn't time. He'd received an urgent call the previous afternoon from the Colorado Historical Society alerting him of a historic house in Idaho Springs about to be demolished. In a transparent attempt to thwart regulations, the developers delayed giving notification until the eleventh hour. Several calls later, Duncan finally got the demolition company to agree to halt work for the day so he could examine the site. He'd better get himself in gear.

Three more days, he told himself. Only three more days. It would be over on Monday. All he had to do until then was avoid the insurance adjuster. And since he'd be in Idaho Springs most of the day, that shouldn't be too hard.

Evasion wasn't his preference, but then again, the situation wasn't a matter of choice. After all, no Irish son worth his salt turned in his own sainted mother for grand theft.

With a heavy sigh he reached for his well-used buckskin fedora, preparing to leave the building. Just as he plopped on the hat, he heard his door open. Only one person he knew entered his office without knocking, and the man had already done it once today. Duncan wasn't about to let Alistair get away with it a second time. Getting a firm hold on his anger, he slowly swiveled his chair around and found himself staring into the face of an angel.

THE INSTANT VICKY MET those scowling electric-blue eyes her heart skipped a beat. Her stomach tumbled. She found herself unable to speak.

Good heavens. Was she awestruck about meeting this famous archaeologist and anthropologist?

No denying it was a possibility.

She'd been attending night school at Metropolitan State in Denver for several years, studying art, antiquities and insurance law in preparation for her promotion. She'd read Duncan Mulcahey's textbook and had even tried to get into one of his infrequent seminars. What's more, the tales of his exploits had always intrigued her, even though she regarded them with a degree of skepticism.

Had he really wrestled a crocodile in the Ganges River?—no, she didn't think the Ganges had crocodiles, maybe it was an alligator. Regardless, the story definitely included a large body of water and a dangerous reptile.

She shook her head. For heaven's sake, she only needed his signature on a routine claims form. This wasn't a job interview, the doctor wasn't actually a celebrity, and she really did need her voice back.

"D-Dr. M-Mulcahey?" she finally stammered.

Sometime during the drawn-out silence, his scowl transformed to a quizzical expression. Now he tilted back a soft wide-brimmed hat banded by something snaky and regarded her with curiosity.

"Visitors aren't allowed in the basement, miss." His rhythmic voice made the mundane information sound like something spoken by the bard. "Can I show you the way out?"

He stood up, as if offering to guide her, reaching an impressive height that again struck her mute.

Whenever she'd heard Duncan Mulcahey spoken of, two images came to mind, both of older men. One was of a stoop-shouldered man, wearing a soft gray sweater, perhaps. Balding, glasses maybe, but very scholarly. The other image was of a man whose face was weathered from hours under the hot sun in the Australian Outback or Sahara Desert, possibly in fatigues and a safari helmet. A character much more likely to wrestle crocodiles.

This man was definitely not academic or weathered. Nor was he older. Close to her age—thirty-five at most—he was tall, with a confident carriage, and he had a strong, square chin and cheekbones to die for. His deep tan emphasized a narrow white scar that ran diagonally across his left cheek and gave him a slightly dangerous look.

An open leather vest revealing a soft blue shirt beneath fell to his waist, and Vicky's eyes dropped lower, taking in his slim hips in their tight jeans. Trying to convince herself she hadn't really paused there, she hastily lifted her head, scanning his broad shoulders on the way up to meet his gaze.

"H-haven't you r-received my messages?" she squeaked, wanting to sound authoritative and knowing she'd failed. "I've been trying to meet with you all week."

She reached into the pocket of her soft-sided briefcase for the folder containing the wedding dress claim. When he still had said nothing, she paused, continuing to stare up at him. "You *are* Dr. Duncan Mulcahey?"

"Yes. And you are...?"

With a nervous laugh, she stuck out her hand. "My apologies...Vicky Deidrich. I'm an insurance adjuster from Global Fidelity Mutual Insurance Company." His handshake felt warm and personal and made her uneasy, and she let go quickly. "Apparently you didn't receive my messages."

"Messages?"

"The Irish wedding gown…"

"You! Global Fidelity! The gown!" He snapped his fingers. "Sorry if it looks like I've been putting you off. It's only…I, um, I just returned from Peru—discovered some magnificent Incan ceremonial ear cuffs and a…" He drew his black eyebrows together momentarily. "But I suppose I'm boring you. What is it you need?"

"Your signature, Dr. Mulcahey. Now that I've caught up with you, if you'd just give me a few minutes of your time and sign these forms, I'll be on my way."

"My signature…?" He lifted a hand and idly rolled the brim of his battered leather hat. "I was going out. An important site is under the wrecking ball and… Can't we do this another day? Monday, maybe? Yes, that would be good. Monday afternoon."

"I've been by dozens of times, and phoned dozens more."

"Have you now? You're to be commended for your persistence."

Somehow Vicky didn't feel as if she'd been complimented, and not knowing what else to say, she simply stared at him. Another silence hung heavy in the air. His excuse for not returning her calls sounded lame. Very lame. Was something funny going on?

Of course not. She was getting carried away again. Her enthusiasm gave her a tendency to see insurance fraud at the slightest turn. But what if she were right? What if she discovered the gorgeous doctor was involved in something underhanded?

Vicky's heart leaped excitedly. Only she wasn't sure if it was because of this man, or because of the boost her career would receive if she found him guilty of fraud.

2

"ALL RIGHT," DR. MULCAHEY said, his tone heavy with reluctance. "Have a seat."

Her feet screamed for a rest, and Vicky quickly accepted his offer. Settling into a stiff antique chair, she offered him the folder. In that short span of time she'd already dismissed her conjectures as hare-brained. Too bad.

But this man had an impeccable reputation as an archaeologist and anthropologist. He'd single-handedly transformed the Whitfield Museum from a small suburban exhibit to one of the most respected museums in the state of Colorado, even the country. A man like him would never risk his reputation on a single artifact.

Duncan took a seat in a wooden swivel chair that squeaked when he turned, put the file on top of the papers cluttering his rolltop desk and removed his hat. An overhead wagon-wheel chandelier glinted blue-black highlights off his collar-length hair, and Vicky had an odd urge to lean over and smooth down some flyaway strands. Instead, she slipped off one of her four-inch heels and massaged her aching arch.

"You sure about this date?" he asked.

"The museum gave it to me. Why? Is there some question?"

"No, not really. Although I did sign the order to have the gown sent out, I was out of the country when it actually happened." He continued examining the paperwork. "It was for the Valentine's Day exhibit. You see it?"

"The exhibit or the dress?" Vicky wiggled her toes and ran her thumb firmly over her instep.

"The exhibit."

"Yeah, I saw it. Nice." She cleared her throat. "Now, the claims form, if you would."

He swiveled around, file folder in hand, and at the squeak of the chair Vicky let go of her foot. "Try wearing something with more support."

"What?" She shoved her foot into her shoe.

"Those heels." He gestured at her feet. "They're hard on your metatarsals. Your back, too. Causes curvature of the spine."

Holding back a frown, Vicky glanced at his feet, wondering how a man who wore hiking boots to work got off telling her how to dress. "Thanks for the advice."

"Don't mention it."

"So," she said briskly, "is that report an accurate representation of how the dress disappeared?"

"Appears to be. Except that some of the preservationists we use aren't on this list. You mind if I make sure they were contacted before signing off on this?''

''Mind?'' Vicky shot straight up. ''Well, actually...yes. The claim's been open for over six weeks.''

''I've been out of the country most of that time.''

''So you told me.'' He'd also been back more than a week, according to Greg.

But he had a point, and she chewed her lip, trying to figure out how to regain her advantage. She'd made so many trips to the museum, and it had taken so long to track him down.... No, she didn't like his suggestion at all.

''Tell you what,'' she said. ''Why not sign off on it today? I'll hold off processing the claim until, say, Wednesday.'' That should satisfy Ida. ''If you find the garment before then, I'll just tear the forms up. That'll save us both some time.''

Duncan gave Vicky a long look, as much to take in the view as to give him time to reflect on her offer. She was such a pretty woman. China-blue eyes. Skin like satin and soft, kissable lips. Topped off with that cap of shiny blond hair the way it was, her face truly did resemble an angel's. No wonder he'd been rendered speechless when she'd opened his door.

He glanced down at the showgirl legs made even more appealing by those impossibly high heels, and the only portion of her slender figure not covered by her stiff business suit. What other charms were hidden by those prim clothes? he wondered, then reminded himself she wasn't here so he could give her a once-over.

Nope. Despite her angelic appearance, this woman's purpose could, in fact, bring down his house of cards. Besides, her prim manner screamed of dinners promptly at six, manicured green lawns, PTA meetings and everything else Duncan studiously avoided. He preferred women with no-nonsense haircuts, who wore khakis and hiking boots, stored a camp shovel in their backpacks and were usually brimming over with excitement about their latest dig. In short, women a whole lot different from Vicky Deidrich.

Unfortunately, he hadn't met any lately, and he found it darkly ironic that the first woman he'd been attracted to in ages not only didn't fit those specifications, but was the very person he'd been avoiding for more than a week.

The phone rang. A quick glance revealed his mother's number on the caller ID box. Undoubtedly she was calling to rail once more about the restrictions he'd placed on Meg wearing the pilfered wedding gown. They were reasonable restrictions, in his opinion, considering the consequences if they weren't followed. No full-dress photos to be sent to the newspapers, guests permitted to the ceremony by invitation only, and—the one that disturbed Meg the most—take off the dress after the wedding waltz.

He wasn't worried about afterwards. If anyone remarked about the dress, they'd just claim it was a replica. But the original needed to be safely returned; he was having a hard time convincing Meg and his mother of that. Well, he'd stop by the house and talk to them before he headed out to the demolition site. As much as he hated the delay, he had to make sure Meg understood. Even as Duncan pressed a button to reroute the call to the front desk, he shuddered at the image of a Grey Poupon stain on that aging lace.

He turned back to Vicky. Should he take her offer? There probably wasn't much harm in it, considering he'd return the dress on Monday. But suppose something damaged the gown? A remote possibility, but if anything happened, Vicky would have his signatures on those forms. And that spelled F-R-A-U-D, no matter how you looked at it.

"Well?" Vicky said insistently, growing uncomfortable under his scrutiny. He certainly wasn't leering, but she had the distinct impression he was sizing up something more than her offer. When he hesitated, she hastily added, "Maybe I could hold it longer."

What a stupid offer. Ida would never go for it.

"Wednesday will be fine," he replied, an answer as surprising as it was relieving.

"Terrific. Now, if you'd just sign the lines highlighted in yellow, Dr. Mulcahey, I think we have a deal."

"How about calling me Duncan? Even my students don't call me Dr. Mulcahey."

"Duncan?" The name stumbled off her tongue. This man was a legend in certain circles, and calling him by his first name didn't feel quite right.

"See, that's not so hard."

She smiled politely, wishing he'd just get on with it.

He picked up a pen, propped the folder on his knees and lowered his hand. She was just a sweep of the pen away from success, a happy boss, her promotion. She could hardly keep her tongue from hanging out.

"Wait!" His pen was still poised above the form. "I need to make copies for our files." He stood up, folder in his hand.

Vicky blew out a weary breath. "Go ahead."

A second later she watched his old-fashioned door close behind him. She gazed dispiritedly at the semiopaque pebbled glass that showed his name in reverse letters and idly wondered why he hadn't included his title of acquisitions director. She searched for his credentials on the walls. A tapestry entirely filled one wall, while photographs and artifacts covered the others. Nowhere among them did she see the framed diplomas or honorary citations she expected. Although who could be sure with all the clutter?

He certainly was an oddball, in a quixotic sort of way, and she supposed a man who kept his office in a basement would put little stock in framed diplomas. A bit unsettled by the attraction she felt for him, she found herself fidgeting. The tales she'd heard about him made her certain he had a reckless streak. Just like her late father, Duncan's passion clearly came first. In the form of Incan cuffs instead of Formula One cars, but the outcome could clearly be the same.

Vicky had been seven when her father died, but that horrible day was etched in her memory. She'd been standing beside her mother, screaming with excitement as her father darted around the lead car to the head of the pack. Her screams turned to ones of horror when his tire blew. The car skidded, hit a wall, burst into flames, and her sobbing mother covered Vicky's eyes as the crew dragged her father from the wreckage.

Her laughing, high-spirited, reckless and charming father never came home. For years, Vicky heard tearful whispers about money problems, about her father's carelessness, and though her mother never spoke of it directly, Vicky got the message: recklessness leads to misery.

For this reason, she routinely crossed off her list any man who put his life in jeopardy before an opportunity even arose. Which was what she now did with Duncan.

Several minutes passed. Except for the hum of a computer—the only modern object in the room—the silence was complete. A lizard served as the screen saver, and she watched as the creature crawled up and off the screen, only to reappear again at the bottom.

More time passed.

Growing uncomfortable, Vicky got up and moved to Duncan's chair. Under the hard-eyed scowl of a shrunken head, she saw a bunch of messages with her name on them. Other documents were haphazardly piled on the surface of his desk, and his calendar lay open on top of one of them. For a moment she was tempted to flip through it. She resisted. Despite Ida's advice, snooping on a man she had no reason to suspect was carrying things a bit far.

After some time she glanced at her watch. Good heavens, he'd been gone more than twenty minutes. How far was that copy machine, anyway?

Well, she had no intention of spending the whole morning in this disorderly office, but she did intend to leave with that signed file. He had to be in the building somewhere, and she had just the means to find out.

Digging the employee list out of her briefcase she picked the first female name she came across to use when she made her inquiries. Greg answered the phone, and she disguised her voice for fear he'd recognize it.

"You got a cold or something, Carol?" he asked. "You sound kind of funny."

"A touch of laryngitis," Vicky said huskily, feeling more than a little guilty. "Listen, Greg, I need to find Duncan, and he doesn't answer his phone."

"Duncan? Let me check." There was a brief pause, then Greg's next words sent Vicky reeling. "No wonder he doesn't answer. He left the building about ten minutes ago."

3

"DUNCAN!"

At the sound of his name, Duncan briefly considered pretending he hadn't heard, then discarded the idea as foolhardy. Approaching him was one of the reasons he'd requested the basement office. The minute you set foot on the main floor, a suit caught sight of you, and this particular suit was the worst of the worst. Alistair Shields rushed across the museum's marble floor, his head and body leaning forward as usual, and quickly caught up with him.

"I'm in a hurry," Duncan said before Shields could even speak. "The contractor at the Idaho Falls site agreed to halt demolition for the day."

"You're risking your neck crawling through a half-demolished building just for a few old clothes and artifacts?" Shields asked with undisguised disbelief.

"Hey, I'm an archaeologist. It's what I do. So why did you stop me? You must've seen I was on my way out."

"I wanted to let you know that the last-round interviews for the permanent director's job have been rescheduled for Tuesday morning.''

''That'll make it rough on Bob.''

''Pity.'' Shields smugly lifted his beaklike nose an inch higher in the air. ''Fulsom is such a *qualified* candidate.''

Duncan knew Shields had deliberately mispronounced the man's name, and he immediately corrected him.

''Fuller,'' he said. ''Bob Fuller.'' His longtime friend and associate—and one of the best administrators in the business—Bob had been scheduled to fly in the following Friday for the last interview. Now he'd have to scramble to make it.

''You arranged this, didn't you?'' Duncan forced his fists to open. Punching Shields wouldn't help the cause.

''I have friends,'' Shields told him, shrugging. ''What you need to remember is you've left a lot of details hanging. If the board knew the wedding dress claim was still unsettled, it would put your recommendation for Bob in a very poor light. You owe me for keeping it quiet, but if I were you, I wouldn't dally anymore.''

Duncan tapped the manila folder he held under his arm, suddenly very glad he hadn't given into his first impulse, which was to shove it in the paper shredder. ''I'm taking care of it. Now, if you'll excuse me.''

He started for the front door.

"Hear your sister's getting married tomorrow evening," Shields unexpectedly said. "Quite a coincidence."

It took all of Duncan's willpower not to pull up short, but he managed to keep on walking as if he hadn't heard. Although he clearly hadn't fooled Alistair. The man's dry, satisfied chuckle still rumbled ominously in his ears even as he approached his MG.

Did Shields know something? The tone of his question implied he did. He couldn't, Duncan assured himself as he slid behind the wheel of his sports car. Making a connection between Meg's exclusive wedding and the common knowledge that the gown once belonged to the Mulcaheys didn't require Mensa intelligence.

The whole dilemma stemmed back over two months ago, just as he was preparing to leave for Tibet. His mother had called the museum administration office to request the loan of the gown for Meg's wedding, and been told she couldn't have it. As she'd excitedly told him that evening, she was so shocked and distraught she hadn't even had the presence of mind to ask the person's name.

At that time, Duncan should have canceled his trip and concentrated instead on getting permission to use the dress, but he'd simply been unable to pass up the rare opportunity to legally rescue some exquisite at-risk icons.

When he'd returned, his mother had shown him

the stolen gown, saying, "Meg will be wed in this gown like every other Mulcahey woman." Her bold statement dared Duncan to argue with her.

He hadn't.

Instead, he'd forged a delivery order, a courier slip, and fairly well made himself an accomplice. All while Shields had been conspiring to take over the museum he and Horace had built on hard work. Duncan's future—his very reputation—was on the line now. And though he'd given consideration to following through on his offer to Vicky, the risk seemed too great. Without Horace's letter to back him up, what he'd already done was iffy at best and, if exposed, would get him into a lot of hot water at the museum. But signing off on that claim—now, that would move him into breaking the law. Three more days, he repeated, as if it were a mantra. Three more days. But even as he added a small prayer that the weekend would pass without incident, he saw a vision of his mother behind bars. An enormous shudder raced through his body, and he knew that, no matter the cost, he'd take the blame himself before he'd see that happen.

"DID HE GIVE HIS destination?" Vicky choked the words out.

"Home first, I think. Yeah, home, then on to Idaho Springs."

Vicky thanked Greg and hung up. Duncan had walked out! With her claims folder in his hand!

Why? What she needed would have taken only a moment of his time.

This just wasn't fair. None of the week's events had been fair. She'd worked her fanny off for Global Fidelity. In early, out late. Three long years of night school. She could recite descriptions of hundreds of antiquities from ancient Cro-Magnon days to early twentieth-century America. Knew insurance law backward and forward. Now a misguided supervisor and a recalcitrant archaeologist seemed bent on taking it all away.

Well, she simply wouldn't let that happen. Come what may, she would get that claims file signed today.

To be on the safe side—who knew what that man had done with her paperwork?—she made a quick stop at her office to print out a new set of forms, double-checked the address she'd found for him on the employee list against a street map, then headed for Dr. Mulcahey's house.

She'd been a bit perplexed when she found two mailboxes on the sidewalk in front of a large house. Since the street number displayed on the front house wasn't the one listed as Duncan's, she'd risked damaging the heel caps of her shoes by walking down a cobblestone driveway in search of a second dwelling.

Now clutching the new claims file in her hand, she knocked on the door of a bungalow. No one answered readily, so she waited, looking around, hoping he really did live here. A pretty little place, tucked back behind a dormant rose arbor, it was painted in colors that echoed the Victorian flavor of the bigger house. A few patches of snow still remained in the shade of a large evergreen, and the first faint green shoots of crocuses were poking up their heads in the many flower beds in response to the unseasonably warm spell of weather.

Vicky knocked again. More time passed. Still no answer.

With a frustrated breath, she pressed her nose to the window in the door, getting a fuzzy glimpse at an empty hallway through the lacy curtains.

She glanced over at the main house, wondering if Duncan might be there. Or maybe he'd already left for Idaho Springs. Should she peek in his windows? She almost felt as if Ida were looking over her shoulder, advising, "Be forceful, be daring, take the risk."

With another nervous glimpse around, she moved to the nearest window. It also had lace curtains, but they were tied back. She leaned forward, squinting to see what the dusky light revealed.

Did Duncan really live here? Only the quirky mixture of furniture and wall hangings made her think so. Not a cobweb could be seen in the corners. Not a speck of dust marred the polished surfaces of the wooden colonial bench, the French provincial side chair, the Mexican cabinet. Vicky didn't see a single paper anywhere—unlikely for a man who kept an office like Duncan's.

Since she saw nothing other than unusual tidiness, Vicky moved on to the next window, which was higher than the first. She stood on tiptoes. This time she glimpsed the kitchen, also spotless under the glaring eyes of an African fertility mask.

The next window revealed Duncan's true nature. At the end of a narrow aisle formed by shoulder-high stacks of dusty cartons sat a desk with a computer on it. Shelves lined the walls, full of objects.

Vicky leaned closer, not sure if she could believe her eyes. Wasn't that a statue of Prince Ginak of Mesopotamia? About third century B.C., she believed. And there! A first-century stone ewer, exquisitely gilded. The shelves were crammed with invaluable objects of all kinds!

Stifling a chortle, she pressed even closer to the window, wanting to be sure. As she did, she noticed a small gap between the window frame and the bottom sill.

Afraid to believe she could have this kind of luck, she tucked the file folder beneath her arm and reached down. The window slid up easily, noiselessly. Vicky kicked off her shoes, opened her coat and tugged up her skirt. Just as she put one knee on the sill, a dog began to bark.

A very loud and very deep bark. And much closer than her pounding heart preferred. She barely avoided snagging her nylon in her haste to get off the windowsill and check out the source of the barks. Her heartbeat eased as she saw that the killer dog wasn't behind her.

Then a cat squalled and the sound of scrambling claws erupted from the roof. A scream followed. Then a slamming door.

Moments later, there was another slam. Quickly shoving her feet back into her shoes, Vicky eased around the corner of the cottage and out of sight.

"Hurry, Duncan!" cried a shrill young voice. "Chelsea's crying. Hurry, before Demon kills her cat!"

"Puff-Puff!" a child's voice screamed repeatedly, sobbing between shrieks.

Someone spoke to the children. Duncan, his voice so calm and soothing that Vicky's own pulse rate slowed. Although the cat continued yowling, the sobs stopped and the dog quit barking.

Soon after, she heard rapid footfalls on the driveway. She shrank against the shelter of the cottage wall and peered furtively out.

An engine came alive and a battered Jeep emerged. Duncan got out of the vehicle, walked back into the garage and returned with a ladder. Soon something scraped against the side of the house, followed by a soft curse. A series of creaking sounds ensued.

Vicky smiled. Apparently Duncan was going after the cat. The Jeep in the driveway gave her no doubt that he planned to leave when he'd completed his rescue, but right now she had new claims forms in her hot little hands and Dr. Mulcahey on a roof. His only escape was the ladder. She had him trapped, her mission accomplished. But even better, she'd glimpsed her ticket to the big time.

If what she'd seen through that window lived up to her expectations, Vicky had a chance to expose the archaeological scandal of the decade.

EVEN THOUGH DEMON HAD stopped barking, he still lurked beneath the eaves. Puff-Puff clung to the edge of the roof, hissing as if she were trapped in a corner. Duncan stepped off the ladder, bending slightly for balance, and crept toward the hysterical cat, crooning, hoping to calm her down, hoping he didn't get scratched to shreds. Or worse, fall and end up crumpled on the ground like a marionette.

He should have just let the animals work it out. It wasn't as though they hadn't done this before. But Chelsea's pleading eyes, along with Shawn's assurance to their neighbor that his big brother could solve any problem, had spurred Duncan on. He hated to disappoint kids. Just hated it. Even more than he hated heights.

Puff-Puff trilled in displeasure as Duncan approached. He dropped to his knees and crawled closer, wincing as the tiles punished his joints.

"C'mon, Puff-Puff," he chanted. "Easy does it. Easy...easy."

Puff-Puff, the ungrateful feline, raised a paw, bar-ing her claws. "Easy, Puff-Puff...easy." As the cat's eyes grew less wild, he slowly reached out and touched her.

When he was convinced she wouldn't attack, he picked her up. In typical cat manner the creature collapsed bonelessly against his chest, allowing Duncan to head back for the ladder.

"Hey, lady, don't go up there!"

At his little brother's alarmed yell, bedlam broke loose. Demon began barking again. Puff-Puff exploded in his arms. As he struggled to keep her from getting away, she sliced his cheek with her wicked claws.

Stifling an oath, Duncan forced calm into his voice. "Settle down, you perverse bag of feline bones," he crooned. "We'll soon be on the ground. Maybe I can find you a nice poisoned mouse to play with." Apparently understanding his words, Puff-Puff graciously batted him only one or two more times as punishment, each swat as painful as the one before. But finally she quieted again.

"Who were you shouting at?" he called out, turning toward the ladder.

If Shawn answered, Duncan didn't hear. The shock of seeing the feisty insurance adjuster had rendered him completely deaf.

4

VICKY DEIDRICH STEPPED off the ladder, still wearing those mile-high shoes. The midmorning light shimmered off her short cap of golden-blond hair, and her wide cobalt eyes held a glitter of appealing determination. Damn, she sure was pretty, he thought again, well aware this wasn't the time or place to be noticing.

He actually felt his jaw drop, and a second passed before he could speak. "What the hell are you doing up here?"

"You left without signing these papers, Dr. Mulcahey, so I figured we could take care of it now."

She waved a fresh folder in front of her, then reached in her purse, moving as if she'd walked on roofs all her life. She came up with a pen, which she used to gesture toward Duncan's Jeep on the ground. "Obviously you're on your way out again. By the way, those weren't nice things you said to that cat."

"Are you nuts?" Her casual movement gave him a fright, and if he hadn't still been on his knees, he wouldn't have been able to resist the urgent need to pull her to safety.

"Oh." She looked around. "Actually, I'm used to roofs. My mother is afraid— But never mind. If you'll just sign these, I'll be gone in a jiff."

"Shawn!"

"Yeah?" Shawn replied from the ground.

"Why'd you let this woman up here?"

"I tried to stop her, Duncan."

"Well, lock Demon in the garage, then come and get this cat."

Vicky moved from the ladder, strolling up the slant of the roof as if it were solid ground. Duncan's breath caught, and he again fought an urge to reach out and steady her. Trouble was, if anyone needed steadying, it was him.

Soon Shawn's head appeared at the roofline. Duncan rose from his knees and cautiously made his way to the ladder.

"Careful," he warned, handing Puff-Puff over to his little brother, relieved to be rid of one burden. But he wasn't any crazier about having his ten-year-old brother on the ladder than he was having Vicky on the roof, and found he'd just traded one worry for another. Not until Shawn reached the ground did Duncan turn back to Vicky, unsure why his concern for her safety was almost as great as his concern for Shawn's.

"Do you have a death wish, climbing up here in those stilts?"

"I'm as in control as you are, Dr. Mulcahey." She cocked her head stiffly, and her eyes darkened with hurt.

Damn it all. He hadn't meant to be so gruff. Besides, he didn't feel all that much in control. Roofs were not his favorite place.

"Sign, please." She stuck out the file and the pen, then moved toward him.

His worst fear materialized. The tip of her heel snagged on the curling edge of a tile. He lurched forward to grab her, but the slant of the roof interfered with his balance. He staggered, barely staying upright, and watched helplessly as Vicky windmilled her arms in a feeble attempt to stay on her feet. She failed miserably and crashed to the roof, rolling toward the edge.

He dropped back to his knees and grabbed at her. One hand caught her under an arm, the other hand connected with a soft, pliable part of her body.

"Sorry," he muttered. But he couldn't let go. She'd tumble right off if he did.

Dear God, he's holding my— As terrified as Vicky was, she still flushed hot from the intimacy of his touch. She couldn't bring herself to call this man by his first name and here he had his hand on her breast. Her entire body was rigid and trembling, but the place he touched tingled with pure pleasure. This was insane! The man could be a smuggler. What's more, she hardly knew him.

Below, she heard the children shouting. The boy

called for his mother, the girl sobbed again. Teetering on the edge of death, she could still only think about how they all could see where Duncan was touching her.

"Move your hand!" she demanded through clenched teeth.

He relaxed his hold. She skidded another inch.

"N-no! D-don't!"

His hold tightened, and he began tugging, the outline of his every finger burning into her flesh. As he eased her up the incline, she clawed for his arms, but the folder and pen in her hands prevented her from gaining purchase.

"Let go of that stuff!" he growled.

"But...but..."

What was she doing? One of her legs already hung off the roof, and gravity was giving Duncan a serious battle. She released the pen and folder, yet even as she clutched at Duncan's forearms she cringed at the sight of her very future fluttering toward the ground. Then her coat caught on a tile and she had to shift her hips to free it. All thoughts of the file evaporated.

Finally Duncan had her. With a sharp explosion of breath, he pulled her against his chest, dropping the hand that enclosed her breast. Vicky's skin felt suddenly cold. Then he wrapped his arms around her stomach. Warm again, she allowed herself to sag against his iron-hard chest.

"You okay?" His breath caressed her cheek. Still

afraid to let go of his forearms, she looked at him over her shoulder.

"Yeah," she whispered. Her heart pounded and her blood raced. She was hot, slightly feverish. Terrified, mortified...exhilarated.

Never in her life had she been so close to a brush with death. But now, in the arms of this perilously handsome possible felon, she felt more alive than she ever had.

He pried an arm free from her grip and ran his fingers down her cheek. "Only a smudge," he said with a sigh that sounded like relief. "You sure now? No scratches, no bruises?"

"I'm fine," she answered breathlessly, meeting his gaze. His electric-blue eyes were filled with her. With fear for her safety, with concern. Several scratches, one beaded with blood, marked the chiseled line of his cheekbone just above the faint white scar. She wanted to touch his injury, to heal it. And her lips, she realized, were just millimeters from his. She had only to lift her head...

He smiled, as if he held the same thought.

She shouldn't do this. This man holding her was reckless, lived on the edge of danger, feared nothing. And he was possibly dishonest. If she should come to care about him...

His bold rescue proved he lived by the same code that had killed her father. But for the first time, as her entire body tingled with intense vitality, she had a taste of danger's lure.

Danger... She ran her tongue over her parted lips.

"Duncan! Duncan! What's going on up there?" The alarmed female voice, thick with an Irish brogue, broke the mood. Full of mingled, conflicting emotions, Vicky jerked her head forward.

"We're okay, Mom," Duncan yelled. Scooting back, he pulled her farther away from the edge of the roof.

"I can do it," she grumbled, letting go of his arms and sitting up straight.

"Take it easy."

"You made me drop my file."

His eyes narrowed. "Look, those papers are the least of your worries. You almost got yourself killed...and me along with you."

"Yeah, well you're used to it." She had a sudden unpleasant thought that her rash act could be used against her. "Are you going to report me?"

"Report you?"

"To Global Fidelity."

Rolling to his feet, Duncan slapped his palm against his leg. "Just say thanks, would you? It's the least I deserve for saving your life."

Vicky didn't know what to say to that. She took off her shoes and levered up. Her fear had vanished. So had the exhilaration. God, this man brought up emotions she'd successfully avoided for years. Embarrassment, excitement...desire.

"Thank you," she mumbled, starting toward the ladder.

"Louder," he said.

"I beg your pardon." She knew what he meant. Turning her head, she met eyes that had turned to blue steel. "Thank you, Dr. Mulcahey, for saving my life. But if you hadn't run off with my claims file, I wouldn't even be here."

"The name's Duncan." He sighed loudly, plucked the high heels from her hand and gestured toward the ladder. "After you."

She backed up cautiously and put one foot on the top rung. And as she climbed down the ladder, unusually indifferent about the way the rungs snagged her new hose, she couldn't help remembering how much she'd wanted him to kiss her up there on the roof.

BEDLAM WAITED FOR DUNCAN on the ground. His mother was demanding explanations for a woman's sudden appearance on their roof. Demon barked incessantly from behind the closed garage door where Shawn had stashed him, and Chelsea squished her peeved kitty against her chest, sobbing with relief on Meg's comforting shoulder.

Meanwhile, Vicky appeared lost in tunnel vision. Even before her hosiery-clad feet hit solid earth, she swiveled her deliciously slender neck in search of her fallen paperwork. When she reached the ground, she stopped to scan the driveway, blocking Duncan's way.

"You mind if I get off the ladder?" he inquired acidly, handing over her shoes.

"Oh, sorry." She took them from him, making him wait while she put them back on, then scurried toward a row of bushes lining the driveway. The scattered sheets hung on various branches like Christmas ornaments, and she plucked them off anxiously, continually shuffling them as the pile grew.

Meanwhile, Meg dried Chelsea's tears, then sent her home with Puff-Puff.

"Duncan Mulcahey," his mom scolded as Vicky feverishly went about her business. "Can't you see the woman is hurt? You should be helping her get the papers."

"Hurt?" The spot where Puff-Puff scratched him stung like hell. He touched it and came away with blood on his fingertips. "How's she hurt?"

"Look at her torn nylons and those scrapes on her knees," Meg interjected.

Duncan watched in stunned silence as his mother and sister collected Vicky's remaining papers. Soon even the manila file had been found, and Vicky was looking quite satisfied with herself. When, as a final triumph, she found her lost pen and came up from the ground grinning as though she'd somehow won a battle, it was all Duncan could do not to groan aloud.

What were the women who'd gotten him in this mess in the first place doing aiding and abetting the person who could send him up the river? Didn't they know who she was?

"Where are your manners, brother dear? You invite a strange woman onto our roof and don't even introduce us?" With the paper harvest complete, Meg joined him at the base of the ladder. Her churlish question didn't surprise him since he knew she was still annoyed over his demands about protecting the dress, but it also reminded him that, no, they *didn't* know who Vicky was.

"I didn't invite— Forget it. I'm having a hard time understanding why you don't find it odd that she followed me up there in the first place."

"You don't know her?" Meg's eyes widened, and she ran her fingers through her copper curls. "You don't think she's a cat burglar, do you?"

"What's this talk of burglars? Surely you're not talking about that sweet young woman." His mother joined them, looking every bit as indignant as Meg. Vicky remained at the edge of the driveway where she was meticulously arranging the papers inside the folder.

Duncan snorted. Sweet? Vicky was as rash and hardheaded a woman as he'd ever met. "Listen," he said impatiently, striving to keep his voice low enough that Vicky wouldn't hear, "by any chance, did either one of you happen to look at those papers you helped pick up?"

"Of course not," his mom snapped.

"We're not snoops," Meg added.

"That's what I figured." He turned his eyes toward Vicky and asked with studied courtesy, "Could you join us?"

She tucked the file folder protectively under her arm, clutched the pen between her fingertips and came forward with a glint of suspicion in her eyes.

"Mom, Meg," Duncan said. "May I present Ms. Vicky Deidrich of Global Fidelity, the insurance company that covers the museum."

Although Meg did only a fair job of stifling her gasp, Duncan's mom didn't even blink her bright blue eyes.

"Nice to meet you." She smiled warmly, invitingly. Too invitingly. "I'm Bridget Mulcahey, Duncan's mother."

"It's nice to meet you, too, Mrs. Mulcahey, and I apologize for interrupting your day." Vicky's voice contained that irritatingly businesslike tone. "If I can just get your son to sign these claims forms, I'll be gone in no time."

"Sure, and he will. But first—" Bridget took Vicky's arm and began guiding her toward the house "—I'll be taking you inside to tend to those scraped knees."

"That's very kind, but it isn't necessary. I have a first aid kit in my car."

"No, really. We insist." Meg moved to Vicky's other side, clearly gleaning her mother's plan.

Duncan watched in outright admiration. Vicky was no match for his mother. Nothing could hold his mother back when she felt she had right on her side. And, by God, she was convinced the museum owed Meg the use of the wedding dress.

Vicky, of course, had no idea what was going on and good manners kept her from protesting too strongly. But she gave it a good try.

"They're scrapes, just scrapes," she repeated in a bewildered tone as the women hustled her toward the door. "It's not necessary. Really it isn't. Honestly."

"Won't take but a bit of your time," Duncan's mom said, picking up the pace. "Then Duncan will sign those forms for you, and you can be going about your business."

Duncan could barely hold back a laugh at the anguished expression on Vicky's pretty face as she kept him fixed uncertainly in her gaze. And when his mom and sister steered her through the door and closed it behind them, he let it loose.

Then he headed for his Jeep, whistling, tossing his keys in the air. A whole day at an excavation site lay before him, and tomorrow was the wedding. Surely, with his family's help, he could hold pretty Vicky Deidrich off until then.

Suddenly, he remembered the odd gleam in his mother's eyes when she'd first seen Vicky stepping off the ladder. His high spirits faded. He was no longer convinced that the only thing motivating her was concern for her daughter.

That spelled trouble, big trouble. Because there

was one thing that galvanized his mother even more than a righteous cause. The sight of a woman she thought was perfect for one of her sons.

Duncan remembered what she'd done to his brother, Michael. He wasn't about to let her do it to him.

5

"I'M FINE," VICKY protested to no avail. "Just fine."

Mrs. Mulcahey was the height of Irish maternalism as she steered Vicky into a small bathroom, where she pulled out antiseptic and bandages.

The scrapes weren't really that bad—hardly any blood at all—and Vicky sensed these two delightful ladies were purposely trying to delay her. But they were being so nice that a prick of guilt accompanied her misgivings, made all the worse when Meg appeared with a package of nylons to replace her damaged ones. Still...

"Duncan *is* waiting for me?" Vicky asked.

"Who can guess?" Bridget replied. "That boy marches to his own drummer."

"It's imperative that he signs those papers, Mrs. Mulcahey."

"Call me Bridget," the older woman said.

"Bridget. But, please, I have to catch him."

The woman looked at Meg. "See if Duncan's still here, will you?"

"Sure."

"On second thought, I'll go with you. Vicky'll be needing her privacy to change her hose."

Too bad these ladies chose such an inopportune time to demonstrate their kindness, Vicky thought as the door closed behind them. She'd bet her morning bagel Duncan had taken off again. But at least she'd rescued the claims file. A few of the pages were dog-eared now, which offended her sense of order, but at this point she wouldn't care if they'd been coffee-stained as long as they sported Duncan's name.

She pulled off her shredded hose and wriggled into the new ones, making a mental note to buy Meg a replacement pair as soon as possible. This done, she put on her shoes, gathered up her coat and the claims file and prepared to go after Duncan.

When she stepped out of the bathroom, she felt vaguely disoriented. As she'd noticed on the way in, lace was everywhere. Not filmy, frothy stuff, but thick tatted sheets of it, hanging over the gleaming wooden handrails of the banister, bedecking a small telephone table, not to mention the tons of it on the windows and furniture in the living room they'd passed through to reach the bathroom.

Idly wondering if Duncan ever tired of the feminine froufrou, she also found herself yearning for this soft, homey look. The color-coordinated decor of the house she shared with her mother was neat, attractive…safe. Like everything else in her life, if she believed Ida's harsh assessment of her character.

As these thoughts danced in her head, Bridget appeared at the hallway door, holding yet another piece of lace.

"I'm sorry," she said contritely. "Duncan got away. He was in such a hurry to get out to that demolition site."

She led Vicky into the living room, where Meg hummed along with a song on the radio as she wrapped lace around some articles in her hand. The small round table where she sat was heaped high with lace scraps similar to the one Bridget held, as well as small boxes of foil-wrapped chocolates.

So they were busy on some kind of project. That was good. It provided Vicky with an easy and polite excuse.

"You think Duncan will be back before five?" she asked after smiling at Meg. "I'd hoped to get this claim settled before the end of the business day."

Bridget shook her head. "Knowing Duncan, he'll probably just be making it back in time to change for the party. Once he gets to digging, he loses all track of time."

"Party?" Vicky echoed absently, already calculating how long it took to get to Idaho Springs.

"Roger's last bachelor fling." Bridget looked over at the table. "Meg's getting married to him tomorrow evening."

"Tomorrow?" Vicky replied. "You're getting

married on Valentine's Day? How ro...how ro-man...tic...."

Even as she said the words, Vicky's smile faded. A missing Irish wedding dress? An Irish bride-to-be? A museum official who had easy access to the gown? And a tableful of items that would have given her this clue if she hadn't been so preoccupied with Duncan's whereabouts.

Apparently her sudden mood change wasn't visible, because Bridget's smile turned radiant. "Yes. And sure if it isn't every girl's dream."

Meg looked up from her work. "Mom," she said a little more firmly than Vicky thought necessary, "we're probably holding Vicky up."

"I do need to head out to Idaho Springs."

"You're driving out after him?" Meg asked with some surprise.

"Yes. Like I said—"

"But it's such a long drive. Leave the papers here instead. I'll make sure they get back to you. Surely a day couldn't matter."

"That's very kind. But I do need it done right away." Vicky backed toward the door. "I'll replace the hose you loaned me as soon as I can."

"No need. Consider them a gift."

"Then again," Bridget countered eagerly, "any excuse to stop by. We'd love to have you visit again, Vicky."

"How nice of you," Vicky replied, continuing to back up.

Still facing the room, she fumbled behind her for the doorknob. She had to get out of here. These women were as delightful as they came, making the information she'd just gathered very troubling. Just as her hand contacted metal, Bridget walked toward the fireplace and plucked an envelope off the mantel.

"Wait!" She hurried forward, gave Vicky a quick hug and pressed the envelope into her hand.

"Mo-o-om," Meg said.

Bridget ignored her. "Come to the wedding, Vicky. I know it's short notice, but please come. We'd love to have you."

"I—I'll try to m-make it," Vicky stuttered, inching her way out.

Smiling broadly, her carrot-hued hair glowing in the reflected sunlight, Bridget wagged her hand in goodbye. "I hope so. Time, address and all that's in the invite."

When the door closed behind her, Vicky stood on the painted wooden porch for a moment, stunned by the discoveries that implicated Meg and Bridget in Duncan's possible crime. Meg's clear warning when her mother gave Vicky the invitation was ominous, nor could the unlikely coincidence between the missing dress and the marriage be ignored. What troubled her most, however, was the specimens she'd seen in Duncan's cottage.

Suddenly, the triumph she'd felt when she'd seen the items fell as flat as a glass of stale champagne. These were good people, too nice to have such a scandal rock their world. As she mulled this over, she heard a chair scrape against the hardwood floor inside. But how? The door was closed. Then she saw the open window.

The chair scraped again, then Meg spoke. "Do you think that was wise, Mom?"

"No harm will be coming of it," Bridget assured her. "And it's time your brother got his reward for all he's done for us. Vicky's the one for him. I can feel it, for sure. Now, I just have to get her hanging around long enough for him to see it himself."

"But Duncan will kill us," Meg moaned.

Bridget only laughed. "Don't worry, darlin', I'll take care of Duncan. Don't you be forgetting, I'm his mother."

Meg moaned again, then all was silent.

Vicky's heart lifted. So that was it. Bridget was a hopeless matchmaker.

With that, Vicky tiptoed across the porch. Suddenly the incriminating evidence didn't seem so conclusive. Meg was most likely worried about exceeding her guest count when she warned her mother about handing out the invitation. And so what if the dress was missing at the same time as Meg's wedding? A lot of gowns had gone out for primping in anticipation of the Valentine's Day exhibit. Losing one wasn't that unusual.

No, these ladies were probably just what they seemed.

But she wasn't so sure about Duncan.

IDAHO SPRINGS WAS AN old gold mining town less than a half-hour drive up I70 on the way to Mount Evans. Most of the town was visible from the highway, so Vicky had no doubt she'd find Duncan. Even if she couldn't see the demolition site upon approach, all she had to do was ask around.

As it was, the house stuck out like a proverbial sore thumb among the charmingly remodeled historic buildings that surrounded it.

Her stomach growled from skipping lunch as she pulled in behind Duncan's dusty blue Jeep, ready to track through the rubble to find him. Ignoring her hunger pangs, she got out of her car and looked around.

This was no place to be dressed like a lady...or a gentleman, Vicky thought. Piles of debris rose from the ground like deformed overgrowth. Pickup trucks were parked at odd angles without any apparent order. A chalky white dust covered everything and lingered heavily in the air.

She glanced down at her clothes. Although her coat hadn't made it through the incident on the Mulcahey roof without damage, she wasn't eager to submit it to more, so she shrugged it off and decided to do the same with her suit jacket. The day was warm enough; she could do without it for a while.

All was idle when she crossed the yard. Workmen sat in the cabs, beds and on the fenders of the trucks, eating, smoking and chatting. As she passed by, one whistled. She ignored the sound, grinning slightly as another man reminded the first that whistling was politically incorrect these days.

Amid the dust and presently quiet mayhem, a house that had once been a beautiful example of Victorian architecture looked as though it had barely survived a blitz. Off to one side, a monstrous wrecking ball hung limp, waiting for action again. A man in a hard hat sat high in the cab, wearing an impatient and disgruntled expression.

It was no easy climb to get to the cab door, and when Vicky stuck her head in, the man looked startled.

"Have you seen Dr. Duncan Mulcahey?" she inquired.

"Who? Yeah. What're you doing up here, lady? You from that historical society or something? You people have no sense."

"Hunting for Dr. Mulcahey," Vicky replied evenly, ignoring the man's irrelevant questions.

"You'll have to get down."

"I will as soon as I learn his whereabouts."

"He's inside the house digging for them artifacts. But you can't go—" he gave her a scrutinizing stare "—hell, I can tell you'll go, anyway." He tossed a hard hat in her direction.

The claims folder secured beneath her arm slipped when Vicky reached to catch the hat, and she teetered just enough to make her heart leap with alarm. Although she immediately caught both the hat and her balance, she felt oddly invigorated, just as she had on Duncan's roof. Her blood seemed hotter, she felt more alive, and for a frivolous moment she wondered if this sensation was the reason some people sought danger. Immediately dismissing the thought, she thanked the equipment operator for the hat, and to his obvious relief she climbed back down to the ground.

She secured the hard hat on her head and set out toward the sadly tilting house. The brisk air penetrated her light cotton shirt, but the sun was warm on her back so she didn't regret leaving her jacket in the car. She wouldn't be in the building long, anyway. Just long enough to get Duncan's signature on the form.

She still didn't know whether to report the articles she'd seen in Duncan's bungalow. What if she'd misconstrued the evidence? If so, she'd end up looking like a complete fool, which certainly would do her career some harm, and she wasn't exactly in good graces now.

Then there was Duncan's request for time to locate the missing gown. What if he did find it? Did that mean his sister had worn it for the ceremony? Should she also look into that?

While these questions darted around her mind like bats in an attic, she reached the half-razed house and was about to duck under a tilted doorway when she heard a timber crack.

As pieces of splintered wood tumbled toward the earth, she jumped aside, catching the heel of her shoe on a rock in the process. Used to navigating on heels, she landed on her feet, thanking her lucky stars that other than a small piece of wood that skidded off her hard hat, nothing hit her.

This place wasn't safe. Not safe at all. Why would Duncan even consider going inside?

But he was here, and she was here, and she wouldn't get these forms signed by standing around worrying about her safety. Taking a deep breath for courage, she went through the crazy-house door, taking solace in knowing her business wouldn't take long.

THE RUSTED LID of the century-old trunk squeaked as Duncan pried it open to find a treasure trove. At the thought of how easily the historic items could have become a casualty of progress, he let out a particularly blistering curse. He immediately heard a feminine gasp.

"I knew you wouldn't be glad to see me," Vicky Deidrich said primly, "but I didn't ex—"

"It isn't you." Her appearance startled Duncan so badly, he almost fell back on his haunches, and he took a second to steady himself before explaining further. "Those jerks almost destroyed a priceless find. *Junk,* the foreman called it. Can you figure?" He lifted up a journal, one of the many items inside the trunk. "Someone's life is recorded on these pages, and that bastard calls it *junk?*"

"He doesn't understand," Vicky replied gently.

"If he knew, I'm certain he wouldn't have been so callous."

"Callous, huh?" Duncan gave a half smile at her choice of words, which made it seem as if he were grumbling about someone who'd criticized his necktie. But the remark had been clearly motivated by kindness, and that realization jarred him from his preoccupation with his own concerns. "Yeah, the brute did hurt my feelings, but I'll get over it."

He returned to inspecting the contents of the chest, careful not to jostle anything that might be dry and brittle, and came up with a porcelain doll. "I suppose you're here about the claim."

"You suppose right. I insist on getting your signature right now, Dr. Mulcahey—"

"Look," he interrupted impatiently. "After what happened on the roof, couldn't you call me Duncan?"

Although the color in her cheeks heightened, she maintained her composure. "All right, *Duncan.* But if you're trying to divert me, you're failing. And I must say, your reluctance to sign off this routine claim looks a trifle suspicious."

"You have a point—hey, be careful!" She stepped over a dangerously jagged piece of wood, looking comically out of place in her impractical heels. He might be prone to laugh if she weren't at such grave risk of injury. Instead he solicitously added, "You can get hurt down here, so watch what you touch. Especially that post." He hitched his thumb at a four-by-four not far from where he crouched with the doll in his other hand. "It holds up the ceiling—or the second-story floor, depending on how you look at it."

"Okay, okay," she said defensively. "But if you'd sign these papers quickly, you wouldn't have to worry any further about me bringing the roof down on your head."

Duncan pushed aside the leather collar of his jacket and rubbed the back of his increasingly stiffening neck.

"The claim's been open for more than a month. Why's it so important to you now?"

"It's messing up our reputation for fast settlements," she replied somewhat sarcastically, moving a few steps closer. "And I have no intention of letting you escape until you've signed."

She clutched the precious claims file against her tailored cotton blouse as she approached, unwittingly outlining her full breasts. This, combined with the hard hat, gave her a rakish woman-in-man's-clothing sexiness that momentarily captured his full attention.

He had to get her out of his life, but she'd hound him without mercy until he gave her what she wanted. Even as the words *insurance fraud* tattooed in his brain like rattling jail cell bars, Duncan asked himself what could be the harm. "Our deal still good?"

"Deal?"

"You'll hang on to the claim until I have a chance to check around?"

She tightened her lips as if reconsidering. Duncan narrowed his eyes. Just as he was about to tell her "no deal, no signature," she said, "Okay."

Duncan put the doll on the open lid of the trunk, smiling uneasily as she handed him the folder for the second time that day. "You got a pen?"

"Oh." She reached to open her purse, then caught sight of the doll. "How beautiful," she said with a sigh. "It must be at least a hundred years old."

"A hundred and fifty," Duncan replied, caught up by her enthusiasm. "Are you a collector?"

"No, no, but I'd like to be." She stared down at the doll with longing. "I had one like this when I was a girl, but it got lost somehow. I know it's fragile, but you think I could hold it for a minute?"

Duncan couldn't have asked for a better diversion. If luck stayed with him, maybe she'd forget about getting his signature altogether.

Right. Still, it was worth a try. With as little fanfare as possible, he put the folder on the floor, then turned toward his tool kit, extracting a pair of plastic gloves.

"Put these on," he instructed. "Worst thing for antiques is the body oil off your hands."

"I know," she said, pulling them on.

"You do?"

She bent over and picked up the doll. "I've been studying art, antiquities and collectibles at Metropolitan State. I tried to get into your last seminar, in fact, but it was closed to undergraduates. Very disappointing.''

''Oh?'' Duncan replied, more flattered than he knew he should be. ''Call me next time and I'll give you an override.''

Jeez, what was he saying?

''Thanks.'' As she gazed appreciatively at the doll, Duncan noticed a speck on her cheek, and he reached out without thinking to brush it away. She lifted her head, looking at him as though he'd done something odd.

''A wood fragment,'' he explained, suddenly flustered by his spontaneous act. ''Did something fall when you first came in?''

She nodded.

''This whole place is unstable. You have to be careful,'' he warned, aware of a protective feeling surging within him.

''I will.'' She regarded him for a long moment, then returned her attention to the doll and lifted the hem of its dress. ''Look at these tiny stitches. You never see work like this anymore.''

''Very true, which is one of the reasons I fight to save these old items. They're a window into the culture of their times.''

''I know exactly what you mean. It's why my promotion into the antiquities fraud division is so important to me. I want to make sure treasures like this aren't stolen or destroyed by unscrupulous people.''

"Promotion?'' Duncan repeated dimly, although he was pretty sure he was getting the picture.

"Yes," Vicky replied, looking up from the doll, then bending to return it to the trunk. Next, she stripped off the gloves and handed them to him. "Thanks for letting me hold the doll. Now, if I could just get those forms signed.''

Duncan swallowed a sigh. He hadn't really expected the diversion to work, but a guy could dream, couldn't he? While Vicky dug a pen from her handbag, he closed up the trunk. He shouldn't be trying to inventory here, anyway. Wouldn't take much more than a clap of thunder to bring this unstable building down.

Although he was tempted to make Vicky bend for the folder he'd placed on the ground, he did the gentlemanly thing and got it himself. Handing it up to her, he said, "Let's go outside. I'm not comfortable here.''

"Goodness," Vicky replied perkily. "I wouldn't expect a man of your reputation to be afraid of anything.''

"I'm not afraid." He felt an edge of testiness coming to his voice. "Just prudent. This house is a wreck waiting to happen.''

He rose to his feet and bent to pick up the chest. Just then he heard a creaking sound. It started softly, rising in volume, then abruptly escalated to an ominous crack.

He saw Vicky swivel her head around, seeking the source of the sound. Duncan saw it before she did—a huge sheet of plaster breaking free from the ceiling.

"Look out!"

Simultaneously, Vicky saw the danger and jumped sideways to avoid it, but tripped on a scrap of wood. She shot out her hand instinctively, searching for something to brace against.

"Noooo! Don't!"

Too late. Vicky's hand hit pay dirt.

Duncan groaned in horror as the full weight of her slender body came to rest against the flimsy four-by-four supporting the roof. The base of the post skidded across the floor with an earsplitting shriek. Duncan reached out and grabbed her, barely managing to snatch her away before the ceiling started crashing down.

Holding Vicky close, he dove for the ground and rolled across the littered floor toward the supporting outer wall. Sticks and rocks jabbed at his skin each time his back hit the floor, and he knew she felt their sting even more acutely since she only wore a thin cotton blouse. He did his best to protect her. But there was no time to think. Just move. Escape. Get this maddening woman to safety. And, maybe, just maybe, manage to save himself, too.

When his back finally came to rest against the

wall, he knew he'd done all he could. If the wall held, they'd be okay. Most of the crumbling second story would fall into the middle of the room. But should the wall collapse, too...

He pulled Vicky closer to his heart.

with, he knew he'd done all he could. If the wall
hadn't they'd be okay. Maybe a disorientating second
were worth, fall into the middle of the room, but
should the wall collapse on them.
he pulled Vicky closer and...

6

THE NOISE WAS DEAFENING. Plaster dust filled her
nose and mouth. An object struck her hard hat with
enough force to rattle her brain. Smaller debris skit-
tered off her arms and shoulders. Vicky coughed and
sputtered. A shriek lodged in her constricted throat
but refused to escape.

Aeons passed before objects stopped falling, although she knew it had actually been only a few
minutes. Sunlight filtered through the myriad gaps
in the collapsed structure, and in the subsequent silence, broken only by their ragged breathing and the
scattered sounds of belatedly falling fragments, she
clung to Duncan's hard shoulders.

Her breasts and belly were crushed against his
torso, and her thighs were pressed tightly to his. She
could feel every dent and angle in his hard muscles,
feel her softer skin almost melting against him. His
heavy breath and rapid heartbeat maintained a
rhythm equal to hers. And in this moment, in this
place, their unseemly intimacy felt right and good
and so, so reassuring that she nestled deeper into the
shelter of his arms.

"You okay?" he asked after some time.

She tilted back her head and looked into eyes that were shimmering with tenderness and caring.

"Yes, I am. You?"

"Other than some bruises, nothing seems broken." He lifted his top arm as he spoke, scattering rubble and causing Vicky to flinch. "Hey, hey, hey. It's all right," he assured. "But here, your hard hat's on cockeyed."

He straightened the hat, then tucked away stray locks of her hair, still studying her face as if to assure himself she wasn't harmed.

"You shouldn't have come here, Vicky," he said in a husky voice. "You could have been seriously hurt, you know."

"I know, but I wasn't."

"Yeah...you weren't."

Something electric arched between their joined gazes, sending a delectable shiver through Vicky's body. Then he put his arm back around her, and again she settled her head on his chest. His heart pounded against her cheek while her own blood thrummed feverishly in her ears. Way off in the distance people were calling out to one another. Settling timber creaked around them. But she was safe here, safe in Duncan's arms. And glad to be alive, glad *he* was alive, glad he was holding her.

In time, the voices got closer, louder, but she only vaguely registered that fact, and when Duncan touched her shoulder she jumped from the shock.

He hissed sharply in response to her movement.

"You sure you aren't hurt?" she asked in alarm.

"Yes," he replied choking the words out on a ragged breath. It was then that Vicky felt the gentle stirring at the juncture of his thighs. Suddenly their enforced closeness didn't seem so reassuring. She pressed her hands on his chest, seeking leverage to move back. Unfortunately there was nowhere to go. A mound of rubble held her fast against Duncan, and he was wedged tightly against the outside wall.

"Vicky," he said hoarsely. "I don't...I don't think you should...do that."

Her movement, it seemed, had served to grind her pelvis harder against him. Heat flushed through her entire body as his erection sprang fully to life.

"I...yes, I suppose not." She forced her every muscle to freeze. "You think...you think help will come soon?" she asked, hating the terrified hitch in her voice. Or was it terror? As much as she wanted to deny it, her body ached to get closer to him, not farther away.

"Soon, I think." He touched the hollow of her throat as if to ease her distress, and the sweetness of it ignited a shudder of need in her body. Duncan moaned involuntarily.

"I'm sorry, Vicky," he said. "I wish I could do something about—"

"It's not unusual," she said, trying to keep her tone clinical. "I've read that life-threatening circumstances often stir...these kinds of impulses. You

know, perpetuation of the species, that kind of..."
Dear Lord, her voice was all quivery. "It's not as
if we..."

There was a long pause before Duncan filled in
her hesitation. "Of course it isn't. Not like
we're...or anything like that."

"No, it's only that we—we—" She squeezed her
eyes shut, too embarrassed to look at him anymore.
What did a person do in this kind of situation?
Where, oh where, was Miss Manners when you
needed her? Talking about it hadn't helped. They
had to find a way to ease their enforced contact.
"We've got to...got to...make room, Duncan."

His answering nod caused his chin to strike her
hard hat, sending a bizzarely erotic pulse through
her scalp. She had to control herself. The diggers
were getting closer. A man yelled Duncan's name,
and Vicky mentally chided herself for jumping once
more.

"Down here!" Duncan shouted back, then whispered to Vicky, "We're going to get out of this.
Honest."

Reaching over her, he began moving pieces of the
wreckage. The pile behind her shifted with an ominous crunch. She blinked, clamped her lips together
again, then clutched at Duncan for protection.

But was it for protection?

Or was it sexual desire?

Dear God, she'd had a few relationships—not
many, but enough to understand lust. But what she'd

experienced before was only a pale imitation of this consuming urge to rip away the fabric separating their bodies and invite him inside to pleasure her, pleasure him.

She didn't even know this man who trembled above her like a lover. Didn't know him at all.

But how she wanted him.

She had to do something to mask her feelings. Start a conversation, maybe.

"Th-the cat scratched you," she said, as if he didn't know. She still kept her eyes tightly shut. Talking, yes. Meeting those startling blue eyes, an absolute no.

"Yep," he said, lobbing something away.

"Does it h-hurt?"

"Not bad."

This wasn't going so well, and it didn't help matters that each time he threw an object away, they bumped. Her own breathing was getting so loud, they both could hear it.

"How did you g-get that scar?"

"An ocelot attacked me."

"In the j-jungle?" At last a subject they could get their teeth into.

He laughed dryly. "No, sorry to disappoint you. I was at a petting zoo in California, and one of the cats escaped. When I helped the owner corner it, the rotten creature paid me back. Never did have much luck with cats."

Duncan could feel Vicky quivering beneath him,

and he tried to work as fast as he could while answering questions he knew were meant to take their minds off their intimate position. It was working, too. Even now he felt his erection fading.

Trouble was, he knew the signs of an aroused woman, and Vicky was exhibiting them all. The shallower, rapid breathing, the faint trembles, the hitches in her voice as she talked. But he wasn't about to embarrass her by bringing it up. Although it occurred to him that by doing so she might forget about getting him to sign the claim, he knew he couldn't take advantage of her distress. She was simply too vulnerable right now. He wanted to protect and cherish her, not exploit her weak moment.

"You can roll away now," he said, giving the last obstruction a long toss.

With a sigh, Vicky turned onto her back, brushing against him one last time. He moaned involuntarily and could have kicked himself if it were possible in such close quarters.

Vicky's clenched eyes shot open. "This is so..."

"Embarrassing?"

She nodded, then shook her head.

"Degrading?" He hoped that wasn't it, and was gratified when she gave her head another shake.

"Surprising? Shocking?"

"Yes," she breathed out unevenly. "And...totally...well, totally inappropriate."

"Inappropriate!" Duncan's tension exploded in a burst of laughter.

"I wasn't being funny," she responded stiffly, taking her gaze away from him. "I was just pointing out that we're only business acquaintances and... well, this simply shouldn't have happened."

He liked her a heap of a lot better when she was more vulnerable, he thought, well past annoyed at her sudden boardroom manner. Sure, he was the one who'd reacted so visibly at first as men often do, but it wasn't his fault the damn roof collapsed. Without meaning to, he took her chin and lifted her eyes to meet his again. Her skin was smooth, damp and slightly heated, revealing clearly what she refused to admit.

"Are you saying you didn't feel anything?" he asked harshly.

A long silence followed, filled only by the sounds of the rescue team and their heightened breathing, but she didn't try to pull away or avoid his gaze.

"No," she finally replied softly, so softly he almost couldn't hear her above the digging noises. But he did hear, and he wanted to hear it again.

"No, what?" he pressed, unsure about why he needed to know.

"No. I can't say that."

The confusion, the pain, the need he saw in her cobalt eyes struck a responding chord inside him. What had happened between them had shattered her controlled self-image. She'd gone beyond control, and this was painfully obvious to the both of them. Not so apparent, however, was how this incident had shown him that Vicky wasn't a woman to be taken lightly. At least not by him.

Dear God, he'd known her less than a day. She'd put his life in jeopardy twice, not to mention she might well have caused the burial of the very trunk he'd come to Idaho Springs to save. She also threatened his reputation and the security of his family. But this, he sensed, was nothing compared to the dangers he'd face if he let himself get involved with her.

He stared into Vicky's distress-darkened eyes. Her lower lip trembled almost imperceptibly, calling out to him to kiss away her pain. Tempting, oh so dangerously tempting, and for one crazy second there, he almost succumbed.

Abruptly, he released his hold on her chin.

"Okay," he said curtly.

"Okay?"

"That's all I wanted to know. If you felt it, too."

"Why?" She sounded deeply puzzled, as well she should be.

"I'm not sure." He took a long, deep breath. "Relax now. The crew'll be here any minute."

Then he rolled onto his back and stared up at the wreckage that easily could have been their tomb.

"Look, Dr. Mulcahey," Vicky heard the site foreman say to Duncan. "I'd appreciate it if you didn't report this. It'd look bad to my boss, and since no one's hurt..."

When Duncan turned to ask Vicky if she was absolutely sure she had no injuries, she deliberately refused to return his gaze.

"No," she replied tersely, still digging through the rubble in search of the claims file she'd dropped during the plaster-and-lumber avalanche. Although Duncan had heatedly urged her to leave while the rescue party dug out the half-buried chest, Vicky refused. She needed to get Duncan to sign those forms now. Today. This very minute, if she could have made that possible.

She never wanted to see him again. Ever.

Then Duncan had his hands on her shoulders, coaxing her to her feet. "Give it up," he said gently. "The papers are buried too deep. You'll never find them."

"You'll go to any lengths to avoid signing that form, won't you?" she said. "Even if it takes bringing down the house."

"Are you suggesting—"

"A bad joke. Forget it."

"Come on," he said, leading her through the destruction toward the light of day. When they were finally outside, he took off his hard hat and squinted down at her through the bright sun. "You sure you aren't hurt? Why don't we go to an emergency room, anyway. Just in case."

"For the hundredth time, no."

"Vicky…" His tone was heavy with concern.

"Return this to the right people, would you?"

She pulled off her hard hat and handed it to him. "And thank them. I'm sure it saved my life." She turned to walk away. "I'll be in touch about the claim."

"I'm sure you will." He no longer sounded concerned, just bitter.

Vicky arched her neck to look at him. "None of this would have happened, you know, if you'd just signed the damned forms in the first place."

"Or if you'd just kept out of places you didn't belong."

Slowly she turned, about to give him a strong piece of her mind. But she couldn't help noticing his badly rumpled appearance. Dirt smeared his face. Plaster dust made his dark hair look almost gray. He held her in his gaze, which simmered darkly with something she couldn't quite identify. Definitely not anger, but what? Confusion? Pain?

He was right. It had been her actions, not his, that had caused the building's collapse. She gave her head a weary shake, suddenly glad he'd reached an agreement with the foreman about keeping this quiet. She didn't want this accident reported, either.

At the shake of her head, he broke eye contact. "Drive safely, Vicky."

Then he left her to watch his retreating back. She headed to her car, trying to decide if she should go back to work and print out yet a third set of forms. She and Duncan had been trapped for over two hours. The dashboard clock said it was now going on 4:00 p.m., and she was heading into rush hour. It would be tough making it in time.

As she turned the key, she caught a glimpse of herself in the rearview mirror. No, going to the office wasn't an option. If Duncan looked bad, she looked worse. So much dust was caked in her hair, it looked like mud, and more covered her face. Her torn blouse was just inches from being indecent, and though her heels had survived the blitz, her nylons hadn't.

Fortunately, she'd reported her trip to Idaho Springs and the reason for it to Ida when she'd stopped at the office earlier to print out a new set of forms. If she didn't get back before the office closed, it would be no surprise. A good example of the wisdom of following the rules.

As she was heading to Denver, she found herself remembering Duncan's expression. Had she really seen pain in his eyes? If so, she had no idea why. She was the one who'd been hurt. She'd thought he was about to kiss her after he'd wrenched that shameful admission from her mouth. She'd wanted him to do it, ached for him to do it.

But he hadn't. Instead he'd left her wondering if his whole purpose had been to humiliate her. If it had been, he'd done a damned good job of it. So what the hell did he have to be hurt about?

Why was she kidding herself? Duncan hadn't humiliated her. She'd done it to herself by admitting she'd been drawn to him. The man could be a thief, and she'd known it all along. Had she no common sense? No instinct of self-preservation? Was she turning into one of those pathetic women who were drawn to bad boys the way moths were drawn to the flame?

God help her. Please, no.

She didn't want to think about it anymore. Wouldn't think about it. She'd broken speed limits getting to Idaho Springs; she could just as easily break them on the way back. Slowing down only to avoid the speed traps in Golden, she made good time and managed to reach her house before rush-hour traffic got serious. She pulled her car into the garage of the neatly landscaped home she shared with her mother and opened a door leading to the kitchen, praying she'd arrived home first.

"My God, Vicky! What happened to you?" her mother wailed, jumping up from her chair at the kitchen table. "You look like you've been through a war zone."

"In a way I have," she replied wearily. "And I'm too tired to talk about it. I just want a bath."

"It's that job, isn't it?" her mother asked, distractedly smoothing Vicky's hair, touching a scrape, pulling at the ragged tear in her skirt as if to patch it together. "I knew it was too dangerous!"

Barbara Deidrich was a good mother in every way, but sometimes her concern just overwhelmed Vicky, and this was one of those times. Although her conscience twitched at the sight of her mother's fretful expression, she simply didn't have it in her to deal with it.

"Please," she begged. "I'll explain later."

To her abject relief, her mother heeded her request. I'll run your bath, honey. You get out of those filthy clothes." She sighed and plucked at the skirt again. "Your lovely Evan-Picone. That gray shade was so becoming to you."

"I can buy another."

Wearily, Vicky limped into the living room, unexpectedly repulsed by the beige-on-beige-on-beige decor. So safe, so suffocating, and it seemed to echo the prudent choices she'd made all her life—at least until that afternoon.

The consequences of which were still pounding on the doorway of her mind when she sank into the steaming bubble bath. Scrapes and scratches covered her arms and legs. Red spots hinted at bruises to come. Nothing major—thanks to Duncan's fast action—and they'd heal in a few days, but at the moment every inch of her body either stung or ached.

She ran her fingers across her lips. They also ached. For the kiss Duncan had all but promised. The realization brought up a fresh wave of shame.

Sneak by museum security, her boss had urged. Tell a white lie here and there if it gets you what you need. Maybe even a few, just a few, teensy-weeny black ones. Maybe steal an ID badge or an address list. Maybe meet a devilishly handsome man who was nothing more than an academic daredevil, and maybe a criminal to boot.

See where crossing the line got you?

Abject failure. Not only hadn't she taken in the signed claims form, she hadn't uncovered a smuggling ring, and would have to return to her office empty-handed on Monday, with a new lie on her lips because she hadn't reported the accident and wouldn't.

See where crossing the line got you?

Level-headed and steady, that was the way. Her mother had been right all along. So why did those solid values suddenly feel like chains?

Lord, she'd felt alive on that roof with Duncan's hand hot on her breast. And, later, pressed against him in that single-bed-size space before he'd moved the rubble, she'd felt agonizing ecstasy. Alive beyond being alive. And she'd wanted more from him. Much, much more.

All these wild emotions were taking Vicky to a place so scary, she wasn't sure she'd survive there.

See where crossing the line got you?

VICKY MANAGED TO PUT OFF imparting the details of her day all through dinner. Later, as she settled beside her mother on the beige couch, wrapped in her robe, she asked about the ski trip her mother was leaving for the next morning in hopes of keeping the conversation off herself.

"I'm thinking of canceling it."

"No, Mom. You planned this trip for months."

"But look at you."

Her mother's worried frown prompted Vicky to quickly reassure her. "I'm fine. Really. Just a little stiff. The bath fixed me right up."

"I've tried to give you time, Vicky, figuring you'd bring it up when you were ready. Won't you at least tell me what happened?"

So Vicky briefly relayed the afternoon events, playing down the danger and trying to skim over how Duncan's evasions had led her to the demolition site in the first place. But despite her alarm, Barbara was no dummy, and she read between the lines.

"Are you attracted to this man?"

"Attracted? Of course not!" Vicky bit her lip. She'd lied to many people today, but she couldn't make her mother one of them. "I mean...well, he has these deep electric-blue eyes, the kind that can get to a woman, and...he's very...male. Manly, if you know what I mean."

Barbara leaned back and sighed. "Unfortunately, I do. That's how I felt about your father. His death was the most horrible thing that ever happened to me." A thickening voice revealed that even after all these years she still felt the sorrow. "Sometimes I think my fear of losing you, too, made me overprotective. Maybe I should have let you make more of your own mistakes."

No news to Vicky, but she was surprised to hear this admission.

"You're a great mom," she said reassuringly, then followed it with a soft self-mocking laugh. "But maybe you're right. I'm pushing thirty. I have a good job. Someday I'm going to have to go out on my own."

Recently, she'd been making overtures about moving out, but her mother's thinly veiled heartache held her back, and she really hadn't intended to bring it up now. Not unexpectedly, Barbara failed to pick up the subject. Instead, she held Vicky's gaze for a second, then got up and walked to an entertainment unit where she slid aside a panel and turned on the television set. *Nash Bridges* would come on soon—her mother's favorite way to spend a Friday night.

Since the show wasn't on yet, she muted the volume, then sat down again. "Someday you will get your own place," she said, resuming the conversational thread as though it hadn't been dropped. "But I don't feel good about it." She patted Vicky's knee. "You have a wild streak, you know."

"A *wild* streak." Vicky burst into laughter, and when it died down she was happy to see her mother was smiling. "*Puh-leeze.* I'm in bed by eleven almost every night. I drive a tan Toyota, and the flashiest color in my wardrobe is maroon. How can you say I have a wild streak?"

"Those high heels you wear. Shoes show a woman's true nature."

Vicky laughed again. "You're a model of restraint, and you wear high heels, too."

"You don't know everything about me, honey. I once led a pretty risqué life."

Vicky looked at her mother skeptically. "You expect me to believe that?"

"Like you said, you're almost thirty. Old enough that such startling revelations shouldn't offend your sensibilities—wait, *Nash* is starting."

The opening gambit came on the screen, the volume was restored, and Barbara settled back on the sofa to watch her Friday night show. Almost absentmindedly she reached out, gave Vicky's hand a soft squeeze, then held on.

Vicky fidgeted, unable to get into the story line. She readjusted her robe, tucked her feet beneath her body, ran her fingers through her hair. Each time she moved, she felt the tug of her mother's hand around hers, but wasn't inclined to pull away.

Wild, huh? she thought, slanting a doubtful glance sideways. If so, what had squelched her mother's headstrong streak? The death of a daredevil husband, or her own fear of taking a leap into a new and unpredictable future?

And what about the wild streak she accused Vicky of having?

If she was right, then Vicky had no excuse for being so repressed. No tragedy, no lost love. Just an untested conviction that if her life ever got out of hand, she'd end up like her mother and spend the rest of her nights watching *Nash Bridges* or some other fictional program where the people lived the kind of life she'd scrupulously avoided.

And though she dearly loved her mother, this kind of life didn't begin to fulfill her nebulous dreams for her future. As she gave their safe and colorless living room another glance, an abhorrent realization struck her.

She already was like her mother.

If she didn't do something—and fast—her promotion would slip away. This would be her life forever more. And it was her fault it had come to this. She'd let the fear of public embarrassment keep her from returning to the office and filling out yet another set of claims forms. Ditto, for her failure to report what she'd discovered in Duncan's bungalow.

But it wasn't too late. Bridget had told her about the bachelor party, and it was a fair guess that Duncan would attend. Maybe that beckoning window was still open.

She'd do it. Yes, she would.

Suddenly she was filled with a sense of power, a certainty she could do anything. Even prove that the esteemed Dr. Duncan Mulcahey was in reality an artifacts smuggler, maybe even a thief.

Gently, she disengaged her hand from her mother's loving restraint.

"I have to go out again," she said.

At the look of protest crossing Barbara's face, she firmly added, "It's business, Mom. Please don't wait up. I'll probably be very late."

7

VICKY WORE BLACK. She hoped it would make her feel in control like the TV detectives played by Stephanie Powers, Stephanie Zimbalist or the wickedly glamorous woman who'd aided the David Niven character in the Pink Panther. Black jeans, black turtleneck, black leather gloves, even a black cap. She wished she'd taken the plunge last fall and purchased that black leather jacket, but since she hadn't, she slipped a heavy black sweater over the rest. Last, she buckled on a black waist bag and shoved a slim penlight and a small digital camera inside.

Now she hugged the shadows of the Mulcaheys' driveway, keeping close to the bushes and slinking toward Duncan's darkened cottage, feeling not at all in control. She prayed the devil-dog was safely locked away, and when nothing barked, she gave thanks for the answer. Still, her pulse raced.

What if Duncan hadn't gone to the party?

Of course he'd gone. He wouldn't let a few bruises keep him from his future brother-in-law's send-off, would he?

She didn't know for sure.

That's what risks are about, she told herself. Not knowing for sure. And, Lord, what an uncomfortable position to be in.

The window she'd been about to enter when Demon had scared her away was still open. Except for the yellow glow reaching over the house from a halogen streetlight, the area was quite dark. Perfect opportunity for her to enter unseen. Maybe. Or maybe not.

Well, it was now or never.

She took a deep breath and lifted the window even farther. Although her pulse beat faster than usual as she climbed in, she was much calmer than expected. Good heavens, was she truly breaking and entering? Shocking behavior, quite shocking, not to mention illegal. Shameful. Disgraceful.

So why was she so thrilled with herself, she could barely stand it?

THE BASH WAS NO MORE tedious than the usual bachelor party, Duncan thought. Located in the back room of a wood-and-brass-decorated eatery and bar, it was filled with every friend Roger had ever made. Booze flowed freely. Jokes and jibes were exchanged. Toasts were made. Fun. Fun. Fun.

Duncan yearned to go home. Already exhausted even before he'd started out that morning, he now also endured the screams of every scratch and bruise he'd received during the hellacious day. Furthermore, he was getting more than a little tired of the remarks. No, he'd batted back when asked about the scratch on his cheek, he hadn't spent the afternoon with a hot fox, just a grouchy kitten, scowling when the answer sparked guffaws.

Sometime after the toasts—or were they roasts?—Roger approached him, full of a bit too much beer and lots of sentimentality.

"I'm a really lucky guy," he told Duncan, draping a brotherly arm heavily over his sore shoulders. "Tomorrow morning I'm marrying an angel."

"Yeah, Meg's a great girl."

"Someday I hope you get as lucky as me," Roger continued, snatching yet another lager off the tray of a passing waitress. "I'll tell you, man, when you finally find the right woman..."

If Roger had been female, Duncan would have described his following sigh as dreamy. "Nothing compares to it."

"I'll bet."

"True fact," Roger said solemnly, leaning over to whisper conspiratorially into Duncan's ear. "This marriage thing's gotten a bad rap. I tell you, man, proposing to your sister is the best decision I ever made. You ever find a girl like her and you'll know what I mean."

"Hey, Roger," some guys near the door hollered, amusement in their voices. "Someone's here to see you."

A buxom storm trooper swaggered in, handcuffs

prominently displayed in her manicured hands, and soon had Roger secured to a chair amid a volley of lewd remarks. Seeing his opportunity to escape, Duncan dashed for the exit.

By the time he climbed into his MG, he ached to his bones with a weariness he knew didn't come from the battering to his body. No, it came from the battering his soul had taken when he'd foolishly contemplated kissing pretty Vicky Deidrich.

Roger's in-his-cups sentiments hadn't helped any, either. Duncan approved of Roger, liked him, actually, and thought he was great for Meg, but he could have done without the sales talk on wedded bliss. The angel thing had struck a discordant note, too. He vividly recalled how that very word had come to mind the first time he saw Vicky.

So Roger thought marriage was the best. Good for Roger, especially since he really was lucky to be getting Duncan's sister as a wife. But, on the other hand, what did an accountant have to lose? It wasn't as if Roger had put his career on the line for Meg, the way their younger brother had. By marrying Sophie, Michael had turned his back on a rising career as a musician.

Duncan rubbed the scratch on his face. Oddly enough, among all his cuts and bruises, the mark left by Puff-Puff's claws stung the worst. How deep those slender claws had cut, and the pain left in its wake reminded him of Vicky. She certainly was as tenacious as a feline, and had proved it by dogging him relentlessly about the insurance claim. What's more, his feelings for her were as tangled as a kitten's ball of yarn—a thread here, a thread there, and they all yanked at his heart.

As he pulled his car from the restaurant's parking lot, he remembered the devastation etching her face as she'd dug through the rubble for the lost folder. When he'd heard her mumble something about losing a promotion, he'd wanted to say, "Look, the dress will be back on Monday," just to make her smile again.

What if he just told her the truth?

The out-of-the-blue thought made him jump so sharply, his battered muscles cried out anew. What on God's earth ever made him consider such a thing?

But why not?

He didn't even know her, that's why not. The risks were just too great. It was enough that the discovery would cause considerable damage to his reputation, but even worse, his mother and sister could easily face prosecution.

There were few things a person could count on in this world, but Vicky's single-mindedness was undoubtedly one of them. No extenuating circumstances would stop Vicky from reporting a crime if she uncovered one, so if he couldn't produce that letter from Horace Whitfield he might just as well call the Lakewood Police Department and turn his mother in.

He was no stranger to risk. He really had wrestled a crocodile—a small one to be sure and not by choice—but he'd rolled around with it until his injured friend had been pulled to safety, then swam like hell to get away. And more than once he'd led a fleeing party away from unfriendly, possibly cannibalistic, natives.

As if to reassure himself, he took uncharacteristic satisfaction in the squeal of tires as he entered the highway with unnecessary speed.

How idiotic. But as he steered the wheels back in line, he decided maybe not, because his courage seemed to be deserting him lately. Never, ever, had he felt the numbing, life-in-jeopardy, heart-tripping, stomach-wrenching terror he'd experienced when he'd been tempted to kiss Vicky. And he knew it had more to do with things connected to his conversation with Roger than with fear of prosecution.

He loved his job. He'd climbed into the rarefied air of the Tibetan mountains and hiked into rain forests in South America, searching the earth for relics of the past. He'd seen evidence of civilizations where man's thought—if not his technology—surpassed the greatest ideas of this century. His work gave him a sense of man's continuity, and a humility born from knowing how insignificant modern man was in the whole scheme of things.

And that took traveling, which took bank-rolling, which had to come from somewhere besides his ample but not bulging bank account.

His thoughts returned to his brother.

Michael played a mean sax. Haunting notes that hung in the air long after the sound was gone. He could have made it big, very big. Then Sophie had come along and lured him into a traditional marriage. The suburban home, the children, the college fund, the IRA.

True, he seemed happy enough teaching music at a local high school, and he still played the occasional weekend gig. At times, especially since his daughter was born, he even seemed fulfilled. But from where Duncan sat, all he saw was that his little brother had traded his lifelong dream for the suburban dream.

Which was something *he* would never do.

Never. Not ever.

Until he'd met Vicky, no woman had even made him consider such a possibility, and he found it ironic that Meg's upcoming nuptials and his family's tradition about the wedding dress had brought them together in the first place. A turn of events that undoubtedly would please his mother very much.

He turned into his neighborhood, glad to finally be nearing home. But he had no intention of pulling into his driveway, where the sound of his engine would alert Meg that he'd jumped the bachelor-bash ship early. Instead, he parked the next block over, cut through the neighbor's yard to his back gate and entered his cottage through French doors that opened off his bedroom. None of the other rooms interested him, anyway. Wearily stripping off his clothes, he dropped them on the floor, then dove beneath the covers.

Just before he drifted off, he found himself wondering what Vicky would look like wearing that fragile, creamy lace? The image of her traffic-stopping body inside the formfitting gown instantly came to mind and took away his breath. Her golden cap of hair gleamed beneath a flowered veil, her blue eyes glittered. She came toward him, hands extended, smiling...

Then handed him a pen and a claims form, sweetly saying, "Go straight to jail, Dr. Mulcahey."

AFTER STEPPING OVER a large case probably filled with illegal gain, Vicky paused a second. All was quiet. Good. She took the penlight from her waist pack and snapped it on. The small beam came to rest on the scowling face of a bearded bronze warrior.

Asia Minor, second century B.C., she automatically cataloged, gratified to see how much she'd retained of her studies. The next item was a limestone Egyptian panel, probably from the fourth century. There were shelves and shelves of priceless specimens. These weren't undisclosed finds from an excavation; these were treasures that surely had been locked and guarded.

Her heart pounded with excitement. What kind of ring had she stumbled upon? This was big. Really big. A discovery of this proportion could give her a worldwide reputation before she'd even earned her title of insurance investigator.

Eager to uncover more incriminating evidence, she moved the flashlight to the next higher shelf. The beam revealed a clay bust of Saint Augustine, Flemish probably, and absolutely exquisite. Feeling awestruck in the presence of such rare beauty, Vicky hesitated. She badly wanted to hold it, touch it... She shouldn't....

But she might never get another chance. And she was wearing gloves. What harm could it do?

All right, then.

She picked it up, trailing the light over the precise detail, engrossed in its magnificence.

Suddenly the room was flooded with light.

"What the *hell* are you doing here?"

Letting out a small shriek, Vicky spun to face Duncan, who stood partly hidden in the shadowed hallway. Her fingers trembled, losing traction on the precious object in her hand. Squeaks of despair vibrated in her throat as she grappled to regain her hold on the slipping artifact.

Her attempts failed.

The fragile and irreplaceable bust of Saint Augustine crashed to the floor and shattered into dozens of flying pieces.

She fell to her knees amid the shards, sobbing, trying to gather them up.

"Oh, my God. I can't believe...look what... omigod, I can't—"

She snatched Saint Augustine's nose from the floor and tried to push it back into the center of his cracked face, but a gaping hole remained. The chin fit only marginally better. Although it seemed like an eternity passed, in truth it was only seconds before she realized the finality of what she'd done. Her sob broke into outright tears and she bent over the broken clay.

"I've destroyed it," she moaned. "It's priceless...priceless...and I destroyed it." Her moan escalated to a wail. "I killed Saint Augustine!"

"What are you doing here, Vicky?" Duncan asked mildly.

Vicky lifted her head and wiped the tears from her face. She'd made a total mess of things, and it was time to face the consequences. See where crossing the line gets you? she repeated to herself, vaguely noticing the odd upward tug at the corners of Duncan's mouth as he stepped through the doorway into the bright room.

Is this funny? she wanted to snap, but before the words left her mouth, she noticed Duncan's—

Lord, what the bright light revealed. A body reminiscent of the statues of gods that rested on the shelves above. Golden tan, sharply sculpted.

And he wasn't wearing a fig leaf.

"You're naked!"

His upward tug formed into a full smile, and a dry chuckle rumbled in his throat.

"Is this funny?" she finally asked aloud.

"In a twisted sort of way."

He moved closer and Vicky reflexively raised her arms. "No! No! Don't come any nearer!"

"Vicky," he said with obviously feigned patience, bending to pick up one of the saint's shattered ears and for a blessed second completely hiding the part of his anatomy that Vicky had scrupulously kept her eyes from. "This is *my* house. I'm the one who should be giving orders."

She turned her head. "At least put on some clothes."

He let out a long-suffering sigh, and she heard the rustle of heavy fabric. Shortly afterward he said, "You can look now."

It took an act of will to turn her head and check out his clothing status—mercifully, he'd wrapped himself in an Incan blanket—and another dry chuckle told her he realized how hard it had been for her to look. Her cheeks began to heat up.

I will not blush, she told herself. *Will not. Will not. Will not.*

"You're blushing, Vicky," Duncan said. "Haven't you ever seen a naked man before?"

"Of course I ha—" She shook her head. "Really, Duncan, that's none of your business!"

His amusement faded. "Look, Ms. Deidrich," he said harshly. "You're in my house in the middle of the night—'' he paused and gave her a scathing once-over ''—dressed like a cat burglar. I'm the one setting the rules here. Can you give me one good reason not to call the police?''

She gave her head a defiant toss. ''How about that your jig will be up?''

''My *jig?*''

''Yes. You know, your smuggling racket.''

Duncan slapped his palm against the side of his head, and as he let go of one side of the blanket— fifth century B.C., Vicky had concluded—it slipped. Her breath caught, only releasing when the blanket came to rest low on his hip. He had a sexy tan line, she noticed, then dismissed that thought and tossed her head again. ''You should be ashamed, Dr. Duncan Mulcahey,'' she said. ''A man in your trusted position betraying it to become a kingpin in stolen artifacts.''

He scowled as fiercely as the bronze warrior, and for the first time Vicky fully realized the precariousness of her situation. A man like that, a man who would smuggle priceless artifacts—what else might he do? Slit the throat of an inexperienced and obviously quite stupid insurance adjuster? Bury her body in the backyard? Or worse, take it high into the mountains where it wouldn't be discovered until the snow melted, causing her poor mother renewed agony and the realization of her worst fear? See where crossing the line got you?

Then the scowl burst into a true belly laugh. The antique blanket slid lower on his hips.

"Stop it!" she shrieked. "This is nothing to laugh about. If you're going to kill me, do it now!"

"K-k-kill you?" His laughter escalated, bringing tears to his eyes. "*Kill* you? Oh, Vicky, you're... one in a...million."

The blanket skidded farther down, revealing the angle of one muscular buttock. Vicky tore her gaze from the sight and glared at Duncan, then swept her arm in the direction of the shelves, following it with her eyes. "You can't deny it! There's the evidence!"

The minute she saw the shelves, she blinked hard. Then blinked again. Something was wrong up there. Something was very wrong.

Because at least half a dozen Saint Augustines smiled benignly down on her, every one of their magnificent faces in pristine condition.

8

"THEY'RE REPLICAS, VICKY. Very good ones, but still replicas."

"Not real," she murmured, picking up the nose-less, chinless visage of the saint. "Not real..." She lifted her head to look at Duncan, her eyes filled with a mixture of confusion and abject relief. "So I didn't shatter a national treasure?"

"No." He couldn't keep from smiling, despite her very real distress. After all, she'd brought it on herself. "Although you did cost me three hundred bucks of gross profit. How you'll make that up to me is something still open to discussion."

He walked over, leaned down and took her arm. "Come on, Vicky. It's time you told me what you're doing here."

She didn't resist as he lifted her to her feet, but when the blanket fell yet another notch, she murmured a panicked "Careful," and tried to lift it back in place. This brought her hand in contact with his bare hip, and her ensuing muffled gasp made Duncan chuckle again. If anything, Vicky was good for laughs, and he only wished he could dismiss her quite that easily.

When they reached his living room, Duncan gave her a gentle push into an easy chair, and stood above her. The time for fun and games was past. This pretty woman was about to unleash complete havoc on his family, his future. The way things stood, he suspected that even when the lace gown was returned Monday, she wouldn't give up on ferreting out the fishy details. He had to stop her, and her intense embarrassment over her enormous error was a good place to begin.

"Talk, Vicky," he said sternly. "I'm sure your superiors don't know about your unconventional investigative methods. Tell me what gave you this harebrained idea, and give me a reason not to call the cops."

Although her luscious lower lip, the one he'd so badly wanted to nibble that afternoon, quivered slightly, tempting him some more, she regained her infuriatingly businesslike composure.

"You have to admit your reluctance to sign the claim forms for the lost wedding dress looks suspicious. In fact—" she pointed an accusing finger at him "—if you ask me, this is all your fault."

Duncan wrapped the fake Incan blanket more tightly around him. It was made of itchy wool, and he wanted nothing more than to scratch himself. But despite his annoyance he had no desire to embarrass Vicky further. He sank onto the sofa and leaned forward. "Would you like to explain that last statement?"

"If you'd taken care of the claim immediately

after the dress was lost, I wouldn't have had any reason to come to your house..." Her hesitation made Duncan wonder if she was remembering all the events that followed her decision to pursue him. "And...*and* I wouldn't have seen the artifacts and concluded—well, wrongly concluded—that you'd smuggled them into the country."

"What I want to know is why it was so important that you get that claim signed off today? Do you realize what danger you put yourself in?" He leaned farther forward, anger suddenly brimming in his heart. "You almost fell off my roof, and we both could have died when that house collapsed. You are the rashest woman I've ever met. Reckless, even. You scare me, Vicky. What if I kept a gun here? I could have shot you!"

"Well, you didn't!" Her eyes widened. "Do you have a gun here?"

"No, but didn't that possibility ever occur to you?"

"I thought you'd be at the bachelor party."

"Where did you learn that?"

"Your mother mentioned it."

Duncan sighed. Where else? Hadn't Meg and his mother put him in a bad-enough position without giving information to a spy? An appealing little spy, too. In contrast to the stiff gray suit she'd worn this morning, the night-stalker jersey under the bulkier cardigan clearly displayed her round, high breasts and tapering waist. Skintight jeans hugged the curve of her hips and the long slim legs he'd already glimpsed. She'd pulled the silly black cap off her head, leaving her tawny hair all mussed, and she'd nervously chewed off her lipstick. Her moist and naked mouth just waited for his kiss.

He knew she wouldn't see it that way, and he bunched the scratchy blanket in his lap, concealing the aftermath of his mental inspection.

"Just tell me why, Vicky. Why today?" If he knew, maybe he could figure out a way to placate her over the weekend. Maybe he could put up a smoke screen so she wouldn't investigate anymore. Or maybe—crazily, insanely, absolutely deranged-ly—he simply wanted to know her better. "Is it about the promotion you mentioned at Idaho Springs?"

She hesitated. Clearly, she didn't want to talk about it. "Why do you care?"

"I just do." He reached toward the phone on the table between them and raised his eyebrows in warn-ing. "Your choice."

His eyes locked with the blue pools of hers, and a bolt of hot electricity passed between them for a long, long moment. The cottage was quiet, very quiet, except for the soft sound of their synchronized breathing.

"It is about the promotion," she finally said. "To investigator in the antiquities fraud division. I've been working toward this for several years. I've studied at the college, and stayed late at night, and done everything I knew to get to this position."

Another pause. Duncan waited.

"On Monday, Ida—that's my boss—told me that I lacked... She said I lacked initiative and daring," she blurted. "She told me to take more risks, and she used the missing wedding dress claim as an example of why she was right." The absolute agony in her eyes as she continued touched Duncan's heart. "She is right. The dress disappeared over six weeks ago, and I let you put me off over and over. No investigator worth their wages would do that!"

"Hey, I was out of the country most of that time, and, anyway, it's just a routine case."

"Which makes it worse! I should have closed the file, Duncan, and when Ida urged me to use any means possible to get it done by today, I took her at her word." She laughed bitterly. "It still took me all week to get to you."

Yeah, he thought, he'd made sure of that.

"I'm sorry, Vicky," he said with unwelcome sincerity. But even if he'd known what the claim meant to her, even now when she was a real person and not just a name on a pink message slip, he wouldn't have done anything differently. As infuriating as his sister and mother were, he'd do anything to protect them.

She nodded her acceptance of his apology, then after a hesitation said, "I know you're the one asking the questions, but would you please tell me why you keep running off without signing the claim?"

Duncan ran his fingers through his black hair. A nearly imperceptible hitch in Vicky's breath alerted him that his blanket had dropped again, and he

quickly lifted it back into place. He didn't like this
tension within him, a mixture of wanting to protect
her, wanting to have her and wanting to keep his
family safe. When his father passed away from a
heart attack nearly five years earlier, it had fallen to
him to watch out for the others. The Mulcaheys were
an independent bunch, and it hadn't actually been
that much of a burden, so he'd never resented it.
Until now.

"It wasn't intentional," he said, trying to devise
a credible reason on the fly. "I've been preoccupied
with running the museum—not a job I'm cut out
for—and also Meg's wedding. You showed up today just as I was heading out to Idaho Springs and,
well, Vicky, truth is I just got..."

"Distracted?" Her skepticism was obvious.

"Yes, distracted." Nope, that wouldn't do it. He
had to offer her something more. "But I promise to
check with the rest of the preservationists on Monday, first thing. And if I haven't found the dress by
early afternoon, you just come on down to the museum and I'll sign off on the claim."

"Really?"

"Really. I'll even backdate it to today if you'd
like."

He saw wheels turn behind her eyes. "Thanks,"
she finally said. "But I couldn't do that."

Why wasn't he surprised?

Her answer confirmed that he'd done the right
thing by keeping the truth from her, but for some
reason he also found her unequivocal honesty sexy.

He stirred again beneath the bunched-up blanket. To ease his discomfort, he stood up, tying the top ends of his makeshift garment over his shoulder to keep it from slipping again.

Reaching out, he took Vicky's hands and lifted her to her sneaker-clad feet. Without her heels she barely reached his shoulders, which made her seem small and defenseless, and the sheen covering her round blue eyes as she stared up at him only added to that impression. "Then it's settled. Monday afternoon."

"Okay," she said, nodding distractedly. After a brief pause, she said, "Can I ask you one other thing?"

He grinned, getting suspicious again. "Depends."

"Do you really think I'm rash and reckless?"

"You actually want an answer to that?"

She nodded.

"Yes, I do."

He wasn't sure what he expected, but the wide grin practically splitting her face wasn't it.

"I just insulted you. What are you smiling about?"

"Remember how I told you Ida said I lacked initiative and daring?" she replied, still grinning like mad. "Well, I can't think of anything more the opposite than being rash and reckless, can you?"

Duncan stared at her blankly.

"That means Ida is wrong, don't you see?"

"Yeah." He rubbed his chin reflectively, fascinated by her elation. "But maybe you could find

something in the middle before you kill yourself...or me.''

God, what beautiful eyes, and her jubilant mood
made them glitter like blue jewels.

He didn't mean to, truly he didn't, but it somehow
seemed choreographed. His head dipped forward
just as hers tilted back. And then he kissed her.
Light, feathery, savoring the feel of her soft mouth
against his own. She didn't protest. Instead she relaxed and slightly parted her lips, breathing out a
little sigh as she did. It was so sweet, tasting her.
Like drinking nectar from a morning glory, and he
wanted to drink longer, deeper.

She was willing, he'd bet, judging from the subtle
tremor he felt beneath his hand. But even if he ignored his better judgment that told him a woman
like Vicky was sheer danger, he couldn't follow
through with this lie between them.

He released her chin and looked into her lovely
eyes.

''You go on home now, pretty Ms. Vicky Deidrich. Rest easy over the weekend. I'll call you
Monday.''

She opened her mouth as if to protest, then shut
it, apparently seeing the wisdom in his decision.
''Monday,'' she said. ''No surprises.''

''None.''

She started to move back, then hesitated. A stubborn expression replaced her wistful look, and she
abruptly tapped his chest. ''You'd better be telling

the truth, Duncan. If you aren't, I won't rest until
you end up in court.''

Duncan swallowed his pained sigh. It seemed his
crazy vision wasn't quite so crazy, after all.

VICKY STARED AT the door Duncan had just closed
for a minute, then turned to press herself against the
shadows of the hedge and slink back up the driveway. It took all her will not to touch her well-kissed
lips.

Why hadn't she protested?

Why, indeed. Kissing him had been all she'd
thought about since that afternoon. Which was outrageous.

She halted a second to free a twig that had
snagged her sweater, telling herself that, okay, so
Duncan wasn't a thief. He was still covering up
something about that wedding dress, though. She
knew it in her heart. She freed the sweater and continued toward the street.

Yes, oh yes. Under the circumstances, she should
have protested the minute Duncan made his move.
Except...well, it had almost seemed beyond her
control.

She let out a scoffing sound that alarmed her so
much, she stopped to make sure no one had heard.
All looked quiet in the big house, and nothing indicated that anyone was coming to check on the
noise.

Light filtered through the lace curtains covering
the window facing the driveway. She pictured the

table she knew rested on the other side, saw it brimming over with lace party favors.

What was it like, she wondered, assembling favor packets with your mother, knowing the act signified a relationship forever changed?

And what was Meg doing now? Dreaming of her wedding the next day? Or was she even now trying on her wedding dress—possibly *the* wedding dress—one last time, handling that fragile lace with the extreme caution it demanded, careful not to pull a single thread? Was Meg picturing Roger's expression when he saw her walking up the aisle awash in antique lace? Did her heart pound with anticipation and perhaps a little apprehension?

Vicky's loud sigh startled her back to the present, and with it came a startling realization.

Meg Mulcahey really would be wearing the missing dress tomorrow. It was the only explanation for Duncan's odd behavior. What's more, Vicky had known it from the moment Bridget mentioned the wedding, but she'd been hiding it from herself.

Why? she asked, knowing she needed to start moving again, but oddly unable to do so. Why would she ignore so obvious a fact?

Because it was easier that way. Because she was nothing if not a romantic. Because, even though she'd only spent moments with Meg, she wanted her to have that storybook wedding.

What was that basketball term? No harm, no foul. It applied in this case. If the dress was returned undamaged, no one would have been hurt.

Under any other circumstances, Vicky might have kidded herself into ignoring the evidence of wrong-doing. But the intended bride's brother had just kissed her, and she feared he'd only been trying to woo her into looking the other way, a possibility full of misery. The rules had changed now, and she had to find out the truth.

Then what would she do? Report Duncan for theft? His mother and sister as accomplices? All because they'd wanted Meg to have the wedding of her dreams?

A sudden woof-woof-woof shocked Vicky to action. Demon! Lord, she hoped not. But this was no time to hang around musing about her course of action. Rejecting the protection of the grabby hedge, she broke into a soundless sprint and only moments later jumped behind the wheel of her car. And though she prayed no one would report seeing some-one dressed like a cat burglar racing down their street, she still took time to rummage in her glove compartment.

She had put the invitation there just this morning, never dreaming she'd use it. Now it was her key to the truth.

9

VICKY SPENT ALL DAY Saturday wallowing in indecision. No, she wouldn't go, she told herself as she saw her mother off to Lake Tahoe, trying not to put too much stock in the hurt look caused by her failure to reveal the details of her late-night excursion.

Indecision was still with her even after she'd decided she would go to the wedding and had unaccountably driven to the nearest mall to buy a dress as if the night were a big occasion. Once she got home and pulled the protective covering off her purchase, she knew for sure she wouldn't go. What had possessed her to buy this spaghetti-strap dress? That short flirty skirt was almost indecent. The impulsively chosen matching purse was worse. She never wore red. It was flashy and impractical. What's more, etiquette decreed a woman should never dress for a wedding in a way that competed with the bride.

No, absolutely not, she wouldn't go!

This decided, she sank into a bubble bath. Afterward, she took special care with her makeup and hair. Next, to her dismayed surprise, she slipped on the slinky dress, got into her highest dressy heels, then picked up her coat and handbag and got into her sensible Toyota.

What was she doing here? she wondered, as she hunted for a place to park in Saint Bernadette's already crowded parking lot. No answer came as she entered an open spot beside a large van she hoped would hide her car from Duncan. She hadn't seen his Jeep, but that didn't mean he hadn't arrived in another vehicle. And even if she wasn't sure why she was here, she did know she didn't want him to become aware of her presence.

The sun was beginning to set as Vicky nervously entered the church. The engraved invitation stated that it must be presented for entrance, so she held it and the red purse tightly in her damp hand, wishing she'd had the sense to stay away.

But she was here now. The only thing left to do was to hide her inappropriate ensemble under her black dress coat and sit discreetly in the back of the church, quiet as the proverbial church mouse, and gather her information. If Meg didn't appear in the antique gown, then Vicky would disappear into the crowd after the ceremony, assured of Duncan's truthfulness.

There was a line in the vestibule leading to the sanctuary, probably caused by the need to present the invitations. Why had the Mulcaheys imposed this requirement? Possibly in fear of gate-crashers because of Duncan's modest celebrity? But then again... Maybe he didn't want reporters photographing the gown.

What if her intuition was right? What if Meg did come down the aisle wearing the gown? What then?

A fresh wave of indecision grabbed her. Ignore it. No, yes, no. Turn them all in. Yes, no, yes. No. Her head was beginning to ache from the thoughts boomeranging in her mind.

All this was going on while she simultaneously kept an eye out for Duncan. Regardless of what she found, she didn't want him knowing she was here. With the size of the crowd, that wasn't likely to be a problem.

The reassurance wasn't helpful, and she clutched the invitation and her handbag close to her body. Nervously pressing the lapels of her camouflaging coat together, she looked to one side, then the other. She looked behind her, she looked in front of her. All while she moved with the crowd waiting to be seated.

She was checking over her shoulder one more time when a melodious male voice asked, "Bride's side or groom's side?"

Vicky turned and met a pair of electric-blue eyes.

"WHAT ARE YOU DOING HERE?" Duncan demanded sharply, ignoring the puzzled faces of the couple waiting behind her.

"Don't be rude," she said sotto voce, peeling

what looked like an invitation off the bright red handbag in her hands. "I was invited."

In his agitation, he practically ripped the envelope from her hand, then opened it and inspected the contents thoroughly before handing it back to her.

"It doesn't have your name on it. Where'd you get it? Did you steal it?"

"S-s-steal!" She glanced back quickly. "Duncan, please. People are, well, they're..."

A murmur Duncan had failed to notice until now passed through the line behind Vicky. In the vestibule, his mother chatted pleasantly with waiting guests. She looked every inch the formidable matriarch in her brocade suit, with her auburn curls tamed into an elegant upsweep, but she betrayed the image by winking at Duncan. Next, she gestured toward Vicky, and in a voice that was meant to carry said, "She's a special friend of Duncan's. Isn't she lovely? She'll be sitting with the family, she will."

A relieved sigh passed through the crowd. The couple just behind Vicky smiled.

"Everyone's waiting, Duncan. Would you please seat me?"

Since he had little choice, he stiffly led her to the aisle where his mother had not so subtly instructed him to seat her.

She hesitated at the end of the row. "I can't sit here."

"You heard my mother," Duncan replied. "You're to sit with the family. And if that invitation's a fake, you'll be hearing from her again. Real soon.''

"Get lost," she mouthed, a clearly false smile pasted on her face. Then she moved down the row, claiming a place near the outside, where she sat up exceedingly straight and held the incongruous red purse primly on her lap.

What was she doing here?

One person knew.

He charged back up the aisle, pausing only long enough to turn over his temporary usher duties, and went to find his mother.

She was chatting with another group of guests. Duncan manufactured a problem with the caterer and excused them both, then swept her into a somewhat secluded alcove.

"What are you doing?" he demanded. "When Vicky sees that gown, we'll all be dragged before the magistrate."

"You're working yourself up over nothing. I'm sure when you tell Vicky the truth, she wouldn't dream of turning us in. Besides, it's not good to keep a secret from your future wife."

"My fut—look, Mom, the only part Vicky's going to play in my future is sending me to jail. And maybe you and Meg, too."

"I'll be putting my faith in human nature today, Duncan, and you should do the same. This is your sister's wedding day. The saints wouldn't be letting anything bad come of it. At least, nothing worse than the flowers being late.''

Just then a woman Duncan recognized as the church's wedding coordinator came forward. ''Time for family pictures,'' she said cheerily.

''We're coming.'' With a look that told him the conversation was over for now, his mother gestured for him to follow, grumbling all the while about how upset Meg was that the bouquets hadn't arrived yet.

As he posed with his family for Meg's wedding album, Duncan again asked himself why he was so shaken. He was a legend, for crying out loud. True, the stories of his dauntless courage had been blown way out of proportion, but they contained enough truth that he shouldn't be quaking because of three lovely women.

Flashbulbs went off repeatedly, blinding him each time they popped, and making Michael and Sophie's baby cry. Meg told Shawn to stop making funny faces. The photographer told a bad joke. Shawn said he didn't get it, while all the adults forced a laugh.

Except Duncan. He couldn't have forced so much as a chuckle if his life depended on it. If he'd been shaken when the photo session started, it was nothing compared to how he felt now. Because with the last blinding flash of the camera, he realized exactly what scared him so much.

When Meg walked down that aisle, Vicky would know he'd lied to her. Although she'd be wounded by his deception, it went well beyond that. His lies would destroy the tiny degree of trust they'd built between them the night before.

So why should he care? She was a woman working for an insurance company, a business acquaintance, an adversary, even. She'd live. Her life wouldn't be ruined forever.

No, but his might. Because at this very moment, with circles left by the photographer's camera still dancing before his eyes, Duncan realized that sometime during the previous crazy day, he'd fallen in love with pretty Vicky Deidrich.

VICKY STOOD UP AS MEG floated down the aisle on Duncan's elbow. A lump formed in her throat and she wasn't sure why. Maybe it was because the antique gown was even more stunning than she'd envisioned and Meg looked like an angel in it. Or maybe it was because she now had proof Duncan had deceived her.

He had his reasons, of course. He'd lied to protect his family, risking his hard-won reputation in the process, and his sister was having a once-in-a-lifetime dream wedding as the result. An old-fashioned, chivalrous act, she supposed.

This confirmation still hurt like hell.

And it put her in an agonizing position. She knew her job. She knew what the law said. She'd studied it long enough. Come Monday she had no choice but to abide by it.

Duncan presented Meg at the altar. She glowed

as she ascended the stairs, miles of lace billowing behind her. *Look at her,* Vicky said to herself. *Look at the dreamy gaze she's giving Roger.* It was enough to make a woman cry.

She dabbed at her eyes with a tissue that suddenly materialized in her hand, then turned to see Duncan's mother smiling fondly. How she'd ended up seated beside the mother of the bride was beyond her, but she did know Bridget was a nice woman. Too nice to be charged with a crime.

As Meg and Roger exchanged the personal vows they'd written themselves, Vicky sniffled and the tissue again made its way to her eyes. Weddings were so beautiful. Especially Valentine's Day weddings where the bride wore a gown crafted from handmade antique lace.

What had Ida said about bending the rules? Vicky sniffled again, knowing very well what Ida had said, then returned her attention to the unfolding pageantry on the altar.

SINCE SHE WAS SEATED with the bride's family, Vicky left the chapel right behind the wedding party. The ensemble traveled to the reception hall along with the family, where she knew they would form a reception line.

A very long, very time-consuming, reception line. At least this was Vicky's hope as she sidled toward the exit. Indecision was becoming her middle name. At one point, she firmly decided to keep her knowledge to herself. The dress would be returned. Meg's fairy-tale wedding had come true. No reason to mention what she'd seen this evening.

But as the ceremony had wound down, she'd remembered her fiduciary responsibility to Global Fidelity, and by default to the Whitfield Museum. Good intentions aside, Duncan had removed museum property without permission and subjected it to the possibility of damage. Could this go unreported?

Well, she still had a long, quiet day ahead of her where she'd have the house to herself, which gave her plenty of time to think about it. If she just didn't have this sinking feeling that she wouldn't be any closer to a decision by the time her mom got back from her ski trip.

For now, though, escape was just ahead, and she tightened her coat around her, preparing for the chill of night air.

Suddenly she felt something poking into her back.

"Freeze!" a young voice said.

Vicky looked over her shoulder and saw Shawn grinning at her. "Mom says I should make sure you don't leave," he explained. "Did I do good?"

Engaging grin, Vicky thought. Despite the missing tooth, the kid sure did look like a miniature of his older brother. She couldn't help smiling back. "I'm still here, aren't I? But I can't stay. Would you just tell your mother I had to leave?"

"I'll get into trouble."

This was blackmail, pure and simple. She was about to tell him so when footsteps sounded behind her.

"Thanks, Shawn," Duncan said. "I'll take it from here."

"Sure thing." But Shawn stayed where he was, looking at them with open curiosity.

"Alone," Duncan added.

"Oh, right." Shawn scuttled back slowly. Duncan continued staring at him. In a few seconds, the boy gave up the game and headed off toward the reception hall.

Vicky's heart had been pounding too hard for her to appreciate the obvious humor in the situation, and it still pounded when Duncan turned back to her.

Aiming for offhand sophistication, she asked, "You here to accuse me of more forgery or theft?"

Her squeaky delivery told her she'd failed.

Duncan regarded her for a long moment, giving Vicky time to take in his appearance. He wore a tuxedo and had slicked back his dark collar-length hair, but it did nothing to mute his blatant virility. Even the dark shadows under his eyes seemed designed to point out their compelling color. If anything, he was more handsome than ever.

"You ever going to take off that coat?"

She stiffened at the idea of him seeing the dress. "I'm not staying that long."

"You started it, Vicky." A muscle throbbed visibly in his jaw as he took hold of the lapel of her coat. "Aren't you going to hang around and finish it?"

People were still milling in the vestibule, and to avoid a scene, Vicky gave a half turn and let him slide the coat off. As she circled back in time to see him folding the coat over his arm, she heard him catch his breath. His azure eyes suddenly held the terrorized look of a deer caught in a headlight beam.

"That's, uh, that's quite a dress."

Vicky's stiffness vanished. She felt a smile explode on her face. The muscle in Duncan's jaw relaxed, his wide grin mirrored hers, and he blurted out, "I'm sorry I lied to you."

"I know." And as she took in his contrite expression, she wanted to tell him it was all okay. But such an answer didn't feel right to her. Not yet. She looked around, checking to see how many were still in the vestibule. A couple walked hand in hand toward the reception hall, and a woman entered the sanctuary. Other than that they were alone.

"It might help if you'd tell me why you took something that wasn't yours in the first place," she said.

"Because it does belong to me."

Vicky felt the shock like a punch, which Duncan must have noticed because he added, "Well, it belongs to my family. My grandmother donated the dress to Horace just after my mom married my dad. He gave us a letter guaranteeing we could borrow it back for every Mulcahey wedding."

"Then why didn't you simply go through channels and present the letter?"

A pained expression crossed his face. "I lost it."

Vicky leaned forward. "You, uh..."

"Lost it. That's what I said."

"How?"

He waved his hands. "I don't know. But with Horace dead, and Calwood taking over, and all the trips I had scheduled—well, I figured the easiest solution was to just take the damn dress without asking."

"And report it lost in transit?" Vicky asked, more troubled by that aspect of his story than any other.

"I didn't. When the staff started putting up the Valentine's Day exhibit, they discovered it was missing. Someone submitted the claim while I was in Tibet." He regarded her levelly, as if emphasizing the importance of what he was about to say next. "What you need to know is that I took the dress, and I manufactured the order to send it out, as well as the delivery pickup request. I acted on my own, knowing full well what I was doing. If any charges have to be leveled...well, I'm your man."

"It's no good heaping lies upon lies, Duncan Mulcahey."

It was Bridget Mulcahey's unmistakable brogue. And the woman approached with equally unmistakable determination on her face. "I won't be letting you take the rap for me, son."

"Don't, Mom!"

As if her son hadn't spoken, Bridget turned toward Vicky. "I took the dress."

Duncan groaned.

"You?" Vicky hardly believed her ears.

"Meg's wedding was approaching fast, and Duncan wasn't getting to it quick enough and... Well, my husband used to say I was a hothead. Proved him right, I guess."

"It's not true, Vicky," Duncan protested. "It was me, not her."

"Shush, Duncan. You weren't even in the country when I did the deed." Bridget stuck out her hands. "Handcuff me if you must, but don't be ruining my boy's career because of my foolishness."

Vicky smiled from the incredulousness of it all. "Do you really think I'd handcuff you—" she shook her tiny red bag "—even if I had some in here?"

Bridget grinned as if she'd been caught with her hand in the cookie jar. "I kind of hoped you wouldn't. That mean I can return to my guests?"

Vicky nodded. "For now. But I might need to talk to you later, so stay in town."

"That I will. All's well that ends well, I always say, and now that you two have patched up your lovers' quarrel, I can see it'll only be getting better and better."

That said, Bridget spun around and bustled back to her wedding guests.

"Lovers' quarrel?" Vicky lifted an eyebrow at Duncan.

"Mom suffers from delusions," he answered. "That much must be painfully clear." The corners of his mouth strained to rise despite his efforts to hold them down. He quickly lost the battle. With a smile on his face, he extended the arm that didn't hold her coat and with mock formality said, "I believe we're expected at a wedding reception."

10

DUNCAN'S PLACE-MARKED SEAT at the bridal party table remained conspicuously empty, and it seemed just as conspicuous to Vicky that no one was sent to look for him.

He'd snagged a pair of chairs at another table, draping her coat over the back of hers, then went off for some wedding champagne. He returned with two flutes. Handing her one, he then lifted his in a toast. "To happy endings."

"And a fine paraphrase of your mother's words, it is," Vicky replied playfully as the crystal clinked.

The band started playing, signaling the wedding waltz. Guests gathered on the perimeter of the floor, waiting for the couple to appear, and their turned backs gave Vicky and Duncan the illusion of privacy.

"So it's certain?" she asked. "On Monday, the gown will show up at some obscure preservationist's?"

"A sure thing."

Vicky took another sip of champagne. "Then I'll

give thorough consideration to reporting that the claim was dropped.''

''No investigation? No charges?''

''None. I never had any interest in dragging your mother to court. Just you.'' She winked at him, a bit startled by her own bold behavior. ''I think you might look good in prison stripes.''

His rich laughter held as much relief as amusement, and they both basked in the sound for a moment. Her decision had clearly lifted a weight from his shoulders, and though she still wasn't quite sure she'd made the right one, it felt good.

He put down the glass and took her hand, holding on to it with both of his. The silence should have been uncomfortable, but Vicky didn't give it a thought because she was lost in Duncan's eyes and the electric energy running from her head to her toes. She could have stayed that way forever.

But it was not to be. Duncan stood, giving her hand a gentle tug. ''Come on. Let's go watch Meg and Roger dance.''

She set down her glass and rose to join him, hoping her disappointment didn't show. ''It's nice to see you so interested in your sister's happiness.''

''Well, yeah, but that's not my real reason. I want to make sure she takes the gown off afterward.''

''Duncan! You really aren't going to make her change before the reception's over, are you?''

He checked quickly for eavesdroppers. ''Hey, it's stolen property, remember? Even if it weren't, the gown's three hundred years old and held together with a promise. Wouldn't take much to make it disintegrate. You've studied antiques. Can you imagine what would happen if Meg spilled champagne on that fragile lace?''

I'd never get to wear it. Vicky shuddered, both from anticipating the damage and from shock at her inappropriate thought. But Duncan had succeeded in making her see his point.

She accompanied him to the dance floor where they squeezed through a hole and watched the couple dance. Again, Vicky was awed by the exquisite grace of the gown. The lace almost took on a life of its own as Roger and Meg glided around the room.

When the waltz ended, Duncan took a few steps onto the dance floor, raising his arm to catch Meg's attention. On seeing him, she grimaced ruefully, then gave a crisp salute against her tiara.

Duncan grinned. She grinned back, then whispered something to Roger and headed for the exit from the reception hall.

''Assignment complete,'' Duncan said.

Guests milled about. Some returned to their tables, some headed for the buffet. Still others remained standing, waiting for a new song to begin. Soon the melody of ''The Rose'' filled the hall.

''Dance with me,'' Duncan said, his voice oddly husky.

She nodded, and soundlessly moved into his waiting arms as a vocalist launched into the words. Duncan wrapped a strong arm around Vicky's waist and guided her across the room, the heat of his fingers warming her skin through the flimsy fabric of her dress.

Like everything else he did, it seemed, Duncan was an excellent dancer. He led her with such firm and subtle pressure, it felt as if they were floating. There was no other word for it, because she was certain her feet weren't touching the floor. Each dip and sway brought their bodies in faint but delicious contact. The singer sounded like an angel entertaining them from on high.

Vicky must have entered heaven when she'd stepped into Duncan's arms, she was sure of it, and she forced herself not to think about how far she now could fall.

Take more risks. Take more risks. The words thrummed inside her head in harmony with the song, alerting her that she was about to take the biggest risk of her life. *Oh, Ida,* she wailed inside, *I don't think this is what you meant.*

God help her, she was falling in love with Duncan.

"I'LL BE BACK AS SOON as I get the dress."

Duncan disappeared into a hallway leading to the bride's dressing room, while Vicky waited in the vestibule. She moved around a corner into an area somewhat sheltered from view so she could lean against the wall and slip off one of her strappy, spike-heeled sandals. While she massaged her aching arch, she thought of what her mother had said. Did impractical shoes truly reveal a wild streak? She giggled as she stepped back into the shoe. She might very well find out for sure that very night.

Just as she lifted her other foot to give it similar treatment, a man barreled around the corner, brushing her hard enough that she almost lost her balance.

"Excuse me," she said, wondering not for the first time why she had a habit of apologizing for something that was clearly the other party's fault. He looked at her indifferently, giving her a brief and nondescript impression. Hatchet nose, an oddly shaped birthmark on his jaw. Not an ugly man, but not handsome, either. And apparently he hadn't heard her apology, because he kept on moving without responding, head bowed, clearly in a hurry to get the package he carried to God-knew-where.

His appearance and manner evoked a brief sense of déjà vu that Vicky immediately dismissed. He probably worked for the caterer or photographer, or she'd seen him during the reception.

Soon after, Duncan returned with a large white carton. "Best archival box money can buy."

Vicky giggled again. The naughtiness of their harmless deception now seemed exciting, though she was well aware that even that morning such indifference to the rules would have seemed unthinkable.

"Come on," he urged. "Let's get out of here."

With yet another giggle, Vicky gathered her light-weight dress coat against the cold and hurried with Duncan to his car.

"I LOVE YOU IN THAT DRESS," Duncan murmured, helping Vicky out of her black coat for the second time that evening. He grinned. "You look... wanton."

"Wanton?" she countered with a husky laugh. "I don't want to disappoint you, but—" The laugh died in her throat as she caught Duncan's smoky look. "Well, maybe I could give it a whirl."

"I hoped you'd say that." He tossed her coat carelessly on his sofa, then turned back and cupped her face with his hands.

"Kiss me again, pretty Vicky Deidrich."

Vicky tilted her head back. She'd slipped out of her shoes the moment they stepped inside Duncan's cottage, taking away four inches and leaving her at the mercy of Duncan's considerable height. But rising on tiptoes to meet the challenge, she put her mouth on his.

Her sigh came from her heart, rising with an ache she didn't understand. Or maybe she did. This man ignited something hot and dark in her, something beyond mere sexual need. Until now, she hadn't realized she'd felt half a person or that the other half resided inside him. She wanted to be closer to him, burned to get closer, to give herself over to him, while at the same time reclaiming the rest of who she was.

"Oh, Vicky..." He'd heard the throb in her sigh, knew his own whispered plea held an echoing ache. She felt so slender, so fragile in his arms, and he wanted her with a desperation he'd never before known. They were going to make love, no doubt about it. Sexual hunger pulsed between them like a voracious tiger. And so did their unspoken doubts.

Even as she parted her lips to accept his exploring tongue, even as a half-expressed whimper vibrated in her throat, he felt her hesitation. He didn't know where it came from, or why, but it mirrored his own so perfectly, he felt as though he'd found his own reflection.

In his arms was a woman who represented everything he feared. Saints above, a woman his mother approved of, one she'd possibly picked out for him.

Love, honor and cherish. He'd heard those words just that night.

Vicky stirred, slid her arms between his hands and clasped them around his neck, deepening their kiss. She nibbled greedily at him now, the whimpers growing audible, and the silky red dress rustled softly, mingling with the whimpers into a tantalizing song.

This was a woman a man loved, honored and cherished. Married. Had babies with. She deserved that even though she showed no outward sign she was seeking it. And if they made love, he'd want to give it to her as sure as the sun would rise the next morning. He should stop this right now, let her go and send her sweet little red-clad figure out that door.

He dropped his hands from her face, preparing to release her. A moan escaped her lips; her hands dug deep into his hair, entwining with the strands.

Against his own volition, Duncan picked up the sliplike strap of her dress, slid it over her shoulder and down her arm.

"Oh, Vicky," he whispered hoarsely. "Oh, Vicky."

The sound waves of Duncan's voice vibrated like thousands of needles of delight against Vicky's mouth, and the soft fabric of her dress caused screaming tingles in her arm and breast as Duncan slowly pulled it down. She shuddered with wanting, savoring sensations so intense, she also wanted to pull away.

Was this what happened when you found the perfect one? she wondered dizzily. Was this sense of inevitability, this headlong rush into a mating that couldn't be stopped what love was all about?

"No, no, no," she mewed as he broke their kiss. Then his lips touched her arched neck and she let it fall back, relaxing into the support of his other hand.

Or was this merely lust? a marginally detached part of her mind inquired. A primal, hormonal hunger that civilization had struggled for aeons to bring under control? Was that it? Was love simply a matter of estrogen and testosterone?

She had to learn for herself. If that meant being "rash and reckless," if that meant discovering she had the "wild streak" her mother had declared was inside her, she would take this risk with Duncan and find out. To do otherwise was to let her heart wither away, unripened, unplucked...unloved.

Duncan's lips moved relentlessly down her neck, slowly, leisurely. She arched her body, offering it to him without reserve. Finally, unbearably, deliciously, his mouth traversed the mound of her breast until it came to close over her hard and aching nipple.

All detachment exploded into exquisite sensations.

"Vicky," he murmured once more, tracing his tongue over the pebbled surface, tightening then releasing, tightening then releasing.

She was squirming now, pushing her hips sweetly against him and driving him totally mad. He'd been trying to hold back, to prolong the sensory smorgasbord of kissing and stroking, but her swiveling torso ignited him, and he sprang fully alive. His hardness met her softness, and the quickening of her hungry movements told Duncan his arousal had increased hers. She lifted one leg, draping it over his hip and pushing as hard as possible from that precarious position. Her soft, hungry sounds sent his mind reeling, and the growing intensity of her response would soon send him over the edge, beyond control.

"Vicky," he said, trying to warn her, wanting to warn her, yet so beyond that now, almost unable to hold back.

Abruptly, she arched her spine and looked at him, trusting him to keep her from falling. Her pupils were so dilated, her eyes almost looked black, and her lips were round and moist, begging to be kissed again.

"Take me now, Duncan," she breathed. "Now, please."

With a low growl, Duncan pulled her against him, then lifted her remaining leg with his other arm. Although almost beyond such caution, he inched back carefully so as not to fall and sank onto his overstuffed couch, bringing Vicky down to rest with her legs straddling his hips.

Who would have guessed this prim kitten would be such a tiger? he thought. And then thought escaped him. Panty hose and a satiny thong bikini were no barrier to their unleashed passion. Writhing with denied hunger, they were like a starving couple at a banquet, and when Duncan entered Vicky, large and full and almost afraid he'd hurt her, she sheathed him completely, taking him inside her as though to fill up some empty place.

Duncan had never realized how alone he'd felt until Vicky rose and lowered upon him, completing him physically, emotionally and, inexplicably, spiritually. When finally their joining caused her to shatter atop him, filled with shudders and moans and pleasure cries, he knew that no matter what Vicky Deidrich might expect from him, he, Duncan Mulcahey, would want to give her the same completion. And much, much more.

Then his own pleasure exploded inside her still-quivering body, and he realized he could never give her enough to match what she gave him.

"MMM..." VICKY STRETCHED like a cat, luxuriating in the feel of her satiated body. The pleasure of being so close to Duncan moved her to touch him everywhere, and she succumbed fully to that impulse.

"My thoughts exactly," he said, putting a feather kiss on the tip of her chin. "Where have you been all my life, pretty Ms. Vicky Deidrich of Global Fidelity Mutual Insurance Company?"

Waiting for you. I just didn't know it. But she kept that answer to herself. Snuggling against his now-bare shoulder, she said breezily, "Adjusting claims, sir. And now that you bring it up..."

"Hey," he said half-jokingly, "that's not where I was going with this."

She returned the favor of the chin kiss, then tucked her head back on his shoulder. "But I want to know more about the gown. Things like, exactly what permissions did the letter grant you?"

He sighed. "After what you told me last night, I'm very aware of how much your job means to you,

Vicky. I know the sacrifice you're making, and I'd tell you not to do it except—"

"Your mother would be in deep water."

"Exactly."

"I'd feel a lot easier about this if I understood why you didn't at least try to go through proper channels. For heaven's sake, Duncan, you're the acquisitions director, not to mention the acting director of the museum. Couldn't you have done this legally?"

Duncan laughed. "Wait until you get to know my mother better." He grabbed her around the waist, lifted her up to sit on his lap. "Get comfy. It's a long story."

She settled against his chest, running a hand down his arm as he stroked her hair with his other hand. "The lace gown is a Mulcahey family heirloom made by my great-great-great—hell, who knows how great?—grandmother. It dates back to the seventeenth century," he began. "Since then, every Mulcahey bride—daughters and daughters-in-law alike—has worn the dress at her wedding.

"The trouble started twenty years or so ago when my grandmother decided to donate the wedding dress to the Whitfield Museum. Horace Whitfield, the original owner, was an old family friend, you see. Some suspected Nana and Horace were having a thing after their spouses died....

"Anyway, my mother threw a fit, but it didn't do

any good. However, she did manage to make Nana get something in writing.''

He went on to tell her about the letter he'd kept over the years, but hadn't given much thought to, because as long as Horace owned the museum, it was only a formality.

''Nana died about four years ago, and Horace passed away last summer. His kids wanted nothing to do with the museum, and they sold it to Calwood Entertainment. Just about the time Meg and Roger got engaged.''

Duncan paused and buried his hands in his hair. ''I hate this gel gook,'' he groused, interrupting the story to brush it out with his fingers.

''Duncan,'' Vicky said, growing fascinated with the story about a gown worn by a whole family of women. What continuity. What romance.

''Hell,'' he said. ''It's all my fault, anyway. I kept putting off submitting a request. The museum got sold almost as soon as Horace died, and new management came in. I had several very important excursions booked, Tibet and Peru. Alistair showed up—''

''Alistair?''

''My archrival,'' he joked. ''But that's not important. Anyway, I finally got around to looking for the letter about Christmastime.'' He blew out a breath. ''I looked everywhere, even under my computer, but that damn letter was nowhere to be found and the wedding date was getting closer and closer.

I considered asking permission without it. But the change in management had made everyone tense, and I was waiting for a window of opportunity. Then I left for Tibet. When I got back, the dress was gone.''

''That's when your mom took it.''

''Uh-huh,'' he replied grimly. ''And made my life a living hell, too. Seemed while I was out of the country, she got impatient. She called and talked to somebody about the dress, and got a very insulting response. Whoever it was told her they didn't lend museum property to peasants.''

Vicky cringed. She didn't know Bridget well, but she'd have guessed that didn't set very well with her. ''Who'd she talk to?''

''I don't know. Someone in Administration. A man. She was so upset, she hung up before she got a name. Instead, she sneaked into the museum that very night and just took the gown without permission.''

''How did she get past security?''

He arched his neck to look at her. ''Yes, indeed. You *do* work for an insurance company.''

Vicky laughed. ''And the very same one that insures your exhibits. I have a feeling my management wouldn't like this breach.''

''True. But it's not as bad as it sounds. All the guards know Mom. When she told them I'd forgotten some notes and wanted her to mail them to me, they let her in without question. Then she just packed up that dress and walked out with it.

"If our staff hadn't decided to use the gown in the Valentine's Day costume exhibit, we would have returned it before it was even missed. But its 'disappearance' forced me to do some fancy footwork." He laughed out loud. "I got away with it, too. At least until you showed up. Do you have any idea how many message slips I have with your name on them? I could paper the men's room."

Vicky swatted him. "Don't you dare."

"It's my remaining weapon," he teased, his laugh subsiding into a soft, sexy rumble. "Please, please don't turn my mother in. I couldn't bear to see her go to the chair."

She kissed the tip of his nose. "Rest easy, my dear. Neither could I." Then she sighed. "This is the most romantic story I've ever heard. It's got it all. Family loyalty, a wedding, an heirloom gown and a deep, dark secret."

"Romantic?" He dropped a soft kiss on her lips. "Hmm, maybe we should pursue this."

"Uh-uh," she said. "Business first." She chuckled a bit dryly. "You know," she said, "I absolutely adore the way this all turned out, but in a way I'm disappointed."

"In me?" he asked with mock offense. "What can I do to make amends?"

"Stop joking, Duncan. You're going to get a big enough laugh when I tell you."

"So tell me."

"When I saw all those replicas in your storeroom, I honestly thought I'd stumbled onto a *huge* ring." Heat rose in her cheeks when she just thought about her foolishness. "Can you imagine the jump start my career would have gotten if you'd actually been the kingpin of an antiquities smuggling scheme?"

"Sorry to let you down. But, shucks, ma'am, I'm just an honest, hardworking archaeologist."

"Yeah," she said with a sigh.

"You don't have to sound so distraught." He shifted and rearranged her in his lap. She felt a muscle in his thigh jump. Or maybe the muscle wasn't exactly *in* his thigh. "Tell you what," he murmured into her ear, his warm breath somehow managing to send chills down her spine.

"What?" She tilted her head so his mouth could travel down her neck.

"What if you take the gown in? You could say you'd been checking out preservationists. Maybe I could get a friend or two to vouch for you."

"Actually, I did check some out."

"All the better. Umm, you taste good." His lips were now at the hollow of her collarbone. "Anyway, you could claim you picked it up at the obscure shop I'd already planned to cite, and be the hero of the day." Now he nuzzled the valley between her breasts. "Would that handle some of your disappointment?"

See what crossing the line got you? she thought,

sinking into the electrifying, enervating, deliciously sensational feelings his mouth created. It got you strange, wonderful, exciting and terrifying experiences. And, though her conscience wagged a finger at her, the scheme was so outrageously perfect that she refused to pay it any attention.

"You're a genius, Duncan," she whispered, succumbing to his gentle pressure as he pushed her down on the sofa. "But no more talking now, okay?"

"Mmm," he purred, moving to lie on top of her.

11

"MMM," VICKY HUMMED, picking up on their fascinating earlier conversation as Duncan nuzzled her neck one last time before seeing her off.

"Ditto. Wish you could stay."

"Me, too. But my mother will be home from her trip in a few hours, and she isn't quite ready for me to stay out all night. I have to admit it makes me feel kind of silly...at my age."

"I think it's charmingly old-fashioned," he reassured her.

"Sure you do."

Duncan laughed. He looked so sexy in the crisp sunlight of the late winter afternoon, like his archaeologist self again, with his soft leather hat back on his head and a fleece-lined denim jacket topping his close-fitting jeans. Duncan in a tux was sexy, and Duncan in jeans was...even sexier.

Vicky smiled at both her own whimsy and the new surge of longing it had sparked, then drew on all her willpower to say, "I have to go."

He nodded, gave her one lingering, toe-curling kiss, then put the carton with the wedding gown on the back seat of her Toyota. They were standing in the empty parking lot of Saint Bernadette's where Vicky had left her car the night before, and with no one around she was tempted to sink into another long kiss. Instead, she slid into the driver's seat, turned the engine over, then drove away before she changed her mind, waving at Duncan no more than half a dozen times before he vanished from view.

Sometime around dawn they'd gone into his bedroom and fallen into a limb-entwined sleep. Vicky hadn't awakened until after one o'clock, and found Duncan just returning from a trip for gooey doughnuts and hot coffee.

Vicky never ate doughnuts. This time she ate four. They'd been so delicious, she could still taste them.

As she and Duncan stuffed their bellies, they talked some of how Vicky would return the gown. His preservationist friend would back up her claim, and to add credence to her story, Duncan would eventually produce the phoney claims check that had *inadvertently* been mislaid. In the light of day, she wasn't quite as comfortable with a scheme they'd hatched at midnight. But Duncan was convincing in his claims that this outcome was more believable than his original plan, because Vicky's efforts would have unearthed the dress rather than a coincidental discovery.

As she made the turn onto the freeway, Vicky let herself acknowledge the even deeper worry running beneath their pending deception.

She'd crossed yet another line last night, one that opened doors to entanglement, caring, possible commitment. But like her father, Duncan made his living by taking excessive risks. If their relationship deepened—and everything hinted it would—she faced the specter of long nights fretting about his safety, wondering if he'd drowned in some turbid waters or been slain by unfriendly natives or shot in some war-torn zone. She'd heard her mother's tales too many times not to know the agony such fears brought.

Yet even as these worries nagged at her, she felt the afterglow of their transcendent lovemaking and couldn't help but smile. What an idiot she was to have been scared half-silly by her mother's stories.

Duncan and her father were not all that much alike. Sure, they took greater risks than most in their work. But hidden between the lines of her mother's tales of her life with Vicky's father was the fact that he'd been a high-rolling man. He'd gambled both on the racetrack and off, and though he'd won more than his share, making it fairly high into the national standings before his tragic accident, he was more likely to put those purses into a high-tech race car—or, worse, on the black or red square on a roulette table—as he was to pay the rent.

Duncan, however, had roots. Despite his globe-trotting job, he had a family who relied on him. And he cared enough about them to risk everything, even his career. No, unlike her father, Duncan wasn't a man who took risks lightly. He wore a seat belt in the car, he'd worn a hard hat at the demolition site, and she suspected he avoided danger whenever he could. He just didn't let the possibility of risk paralyze him the way Vicky's mother did.

A car behind her tooted its horn, and Vicky realized she'd let her speed slack off. As she upped the gas, she saw her exit. Her woolgathering had almost caused her to miss it.

No, she repeated to herself a bit later as she parked her car in the garage, Duncan was nothing like her father. Most likely the stories of Duncan's exploits were grossly exaggerated. He was what he seemed—an archaeologist working for a small prestigious museum and a respected member of the academic community.

Who wore a leather hat banded by the skin of a poisonous snake she'd heard told he'd killed with his bare hands.

She sighed, then reached over her seat to get the box with the wedding dress from the back. When she got out of the car, she surprised herself by slamming the door with more force than necessary. Yep, she thought sardonically, that was Duncan, all right. Just your average dull guy with your average dull job.

And she'd had the luck to fall in love with him. Oh why, oh why, hadn't heaven seen fit to send her a nice certified public accountant like Meg had married?

"MORE POTATOES, MOM?" Vicky asked.

"Just a few." Barbara dished out three or four of the small red spuds. "It was nice that you cooked tonight."

"I figured you'd need a big meal after two days of burning up the ski slopes," Vicky said. But the real reason was that she felt guilty. As she'd hurriedly yanked off the impulsively purchased red dress and hidden it in the back of her closet, she'd decided not to tell her mother about the weekend. She hated the idea of hiding it from her, but she didn't want to hear the warnings.

"I hardly burn them up these days." Her mother cut into one of the potatoes, stabbed a piece with her fork, but paused before she put it in her mouth. "The way your cheeks are glowing, honey, you look like you spent some time on the slopes yourself."

"I do? Oh. Well, I took a long walk before you got home. Must be the cool air."

"Must be." This was said in a skeptical tone, which hung unchallenged in the air as Barbara ate the potatoes. When she finished her plate, she leaned back in her chair. "So you're really not going to tell me, are you?"

"Tell you what?" Vicky grabbed her plate and jumped up. "You done?" When her mother nodded, she took that plate, too, and carried them both to the sink.

"Tell me what you did this weekend."

Vicky hesitated at the sink. She turned on the water, letting it wash over the plates. A pivotal moment of truth had arrived. Cross the line? Yes, she'd done it again and again these past few days. But where did it end? It was one thing to keep things from her mom. It was quite another to tell her an outright lie. Yet she knew where the truth would take her. To a long list of warnings about daredevil men.

"I called last night, then tried again several times today."

"I was out."

"Obviously."

Vicky let rushing water fill the long pause that followed. She'd arrived at a crossroads. How she responded now would define the direction of her relationship with her mother for all time to come. She bent over to give one of the plates a vigorous scrub, then finally placed it on top of the other in the sink. With a decisive twist, she turned off the water and circled around to face her mother.

"I turned twenty-eight last month, Mom. I'm closer to thirty than twenty. You're my mother and you love me—I love you, too—but it's time I led my own life."

She expected protest, probably tears, possibly even mild hysteria, but her mother regarded her evenly. "Come back and sit down, Vicky, so we can talk about it."

Vicky hesitated.

"Please."

It was a short walk, but it seemed interminably

long, and during it Vicky realized she couldn't back down during this conversation. She couldn't and wouldn't. And she wasn't even quite sure why. When she settled in the chair, she put her hand on the flecked Formica surface, suddenly and acutely aware that while this type of chrome-legged table had come back in style, they'd had theirs as long as she could remember. Mysteriously, this realization filled in the "why." She didn't want to live a life with that little change in it.

What had gone on between her and Duncan was her business and her business only. She wasn't a little girl anymore, sharing and confessing her secrets to her mom, hoping to be supported or forgiven.

"Most of what happened this weekend doesn't concern you," Vicky said as gently as possible. "Much of it has to do with my job, which I can't talk about at this time."

Yet she could talk about some of it, she suddenly saw. And as that possibility occurred to her, she realized she wanted to talk about the dress, wanted to show it off. The need to reshape their relationship was hurting her mother, and the dress was so beautiful, it could do nothing but cheer her up. It might even be a means of holding on to the best of their relationship. And though Vicky knew this feeling might have no solid foundation, she nevertheless blurted, "I closed the wedding dress case this weekend!"

"You closed it?" Her mother's expression of absolute delight was exactly what Vicky had hoped for.

"Yes. And the gown's in my bedroom. It's the most exquisite creation you've ever seen. Would you like to see it?"

In response to Barbara's answering nod, Vicky jumped up from the chair and grabbed her mother's hand, almost dragging her down the hall to her bedroom, where she asked her to wait while she got the dress. By the time she pulled the box from the shelf, a thousand sugarplum visions of herself in the incredible gown had raced through her head. Foolish visions, exciting visions, dream-fulfilling visions. And in every one, Duncan's handsome, sculptured face loomed large.

She plopped the carton on the corner of the bed, then reached forward and lifted the lid, using it as a backdrop to display the gown, even though it blocked her own view.

"Isn't it breathtaking, Mom?"

A long pause sliced into her euphoria, and the sugarplums fell away from Vicky's eyes. Something wasn't right. Her mother was staring at her blankly when she should have been staring in awe.

"There's no gown there, Vicky," she said in a puzzled tone. "Just a bunch of bath towels."

"DID YOU SIGN THE CLAIMS forms?" Alistair demanded as he barged into Duncan's office without knocking. Nothing new, this barging act, but he then proceeded to loom over Duncan like a vulture.

"Give me a little breathing room, would you, Shields?" Alistair scooted back a few feet while Duncan thumbed through a plethora of folders crammed into the cubbyholes of his antique desk in search of the file Vicky had given him on Friday. He'd carried it with him in the MG all weekend, and had brought it in when he'd arrived at work. But the morning was already getting away from him, and for the life of him he couldn't remember which slot he'd put it in.

"Oh, here it is. Ms. Deidrich will be stopping by after lunch to pick it up."

Actually Duncan was hoping to take her *to* lunch.

"What a relief." Alistair made a mocking sweep across his forehead with the sleeve of his jacket. "For you, anyway."

Duncan knew better than to ask what Shields meant by that.

"This claim could've gotten you in deep doo-doo."

Duncan sighed. Apparently the man was going to tell him, anyway.

"Could've," Duncan replied offhandedly. "Didn't."

"Lucky you. You realize the gown wouldn't have been lost in the first place if I'd been here to institute adequate controls?"

"Maybe." Duncan swiveled toward his desk, gesturing to the door as he turned. "You mind? I've got a busy day here."

He heard Alistair's footsteps on the floor, heard him pause, and was very careful not to respond. Shields's superior tone had an I-know-something-you-don't-know ring to it that sent off warnings in Duncan's head. Despite his frequent Machiavellian maneuvers, the man wasn't all that bright and didn't even begin to know how to bluff. Something was up.

Shields cleared his throat.

Here it comes.

"My sources tell me I'm a shoo-in for the director's job. Which means you'll soon be out of your office for good."

"You want my office?" Duncan asked, spinning in his chair and planting his boots on the floor with deliberately excessive force. Rising to his feet, he moved closer to Alistair, purposely towering over him, and smothered a gratified smile when the man flinched and scuttled backward.

"You want my office?" he repeated, sweeping his arm to take in the crammed and cluttered basement room. "Take it."

Alistair wrinkled his beak in distaste. "Don't be dense. I was speaking about the position. I'll be your boss soon. Now, won't that be sweet?"

"You dream big, Alistair, but you're just a little man, and I think even Calwood's management is bright enough to see it. Bob Fuller will get the job hands down, but if he doesn't, there's still me. I've seen what you do to museums, and I'll be damned if I let you tear down this one.''

Nostrils quivered. Beady little eyes narrowed. ''Fulsom doesn't have a chance.'' He backed warily toward the open door. ''Just get the claim settled today, or I'm making good on my promise to take this mess before the board.'' Then he whirled and left the office. The glass rattled from the force of his slam.

Duncan sank back into his chair. He got no gratification from intimidating Alistair. Dealing with the man was sort of like dealing with a cockroach. And while he didn't necessarily relish squashing insects, it was often necessary to prevent disease.

Beneath Shields's archaeological credentials beat the cold heart of a bean counter. The bottom line was what he worshiped, and if it started to falter, he sold off specimens to shore it up—usually the rarest and the best. Early in their careers, they'd worked for a small facility specializing in early American pieces. Shields had wielded his way into administration, and when challenged about dwindling receipts and donations he had surreptitiously tried to sell off a prime, unblemished late seventeenth-century carriage. Duncan had gotten wind of it, and with quick action had quashed the deal. Shields never forgave him for that.

Duncan tapped the crisp manila folder lying on his desk, then checked his watch. Not even ten. He wished Vicky would show up early. Alistair was breathing down his neck, and the conversation they'd had in the entry hall on Friday when Duncan had been headed out still left him uneasy. If the man knew something...

Duncan shook his head. What could he know beyond sheer conjecture? Nothing. Nothing at all. Besides, even as he sat here worrying, Vicky was undoubtedly presenting the dress to her supervisor and proudly announcing she'd solved the case.

12

THE LAST WORDS VICKY SAID the night before had been "*No*, I don't want to talk about it." The first words she'd said that morning had been "I'll be late to work."

Now she was barreling toward Duncan's office with the towel-filled archival box tucked awkwardly under her arm. She'd clipped on the museum guest badge and sneaked in through the employees' entrance just as she'd done the previous Friday, only this morning she didn't have to worry about her feet.

In her haste to reach the museum she'd pulled on her jeans and sneakers instead of taking time for business dress. As noncommunicative as she'd been since discovering the missing dress, all that was about to change when she hit Duncan's office.

Because she sure wanted to talk now. Boy, did she ever want to talk.

As she rounded a corner into the corridor that led to Duncan's office, she heard raised voices echoing off the exposed pipes. The argument didn't last long and soon a man rushed out, slamming the door behind him. Head down, he rushed in her direction.

She expected him to stop and question her, but he paused only a second, a grim smile flashing across his face, then continued toward the stairs without a word, clearly in as big a hurry as she was.

Because of the unusual mark on his jaw, Vicky recognized him as the man she had hidden from on Friday, and she'd seen him somewhere else recently.

Meg's wedding. The man who'd almost mowed her down. No wonder he seemed familiar at the time. But he was clearly a museum employee, most likely a good friend of Duncan's. Considering the wedding gown situation, he certainly wouldn't have been invited to the ceremony otherwise.

Something about that conclusion felt false to Vicky, but she ignored it. She was too busy contemplating the shocked look that would undoubtedly cross Duncan's face when she confronted him. But even as she tried to take pleasure in his reaction, she knew she hoped for something different.

Joy at her unexpected appearance? Maybe. Honest bewilderment when she showed him the contents of the box? Yes.

It was too much to hope for. The finger of suspicion pointed directly at Duncan. Only he and members of the wedding party had access to the dress after Meg had taken it off. She trembled to think how devastated she'd be if she let herself give in to her shaky hope and Duncan disappointed her.

So she fueled her fiery anger, knowing deep down she was really trying to smother the wailing voice inside her that railed against his betrayal. Why had he used her this way? What did he have to gain?

She was about to find out.

The door lay straight ahead.

Righteous indignation exploded inside her, and she grabbed hold of the ancient brass knob, gave it a sharp turn, then crashed through the door, the unwieldy box banging against her hip.

"Vicky," Duncan exclaimed, turning to give her a delighted killer smile that made her heart leap and rendered her momentarily mute. It faded as quickly as it came. "Something's wrong."

She marched straight forward, bent over and poked her finger in his chest. "You bet there's something wrong, mister. Look at this."

With that she opened the box and turned it upside down.

The look on Duncan's face was amusing and puzzling at the same time. He jumped up to stop the absent dress from hitting the floor. But when he grabbed a towel instead, he flopped back into his chair, which tilted and thudded against his desk.

"Where is the dress, Vicky?"

"You tell me. Can you imagine my embarrassment if I'd taken this to Ida and announced my big triumph?"

Duncan nodded. "Not a pretty sight. So where is it?"

Letting the box fall to the floor, she jammed her fists against her hips. "You tell me, Duncan."

"You think I gave you a box of towels?"

"How else would they get there?" Sarcasm weighed so heavy in her words, he was surprised they stayed in the air long enough to be heard.

Duncan stood up. Sometimes he was thick, but the reason for her behavior was sinking in. She thought he'd tricked her. As surprising as that realization was, it didn't even match his shock at the utter despair swelling up inside of him. She thought he was a low-down cheat, playing with her trust. He'd held her, kissed her, made love with her, and let her into his heart despite his better judgment, yet she still believed he was capable of such treachery.

"I don't know." He searched his memory out loud. "I went to the dressing room area after the reception. Mom went into the bride's room and got the box. Do you think...?"

"Don't you dare blame your sister!" Vicky cried in outrage.

"I wasn't blam—" He'd been about to say that maybe Meg forgot to pack away the gown. "Oh, hell, this won't work. If you can't trust me, if you'd just automatically assume I'd do something this dirty, well, lady—" he pointed a finger at her "—you don't know the first thing about...about... integrity!"

"Integrity?" She didn't exactly stumble backward, but her jerky movements gave that impression. "You talk about integrity? After what y-you just d-did? Well, I'll tell you this. You can forget our little deal. As soon as I get the gown back, I'm writing a full report that will include every dirty fact.''

Vicky could hardly contain her fury, yet a wave of pain still rolled through her body. He was the one who'd taken the dress. He was the one who'd proposed she claim credit for finding it. Yet he had the nerve to speak to her of integrity? Well, she was nobody's victim. She'd be damned if she'd let him see how badly he'd hurt her.

Not that he was looking at her, anyway.

He'd turned his back on her and was now leaning forward to get something from his desk.

''Ahh,'' she said, when she realized the target of his search. ''The mysteriously missing folder.''

''I had it all along, Vicky,'' he intoned. ''But you already knew that.''

''My point.''

''I know.''

He opened the folder. After shuffling through a page or two, he picked up a pen. Was he about to sign the claim? Why? This would give her hard evidence of insurance fraud, and put his career on the line.

''Here's your precious claim. I even used black ink. Neat, crisp, just the way you like things. You can say whatever you like in the report. I don't care, although I'm sure it'll make Shields happy.'' He slapped the folder shut and jabbed it in her direction. ''Now take it and get out of here.''

Vicky's mind felt like a sieve, with tiny pieces of a bigger picture falling through the holes. None of this made sense. If Duncan had kept the dress, why would he sign off the paperwork? And why did that name he'd brought up jiggle something in the recesses of her mind? What's more, she still couldn't figure out what Duncan stood to gain by keeping the gown.

Think, Vicky, she said to herself. Who else would benefit if the gown disappeared? Who else even knew the Mulcaheys *had* the gown?

"Go on, Vicky," Duncan said harshly, but her mind was spinning so fast, she barely noticed. "Go on."

Then it came to her. "Who is that man who just left your office?" she asked.

"It's not important, Vicky. Would you just take these papers and leave?"

"No, really. Who is he?"

"Alistair Shields," he answered brusquely, walking to his door and waving the folder as he opened it.

"Alistair Shields, your archenemy?"

"I'm not in the mood for jokes, Vicky."

He pointed at the open door, but Vicky barely noticed. Duncan invite Alistair Shields to his sister's wedding? No way! Which meant Shields had been there for another purpose. With that final piece, the big picture fell into place. Vicky squared her shoulders resolutely. She now knew what she had to do.

Duncan noticed Vicky's expression turn stubborn, and was prepared to physically escort her through the door. But just then she ripped the file from his hand, thoroughly startling him. It wasn't until the manila folder fell empty to the floor and she turned the documents sideways, then took hold of either end, that he realized what she meant to do.

"Don't!" Duncan stilled her hands just as she was about to tear the papers in half. "What the hell are you doing?"

"Making sure you don't commit insurance fraud."

"You're crazy, Vicky, you know that?"

He wrenched the documents from her hand so quickly, she didn't have time to put up a fight. So perplexed he could hardly think straight, he bent for the folder, slipped the forms back inside, then walked to his desk where he laid the packet down. "They'll still be here when you come to your senses."

"I won't," she replied firmly. "Because I now know you didn't have anything to do with the dress disappearing."

"Then who did? Tell me and I'll take care of it."

"No." She stared at him rebelliously. "No. This is something I have to do myself."

With that, she swept the storage box from the floor and left Duncan staring wide-eyed at her retreating behind.

He blinked several times before the storm inside

his head subsided enough to let him think. What was going on in Vicky's clearly muddled mind? After seeing her climb onto one roof and bring another one down on their heads, he knew she was capable of almost any caper.

And he was scared half to death she wouldn't survive this next one. Where was she going?

He went over their disjointed conversation, seeking an answer. When it finally hit him, he uttered a curse, furious at himself for taking so long to figure it out.

HOW CONSIDERATE of Alistair Shields, Vicky thought, as she swung open the unlocked side gate leading to his backyard. She paused a minute before proceeding, scanning the nearby houses, listening. Birds sang in the trees above, and the hum of traffic came from the main street a few blocks south.

No barking dogs, which was good. No one rushing through their front doors demanding to know her purpose. Even better. She'd get what she needed to get, then be out of here in a jiffy.

After leaving Duncan's office, she'd hurried to her car, where she'd taken the Whitfield employee list from her briefcase, and searched for Alistair Shields's home address. Turned out his house was only a short drive from the museum.

She still found it hard to believe she hadn't made the connection immediately. After all, she'd encountered Shields in the hallway only moments after hearing an argument coming from Duncan's office. But she'd been too focused on setting Duncan straight, never once giving him the benefit of the doubt. Well, this was her chance to make up for it.

Now, as she slipped through the gate and headed to the back of the house hoping to find an unlocked window and test out her newly developed skills, it barely registered that mere days ago she wouldn't have even conceived of her present plan.

To her glee, the first window she checked was open a crack. Denver's warm spell was certainly working to her advantage. Even better, there were no bushes or muddy flower beds to hinder her entrance or cause her to leave betraying footprints inside. Her plan was to get in, snag the gown, get out. She was a hundred percent certain the gown would be inside...well, maybe eighty percent. No, seventy.

For heaven's sake, she chided herself. Of course it had to be there. Shields certainly wouldn't keep it in his office at the Whitfield. It *was* in there, and it was time she climbed in after it.

She lifted the window until it was fully open, threw one leg over the sill, then gripped the bottom of the raised panel and lifted her other leg. When her feet hit the floor, she leaned back and shimmied the rest of her body through. Just as she ducked her head to clear the window she heard a sound.

Her heart went off like a trip-hammer.

"Why, hello, Vicky. What a pleasant surprise."

"Duncan, you scared me!" she exclaimed in a

whisper, although she knew the house was empty. "What are you doing here?"

"I could ask you the same."

His hands were so full of lace, he almost appeared to be wearing the dress, and for a second Vicky wondered if he were in cahoots with Alistair. "You...you've got the gown."

"Yes. I do."

"That's what I said. You do."

"Yes."

"What are you going to do with it?"

"Ah, Final Jeopardy. Category, antiquities. And the answer is, take the antique dress to museum management and confess all."

"What? After all I've done? You can't do that." She charged forward and fisted her hands around a bundle of frothy lace. "Give it to me."

"Why? What are *you* going to do with it?"

"Take it to Global Fidelity like we originally planned."

"No, Vicky. It's gone too far now. I won't let you jeopardize your job for me."

Vicky tugged on the dress. "Yes, you will!"

"I won't!" Duncan replied, tugging back.

"You will! It's the only way!"

"Forget it, Vicky. I won't let you do it!"

She tightened her grip on the fabric and stepped back, pulling the dress with her. Duncan took a counterstep in the opposite direction.

"This is my family's problem," he said heatedly.

"I'm not dragging you in any deeper. Now, give me this dress!"

"No!"

She gave the gown a furious yank, determined to wrench it out of his hand. Duncan resisted just as forcefully. Their eyes locked in a battle of wills, a yard of taut lace spread between them. Then, as if with one mind, they simultaneously froze.

"Oh, my God," Vicky gasped, afraid to look. "D-did we…did we tear it? Did we?"

Duncan's outward breath was audible. "No. No, we didn't."

His dark blue eyes had paled, and she knew if hers hadn't, her skin sure had. She felt white as a ghost, and the horror of what they'd almost done filled her with shivers.

Still trying to recover, she heard an incongruous sound. Then another. And another. They were coming from Duncan.

"You're laughing," she said in astonishment. "You're always laughing at the most inappropriate times. This just isn't funny, Duncan."

Chuckles burst from his throat. He staggered toward the bed, where he dropped the wedding gown, then collapsed beside it, holding his sides as he rocked left and right.

"Oh, Vicky. This…this whole wedding thing's been…such a mess. T-tearing the gown—" a new burst of laughter consumed him "—would've just…just capped it off."

Vicky dove for him, knocking them backward on the bed. Infuriated, she pounded on his chest. "Stop," she wailed. "It isn't funny."

Duncan grabbed her pounding fists and held on. He was trying to stop, she could tell, but stray chuckles vibrated through his body. No longer able to beat him to a pulp, she laid her head on his chest. He chuckled again, and the sound waves tickled her ear.

"It really isn't funny, Duncan," she said, although talking reason into him was an apparent lost cause. "We're in Alistair's house illegally. You're about to commit career hari-kari. And I probably already have. What are we going to do?"

He gave another chuckle, and she made a move to hit him again, but he held her hands fast to his chest. "I have no idea. And you know what the hell of it is? I wouldn't change a thing that happened."

He transferred her trapped fists to one hand, then put his other hand behind her head. "Because if I did change things, I wouldn't have met you."

His eyes were no longer pale. They were smoky and sparkling, dark and filled with light, all at the same time, and the look in them was just for her. She knew his intention even before he kissed her.

Time stopped as Vicky sunk into the incredible embrace of the man she loved. It was so amazing the way their mouths, their bodies, fit together as if halves of the same whole, amazing the way their tongues thrust and parried, as if each of them knew what the other would do even before it was done. This man was of her heart, of her soul.

Duncan broke the kiss. "Vicky," he huskily reminded her. "You're right. We have to get out of here."

With reluctance, Vicky moved out of his embrace and stood up. "So, it's settled? I'll take the gown to my office just as we planned."

Rising, he faced her and took firm hold of her arms. "It's too risky. Besides, if I don't own up to this, it will hang over my head like a French guillotine."

"But it's not fair." She gazed down longingly at the dress. "Meg had a right to be married in the gown." *And so do I.*

But she never got a chance to say those words, even if she'd wanted to, because when she looked back up at Duncan, Alistair Shields was standing directly behind him.

"Don't move, lovebirds," he said, "I have a gun in Duncan's back."

13

DUNCAN FROZE; HIS GRIP on Vicky's shoulders tightened. Whatever happened, he had to make sure she wasn't harmed. But she hardly noticed his re-action, instead she stared at their captor in appalled disbelief.

"A gun?" she scoffed. "Don't be absurd. You don't have a gun."

It felt like a gun. Shields had said it was a gun. Fair bet it was a gun. "He could have a gun, Vicky."

Alistair pressed the object in question deeper into Duncan's spine. "I do, and I'll use it if you don't do what I say. And right now I say phone the po-lice."

Vicky looked at the man as though he were crazy, which in Duncan's opinion he well might be.

"Do you know who I am?" she asked haughtily. "I'm Vicky Deidrich. I work for Global Fidelity. And if you think I won't report this, you're sadly mistaken."

Duncan gave out a choked laugh.

Alistair gave out a satisfied one.

"Perfect. I went back to Duncan's office and found the signed claim, which led me here for the dress so I could turn him in. And look what I find. The adjuster and the thief conspiring to commit insurance fraud. Couldn't be better if I'd planned it myself.'' He prodded Duncan's back again, and waved a manila folder with his free hand. "The papers. All the proof I need. Now, if you don't want me to blow your boyfriend away, you'll make that phone call.''

"You don't have a right to that file," Vicky blustered. "It's Global Fidelity property. Hand it over right this minute.''

"Are you nuts, lady?''

"I've asked her the same question," Duncan muttered. "Vicky, do as Alistair says, would you, honey?''

"No, Duncan, I certainly won't. This whole thing is ridiculous. He *doesn't* have a gun. He's an archaeologist, for heaven's sake! What would an archaeologist be doing with a gun?'' She shook her head as she spoke, sending golden waves dancing everywhere, and scaring the hell out of Duncan. He'd seen her in this stubborn mood before. "Vicky...honey.''

Even as the plea left his mouth, Vicky brushed his hands off her arms in a martial arts move, did a kind of half step thing around him, then threw her weight at Alistair.

"No-o-o!'' Duncan roared, whirling, prepared to

take the shot, prepared to protect Vicky even at the cost of his own life.

A horrified squeak left Alistair's throat at the same time the strangled laugh left Vicky's. Even as Duncan's fist headed for Alistair's beaklike nose, he knew something was odd.

"He's got..." Vicky tittered. "It's only a banana."

"A *banana?*" Duncan's blow smashed into their captor's face, the sound punctuating his question.

Alistair reeled, staggered back against the wall, then sank to the floor where he cowered with the banana in front of him as though it could actually do some harm. Just as Duncan began seeing the humor in the situation, Vicky's amusement vanished.

She marched over to Alistair.

"Give me those!" she ordered, snatching the fruit and the claims folder from his hands. Then she whirled back to Duncan. "I think it's time we call the police."

"No police," Alistair whined. "Damn, Mulcahey, I think you broke my nose."

"It was long past due," Duncan snapped. "Go ahead and make the phone call, Vicky."

"Wait!" Shields cried. "Think about what you're doing. It's just your word against mine. I made copies of those signed forms. Even if you destroy the file, I can still prove you and your little sweetie conspired to commit insurance fraud."

"Your little sweetie?" Vicky parroted. "I don't think I like this guy, Duncan."

"Me, neither. But he does have a point."

"So what do we do with the creep?"

Shields glared up at her from the floor. "No need to be insulting."

"Oh, I could say much, much worse. So what do you think, Duncan? A crime's been committed. No question about it."

"Still my word against yours," Shields repeated.

"You know what?" she remarked. "I don't think you made copies. After all, you said you had a gun when you didn't. You think he made copies, Duncan?"

Only then did she realize Duncan hadn't responded to any of her questions. She took her eyes off Shields and turned to find Duncan staring morosely at the gown on the bed. "Duncan? You okay?"

"What? Oh, yeah, I'm fine." But he looked somewhat stunned, and he had his mouth slightly open as if he was about to say more. Vicky waited to see if he did. "Shields is right," he finally said. "It's his word against ours. Besides, all these lies are haunting me. They'll just rebound on us someday."

"You're going to confess?" Alistair said in alarm. "Don't be an idiot, Mulcahey. Our names will be smeared, and for no good reason, none at all."

"Well, I still don't think he made copies," Vicky said. She handed the file folder to Duncan, who accepted it listlessly, then looked down at the banana still in her hand. Suddenly she remembered she'd left the house without breakfast. "I think I'll just have a look around."

Stripping back the peel, she nibbled on the banana and headed out of the bedroom in search of Shields's office, his briefcase, or both.

"You hooked up with a crazy woman," she heard Shields grumble.

She waited for Duncan's response, but he spoke so softly, she couldn't understand his words. From her spot in the living room she saw another open door, and through it, the corner of a desk. Alistair's office. Taking another bite of the banana, she hurried to see what she'd find.

The office was sterile and tidy. Above the desk was a bulletin board filled with papers held up by pushpins. A hard-sided briefcase sat on the desk. She decided to search it first, since it was the obvious place Shields would have put the copies, especially since he hadn't counted on running into them in his own house.

"I don't believe you'll take this mess to management, Mulcahey," she heard Alistair say from the other room. "You aren't that stupid. Besides, why? I don't get it."

"I may go down, but I'll take you with me. You have no respect for our profession, and I don't want you ruining what Horace took so many years to build.''

"You just don't get it, do you? Antiquities are about prestige, gate receipts. Money with a capital *M*. They're not about preserving the past anymore. Calwood understands that, which is why I'm a perfect fit for their organization.''

"Yeah. Well, they won't be seeing gate receipts or donations for long. If I know you, you'll sell all the exhibits to the highest bidder within the year to boost the bottom line.''

"Yeah, but by that time I'll already have my ticket to a better job.''

Vicky tuned out the bickering men to concentrate on going through Alistair's briefcase. If he really had copied the claims file...

Well, she simply wouldn't let that thug in archaeologist's clothing destroy Duncan's reputation.

None of the files in the body of the case contained anything resembling the insurance documents, so she began searching the pockets attached to the lid. Records of meetings with Calwood Entertainment's board of directors. An inventory of Persian pottery. Another covering fourth-century Rome. Maybe Alistair was already selling off antiquities.

"Dammit! What do you want?" Shields's shout pierced her filtering system and she paused a minute to hear what Duncan would say.

"Withdraw your name from the running for the director's job and I'll forget what I saw here.''

"No weepy confessions? No accusations?"

"That's right."

"What? So you can bring in your buddy Fulsom."

"Fuller," Duncan corrected him harshly. "And he's a hell of a lot more qualified than you."

"Whatever." Shields made an impolite sound. "In your dreams, Mulcahey."

Vicky tuned them out again. But Duncan's answer to Shields's question gave her hope that he'd soon give up his need to tell all. It just wasn't a healthy choice he'd been about to make.

Now, if she could make sure Shields hadn't copied the signed claims forms, it would go a long way toward helping him make the right one. Impatient, she pulled everything out of the briefcase.

Nothing.

She slammed the lid shut, prepared to search all the files if she had to. Sitting down at the desk, she pulled out the attached file drawer, than gave the room a quick glance to see how many drawers she'd have to search.

Her heart sank. Three filing cabinets, four drawers each. This on top of the drawer in the desk. She could search all day, and even then, she couldn't be certain that if Shields really had made the copies he hadn't stored them in his office at the museum.

"Vicky," Duncan hollered. "You going to be all day in there?"

Probably. "I want to look in one more place."

"Don't take too long. I'm about to kill this guy."

From the tone of their interchange, Vicky didn't doubt it. But at least she could search the desk before giving up. She lifted up a desk pad featuring a calendar. Nothing underneath it. A check between the sheets of the calendar didn't unearth anything, either. Next she started with the drawer.

Folder after folder, and no copies.

"Vicky!"

"Be right there." She leafed through the last folder. Again she came up empty-handed. Frustrated, she flopped back in the chair, staring vacant-eyed at the bulletin board above the desk. Business cards, flyers, memos and other not-so-easily identifiable scraps of paper covered the board like patches on a crazy quilt, in stark contrast to the office, which was so neat as to be impersonal. The incongruity piqued Vicky's curiosity and she stood up to take a closer look.

An unpaid bill, due the upcoming Tuesday. A business card from a secondhand dealer. A notice about a meeting of a professional society.

"Vicky…"

Duncan sounded stretched to his limit, but she couldn't stop scanning the board. It was like a biography, or like going through someone's photo album and seeing snapshots of their life.

Most of the papers were in reasonably good shape, indicating that Shields maintained the board on a regular basis.

Duncan called for her again. She moved to leave the room, then something caught her eye. Out of place, she thought, very out of place. She leaned closer to get a better look.

The paper was a bit yellow, but that wasn't what caught her attention. No, it was the type, which was uneven and had missing serifs. This wasn't something printed out from a computer, it had been done on a typewriter. She lifted up a flyer that covered most of the sheet, and saw the Whitfield Museum logo printed across the top. At the bottom was a large scrawled signature.

Horace R. Whitfield.

Above the signature was the line that gave Duncan and his family the right to the antique wedding dress: *and in exchange, the Whitfield Museum, its predecessors and successors, give the Mulcahey clan permission to use the gown at all marriages into perpetuity.*

Tears rushed to Vicky's eyes as relief flooded through her body. Until that moment she hadn't acknowledged the small part of her that had doubted Duncan, had even doubted his mother. But here was proof they'd been telling the truth.

She pulled out the pushpin securing the letter, being very careful not to hurry for fear of tearing it, then sped toward the bedroom, pausing only long enough to discard the banana peel.

"Duncan," she said softly as she entered the bedroom.

"Where are your scruples?" he was asking Alistair, who now sat on the bed.

"Duncan," Vicky repeated, louder.

"Success isn't built on scruples," Shields replied.

"*Life* is built on scrup—"

"Duncan!"

He jerked his head in her direction. "What?"

"I found the letter." She waved it in the air.

"Letter?"

"Letter?" Alistair echoed.

"From Mr. Whitfield."

Alistair groaned, but Duncan just stared at her in confused disbelief.

"You...you found the letter?"

"It was tacked to Alistair's bulletin board."

Duncan took the letter from Vicky's hand, stared at it a second, then spun toward Shields. "Where did you get this?"

"A hint," he replied sardonically. "Don't ever mark a file folder Personal. It's a dead giveaway."

"How did you even know the letter existed?"

"Oh, that." As Alistair responded, Vicky would have sworn his chest puffed out with pride. "I was at a conference a few years ago, had lunch at a table with old Whitfield. He talked about what a treasure the Mulcahey gown was, and how all it had cost him was a promise to lend it back when any Mulcahey got married." A sly wink followed this. "Even hinted he had a thing with your grandmother."

"Well, of course. He was crazy about her!" Vicky snapped, then bit her tongue when Duncan slanted a squelching look in her direction. "Besides," she added, wheeling on Shields, "I can't believe you remembered the conversation."

"You never know when you can use that kind of thing. Imagine my delight when your charming mother phoned for permission to use the gown." Shields chuckled. "Amazing how rash people can get when you insult their heritage."

"That was you!" Vicky said heatedly.

But Duncan only turned away in disgust. "Well, now I can prove Mulcaheys aren't thieves."

"You're still going to report what you did?" Vicky asked in shock.

Looking confused, he ran his hands through his hair. "Yes. Why, did you think that had changed?"

"I could hear you talking in the other room. You offered Alistair a deal."

"No deal," Alistair said.

"No deal," Duncan echoed, still looking at Vicky. "So back to plan A."

"Why are you being so stubborn?" she asked.

"Me stubborn?" Duncan's eyes narrowed. His temper was badly frayed, and her accusation felt like a slap in his face. "You're the stubborn one. What if Shields had really had a gun?"

"He didn't!"

"But he could have, and you could've gotten shot." His hands suddenly trembled as though the incident just happened, bringing back the full horror of thinking he would lose her. "Don't you ever do that again, ever."

Suddenly Vicky's eyes widened. "Watch out!"

Shields leaped off the bed, surprising Duncan, and snatched the Whitfield letter right out of his hand. Then he bolted through the bedroom door, slamming it behind him.

"Catch him, Duncan!" Vicky said, even as she yanked open the door and pushed him aside, squeezing through the bedroom door ahead of him. The minor collision cost Duncan some time. Before he could act, Vicky dove for Alistair, catching him around the legs as he yanked the front door open.

"Get her off me!" he bellowed, crashing to the floor with Vicky clinging as tightly as humanly possible and grinning in wild triumph.

"Oh, Vicky," Duncan said, sighing. "What am I going to do with you?"

He walked over to the pair, leaned down and extended his hand. Vicky released Shields and let Duncan pull her to her feet. She was still grinning madly, and he wanted to kiss that smile off her face, but Alistair was attempting to wiggle through the door. Duncan put a foot on his back.

"Going somewhere?"

"Okay, Mulcahey, you win. I'll withdraw my name from consideration and let Fulsom have the job. Now let me up."

"Not yet." Duncan looked at Vicky sternly.

"Now, Ms. Vicky Deidrich, we've got to get a few things straight. You are the most foolhardy, daredevil woman I've ever—"

"I'm not the daredevil. You're the daredevil, and I'm so scared something will happen to you."

"Now you know how I feel," he snapped. "Honey, I'm not even in your league when it comes to taking risks. And if you ever do anything to endanger your life again, I'll…I'll—oh, hell, Vicky, I don't know what I'll do." He pulled her close to his chest, where she sweetly laid her head against him.

"You think I take too many risks?" she whispered against his chest.

"Think? I know." He stroked her hair. "You're so crazy, Vicky."

"Amen," Shields interjected from the floor.

Duncan applied more pressure to Alistair's back.

"And you've just got to stop. I can't have the woman I love constantly in danger. I'll be dead from stress in a year."

Vicky's head jerked back involuntarily, causing a painful crack. "What did you say?"

"I'll be dead in a year."

"No, not that. The part about the woman you love."

Duncan's electric-blue eyes momentarily sparked with sheer terror, making Vicky fear he'd take his words back. Instead, he stroked her cheek, softly, gently, letting his finger drift down to the swell of her lower lip. "I love you, Vicky."

Then he leaned forward and kissed her.

"Ah, jeez," Alistair groaned.

Vicky gave the man's ribs just a teensy kick, and kissed Duncan back. Good heavens. He loved her. He thought she was a daredevil. He wanted to risk his life for her. As much as she wanted to, it was all too much to believe.

It had been *such* an emotional day...weekend, really. Up and down, not at all levelheaded and steady, and she wasn't sure her nerves could stand this roller coaster anymore. Abruptly she broke their kiss.

"You really love me?"

He nodded. She grabbed the points of his collar, kissed him hard, then pulled away again.

"You better mean it," she said fervently, jerking hard on the collar.

"I do. I love you."

"He loves you," Shields interjected impatiently. She kicked him again.

"If you don't..." She yanked at Duncan's shirt with increasing ferocity. "If you don't, I'll kill you. I swear it, I'll really kill you."

"Vicky," he said. "Shut up for a second." He put his hand over her mouth, assuring her compliance. "Do you realize you haven't even said you love me, too."

"For crying out loud, she loves you," Shields insisted. "Any fool can see that."

A pained "oomph" followed, but Vicky barely noticed. She'd been so terrified of loving Duncan, terrified his job would someday snatch him from her, terrified she'd somehow lose his love. But today's events showed her that the same thing terrified Duncan. Yet he'd found the courage to go forward. He thought she was a daredevil, but he was wrong. She'd been a coward through and through. But no more. No more.

Mewing "oh, oh, oh," she brushed his silencing hand away and rained small kisses on his face. "I do, Duncan, oh, I do. I love you so much, it scares me to death."

"Obviously, considering your tardiness in saying so." He sighed with heavy relief, then covered her mouth with his in a sweet kiss that Vicky knew sealed their love for eternity.

"Oh man, oh man" came a wail from the floor. "I'll be down here till doomsday."

Epilogue

Valentine's Day, a year later

"YOU'VE GOT TO STAY still, darlin'," Bridget Mulcahey mumbled around the plastic clips between her teeth.

"Oh, sorry."

Despite the popular opinion that people in earlier centuries were smaller, it seemed the original wearer of the antique gown had been a buxom lass, and Bridget was using pH-balanced clips to mold it to Vicky's more petite form. She'd been at it quite a while, too, and Vicky was getting a bit fidgety.

She twisted her neck oh-so-carefully to check the progress.

"Still," Bridget repeated. "Very still.

"Never did mind very well," Vicky's mother joked, picking up the bridal headpiece and fluffing up its miles of organza.

"Puh!" Vicky countered. "I was the perfect child."

"Be sti-i-ll."

"Oops."

They all laughed, and Vicky felt her heart swell

yet again with happiness. The Mulcaheys had welcomed Vicky and her mother as their own. To be part of such a family, after years of just the two of them, felt like reaching out to the larger world. She suspected her mother felt it, too, because she and Bridget had already started forming a fast bond that Vicky feared might someday be used to her detriment.

Just then Meg burst through the door, carrying a box filled with bouquets. "Thank God, they made it in time. I thought it was going to be the same nightmare as my wedding, where we were already in the vestibule before the flowers came. Why do you keep using that florist, Mom?"

"They're friends from Ireland." Bridget paused in her work to look up. "Who keep asking me why you and Roger haven't given me any grandbabies yet."

Meg slanted a glance at Vicky. "See what you have to look forward to?" Then a glance at the mothers. "I can't believe you two are going on the honeymoon." A glance back to Vicky. "At least Mom didn't do that to Roger and me."

Vicky tittered. Her future mother-in-law gave a sharp pull on the dress.

"Not all the way to Greece," Barbara protested. "Just to New York, where we'll go on to Ireland."

"You *will* stay out of Belfast, won't you?" Vicky asked, since the subject had crossed her mind. Ever since her mother and Bridget had made plans to go to Ireland, Vicky had started worrying.

"You've become quite the fussbudget since deciding to get married," Barbara said in a half-jesting tone.

"Mother, that isn't true!"

"Be still!" Bridget hissed, causing them all to break up.

When the laughter died down and Meg had left the dressing room with the bridesmaid bouquets, Bridget patted Vicky's waist in a final inspection of her work. "Done," she exclaimed, heaving to her feet. "Now, let's take a look at you."

Vicky turned to face her, basking in the acceptance she saw in the misting blue eyes that were so much like Duncan's. "You're such a beautiful bride."

"She does look beautiful," Barbara crooned, fluffing the headpiece again and giving a few sniffles. "This is the happiest day of my life."

"And mine," said Vicky.

"And mine," said Bridget. "Well, except for when Meg was married...and Michael. But it is right up there, to be sure."

They all shared another laugh, then Bridget moved away.

"Now, put on your daughter's headpiece, Barbara. Her groom is waiting."

Her mother's eyes brimmed with tears and her smile was tremulous as she carefully secured the band of pearls and sequins on top of Vicky's sleeked-back hair. Next, she arranged sheets and sheets of fine pink-tinged voile around Vicky's shoulders.

"Look at you," her mother said, turning Vicky so she could see in the full-length mirror. Vicky let out a little sigh. A fairy-tale bride stared back at her.

"Oh, Mom," she whispered. "Oh, Bridget."

Both of the women beamed, but neither spoke, and Vicky knew why. When she stepped out the door, nothing would remain the same. Her mother would be on her own for the first time in her life, and Duncan would leave the bungalow from which he'd stood guard over his family. Even now, Vicky had felt the subtle changes. For one thing, she was worrying more about her mother than her mother was worrying about her. *Belfast?*

But two women who were losing their children were also gaining a fast friendship, and the marriage was making Vicky and her mother an integral part of this delightful family of thieves.

She'd been blessed, Vicky realized, totally and completely blessed, the day fate had sent her marching into the Whitfield Museum, determined to settle the case of the very gown she now wore.

In the vestibule, a fair distance from the dressing room area from where Duncan had been banished, he paced the floor, waiting for the fussy little woman who oversaw weddings to call him to the vestry where he'd again wait until it was time to go to the altar.

"How did you stand this part?" he asked Michael, who leaned against a wall, grinning. "You have the rings?"

"Yes, just like I did the last time you asked. Chill, big brother. You'll sweat all over that classy tux of yours."

"What if she changes her mind?"

Michael's grin widened further. "If ever I saw a woman in love, it's Vicky. Trust me. Besides, all grooms feel like this. I did."

"You? No! Sophie adores you. It's as plain as the nose on her face."

"My point. It's just as plain on Vicky's." Michael turned his head toward the door. "Say, isn't that your boss?"

"Where?"

"There."

"Oh, yeah." Duncan waved and Bob Fuller began walking toward him.

"Boy, you must've been relieved when Shields withdrew his name so suddenly," Michael remarked. "You ever find out why?"

"It's a long story. I'll tell you later over a pitcher of beer."

He'd already told it to Bob, who'd run interference with Calwood's board with the help of Whitfield's letter. He'd felt a lot better with the truth out, and when emotion settled down, so did Vicky. As it turned out, her boss had been so pleased with the way she'd handled the case, she'd turned in her promotion recommendation. Of course, Vicky hadn't told her boss everything, but she'd kept pretty close to the truth.

Now Duncan extended his hand to accept Bob's handshake. They exchanged a few jibes about Duncan's formal attire, then the birdlike wedding coordinator appeared—so suddenly, Duncan was sure she'd walked through the wall—and told him it was time.

"You're a lucky dog," Bob said, hurrying off to take his seat.

The next moments were a blur. Duncan was whisked to the vestry, where the bird woman gave him final instructions he barely heard, and he turned to Michael at least two more times to ask about the rings. Then he was standing on the altar, facing the pulpit, and the music began and a hush fell over the church and everyone stood and Duncan slowly turned around, his heart in his throat, certain he'd discover Vicky's mother running up the aisle, saying it was all a mistake and—

Dear God in heaven, she was beautiful!

Netting billowed around her head like clouds kissed by a sunrise and fell over her creamy shoulders to drape the rich patina of cascading lace that made up the gown. Yet the clothing itself faded away and seemed to have one purpose and one purpose only: to cameo Vicky's radiant face. Michael was right. She loved him, and she was walking toward him with a serenity he'd only prayed for.

He met her eyes. The tension left his body. He smiled.

Duncan's smile erased the remainder of Vicky's anxiety. Before walking into the nave, holding on to her mother's arm, her heart had trip-hammered with fear that Duncan regretted his decision. But now, looking at his smiling, expectant face, she knew he didn't.

He looked so incredibly handsome in the pearl-gray tuxedo, and carried it with a natural grace that made it seem he was born to wear such clothing. Her smile widened at that thought. No, Duncan would soon be back in jeans, leather vest and hiking boots, and he would still traipse through dangerous regions in search of ancient civilizations. But he'd take fewer trips, she was willing to bet. And she'd join him sometimes, though her own investigative duties at Global Fidelity were quite demanding these days.

Then she was at the base of the altar.

"Who gives this woman to this man?" asked the priest.

"I do," replied Vicky's mother, her voice thick with emotion.

Vicky gave her mother's hand a loving squeeze, then climbed the stairs and took her place beside Duncan.

He only had eyes for her.

She only had eyes for him.

They joined hands to say their vows, gazing deep into eyes all the way to their souls, and Vicky suddenly realized that if it weren't for the wedding dress mess, they wouldn't even be standing at the altar.

As the priest recited the marriage mass, Duncan leaned his head toward her and whispered, "You know why we're here?"

Worried as usual about offending someone, she mutely tilted her head in question.

"Because of the wedding dress mess."

Startled that he'd said the very words she'd been thinking, Vicky felt a wild grin cross her face. A chuckle bubbled in her throat. Another followed. Then, right there, in front of the patiently waiting priest, several hundred guests and God above, she totally lost it.

Later, after tear-jerking vows, a lingering kiss and a long stand in the receiving line, the new Mrs. Mulcahey's deliciously scandalous laugh up there on the altar was the talk of the whole reception.

**Start celebrating Silhouette's 20th anniversary
with these 4 special titles by**
New York Times **bestselling authors**

Fire and Rain*
by Elizabeth Lowell

King of the Castle
by Heather Graham Pozzessere

State Secrets*
by Linda Lael Miller

Paint Me Rainbows*
by Fern Michaels

On sale in December 1999

Where love comes alive™

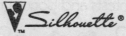

HEART OF THE WEST

Every Man Has His Price!

Lost Springs Ranch was
famous for turning young
mavericks into good men.
So word that the ranch was
in financial trouble sent
a herd of loyal bachelors
stampeding back to
Wyoming to put themselves
on the auction block!

July 1999	*Husband for Hire* Susan Wiggs	January 2000	*The Rancher and the Rich Girl* Heather MacAllister
August	*Courting Callie* Lynn Erickson	February	*Shane's Last Stand* Ruth Jean Dale
September	*Bachelor Father* Vicki Lewis Thompson	March	*A Baby by Chance* Cathy Gillen Thacker
October	*His Bodyguard* Muriel Jensen	April	*The Perfect Solution* Day Leclaire
November	*It Takes a Cowboy* Gina Wilkins	May	*Rent-a-Dad* Judy Christenberry
December	*Hitched by Christmas* Jule McBride	June	*Best Man in Wyoming* Margot Dalton

HARLEQUIN®
Makes any time special ™

Visit us at www.romance.net

PHHOWGEN